Also by Graham Dinton:

The Note in the Bodleian (And other Oxford mysteries)

The Jasmine Gate (And other Jazzie adventures)

About the author:

Graham Dinton was born and raised in Cornwall, England, then trained as an electronic engineer, before pursuing a career in computer software and IT. He started writing fiction in 2004 and has written many short stories, publishing with the Turl Street Writers and as himself. As well as creating fiction, these days Graham also spends time helping his wife take care of their wonderful granddaughters on Mondays and Fridays.

You can find all of Graham's books on Amazon stores around the world or from links on his website.

You can connect with Graham at:

Website: http://grahamdinton.com/

Blog: http://grahamdinton.com/wp/

Twitter: @GrahamDinton

Facebook: Graham Dinton

Held to Ransom

Graham Dinton

For Meryl, whose enduring love, patience and indulgence
have sustained me.

Prologue

Amanda Brown released the catch on the blind and pulled it up in stages to ensure it didn't snag on the small shop window ledge that was home to a collection of fluffy toy bunny rabbits and ducks. She glanced through the glass and stopped to watch her husband roll the security shutters away outside, allowing the sharp morning sun to light up the gossip magazines and puzzle books. Then she turned away and went through to the small kitchen, where she turned on the kettle.

She heard him walk in behind her and hang the shutter keys on their hook.

'Another day, another dollar,' he said.

She yawned and put a teabag into each mug that sat on the worktop. She had purchased the large white one for David in a charity shop further along from their frontage on the Cowley Road last winter when she was looking for a scarf - it read *KEEP CALM AND READ A NEWSPAPER* and he loved it. She preferred hers to be china with a fine English rose pattern. It was 5:55am, the same time she had boiled the water yesterday and the day before that. Sunday was the only different day of the week when they opened at 7:30am instead of 6am.

Amanda avoided talking until after her first cup. There wasn't any need. They busied themselves unwrapping bundles of newspapers and sorting them into rounds, ready for Luke,

Lisa and Jess, who were the current crop of delivery kids.

The Wednesday headlines were the same across all the newspapers. A plane crash near Iasi in Romania, close to the border with Moldova, 180 feared dead. Amanda read the front pages carefully, catching a fresh paragraph each time she labelled a new paper for Jess's bag. She didn't want David to be alerted to her interest. Not that she need worry, he looked to be totally absorbed in refreshing the stocks of cigarettes and boxes of matches.

The day moved hour by hour.

Six to seven, the early birds, fresh-faced joggers, shift workers, Penny from the café next door-but-one, and George the lollipop man.

Seven to eight, the school kids. Sweets, snacks, cans of drink.

Eight to nine, the commuters rushing to work, picking up cigarettes, water, papers.

Nine to ten, the parents after the school run, magazines, chocolate, cans of Coke.

Amanda knew a few dozen by name and many more faces. She prided herself on remembering their favourite sweets or reading materials.

By ten they were ready for their third cup of the day, coffee this time, and she went through to the back to put on the filter machine. David stood behind the till. He looked so much older than when they'd married in a rush over ten years ago, swept away by something she couldn't really put her finger on now. She told herself the eight-year age gap was really starting to show. She liked to keep herself in shape and on-trend, ready to party, game for a laugh. David was the respectable type, a member of the Chamber of Commerce.

She heard the shop door buzz open as she sprinkled the second spoon of coffee powder onto the filter paper.

'Good morning,' David said. He always greeted every customer, something she never concerned herself with. They rarely responded. This one did.

'Good day.' The accent was heavy, the voice jolting her heart rate. Sergei. Amanda's face burned as she gripped onto the kitchen worktop, and she felt an immediate faintness. Sergei, here. Not possible. Her hand went to the sapphire pendant on a gold chain around her neck. She shuffled her feet towards the cupboard on the side wall, out of sight, and held her breath.

'Twenty Bensons, please.' Sergei's voice was older, deeper, dangerous.

Amanda leaned forward to peep through the gap beside the hinge of the door and saw David retrieve the packet and hand it across, taking the note in return. As David rang up the till, she could see him across the counter, tall, powerful eyes, familiar. She waited and she watched him turn and walk back to the shop door.

As he left, she reentered the main shop to get a better look. Sergei had developed a slight stoop as he walked. When he reached the Cowley Road pavement outside he glanced through the window, past the souvenirs on display, directly into her eyes. His face flickered a smile without any break in his step, then he was gone.

1

I was deep in thought about the universality of family values across cultures when the stripy blue tape snagged on my handbag and held me back. It stretched from the butcher next door to the lamp post on the corner of Rectory Road. A crime, a story. I took out my phone and snapped. PC Average emerged through the door of the convenience store, dipped under the tape, and approached me.

'Excuse me. No photos.'

I shaded my eyes from the sun that reflected from the shiny pavement, the slabs still wet from overnight downpours. A white fog of condensation floated on his breath.

'What happened?' I offered my card which he took and examined.

'Ah, the *Gazette*. I thought it wouldn't take you people long.'

'I only came by for a bottle of water on my way to an appointment. Coincidence.'

'Your lucky day then, Miss Hawkins. Not lucky for the owners.'

He was taller than me and I moved into his shadow to observe him fully. An inspector, no less – nothing average about this crime. I peered into the gloom of the shop but could see nothing wrong. It was 8:30am and the street was awash with office workers and school kids. A small crowd was gathering, those with no urgent destination and those simply unable to pass the intriguing scene.

'Care to comment? Something I can go on?'

I offered up a playful smile, and held my phone at arm's length beside him, ready to capture us together with the shop as a backdrop. He grabbed my wrist and glowered. Inspector 4385, clean-shaven, slim, not to be messed with. He had a lovely grip. I muttered about the Bill of Human Rights, until he let go my arm and we stood facing each other in a Mexican standoff.

'Our media statement will be at a press conference in the lobby of the town hall at 11 o'clock. All press are welcome,' he said, looking over my shoulder.

'I could make a guess. Raid gone wrong. Shopkeeper in self-defence stabbing. Blood on the till.'

'You would be wrong. Missing person.' He turned and walked back under the tape.

I retreated to the coffee shop that was three doors along the Cowley Road, where the bean-grinding machine was suffocating any conversation. When it stopped, the man ahead of me in the queue was talking in a loud voice, asking what was going on, but it was clear the barista knew nothing. While I waited to order a croissant and black coffee, I messaged Jamie to say I would be late back from my meeting. If I told him any more than that, he would be down here stealing the story for himself, and telling me I had to focus on my ongoing series about social justice for immigrants. Maybe I could find a connection between the two, if I delved deep enough. This was the Cowley Road and the central area of my study.

I took my order and grabbed the stool in the window. At the table in front of me, three students were discussing the merits of Charles I and what he achieved for seventeenth-century Britain. Apparently it wasn't all bad. To my left, a white-haired man was reading his Kindle, slurping at a latte. The world of Oxford passed outside our window. I pulled off a piece of my croissant, dunked it in my coffee and swallowed it down. From my bag, I fetched my iPad and began to research.

The shop was rented by a Mr and Mrs Brown, who had taken it up in 2008. She was a runner, various charity events over the years showing her to be fast for an amateur, at least in half-marathons. There was no information regarding children. I managed to find one photo at the annual ball of the chamber of commerce, him smiling in his black tie, and her stunning in an evening dress. So which one was missing? And why the crime scene tape?

I phoned Gary.

'Emma, how's my beautiful one? Long time. What do you want?'

Gary was a date once. We lasted four months but his heart wasn't in it. The shift work did for us, mainly his nights out on patrol. We'd agreed we might be able to help each other, so we parted on good terms, and he'd been invaluable ever since. I knew how to work him, despite a new girlfriend on the scene.

'How's Alice? I think that was her name.'

'Ah yes, the wonderful Alice. She came and went sadly. How about you? Married yet?'

'As if.'

'I'll be back for you when you're forty.'

'I'll save myself. In the meantime can you tell me who Inspector Tall is? Handsome chiselled face, fair hair, 4385?'

'Um, that'll be Richards. Why? You're not, are you? I can't keep up with you. And I thought he was married.'

I cleared the last few crumbs from my plate. The window had steamed up again so I wiped it clean to survey the pavement. A police car had pulled up outside the Browns', the driver sitting waiting, talking on his phone.

'He most probably is. I only met him this morning. Friendly, witty, big smile.'

'That's not the normal Richards. Must be the effect of your charm.'

'That was my best irony. He's at a crime scene. I was hoping you could tell me what has happened.'

Gary coughed and laughed at the same time. I could picture his heavy face and smell the stale tobacco jacket hanging on the back of his chair.

'Well, if Richards is there personally, it's probably the case about our missing wife. Are you on the Cowley Road? She was kidnapped in a raid last night. Break-in about 2am. Both threatened with an iron bar. Man beaten up pretty badly. That's all I know.'

I put down my cup and scribbled some notes. Kindle man looked up at me. Was I more exciting than his novel? This wasn't the place to discuss a kidnapping. I stood and walked outside, then faced into the café to keep an eye on my bag and papers. He watched me back through the glass.

'How many?'

'Two men in black. Dark car out the back. We're trawling through CCTV right now.'

'Mr Brown? Has he gone too?'

'No, he's injured and in shock. Sedated I believe. I'm not on the case, it's just corridor talk.'

'I owe you one.'

'You owe me six. Now hop it.'

I returned to the warmth inside. It was nearly 10am. I just had time to post my piece - better to go with what I had already. If Jamie was in a good mood, and the tech boys had their servers warmed up, we would have it on the web before any formal announcements.

***

I reached the office at 12:30, where Jamie was marking Henry's card. This was a daily occurrence. Henry could find the wrong side of Jamie even with the most glowing, positive story about some charity fundraising do-gooder.

I threw my bag under the desk and logged in, keeping my eyes on the screen. Henry sat opposite. The *Gazette*'s office was a converted mansion house on the Banbury Road and had been refitted in light oak and glass throughout. Workstations were numbered and supposed to be hot-desks but I always sat at U1-5 with Henry at U1-6 - some weird numbering system invented by the management to help you appreciate how important and individual you were. Jamie's deep voice rose above the hubbub of the large open newsroom.

'That part about the Chief Exec, that's complete rubbish,' he said.

'I found it in the archive. Back in 1982.'

'That's as may be, but you can't use it there. It's not

relevant.'

Jamie stood at the side of the desk, slightly raising himself up on his toes, giving him a somewhat rugged, striking profile. His face was beginning to flush with annoyance, his Glaswegian accent more pronounced as it always was when he got angry. He hadn't been that way with me since last year, when I got the Oxford United report back to front and awarded them the win. Today it was hapless Henry's turn.

I retrieved my messages and checked email. I already knew the story was live and when I looked at the website, it was the most popular article in the previous hour. The other local papers carried similar pieces, the press conference confirming what I'd already discovered. Amanda Brown, 43, was missing, presumed kidnapped.

'My office, Emma,' Jamie said.

I gave Henry a look as I stood up, and he smiled his relief in return. Jamie and I walked through the open office together, then along the corridor to what he called his den, a room lined with half-height mahogany panelling, with a photograph of the Queen on the wall behind his matching mahogany desk with inlaid leather. It was a complete contrast to the rest of the modern refit, and we could have been in the eighteenth century, except he wore black chinos, and I had a short, tight green dress with opaque tights and heels.

'So why would an ordinary British shopkeeper's wife be taken?' he said.

He sat in his dark brown leather chair while I stood. Eventually, he indicated at the seat opposite him, so I plonked myself down, crossed my legs and smiled. He was stressed because I was ahead. I opened my iPad and talked through my notes. When I glanced up, he was grinning in an annoyingly engaging way.

'What?' I said.

'You're enjoying this.'

Jamie's familiar aftershave floated in my direction on the breeze from the air conditioning unit. He preferred his den cooler than the rest of the building and my arms shivered of their own mind. He looked trim, in a smart pastel salmon shirt with a designer motif on the pocket. His dark hair was trimmed short, fuller and wiry on the top and he had deep brown eyes that shone when he spoke to me.

'It's a big story. She could be dead,' I said.

'What do we know of the attackers? Any sightings?'

'It was too dark. No cameras. The shop system was turned off for the night. They broke in round the back by forcing a window.'

'Mr Brown must have something on them. Were they white, black, brown or yellow?'

I rolled my eyes, not smiling. 'You have a way with words. I think what you're looking for is Caucasian, and yes they were white Caucasian.'

'European, I bet. Ties in with all those articles of yours about the attacks on Muslim women and the impact of immigration. It'll be one of your lot.'

He was making a ridiculous generalisation. I stood up. 'What did you actually call me in for?'

'This is a job for someone more experienced. I'll investigate it while you get back to your social justice,' he said.

My cheeks felt hot as I stared back at him.

'You can't do that. I'm on it already. I have a police

contact and plenty of background information.'

'It's a great start. No harm done. I can pursue it from here.'

I tried smiling at him, dismissing it lightly despite his commanding style. He knew full well that I had broken big stories before, like the public services expenses fraud last year.

'You're teasing me. How about you give me a few days anyway?' I said.

He stood up as well then, facing me, and spoke more quietly. 'OK, perhaps we can work together on it.'

'I'm sure I can learn from you,' I said, grinning at the perfect result.

'There's one other thing. I did just want to see you. I have a card for you.'

He took an envelope from his top drawer and handed it across the table. I opened it and on the front was a black and white photo of a woman holding the handset of a telephone, probably from the 1950s. She looked elegant, in a cocktail dress of the period. Underneath the caption said: *The only reason she had a landline was so she could call her mobile to find it.* Inside, it simply stated 'Happy Birthday, regards Jamie.'

I laughed at the card.

'It's kind of you to remember. I ... well, I'll go and investigate *my lot*, as you call them,' I said.

***

Aunt Hazel was sitting at the corner table with two pints of cider, presumably one of them for me. She still thought of me as sixteen, but she meant well. The pub was surprisingly quiet for a Friday and the perfect place to celebrate the totally uninspiring age of thirty-one.

We talked jobs, health, money, alcohol, and men of course. Uncle Jack was away for the next two weeks at a conference so Hazel was happy to have a fun evening out.

'Fancy moving on to a bottle of Sauvignon – my treat?' I said.

She nodded as she started on me. 'So you're telling me you like being single.'

'You make it sound like a disease.'

'Well, when you're over thirty, it's certainly not healthy,' she said.

'I like the thrill of the chase and then I get bored too quickly.'

She laughed and ran her hand down my arm, smoothing out the green lace of the sleeve and adjusting my favourite yellow gold bangle which she had given me for my twenty-first.

'Your mother would be proud. She was a flirt too.'

'That doesn't sound quite right, not for me, nor her.'

I smiled at Hazel. I loved the way she talked of her sister in such an adult way. She always had, ever since she took me into her home from the age of six.

'You'll meet someone you love eventually. Just like she did. It takes time.'

'There are a few frogs on the horizon.'

I drank the last mouthful of the remaining cider and put my glass down next to hers. There was a commotion at the bar and we both looked across. It was Andrei, one of the frogs from recent work-related interviews, and he was drunk.

'Oh God,' I said.

He stood up and pushed the bar chair to one side, scraping it over the floor. He swayed a little, then slapped the other guy on the shoulder.

'She was really lovely.'

'Sure she was, bud, sure she was.' The second man remained on his bar stool, arms resting on the beer cloths. He held his head in his hands.

'No really, she was, totally.'

I wondered who he was talking about. There'd been no mention of girlfriends when we had met for coffee a couple of times. He'd been most helpful in my research about the Romanian community in the Cowley area.

Hazel was straining to see and hear, her back to the action. We had to go, before we were spotted. I rose to my feet and grabbed her coat, offering to help her with it.

'Next pub?' she said. I had promised her a crawl through the King's Arms, the White Horse, the Mitre.

I tried to keep hidden behind Hazel as we left, but we had to squeeze past the bar and he spotted me immediately. My face flooded with hot blood. He gazed from one to the other of us, taking in my aunt from foot to head in one movement of his eyes, then returning his focus to me, to some vague point midway between my breasts and my face.

'Well, well. Emmy isn't it? I'm a bit drunk. I'm so sorry. Who's your lovely friend?'

He smiled and put his hand out to Hazel.

'Pleased to meet you. I'm Andrei. Emmy's could-be boyfriend.'

I should have cleared up the situation faster but while I

was forming the words, Hazel spoke up.

'Pleased to meet you too, Andrei. Emma's mentioned you, I think. She's a lucky girl.'

A lucky girl? What was she playing at? Fitting me up? Flirting herself? Totally wrong.

'She's beautiful, that's for sure. I would be very lucky.'

Andrei stumbled in my direction and put his arm around my waist and kissed me on the cheek, then he let go again and turned back to Hazel. He stepped towards her and put his arms around her neck and pulled her close to him so he could kiss her on each cheek.

'Any friend of Emmy is a friend of mine,' he said.

Then he surveyed us in turn.

'Lovely to have met you Andrei, but we must be going. Emma's birthday pub crawl. Perhaps we'll meet again soon,' Hazel said.

2

The next morning Andrei was sitting outside the coffee shop on the High Street at one of the metal tables. The street, traditionally known as the High, was quiet except for a couple of slow-moving buses to London and some delivery vans. It was term-time but the usual myriad of student bikes which added to Oxford's charm were absent on a crisp Saturday morning and it was still too early for tourists to have finished their full English breakfasts and boarded the open-top buses.

I surprised him when I approached from the opposite direction from where he was looking for me. He leapt from his chair and gave me a hug, both of us wearing fleece-lined jackets that helped keep us at a polite distance. I recognised the hint of his lemon aftershave, slightly less masculine than it ought to be. He'd grown stubble since last night, but he'd sobered up and was fresh and bright-eyed with that familiar lopsided grin.

'Let's go inside, too cold here,' I said.

I queued and paid for the coffees while he found a table near the back. When he took his jacket off, he looked slim and confident, a striped shirt collar peeping from under his plain grey woollen sweater.

I put the tray on the table between us and sat down.

'So good to see you, Emmy,' he said.

'Emma, try Emma, and thanks for coming to see me so

early.'

He laughed and took his cup of latte.

'Em ... ma, my Emma,' he emphasised.

The heat in the café was almost oppressive. Each new entrant brought a fresh wave of cold air from outside but when the door shut, the heaters refilled the room with an intensity of warmth that was the main attraction of the place. The coffee was average, made from stale beans, but the fresh croissants and pastries were excellent. I often used it to meet people, mostly because of the anonymity and its proximity to my bus stop for the office.

'How are you, Andrei? Hangover?' I said.

'No lasting effect. When I saw you last night, I was a bit drunk. Sorry. Happy birthday for yesterday. I had no idea. Was that your sister? You have her lovely looks.'

'Oh ... thanks ... that was my aunt. She was out of order at the end there. Best forgotten. I don't want to mislead you.'

'Oh, OK. Then keep me on your most desirable, maybe in the future, shortlist, perhaps.'

He could make me laugh but Andrei was not dating material. 'I was hoping for your help.'

'How can a poor Romanian waiter, chained to his father's rather modest café, an expert in the art of table clearance in one visit, possibly help such a capable lady?'

'Did you read about the attack at the newsagents?'

'Ah, you want me for my ears and eyes, to be your spy on the street, your informant.'

'Only if you know something, of course.'

He opened the newspaper that was lying on the table between us. There on page five was a photograph of Mr and

Mrs Brown, standing outside their shop. They were holding the flag of St George: the picture taken on the day that England had played their last World Cup match. The headline read 'Mystery of Missing Newsagent'.

'I don't know these people,' he said.

'But maybe you could ask around. Find out. Any word on who the perpetrators are? Listen to the gossip at the café, perhaps? The rumour is that it is an Eastern European gang.'

He looked up at me and became serious, stroking his unshaven face. He had an angry look I'd not seen before. Andrei had helped me with a great deal of research for the series of immigration articles that I'd written over the last three months. Throughout that whole time, he never once was short, ill-tempered or impatient.

'Emmy, you don't understand. You still don't understand. Why do people always assume? Something bad has happened. Oh ... it must be the foreigners. Come on.'

'I know it looks like that. But really, a source has told me that it's a gang, probably Romanian, getting payback for the storekeeper's right-wing views.'

'What source?'

I glanced at my watch and wondered whether I should cut and run. Andrei was not looking hopeful and I could use the time in the office to research the Browns' business interests.

'Not expecting me to argue? I don't know anything about them at all,' he said.

'Can you keep your eyes peeled?'

'Peeled eyes? What are these peeled eyes?'

'I mean, can you just keep a lookout ... in the café, in the community? You have lots of connections. If you hear anything, could you call? Please?'

I reached out and put my hand on his, and smiled at him. He turned his hand over and grasped mine.

'Emmy, of course I will. You are my sweet.'

'It's Emma.'

***

Even on a Saturday, the newsroom buzzed with activity. The *Gazette* never stopped. Five minutes after I sat down at U1-5, Henry arrived full of bluster and full of virus. He sneezed as he took off his coat and hung it on the back of the chair next to him.

'Don't you dare bring that in here,' I said.

'Don't worry. It's four days old. Never catch it now.'

He sounded phlegmy and hoarse. I held my hand up to my face until he had settled into his desk, the air thick with the smell of decongestant.

'Night Nurse, swear by them,' he said.

'You should be at home,'

'I'm working on an important piece, and I need to be seen to be here with my career on the line.'

'You'll be fine. What's it about?'

'Library closures. Vital. What next in the cutbacks? If we lose our libraries, we lose our heritage, our culture, our soul.'

'You read books?' I said, then regretted it immediately. Of course he did.

Ten minutes later, after a rant that included the home secretary, the evil Amazon, the genius of William Caxton and a mention of Sir Thomas Bodley, he finally settled back and explained that his career depended on the retention of village libraries in Oxfordshire.

'This is about Jamie, isn't it? Don't let him get to you, you're doing fine.'

'Really? You think so? That's so good to hear ... from you, you know. You're the one on the way up.'

'Not really. Just a bit of luck, that's all,' I said, although I knew I'd worked tirelessly on bringing various rogue public servants to justice.

Henry and Lady Luck were on different pages altogether, probably completely different newspapers. Henry was the one who could spend three hours on a piece about the improving crime rates in the town, only for three murders to occur on the night before it appeared in the features column. Someone drove into the back of Henry's car the day after he bought it. That was Henry.

'I'm looking for details and dirt about the Browns,' I said.

'Jamie says they were attacked by thugs. Foreign thugs.'

'But why? That's what I need to resolve.'

I turned back to my screen and pulled together what I had already. The accounts for the shop showed it to be profitable, very profitable. I couldn't understand why until I searched a little deeper and found there was no mortgage on it. The Browns had paid cash back in 2008 when the price of small businesses was at rock bottom.

Henry sneezed again, prompting me to stand and withdraw towards the corner.

'Sorry Henry, but I won't take the chance. A cold is the

last thing I need right now. I'll go and work over there, I think.'

He waved approval after I'd already cleared my stuff into my bag and was getting up.

'You're probably right. I shouldn't be here. We don't want Jamie succumbing, do we?'

I started again on reviewing all the archives I could find in the *Gazette*, all online and searchable on the database, then I went through the council records, any planning requests in the area, any history of break-ins. There was very little to go on; they seemed the perfect owners.

Amanda had been a dancer before she met David Brown in 1999. She had worked in the clubs in Brighton before moving to London and appearing in the West End and nightclubs, then moving to Oxford to set up a dance school. They married in 2002, no children. An age gap of 8 years, putting him at 51. He had always worked in the retail corner shop trade, his father having owned a place at the top of the Iffley Road until he died in the early 2000s, when David Brown took over.

I called Inspector Richards, on the off-chance of finding another weekend worker. Perhaps I could exchange some information.

'Emma Hawkins, the *Gazette*. You remember me?'

'You managed to find yourself some water, I take it,' he said.

'I did, thanks. And a good story. I thought I might be able to help your enquiries. It appears Mrs Brown was once a dancer. Perhaps there's something in her past that's relevant.'

'What makes you think I'm at all interested in your research, Miss Hawkins?'

'You can call me Emma. Most people do. I understand there could be a link back to foreign nationals. She might have been taken out of the country.'

Share a snippet, gain a snippet, I thought.

'Well, thank you for your speculation but, as you can appreciate, I won't be sharing mine and I can assure you we are working very actively on this case right now, and will have more to report to the media in due course.'

There was nothing else for it: I would have to talk to Gary.

I got a coffee from the machine and carried it back to my desk. Before I resumed, I fell into a message exchange with Becky, my best friend, the person who had rescued me from countless disasters since I was six years old and now a maths teacher responsible for the numeracy skills of some of Oxford's finest teenagers.

<Yes, I did meet Andrei again.>
<No, we didn't arrange a date.>
<No, I'm not seeing him again.>
<Yes, he is cute, I suppose, but he is a source.>

Her questions never stopped, presumably a way of entertaining herself on a quiet Saturday morning. Eventually I called her.

***

'So, come on then. What about Andrei?'

I pulled the phone tight to my ear, sat up straight in my chair and accidentally knocked my knee against the edge of the desk, muffling a squeal. Henry had gone to replenish his Night

Nurse.

'There is no Andrei, not in that sense. He's a help for big news stories,' I said.

We discussed the kidnapping and the fact that the shop closure would impact her Year Nines' ability to buy snacks on their way to school on Monday.

'We go back next week for the summer term. Apparently there's escalating violence in that area. Some kids have tweeted about seeing abuse in the street aimed at a group of Indian women, but they could be exaggerating. I've already seen concerns from some teachers on Facebook,' she said.

'Does anyone have any theories of who might be responsible?'

'None with any foundation of fact. We'll leave that to you, the professionals. Have I told you about Daniel?'

We both knew she hadn't. Daniel was her new boyfriend, a solicitor apparently famous for his prosecution of corporate fraudsters. I would google him later. The important fact was that he was enchanted by her, and I just had to meet him as soon as possible. That brought her full circle to Andrei.

'Andrei sounded amazing. We're meeting up with you guys tonight. Me and Daniel, you and Andrei.'

I stabbed my pen into the pad in front of me.

'How on earth did he get to talk to you?'

'We haven't talked. He just emailed me an hour ago, to introduce himself. Sent me a picture and everything.'

'That'll be Hazel's doing. But there is no me and Andrei.'

'Emma, you need a man, you know you do. It'll be fun, give it a go. And you must meet Daniel.'

After the call, I walked through the offices of the paper, floor by floor. I needed to think. People smiled, familiar faces. I'd been a qualified journalist for three years and on the news desk for two. News gathering is not a team sport, and there were few I could call friends. Who did I like? Certainly not Andrei. I had to navigate between gathering information and fighting off his interest.

***

In the afternoon, I sat in the reception area of the Golden Locks salon waiting to have my hair turned neither golden nor locked. Straight black, centre parting. The national newspaper headline declared another Muslim woman injured in a random attack on the street in Oxford, although I knew that was deemed to be a family argument by the local police.

My stylist called me over to the chair. 'Date tonight Emma?'

She always asked and I had always said no, so I surprised her this time.

'Just meeting some friends, but I suppose you might call it a date. How about you?'

'Na, telly night with boyfriend. Chocs and *Casualty*.'

'Nice.'

When I got back to the flat, I loaded the washing machine, then I started to get ready. Becky had booked a table at Le Bistro on the Cowley Road and we were meeting in the pub on the corner beforehand. It was near the Romanian café where I had interviewed Andrei a few times for research.

Becky had been persistent, so I resolved to go, and put

him straight when I found the right moment. How had he found Becky anyway? Hazel denied all knowledge.

Sparkly understated top, jeans, heels. I dressed down. I didn't want any misunderstandings.

***

Becky called Sunday morning.

'Well?'

'Well, what?'

'Daniel, hot or what?'

'Hot,' I said.

She giggled down the phone, then I heard a male voice in the background.

'He's making scrambled egg,' she whispered.

'A keeper.'

'Breakfast in bed?' she said.

'Not here. I'm ironing and watching a box set about the Tudors.'

'Not again. Don't miss out, Andrei's a keeper too I reckon,' she said.

'There is no me and Andrei, Becky. I told him again last night. Right after you two left. He walked me to the taxi rank. I told him straight this time.'

'But we're meeting later ...'

'Meeting later? Again? How can you possibly be meeting him again later?'

'You are too. At your Aunt Hazel's. Lunch.'

The buzzer of the flat rang, giving me the excuse to cut her off. I would need to call Hazel. I pressed the intercom, and decided to face him down.

I threw on my thickest, woolliest, shabbiest comfort sweater to cover myself and walked downstairs to open the external door. Mine was the upstairs flat and fortunately the Marsdens from down below were away for the weekend, so the shared hall was empty.

Andrei had a bottle of red in one hand, white in the other and a grinning face.

'Andrei, I appreciate we may have translation difficulties. I don't speak Romanian. How clear do I have to be?'

'I know, I know, but your auntie has invited us for lunch.' He stepped forward and I blocked him with the door.

'It's off.'

His face looked eight years old, like I'd taken away his Lego box. His bottom lip pouted.

'We all need to eat,' he said.

'Not all together though. When did she invite you?'

'This morning, on Facebook. You must have seen it too.'

I sighed and shut the door. Hazel and Facebook – what a nightmare combination.

3

At the point where the Banbury Road, the Woodstock Road, and St Giles meet is the Oxford War Memorial, in memory of those who fought and those who fell in two World Wars. As I walked towards it on my way to meet Gary, I could see the wreaths still lying there from last November, wrapping the base of it in a red poppy blanket to shield it from the deep freeze of winter, each one no doubt laid with appropriate reverence for those who had battled to protect our freedom.

I stopped to read the simple inscription on the surface facing towards the city. It was a still, sunny morning, the damp of the dew glistening on the petals of the flowers, and there was a break in the Monday commuter traffic behind me, so I could hear the birdsong.

Gary punctured the mood.

'Hey Emma, my beautiful one, how are you today?'

He bounded up like a Labrador and put his arm around me, and I let him kiss me on the cheek. He was my height when I wore my heels, and had a faint scar down one cheek, from some scrap at school apparently, which he often hid with three days of facial hair. Today he was clean-shaven, and wearing a suit and tie.

'Interview?'

'Funeral. Not family. Friend of friend. You don't want

to know.'

Gary's friends were usually from the dirty side of the grid, slippery and dangerous, so by 'friend of friend' I assumed he meant criminal. He always walked a fine line between police work and the criminal world.

'Let's go and sit. I've brought you a coffee.'

I let him take one of the steaming polystyrene cups that were carefully stuck into a cardboard holder I had carried up from Taylor's coffee shop.

'Skinny latte, double shot?'

'Of course. I know what you like,' I said.

'You do. You're the perfect woman Em. Why did I let you go?'

Before we reached St Giles' Church, we entered a small graveyard where there were a couple of benches. We often met here, after we'd split up, to exchange information about crimes we were working on. The graveyard was set back from the path and very seldom used, especially on freezing nights like last night. The police kept the benches clear and there was a tranquillity about the place that enabled us to speak in private.

'What can I do for you?' Gary said as he sat down beside me.

'The Browns. I thought we could share.'

'Go on then, you first.' He laughed, then sipped his coffee through the small hole in the lid.

'Well, she's a dancer, or more accurately, she was. He's in the Ku Klux Klan, I believe.'

Gary snorted, nearly dropping his cup.

'A nationalist party for England, nothing illegal. Not from what we can find,' he said.

'Ok, well not quite the KKK but he would if he could.'

I looked across at the graves opposite, the headstones at awkward angles and overgrown with moss and weeds. The names were fading, lichen covering the dates and inscriptions.

Gary continued, 'He's a successful businessman. He inherited from his father and has developed it further since. He's a nationalist, anti-European. Many would say there's nothing wrong in that. He was done once for selling sweets in 1/4lb bags rather than metric, that's all we've got on him.'

Gary had been a policeman for ten years, ever since school, and was passionate about people's rights; innocent until proven guilty and all that. He'd not yet caught the cynicism of his seniors or elders. He smiled at me when I pulled my doubtful face.

'I can't stay long. We shouldn't be seen together,' he said.

We both looked around like spies and took another gulp of coffee. The traffic was stationary on the Woodstock Road to our left and a man in a black BMW stared at us from the passenger seat. He could have been with the CIA. I leant into Gary's shoulder, then turned to him, put my free hand on his knee and kissed him on the cheek. When I looked back, the driver smirked.

'Em, stop that. I might take you seriously.'

'What about the woman?' I said.

'His wife. Yes, she was a dancer as you say.'

'Part of a chorus line, a dance troupe.'

'Well, maybe. But she also pole-danced in London, at various clubs. Had some dodgy management apparently. We're checking with the Met about all that, to see if there's any connection.'

'Hardly makes a motive, not after all this time, surely? A long lost admirer of her skills with the pole returns to grab her and take her ... where?' I said.

Gary put his arm round me again and squeezed. He was shivering in his suit.

'One more thing. How much money was stolen?' I said.

'We don't know. Mr Brown has reported twenty thousand, but we think it could be more like fifty.'

'What, fifty thousand in cash in a house-safe? Now, there's a story. Why do you think that?'

'His bank records, and his fancy business friends.'

Gary stood to leave and dragged me by the hand. We walked together to the path back to the Banbury Road, then he kissed me on both cheeks.

'I didn't see you, remember,' he said, then turned and paced away towards the city centre. I put the coffee cups into the bin and walked the other way towards my office. The London underworld demanded my attention.

***

Googling pole-dance clubs while sitting at U1-5 didn't seem the best of ideas. Apart from Henry, the newsroom was more than half men and there was no way I would avoid banter about moonlighting, job applications, how they could interview me, or help me prepare for the audition.

'Need a bit of extra cash, Emma?'

'Want me to check your moves?'

I could hear it all. Anyway, I didn't want to divulge my

information yet. It might lead nowhere fast.

Gary had given me a long list of clubs that existed back in the Eighties where Amanda Brown had probably worked. There were scores of names and it would be like finding a needle in a haystack, so I decided to review other lines of enquiry first. I put my bag on the desk and hid the folded piece of A5 paper in the outside pocket.

'There's been a crash on the A34. Oh, and Jamie wants you in his office.' Henry said when he looked up from his screen opposite.

'Let me see, is that the forty-eighth or forty-ninth so far this year? Breaking news.'

'Ha ha. We can't all be working on the crime of the century you know. Anyway, don't joke about the dead. The fog early this morning killed four.'

'Possibly someone's dangerous driving. Anyway, sorry. I didn't realise. Yes, it sounds big.'

I walked around to his side of the workstation and looked at his screen. He'd written two hundred words and had a few thumbnail images he was using as reference material.

'Any names?' I said.

'A couple only so far.'

'Be super careful. You know the drill. I got a name wrong once. The guy was still in hospital, not dead. Apart from the grovelling to the bosses, the worst is the phone call to the relatives.'

'Better than the other way round I suppose.'

I sighed and put my hand on his shoulder. There was never any fun in reporting these kinds of event. A murder or abduction had a fascination about it, a whodunnit, a Morse.

But car crashes, lorries squashing vans into a quarter of their size, vehicles strewn around the road like in a children's playground – that was really dark.

'Jamie is waiting, you should go. He sounded anxious.'

I squeezed his arm and laughed.

'Jamie doesn't do anxious very well. Something must be up.'

I walked to Jamie's door and knocked. While I waited, I straightened my hair, pulling it back from my face, and I brushed down my jacket and skirt. I was wearing a navy suit and white blouse, I wanted to look my best.

He summoned me in.

***

His laptop was giving trouble. That seemed to be the focus of our meeting.

'What did you want me for?' I said, as I sat with my fingers poised to take notes.

Jamie was dangerously interesting, but he was also the boss. Although sometimes awkward, he never failed to notice any small change I had made, complimenting my hair or saying my outfit suited me, always in a professional manner. I could tell he genuinely liked me. He looked as if he was really making an effort with his clothes and lately he had invested in a new range of fragrances.

'That was an hour ago. Things have moved on. Where have you been?'

I told him what I had discovered from Gary, leaving out the lap-dancing club.

'You dating Gary again?' he said.

'No, I'm working on a story.'

'Good. Well, apart from the fact that apparently there's a whole new batch of Romanians arrived, my laptop has died.'

I wasn't sure which to react to. He spoke as if they were a consignment of imported eggs but I forgave him that. Laptops were personal things and I knew better than to mention backups.

'Have IT taken a look?'

'Oh yes, of course. You know how it is. *Rebooted it Mr Wilson? You have it backed up, Mr Wilson?* Very helpful, I'm sure.'

I stood up and walked around to his side of the desk and, without asking, I put my hand on his shoulder as we looked at the screen together. It was like dealing with Henry or a child, except this was a sinewy, athletic shoulder.

'Let's see if we can work this out,' I said.

'Don't patronise.'

I leaned forward a bit and he pressed his arm against me as we looked. There was a window on the screen with a strange message about inappropriate activity on the network.

'Have you been looking at something that you shouldn't?'

'As if. Of course not. I'm careful to do that kind of thing on my desktop at home. What do you look at, by the way?' He looked up at me with a big grin on his face.

'Been gambling?'

'Nope.'

'Hacking into GCHQ?'

'Not that either. I've been doing a piece on the benefits

of working beyond sixty and how the jobs that sixty-year-olds would be prepared to do are being taken by the migrants.'

I stood back and snorted in disgust. Jamie always found the same angle. The trouble was that the readers loved him. The Summertown battalion of neo-conservatives. The North Oxford Tea Party.

'Perhaps the socialists have hacked into your hard drive,' I said.

'It could happen.'

'Call IT again. Tell them the commies have landed. Order a lock-down. They'll love it.'

My phone beeped with a message inside my bag.

'That'll be them, the reds,' I said.

I read the screen and it was Becky. I hadn't spoken to her since Sunday lunch. I sat back down to read it properly, leaving Jamie to press random letters on his keyboard. At one point he looked up and smiled, then cast his eyes over me inappropriately, causing me to blush and adjust my skirt.

'Mr Brown was pretty wealthy. We will need more on his finances,' I said.

'I've ordered a report. Business, personal, the lot. It'll take three days.'

Jamie shut his laptop and slapped it hard on the lid. He straightened his tie and cleared his throat. There was something coming. Something else. The Queen looked down on us from the wall, sitting sideways on a chair and smiling. Next to her, the JPS Lotus was captured with four wheels off the ground at Monza in Italy. Jamie could only have been about four years old at the time, and already a car enthusiast and a royalist.

'So, what did you want?' I said.

He walked over to the window and looked out. Jamie's office overlooked the back, a quiet garden area stretching down to some trees that separated us from a quiet suburban street. The lawn was maintained by a contract garden company and always looked neat and tidy all year round.

'We need to be sure to maintain professionalism,' he said.

I could not see what he was getting at. Had I done something wrong? He carried on talking to the glass.

'There's always conflict at work, a sort of conflict of interest. It is difficult sometimes. We must be careful to maintain a certain level of behaviour that is appropriate,' he said.

'Of course. That's vital,' I said.

He turned and smiled, like he'd just been given a big bag of sweets. Then he returned to his desk.

'That's all for now, thanks. Keep digging. We'll go to see David Brown together this afternoon,' he said.

***

The sign on the shop door was a sheet of white paper, taped on with parcel tape. *Closed for at least a week* was printed in a large typeface. The police had gone; normal life had resumed. Regular shoppers would find their daily cigarettes and bottles of Coke further afield.

When David Brown opened the door to us, a wave of heat spilled onto the pavement carrying the aroma of a corner sweet shop, heavily laden with sugar and liquorice. We stepped inside and he double-locked the door behind us, then pulled the blind down.

'Can't be too careful. So many kids around causing me hassle,' he said.

He was a man of medium height with a heavy build, slightly balding and short, tidy greying hair. I wondered whether he'd been to get his haircut that morning or whether he owned some clippers. He wore dark-rimmed glasses, almost round, giving him a retro-fifties appearance. He just needed braces and armbands to complete the look. His face was badly bruised around the eyes and his left cheek, and his arm was encased in a bandage and resting in a sling, although apparently not broken. Fortunately, there was no blood visible.

'I'm Jamie and this is Emma. We're very sorry for your situation,' Jamie said.

Other than the newspaper rack being empty, the shop looked normal. It had been shut for three days but there was nothing that would go to ruin. Jars of sweets lined the wall behind the counter and a rack of cards and magazines sat over to the right beside a door to the back room. Last month's *Hello* magazine lay in a pile next to the till, the beaming face of a pregnant celebrity standing next to her man outside a castle gate smiling out from it.

'I'll have to reopen eventually I suppose. People will find shops elsewhere, there's no loyalty these days.'

'Don't worry. They won't divert too far from their commute. I know I won't. There's always room for a corner shop,' I said.

'You'll get the ghouls and nosey Nellies, at least for a while. You'll probably notice a boost to takings,' Jamie said.

Mr Brown showed us through the door at the back into

a small corridor. The walls were a deep shade of purple and there were no windows, so the light cast sharp shadows. There was an open door off to the right to another room where I could see boxes of stock piled up across the floor. Crisps, cigarettes, dark chocolate bars.

At the end of the passageway he led us into an oblong room that looked to be their living room. It was warm and comfortable, softly furnished with a modern dark leather couch, facing a television with extra loudspeakers each side. An office desk and chair were on one side, and at the back of the room was a dining table where he took us to sit.

'Tea?' he said.

We declined and got out our notebooks.

'We prefer to just get on with it if that's OK, Mr Brown. I'm sure you don't want us in your life any more than need be,' I said.

Jamie led the interview. He was dressed in a blue suit and tie, and sat comfortably with his leather Filofax open on the table in front of him. David Brown did well to follow Jamie's brogue as he rehearsed his opening questions. I usually observed people struggling when they first met him.

'I suppose you want to know what happened,' David said.

'That, and any thoughts you have about the perpetrators,' he said.

'I've told all I can to the police. I didn't want to talk to you people but I suppose I am in the trade, and I can see that it might help find her, if you publish front page. Keep her in the news.'

'It'll be front page as long as it takes. We'll do all we

can.' Jamie smiled at him, scribbling as he did.

David related the events. The back doorbell had rung repeatedly, around 2am. He thought perhaps there'd been some kind of incident directly outside his shop. He left Amanda in bed and went downstairs and opened the door.

'That was my first mistake. All those training sessions about security I attended at the police a few years ago, and I simply opened the door to them.'

His voice wavered as he spoke, and he looked like he hadn't slept. Three men in balaclavas had burst in. It was amazing he hadn't had a heart attack: he looked unable to deal with any kind of stress.

'At first, I didn't see the weapons. Then one of them waved this metal bar at me and shouted for me to get into the storeroom. At that moment, I thought it was a raid and I would die if I didn't do what they said. I also thought I'd get it over with fast and hoped that Amanda didn't come down to see what the commotion was.'

I asked to see the empty safe in the storeroom once we'd finished the interview and suggested we took a couple of photos of him alone.

'Do you have a photo of Amanda we can use? Something we can publish? I don't want to be indelicate, but perhaps a smiling, attractive one, please. Something attention-grabbing?' I said.

'I have plenty of those. Amanda is a stunning woman. She is younger than me and has a beautiful face.'

'Did they force the safe?' Jamie asked.

'No. I opened it. He kept threatening me, the one who was the leader. The other two hung back and never said a word. They were young though, younger than him. Could even have been teenagers.'

'Did he have an accent? When he spoke?'

'Foreign. Europe. East. No doubt in my mind,' he said. 'He demanded the contents. Said it was payback time.'

'Payback time? For what?' I asked.

David stood up and walked over to the small window that looked out on the back yard. He had a slight limp.

'I have no idea. Where the hell is she? What have they done? They took the money and just as we walked back into the hallway, she came down the stairs. She had wrapped herself in a coat and put on some trousers and shoes. She had the big torch in her hand.'

'Do you have an electric alarm, Mr Brown?' I asked.

'I used to. It stopped working about a month ago and I've been meaning to get it sorted out, but that's me isn't it. Useless. I leave all that stuff to Amanda.'

'So the bastards took her with them?' Jamie said.

David Brown turned back to face him and stared. The room was hot; he must have had the heating on all weekend. He had a sheen of sweat across his forehead. His hands were shaking.

'One of the lads grabbed her and held her arms behind her back while the other one put cable ties around her wrists. I leapt forward but the one with the iron bar took a swing at me, hitting me across the stomach, then he kicked me hard until I fell on the floor and he kicked me again, in the head and face. There was lots of blood and the swelling was closing up my left eye. Two minutes later they were gone, bundling her out the back door. She was screaming.'

I scribbled notes to stop me thinking about the blood, otherwise I would be sick, then I went into the next room to take some photos on my phone of the empty safe. Jamie and David continued to chat quietly and reviewed some snaps of his wife. When I came back, Jamie showed me two he had chosen, both of Amanda at functions wearing formal blue gowns with matching gold and sapphire jewellery to complement her striking features.

***

Back at the office, I sat at U1-5 and tried to focus on my research into East European criminals. The *Gazette*'s budget didn't stretch to a trip to foreign travel, which, given my challenges with Andrei, was probably a good thing. No doubt he'd pop up and tag along as a tour guide. Sunday lunch had been a disaster: Hazel loved him, and he was charmed by her effort at making Romanian plum dumplings with cream. Becky hadn't helped in the slightest, and the wonderful new Daniel invited Andrei to golf in the week. His feet were well and truly under the table.

Meanwhile Jamie was being demanding. He summoned me to follow him into his office, and he shut the door. There were piles of magazines and old papers on his desk, across the floor beside the window and on the visitor chairs. We stood and surveyed the scene of chaos, Jamie's chaos.

'I know where everything is. I'm having a sort-out,' he said.

'You need the hand of a good woman.'

He grinned and nodded.

'Broaden your research to the entire Romanian community. Resurrect that work you did before, the stuff about the impact on the Cowley Road, when you interviewed that charming waiter of yours. Make it hard-hitting, punchy, balanced but searching,' he said.

'I wish you wouldn't keep on about that. He's not my waiter, nor charming,' I said.

'Do you have a boyfriend?'

'Are you allowed to ask that? I mean, HR and all that. Not sure it's right.'

He walked over to the window to talk to the trees outside.

'I like you Emma, more than I should, probably.'

'Well, if you want to know, then no, I don't have a boyfriend,' I said.

'There, that wasn't so hard, was it? Now, get to your keyboard and get me that story. Remember – a woman is missing, kidnapped by a foreign gang.'

'Yes, boss.'

I returned to my desk with renewed enthusiasm which lasted until Gemma called me from reception, explaining a parcel had arrived. The Georgian mansion the *Gazette* had taken over a couple of years previously retained its period façade, and the reception desk stood in a large hallway with chequered black and white tiling and a vaulted ceiling with a chandelier. Soft uplighting and selective spotlights gave it a modern, warm glow. Julie and Gemma, both twenty-one, set the tone with matching black and white dress suits that gave the paper a 1950s feel. All it needed was a smoky atmosphere, but that would be a sackable offence, the designated area being across the back yard.

They were both laughing as I approached, looking at a card.

'This came with them,' Julie said.

She pointed to three huge bouquets of pink calla lilies. My heart sank as I took the card from her.

Darling Emma, Sorry can't help myself, it's like I'm caught in the headlights. Hope you like them, I know they're your favourite. Andrei x

He was factually correct about the favourite part. I turned the card over to see a print of the selfie he'd insisted on taking with me in his café when we first met.

'Aww, real sweet,' Gemma offered.

It would have been churlish to throw them away, at least not there and then. I gave them to Julie and asked her to keep them hidden in the reception cupboard until I left for the day. Not a word to anyone, on the promise of a drink sometime.

I sent him a text.

<This has to stop now, really it does. But thanks for the flowers. But no more please.>

4

When I arrived at the office the next morning, all thoughts of flowers were forgotten. The newsroom was in meltdown over a spate of fly-posters all along the Cowley Road. Overnight, someone had pasted them to the windows of all the shops that could be considered non-British or foreign. *GO HOME - NOT WELCOME HERE* was emblazoned across each one in large black lettering. It wasn't clear whether this was the work of an individual or a gang. Before I had time to go down there to see for myself, David Brown called. I put down the banana I was eating for breakfast and switched on the voice recorder.

'How can I help, Mr Brown? How are you feeling today?'

'I'm feeling a little more rested. My face still gives a lot of pain. The doctor has me on strong painkillers.'

He sounded downhearted. I scribbled on the pad to check my pen was functioning.

'Have you had posters on your windows?'

'No, and actually, I'm phoning about Amanda. I don't know who to turn to. Not the police.'

'What's happened? We can be totally discreet. One hundred percent guaranteed. It's the journalist's oath,' I said.

'Yes, well ... this is all new ground to me.'

'Have you had contact from Mrs Brown?' I said.

'No, not exactly. Not directly. But I've received an email. From the kidnappers. Or so it seems.'

'Well that's something. Isn't it? Surely the police could help trace it.'

He hesitated. I wrote some notes about kidnap demands, to review historical cases of them. It definitely sounded like a police matter.

'David?'

'It says no police.'

'Yes, well, they always say that. But I'm sure the police could be very circumspect. It's very much looking like a kidnapping for ransom, isn't it?'

He groaned. 'It does.'

'What does the email say?'

'It says they have taken Amanda and don't intend to return her. If I want her, they want money. More money than I have. Fifty thousand in cash.'

'Oh God, that's a fortune. Sorry ... OK, well let's not panic. I could talk to Jamie. Perhaps we should meet you again.'

'I have until Saturday, four days to get the money ready. I've no idea how to do that – they've already cleaned me out. But the fewer people that know, the better. I'd rather you didn't involve anyone else at all. Any suggestions how to find them?'

I stared at the blank computer screen in front of me waiting for inspiration.

'Anything odd about the email? Who sent it?'

'It looks like a made-up name. I'm not sure about forwarding it to you.'

'No. Print it out and I'll come straight over.'

***

After I put the phone down, I wrote a note for Henry, then called Gemma to get a taxi. My hand was shaking, more in anticipation than anything else. It was a big story.

The driver was slow in the rain as he shouted the answers to Ken Bruce's *PopMaster*. He was pretty good at the eighties. I sat in the back and checked through anything useful I could find on the Internet. It seemed there had been plenty of cases of kidnapping over the last few years, many of them ending in the successful return of the victim. Large corporations paying off rogue gangs. I wondered how big this could be, in such a sleepy part of Southern England. But there were fifty thousand pounds missing already and a demand for fifty more.

When I finally arrived, the shop was still closed and I tapped on the front door. The sign had been changed to: *Closed for the foreseeable future, thank you for your patience and good wishes.*

David looked more of a mess than last time. He had not shaved and he wore an old woollen cardigan that he must have had for twenty years. One sleeve hung loose over his injured arm still resting in its sling.

'Emma, thanks for coming. I don't know where to turn,' he said.

I went through to the kitchen and put the kettle on for him.

'Have you eaten?' I said.

'I can't eat.'

I looked through the cupboard and found a tin of

baked beans.

'Do you have any bread?'

'In the fridge.' He pointed to the corner of the room.

'Sit and eat, then we'll look at the situation together. You need food.'

I set about making beans on toast while he made us both a cup of tea. He looked gaunt, lacking in sleep. The blackness of the bruising was coming out on his left cheek.

We sat at the small table, stacked high with old newspapers. David discovered some ketchup at the back of the cupboard and proceeded to devour his lunch in large mouthfuls without speaking. I nibbled at a piece of plain toast, no butter.

'Do you have the money?' I asked.

'I could get it if I have to. Friends, favours.'

'They probably know that.'

'I've no choice.'

We finished up our food and David stood and put the plates in the sink. When he returned he put the printed email down in front of me.

Mr Brown. £50,000 in twenties. By Saturday. No police. No clever tricks. More instructions will follow.

It wasn't signed, but it was from byr2112@gmail.com.

'I'm sure there'll be a way of tracing that. I could get it looked at.' I said.

'Perhaps, but no one must know. Too risky. I'll get the cash somehow. I want her back.'

I made a note of the details and returned the email. He smiled briefly.

'Well, at least she's alive,' I said.

'It looks like it, yes. Also, I've remembered something

else.'

He shut his eyes and rubbed his temples while I watched him carefully.

'That night, when she was taken. She was trying to escape through the front door, I'm sure of it. It might be a small point,' he said.

'How do you work that out?'

'Well, I was thinking. When she came downstairs, she didn't have her slippers on. I found them beside the bed last night. It got me wondering. And I remember, she was wearing her trainers.'

'Is that so surprising?'

'Yes. She must have realised there was a raid, or something very wrong was happening. She came downstairs in some clothes with a coat and shoes. They grabbed her in the corridor there. I think she was trying to creep through to the shop. To escape. To raise the alarm.'

I scribbled on my pad and thanked him.

'Yes I see. This is something you should tell the police.'

'I will,' he said.

I stood and put my empty mug beside the kettle and packed my bag.

'I'll look into it all. Try not to fret,' I said.

***

After I left, I walked up Cowley Road towards the taxi rank. There was a halal butcher with every centimetre of the window covered in the posters. I tried to pull one away but it had been pasted down most professionally. Presumably the police were already checking CCTV of the street. This could not have been done in five minutes and looked like an orchestrated attack. I managed to pull one of the posters away without too much damage and stuffed it into my bag for later analysis.

In the taxi back to the office, I sent a text message to Lou-two.

<Anyone there who could help trace an email?>

I was fortunate to have friends who worked in all sorts of useful places. Louise was a PA in a high-tech company in Summertown specialising in computer security. If anyone knew someone, Lou-two would and she could keep a secret. Louise had been known as Lou-two ever since the first day of secondary school when she met Becky, Louise and me.

'We can't have two Louises in the same gang,' Becky said.

So the name stuck and I had even heard Lou-two's mum call her that when we were round at her house listening to music. Of course, there was no definitive spelling so it became a lottery when writing the birthday cards: Lou-two, Lou-too, Loutwo, Lootoo.

'You know you can call me Louise,' Lou-two said once when she, Becky, and I were out for a drink. We both looked at her as if she was talking in a foreign language and just laughed.

Over the years, Lou-two and I had become much closer, while Louise number one became very busy with her teaching work and missed many of our social occasions.

I also needed to know how David Brown could raise the money. What did he mean by friends and favours? Surely, no friend would lend that kind of money without asking lots of questions. And what of Amanda Brown? Why was she dressed? Was that coincidence, or had she been expecting to leave the building? Had she heard the raiders downstairs?

I was beginning to feel out of my depth, exacerbated by the need to concentrate on my next article, contrasting the positive economic impact of the free flow of people versus the pressure on fair wages locally. I resolved to talk to Jamie when I got back to the *Gazette* and request him to look into the money side of it while I investigated Amanda. It would be exciting to work together on such a high-profile newsworthy item. There was no doubt it would hit the nationals very soon, and we wanted to stay ahead of that.

My phone pinged.

<I can find someone for you. See you tonight to talk about it. L xx>

I'd forgotten it was drinks night. At this rate, I would be the last to arrive.

I pulled out the poster from my bag to review it. Larger than A4, the rough cream paper was filled by the text, professionally printed. In the bottom right-hand corner there was a very small imprint like an emblem or motif that I found difficult to make out. It looked like a series of letters or an acronym. Jamie might know.

5

Becky and Daniel wore matching T-shirts at our First Tuesday drinks in All-Bar-One. They each had a picture on the front: a pear cut in half. His had a logo alongside, 'One half of the Perfect Pair,' and hers said 'The other half of the Perfect Pair.'

It was the first time Becky had brought Daniel to the full gathering of the gang. Men were allowed occasionally but there had to be a special reason, like the first time you showed him off, or when you announced your engagement. Louise's Pete arrived last month and we'd all known straight away. She did the decent thing and didn't put her ring on until he'd made his little speech, spoiled a bit by the waitress whoop-whooping at the top of her voice while she poured the champagne, like we were eight years old at TGI's.

'So, Daniel, this is the full set. Emma, Louise, Claire and Lou-two,' Becky said.

'The famous five ...' he said.

'Not heard that before,' I said.

Claire and Becky were both teachers and Louise was in retail so it was the most convenient place to meet and we'd been doing First Tuesdays since before we all had such responsible jobs. These days it was a case of less alcohol and earlier finishes but we enjoyed staying in touch. Everybody interrogated Daniel for the first hour, but he took it all really well and Becky positively glowed with pride. The bar was crowded and our table was in the far back corner next to a group from the insurance company along the High Street who were having a leaving do.

Service was slow and I offered to get more drinks and stood up. Daniel leapt to his feet, declaring it was his round and he'd come with me. We worked our way slowly through the crowd and I looked back to see Becky watching us with a big grin. Hopefully the bar person wouldn't mistake *me* for the other half of his perfect pair.

'I played golf with Andrei today,' he said as we waited.

I shuffled forward in front of him to take control of the ordering.

'He's a great chap, full of stories about Bucharest. Did you know he has family there? Not a great golfer though. That gave my ego a boost.'

'Bottle of Merlot and two pints of lager,' I said to the barman.

'He wouldn't stop talking about you, Em.'

'Have you got a tray please?'

I stood aside to let Daniel pay, holding the tray close to ensure the wine didn't spill. Did he really think I wanted to hear about that man?

'We're not a couple ...' I shouted as he entered his pin, '... and only Becky calls me Em.'

When we got back to the others, I sat next to Becky and glared across the table at him. I didn't like the idea of Daniel and Andrei becoming friends, there was something just not right about it. Becky seemed oblivious to the problem. She nudged my knee with hers.

'What's wrong, Em?'

'Nothing. Thanks for the drinks Danny.'

He raised his lager and said 'Cheers!' We clinked glasses round the table. He talked about his work, alluding to a big case involving a software company, but he remained professionally circumspect and withheld any details. I sipped at my wine and sulked. Perhaps he could be useful in a future breaking story but for now I was focussed on Amanda Brown and there had been no further information from the police or any of my leads in the Cowley community. My only contact was Andrei, and Jamie was increasing the pressure on me to deliver stronger material about the impact of foreign gangs.

'You OK, Emma?' Claire said.

'Oh it's just work.'

'Ah, the missing woman is it, or is it the immigration? A thorny issue. I spoke to class about it today, you'll be pleased to know. I set one of your articles as a homework piece. "Immigration is good for the economy. Discuss."'

Claire worked at one of Oxford's private schools for girls. It was a long way from the Cowley Road, and I doubted there'd be much balance in their essays. Across the crowded bar, I spotted Andrei. He had just walked in off the High. I didn't want him meeting my friends. Emergency action required.

'Sorry Claire, just need the loo.'

I squeezed past her chair and headed towards him. He was scouring the horde, was he looking for us? I brushed my hair back from my face with my fingers and tied it loosely at the back as I worked my way past a group of students. I emerged from behind a rather large frizzy-haired girl to step in front of him.

'Emmy. Crikey, you made me jump. What are you doing here?'

He smiled and looked me over.

'One of my regular haunts, Andrei. And you? What brings you here?' I said.

He glanced over my shoulder like he was checking the tables for a friend, then he stepped closer and talked into my ear above the noisy bar. They turned the music up at seven in an attempt to rid themselves of the after-workers and attract the party-goers. He was a good fifteen centimetres taller than me and had to bend his head down, breathing on my neck. I shivered.

'I was looking for you, Emmy. You know that,' he said.

I pushed him back towards the door, away from the back corner where he could definitely not go, where he could never go. Becky and Daniel were enough, he was not to meet the others.

'Will you be my girl?' he said.

I felt his hands wrap around me, pulling me with him as I shoved him back.

'Get out, Andrei.'

'Is Lou-two here?'

He pulled away and grinned that lovely lopsided grin again. How on earth?

'Get out, Andrei.' I raised my voice and a couple sitting on a high bench near the window looked across at us. The man made a move to stand up, as if coming to my rescue, but I put my hand up to indicate everything was fine.

When we reached the front door, I walked out onto the

High with him. The door shut and deadened the music. A few smokers were standing in a circle by the front window with coats wrapped around themselves, a cloud of fumes and condensation forming a small smog above them. The pavement was busy with people heading out to see shows, going to restaurants or parties. I grabbed his arm and squeezed as hard as I could.

'Andrei, you are not welcome here. Leave me alone. You're scaring me. You're a nice guy but I don't want you following me. Help me find the missing woman, but keep it professional.'

He laughed.

'Sorry Emmy. I just wanted to meet your friends. I love that look with your hair, by the way.'

I pushed him, then turned to walk back into the bar.

'Sorry, I'll go,' he said, then he sighed and walked away.

'That took a while,' Claire said when I returned.

'There was a queue.'

I took a large slug of wine and sat back, shaking. Daniel looked across at me and could tell I was upset about something, but I wasn't about to sound off about his new best friend. He gave Becky a look and indicated toward me. Becky turned and held my hand.

'You OK?'

'I'm fine.'

'Andrei?'

'Why is everything about Andrei?'

Lou-two heard us talk and broke off her intimate chat with Claire.

'Who's Andrei?' she said.

I grabbed Lou-two's hand and pulled her to her feet, explaining to the others that she was helping me with some urgent aspect of the case. We walked over to a corner table where a couple had just gone and the server was clearing the plates and glasses.

'This is booked,' he said.

'We only need a couple of minutes,' I said and sat down, pushing Lou-two into the seat opposite. I took out the scrap of paper from my bag.

'Here's the email address. Is there anyone at Summercloud that might help? This is highly confidential so don't take any risks,' I said.

She looked at it and assured me that she would try, the place being full of technical experts. There was bound to be someone who could track it to source.

'Who is Andrei?' she said.

'He's just someone I know who is helping with the abduction story. He's a waiter on the Cowley Road. No reason why you would know him.'

6

The next day Jamie came with me to Cowley. He insisted, and I needed some help anyway.

'Just being protective,' he said, but I could tell he didn't want to miss out on any findings.

He drove us in his perfectly clean Mercedes from the car park at the back of the offices down through Marston to the side streets of Cowley. It was a smoother ride than the bus.

'We need to broaden it from just the Romanians and focus on the locals' point of view. What do they really think?' he said.

I looked across the car at him. He'd had a haircut and wore a sharp grey suit that fitted him well.

'You're overdressed for a casual stroll on the street,' I said.

'What are you suggesting?'

'Take off your tie. I'll put it in the glove box. And we should park at the back of Tesco's - it'll be safer than leaving it on the road.'

It was sunny again, and under a beautiful April sky the businesses of Oxford were burgeoning with shoppers. We queued for a space and put our bags in the boot of the car. Jamie also left his jacket and undid his shirt collar. As we walked back down Cowley Road, I briefed him on the task ahead.

'We're looking for real people, and we're not going to press too hard. Informal conversations. It's about all the posters but also Amanda Brown. Where could she–?'

'We need facts and figures,' he interrupted. 'Numbers of crimes, property break-ins, that kind of thing. I want you to focus on the reasons for the crime wave.'

'Jamie, it's my story, just so we're clear. I know what you want but I want to do it my way.'

'Of course, of course.'

We crossed at the lights and I took a few snaps of the scene using my phone. We could get the newspaper's photographer here another time for the proper pictures for the article but I just wanted reminders. I looked around. Three Indian women wearing brightly coloured, silk saris draped over their shoulders peered into the window of a book shop; a Jewish boy wearing a white satin kippah wandered by; Muslim men huddled together talking on the corner of the pavement, pointing to the wanton vandalism of the posters. The area was a thrilling blend of cultures in stark contrast to the traditional Oxford college quadrangles in the more conservative city centre.

As we approached the Victoria pub, the early lunchtime drinkers were out in force. A crowd of lads, probably football fans, were filling the tables and spilling over onto the pavement.

'Why don't you go inside, and I'll work round the outside,' I said.

Jamie eyed me.

'Fancy some sun, do you?'

'No, just easier to work separately, I reckon. Don't

want to scare them, do we?' I said.

He headed through the door and I walked up to the first table, clutching my *Gazette* clipboard. Thirty minutes later, I'd spoken to a dozen people, all happy to give me their views, but nothing new about the kidnapping. I managed to avoid the lads - I could read their thoughts anyway and I didn't want mouthfuls of abuse. I sat at a table on my own and compiled my notes into some sensible order. There was no sign of Jamie - he was probably quietly supping a beer.

All the time, I was keeping a close eye out for Andrei. A sudden appearance wouldn't surprise me. I couldn't concentrate. I kept my eyes on my notepad in case he happened to walk by, although I was beginning to think he didn't just 'happen' to do anything, and it was all carefully planned. He seemed to know my every move and it was beginning to seriously frighten me. Should I go to the police or would that be an overreaction?

Just as I turned the page to write up a quote about the local pickpocketing problem being mainly caused by kids, likening them to a modern day Fagin's gang, a man asked to sit opposite me at my table.

'No problem,' I said, returning to my work.

'You're a journalist then?'

He had a heavy Eastern European accent, white hair swept back and was holding a pipe that he threatened to light as soon as he'd finished pushing the tobacco into the bowl.

'I am. *Gazette*,' I said.

'I am Nicolae Constantin from Jilava near Bucharest. Pleased to meet you.'

He thrust out his hand and I put down my pen and

shook it.

'Emma,' I said.

'You are writing about us, no?'

'I am. Not just you, about the community. We're also trying to find Amanda Brown.'

'The missing lady.'

'Yes, that's right. Tell me about yourself. Have you lived here long?'

'I came here six months ago, with my two boys. My wife, she died a year since.'

'I'm sorry to hear that. Why did you come?'

'No work for my boys at home. Nothing to stay for. Others here first, we followed.'

'You are welcomed?'

'By some, yes, but not by all.'

He finished lighting his pipe, a ritual that took more than a few minutes. He looked more than sixty, portly like a bear. Even with the warmth of the day, he kept his jacket pulled tight.

'Have you suffered any crime? Any theft?'

'No, not me. My boys often have abuse shouted at them, but that's life and could happen anywhere, even in Bucharest ... especially in Bucharest actually.'

I smiled at him. He was right, all cities could be dangerous.

'What do your boys do? You said they work.'

'Grigore, he's the artist, he works in the theatre. Andrei, he's the clever one, computers, very special. But no work here for either of them, so Grigore delivers parcels on motorbike and Andrei, he waits tables.'

I stared at him, looking over his features carefully. He could be Andrei's father, there was no doubt. He had a slightly lopsided mouth when he smiled. I felt my stomach twist. Was this a coincidence? Surely there were plenty of Andreis around.

'Computers, you say? That's a big business. No jobs in that here?'

'Andrei prefers not to talk about it too much. In Bucharest, he worked in computer security, but he got scared. Needed to move out. We came here.'

I scribbled some notes and thanked him for his time.

'How did you know I was a journalist?' I said.

'Oh, I saw your picture in the paper. I always remember the pretty ones. Bright eyes, like the bright lights of a beautiful car,' he said.

I felt myself blush and stood to go. Jamie would be safer company. Too many coincidental meetings: it felt like I was being watched.

'Thanks for your comments,' I said, and walked inside the pub.

***

I persuaded Jamie to head back to the office alone, explaining that I wanted to take some more photographs and soundings along Cowley Road towards the city centre, then I would return to the office by bus. He had grown bored and seized the opportunity to escape.

As I approached the Browns' corner store, I wondered what I might find. The lack of contact since yesterday was not good. I guessed there had been no further word of Amanda.

The front of the shop was locked so I walked down the side to the back gate and tried that. It was open and I went through to the back door and tapped on the wood. While I waited I checked my phone for messages. There was nothing, no word from Lou-two on the email – not that I expected anything yet. Nothing from Andrei either. I banged on the door again, a little harder.

'Who is it?' a voice shouted.

'Emma Hawkins from the *Gazette.*'

I heard a bolt being slid back, then a second, before the door opened slowly and David peered out from the darkness inside, shielding his eyes from the brightness with his good arm. His bruises were continuing to develop and darken.

'You'd better come in,' he said.

I followed him into the back room and was hit by the smell of stale cigarette smoke and alcohol. Empty beer cans were strewn across the table, along with a half-eaten takeaway curry.

'Any news?' he said as he slumped back into the couch where he had clearly spent the night. A stripy duvet lay on the floor beside it along with the TV remote controller and yesterday's *Daily Mail.*

'I was hoping you might. You've heard no more?' I said.

'No. Been checking my email every few minutes but nothing at all. I'm going crazy.'

'So I see.' I walked to the dining chair opposite where he sat and took off a pile of dirty laundry, placing it on the floor so I could sit down.

'I haven't heard from the IT expert about the email address yet. I'm not sure there's much more I can do until we get more from the kidnappers.' I said.

David coughed a smoker's cough, wheezing and spluttering into a tissue he dragged out of his pocket. When he'd finished, he picked up a glass of water and drank half of it. Then he prised out two tablets from a metal wrapper and took them.

'Paracetamol, that's all. Headache,' he said.

'You're not in a good place at the moment. It's understandable. We're keeping close to the community, trying to get word from any locals that may know what has happened to Amanda. Have you heard from the police?'

'A liaison officer called. Nothing new,' he said.

'How about I make you a cup of tea? While you get dressed and ready for what's left of the day? We could go to get some food somewhere perhaps.'

David looked at me as if I was proposing to chop his leg off. He wrapped the blue towelling gown tightly around himself and folded his arms. He was wearing blue slippers, and I wasn't sure what else.

'I can't go out.'

'Of course you can. Fresh air, a walk. You have a mobile phone. Any contact will come through fine. It'll do you good. Now, go and get freshened up,' I said.

I could hear him grumbling all the way upstairs, muttering my name. As soon as I heard the shower, I started nosing around.

Beside his couch was an old wooden desk with a printer on one side of it. There was a plastic box with pens and other bits of stationery, then a desk lamp and a pile of paperwork which looked like bills and bank statements. I worked my way through them quickly, scanning for anything that I didn't know already from the financial investigations we had made.

There were a few mobile phone bills but they didn't show any detailed call records. There was a tax demand for a couple of thousand pounds, not overdue. There was nothing wrong, nothing surprising.

I opened the single left-hand drawer and found a cash box with about two hundred pounds in it. There was also pile of coins in a tray along with a set of keys. I lifted out the tray to look behind it. Underneath was a jumble of old photos, mostly of him and Amanda, but it was the one at the bottom that caught my attention. Four men were standing in front of Oxford's luxurious Randolph Hotel, arms linked and smiling in dinner jackets. It was clearly old and a bit torn at the corners.

I studied the photo closely and could see that David was second from the left, though he looked a good ten years younger. I couldn't tell who two of the others were but the man on the far right was the one who really caught my eye. Could it be Jamie? He looked younger, probably in his early thirties, but had a good resemblance to Jamie. It made no sense.

I heard David coughing at the top of the stairs as he came out of the bathroom. I took out my phone and snapped a picture of the photo, then shoved it back into the drawer and closed it. I hurried into the kitchen and switched the kettle on.

David emerged looking fresh and clean-shaven, wearing a grey woollen sweater and black chinos. He walked with confidence and I could see a hint of the appeal he'd had for Amanda.

'Thanks,' he said as I passed him a mug of tea.

'You should go to the police. About the ransom note,' I said.

'No chance. I don't trust them. You find her for me. They'll mess up.'

'Will you pay? Where will you get the money?'

'My business. Just help me get her back safely. You're being so good to me.'

I was trapped. I knew I should talk to DI Richards or Gary but I couldn't betray his trust. If I did, that would be the end of my exclusive story. And I really should to talk to Jamie.

'OK, thanks. Remember, I want first dibs on any story. I'm just doing my job.'

He laughed. 'Newspaper people - always the same.'

'You've known a few then?'

'One or two over the years. Always looking for an angle.'

'Anyone I know? It's a pretty closed world, journalism, especially in Oxford.'

'Maybe. I can't remember the names now. It was a few years ago. When I first took on the shop.'

I studied his face, unblinking. Nothing, not a flicker of embarrassment. Had that really been Jamie in the photo?

'Come on then. Time for food, my treat,' I said and I grabbed his arm to drag him out the door.

7

My telephone interviews with a handful of Romanians unearthed no intelligence on Andrei, but more importantly nothing about the Browns. The people of Oxford saw the Romanians as a single entity, but when you dug into it, like any other community, it was fractured into a number of segments that had little to do with one another.

After leaving David at the café near his shop, I spent the afternoon researching and writing a piece about the women and how they supported their men to get jobs, as well as endeavouring to earn themselves. Jamie complimented it, but wanted more angle, more edge, something I felt uncomfortable about.

'It's not fair to say they are being shunned, or are unwelcome,' I said.

'But they are taking our jobs, aren't they?'

'They are working, but that's just adding to the economy, building up the area. They are not *our* jobs, they're just jobs.'

'Well, you have to identify whether that would have happened anyway. What about the local unemployment rate?'

I stood my ground but Jamie was the editor, the leader writer, the boss. He'd been with the paper for twelve years, ever since he'd moved down from Glasgow, and had broken many front-page exclusives in his time. My story needed a sharper angle. I was thankful for Jamie's attention to my career, and I enjoyed working with him. I couldn't be certain it was him in that photo with David, and I decided to do more digging before asking him. I opened the photo on my phone and forwarded it to Gary with a note, asking him to name anyone he could recognise.

I caught myself wondering about Andrei working as a waiter in a café. Was that adding to the economy? Did it benefit Oxford? Did it matter? And was he the same Andrei who was a computer specialist?

Becky sent a WhatsApp from school, saying the talk of the classroom was an attack on a Muslim woman on her way to work that morning, just for covering her head. Apparently one of the kids had put up a photo of the altercation on Instagram, but immediately taken it down again. Becky was great at keeping me informed but I didn't want to be distracted so I passed it on to the incident desk to dispatch a reporter.

After reworking the article three more times at my desk, I returned to Jamie to ask for another day, so that I could chat with a couple of my sources before being sure.

'I need it by tomorrow, Emma. Take your time to see it my way,' he grinned.

I packed my laptop and walked out the front of the building into the bright spring afternoon. The wild rose hedging filled the street with a sweet fragrance, and passers-by smiled with the blue sky. I crossed to the gym on the opposite side of the wide main artery into Oxford's centre, and clocked into the card system for my Wednesday workout. Mornings were my usual time at the gym, but I had been too busy lately preparing for my briefings with Jamie. The place was much busier than the regular 7am slot, filling up with the teatime crowd, and I found a locker in the far corner to change, then emerged to the main floor to find a treadmill.

After thirteen minutes of my twenty-minute hill-walking workout program, I glanced up at the window that showed the corridor through to the weights area. One of the staff was giving a tour to the batch of new signees, three men and a woman, dressed in casual clothing with their backs to me, who were peering into the small coffee lounge. Surely not? Yes, it was Andrei. Of course it was Andrei. Joining my gym.

I stopped my machine and scampered back to the ladies' changing room, where I waited for more than half an hour, taking a slow shower and drying my hair fully before daring to venture out.

As I walked back out the front of the building, I chatted to the girl on reception.

'Wow, busy today in there. I don't usually come in the afternoons.'

'Getting more so, lots of new people lately. There's been a promotion.'

'I saw some new ones being shown around. Is there a list of members available?'

'No, they don't give out names. This lot joined yesterday. There's loads of them coming over at the moment and some of them can't even speak English.' She leaned forward, lowering her voice. 'They're probably all on benefits anyway. This country's full up, if you ask me.'

'Does that matter? As long as their money's good and they follow the gym rules. Nothing to say they have to speak is there?'

I felt myself getting sucked along a road I shouldn't. She wasn't Jamie. Anyway, sticking up for Andrei, what was that about?

**

On Thursday morning, the Cowley Road market filled the streets, and traffic was diverted along the Iffley Road. The stalls offered produce from around the world and I looked for possible interviewees amongst the traders and the customers.

'Hi, I'm Emma from the *Gazette*. Care to comment on the growing numbers of people from Romania?'

Each time, my opening line prompted an unexpected response. Traditional Oxford market old-school clientele would welcome them, but recently settled Indians said enough is enough. I noted each response as I wandered through the mêlée. I found myself edging towards the side street which held the Romanian café and realised I had an opportunity to spy.

At the corner shop, I bought a sandwich and a can of Coke, then I settled with my back leaning against a wall along the street from where he worked, and I waited. I wasn't sure what for. It was gone twelve and the café was busy. I could see the outline of Andrei through the net curtains, picking up plates and cups from tables and bringing out steaming plates of Romanian food. I'd eaten there twice before, delicious traditional *supā* and *gogosi*, or deep fried doughnuts to me. I munched on my tuna-mayo sandwich, looking through my notebook and keeping one eye on him.

I came to my senses when an Indian boy, no more than

ten, walked up to me.

'What you doing, miss?' he said in a mix of Indian and Oxfordshire accent.

'Eating my lunch.'

'Got any spare?'

I looked at him, straggly haired and smiling. I passed him the second half of my sandwich and he took it and ate quickly.

'Hungry?' I said.

'Always. Thanks.' He smiled.

'I'm Emma from the *Gazette*.'

'Ishan.'

'Care to comment on the growing number of people from Romania, Ishan?'

He laughed and eyed me carefully. 'Where's that?'

'It's in Europe.'

He shrugged, then gave me the best quotation of the day and my first paragraph changed in front of my eyes.

'All welcome here, that's the beauty of the place,' he said.

After he'd finished off my Coke, I gave him my card and told him to call with any more gems, then he was gone, merging back into the crowd. I felt the need to sit down and was just about to give up when I saw Andrei emerge from the door opposite. He was wearing a black leather jacket and jeans and walked quickly to the corner with Cowley Road. I hurried over to follow and fortunately he didn't look back. I didn't have a plan if he did.

As he walked by the Victoria pub, he passed the gang of short-haired youths in shorts and T-shirts who were drinking on the benches in the sunshine again. One of them called out to Andrei, telling him to go home. The others joined in and Andrei waved his fingers at them, and shouted 'Bugger off!' Two of the lads ran out from the pub forecourt and started shoving Andrei, pointing their fingers into his face. He pushed back and a fist flew, landing on the side of Andrei's face causing him to stagger back. Passers-by stood aside or walked on quickly and I was tempted to run across to him but I shrank back behind an advertising board that stood outside of the door of the pub and watched.

As soon as it had started, it ended. The lads returned to their gang and Andrei walked on, holding one of the café napkins to his face. Blood ran down his cheek and nose from a cut just above his eyebrow.

I followed twenty steps behind as he navigated through the line of market stalls. A series of fabric sellers offering sari materials and silks were busy with ladies from the Sri Lankan community; after them were a small section of Polish delicatessens and then a hat stall with bright red and blue beanies hanging from the support posts, and piles of trilbies and sun hats on the table.

When he stopped to tend to his wound, I waited and rummaged through a few floppy felt hats, maintaining a discreet distance. As I considered my bohemian look in the mirror, my phone pinged a message from Lou-two. Apparently there was no way of divulging any information about the ransom email address due to data protection laws, something her company was very fussy about. So it was back to the beginning with that one.

I was curious about Andrei's destination when he set

off again. He had walked past three bus stops already so I decided he must live around here somewhere. He crossed over and turned down Magdalen Street then immediately stopped at a black door between two shops. I watched as he took a key out and let himself in.

I was shocked but the venture had been worthwhile. On the left of the black door was a gym, so why was he trekking half way across Oxford to join mine?

8

'He probably just wants to get fit.'

Becky was having none of my concerns, when I told her all about it on the phone. Rather than return to the office, I'd gone to my flat to concentrate on finishing my work by Jamie's deadline. Easier to focus, I argued, spending an hour writing up an imaginary doomsday scenario where every migrant worker in Britain took a week off at the same time. It was difficult to quantify the possible impact and then I was easily distracted by cooking and chatting.

'Anyway, you're the one being a stalker, following him around like that, poor lamb. Not even standing up to those thugs for him. You could have taken photos and reported on that,' she said.

'But he's being weird. Why's he following me around like this?'

'He's just being sweet, that's all. He's a cute guy.'

I sighed and gave up, and we moved on to other news of the day, Becky's run-in with the head of year about her views on grammar schools. She never could keep a low profile. I was no further forward on the Browns and I wasn't going to mention the ransom demand to her even though the deadline was looming. Becky filled the rest of her time talking about Daniel. He had taken her shopping after school and bought a necklace from a very fine jewellery store at the mall. I finished up the call with her, turned *Come Dine with Me* back on and returned to cooking my chilli. It was my aunt's recipe that she had taught me when I first experimented in the kitchen as a teenager. I still put in extra dark chocolate to give it her special flavour.

After I'd eaten, I worked late into the evening to rewrite the article, explaining the wide range of views and stress points in the community. I made particular reference to the feeling amongst unemployed youths who had nothing better to do than sit outside pubs on street corners. I had no evidence they were responsible for the posters on the windows, so I only made a very oblique comment about that. Finally, I felt I'd captured it all correctly and mailed it off to Jamie.

My alarm woke me at seven on Friday morning and I showered and dressed and raced out the door, down the dozen steps to the hall. The post had arrived early: an envelope was lying on the welcome mat. I picked it up, ready to put it on the table for one of the other tenants, then realised it was for me. Inside was a postcard. On the back was scribbled: *Emma, my beautiful Emmy, A xxx*

I turned it over to see a black and white aerial photograph of a European city. In the bottom corner was printed 'Bucharest'.

'Bloody man!' I shouted.

I opened the front door. On the step was a brown-paper parcel the size of a shoe box and tied up with string. When I picked it up, I saw it was also addressed to me. I went back into the hall, put down my bag and opened it.

It was the size of a shoe box because it was a shoe box.

A brand new pair with a gift card from him. Size five. My size. How did he know that? They were red, heeled and open-toed, just like a pair I'd admired online recently and put into the shopping basket for later. This man was invading my privacy if he was monitoring my browsing like this, and I needed to get it stopped. I ran back upstairs and put the box into my flat, resolving to return them later, then I set off for work again.

***

Jamie put down the printout, stood up and walked to the window.

'Much better. Add some numbers. New settler counts, number of new businesses – that sort of thing. Try to get more on the kidnapping too. But you're nearly done,' he said.

'I'll call Bill to reserve space in next week's paper.' I said.

'It's well balanced. A bit too balanced for my taste, but enough to wake some interest. We'll track the social media for commentary. Don't want to instigate a riot, do we?'

I smiled at him. He looked pretty good for a forty-year-old. We'd had the birthday party to end all parties last July for him. His eyes smiled back.

'We'll celebrate publication with a drink later,' he said.

'Yes, sir.'

He laughed.

'Get off now wench, I have editorials to write.'

Returning to U1-5, I spent the next hour making the changes we'd discussed, then mailed him a final copy and forwarded it on to the Production department. I felt elated about the piece and Jamie's reaction, but it was twelve o'clock and I needed to think about the Browns and what to do next. It was nearly deadline day and there was no word from David. He wasn't picking up his mobile, and when I called the shop number it rang out for over a minute before I gave up. It was clearly time to see if I could find David at the shop, so I set off for the bus stop, smiling all the way. Investigative journalist writes with a social conscience. I would work on my LinkedIn profile at the weekend.

I clambered aboard the Number 2 and as I looked along the bus, there was Andrei, his head buried in a copy of the *Gazette*. I took a second look, then rushed upstairs. My phone buzzed with a text. I sat down and checked it.

<*Hi beautiful. You look wonderful today. I like the dress.*>

My blood boiled.

I decided to call his bluff and turn the tables. I needed to know more about his apparent technical skills and what he was up to. When we reached the final stop at the Martyrs' Memorial, I came down the stairs with everyone else and waited for him when I got off.

'Hi Andrei, how's things?' I said.

'I miss you. Fancy a beer?'

We settled into a booth in the Mitre. One drink, I thought, although I stuck to diet Coke. I had to rush to find David. I took off my coat and he smirked that lopsided smirk.

'What do you do for a job, Andrei?'

'Well, you know, I'm waiter.'

'Yes but you've not always been a waiter. Are you waiting for something better to come along?'

'I'm waiting tables, that's what I'm waiting. But yes, I suppose so. It's not exactly a career,' he said.

'Did you study? When you were younger? In Bucharest?'

He sipped at his beer and considered me. I was taking him seriously for once.

'What's with all the questions?'

'I'm just curious. Professional interest only.'

'But we make such a wonderful couple. You will see. One day.' He reached for my hand but I pulled away and sat back.

'I'll leave if you don't stop. Now concentrate. What did you study?'

'Well if you must know, computers. I'm a bit of an enthusiast.'

'I thought so,' I said.

A group of Japanese teenagers arrived at the bar, bringing a great deal of noise and laughter. The bartender pointed to the age rules, causing more laughter as they retrieved their documents. They were probably twenty, but looked about fifteen. Andrei leaned towards me to speak.

'How did you think so? Do I look like a geek?' he said.

'No, no, it's just some information I had, that's all.'

'Well there you have it. Now you know all about me. That's good. Did you like the shoes?'

'I did, but they must go back. I can't accept gifts. How did you know I'd like them?'

'Well, I have ways of knowing these things.'

He looked confident, not arrogant, like he had a supreme belief in himself. A self-assured waiter.

'That is totally unacceptable and probably illegal, Andrei. I don't know what you're doing but it's scaring me. I should go to the police immediately. I'm horrified. And the shoes, they still need to go back.'

'Sorry. Please, sorry. I get carried away at times. I will stop. I get bored in the café, it is the fun of the challenge I need. Let me turn it to good, not bad.'

He sighed and finished his beer. Before he had chance to suggest another, I started putting my coat back on. Perhaps I could keep quiet about this and he could be of some assistance.

'I have a request. A couple of things you can help with,' I said.

'Anything for my Emmy.'

'If this is to work, you have to stop calling me that. I can offer you some investigative work, but you must keep it totally confidential. Otherwise I will go to the police about what you have been doing. You must see this as a professional arrangement, I'm not interested personally. I don't know how to make that any clearer.'

He smiled again.

'I don't want any money, but I am eager and willing to help. What can I do?'

'First you must promise total secrecy, and promise to understand there is no us.'

'I do,' he said, putting his hand on his heart as if he was an American making the Pledge of Allegiance. 'I solemnly promise.'

I pulled out the note of the email address that I had from David and explained what I wanted. I didn't go into any reasons, or mention the kidnapping or ransom at all, or that I had given it to Lou-two already, and there were concerns about data protection. I just wanted to find out its source. It was a long shot – it was a made-up email to act as a way of contacting David, but there had to be a real person behind it.

'There's something else. There has been vandalism all along Cowley Road as you know, posters on windows. I need to know their source. There's some sort of symbol at the bottom corner of the posters. What is that? Can you help? Take a look and let me know.'

***

When I arrived outside David and Amanda Brown's shop, it was as I expected, locked and in darkness, the blind down and the shutters up. I tried round the back with no success. I sent a text message to David to try to get some response, then waited a few minutes before deciding I had made a wasted journey.

I headed back to the flat instead of the office to continue my work there, first making a cup of tea and lying back on the couch, putting my feet on the bean cushion, My living room was swamped by the three-seater leather monstrosity that I had inherited from the previous tenants. 'You'll love it,' they'd said. Although I had vowed to get rid of it, the reality was it was too big to get through the door in one piece and I'd have to hire someone to dismantle it and take it to the recycling centre, costing more than it was worth. I just got used to living with something I hated. I'd bought a flowery throw to cover the back of it and resolved to move out in six months. That was two years ago.

At least my television was new. I spent last year's bonus on it, figuring it might encourage Becky and a few other friends to come round more often, which it did for a while. That was until Daniel arrived on the scene.

Halfway through my second cup, I remembered the shoes. I was going to return them immediately, but there was no harm in a trial. After all, that was what online ordering was all about. I took them out of the tissue paper and wrapped the first one around my foot like a glove. My toes fitted perfectly and when I'd done up the thin leather strap around my ankle, I put the other one on and tottered slowly across the room. Perfection in red. I was in love. Tricky. I would just have to pay him for them and eat a bit of humble pie. I made a note of the cost and resolved to withdraw it in cash, ready to give Andrei when we next met.

My phone pinged a message and I reached into my bag to look. Before I got to the phone, I found a small pink box tied with a ribbon with a pink card. My heart sank. What now? He must have slipped it in there when we were at the pub.

The card read:

<Sorry, you may as well have this as well. I bought it before. I promise no more. A x>

I undid the ribbon and opened the box. When I pushed back two layers of pink tissue paper, there was a rose pink silk camisole top, so soft and so gorgeous. I checked the size but, of course, I didn't need to. It would fit perfectly and I would love it.

I checked my messages and there was one from Gemma saying there would be a press conference about Amanda Brown at five o'clock at the police station. I needed to get my skates on. Presumably David would be there. I called him again and it went to voicemail, so I sent another text urging him to reply. As I was putting my coat on, my phone pinged.

<Can't talk, with police. Come to shop tomorrow. 6:30am. I need your help. Time to pay.>

9

The press conference was in the police media centre at the station out of town. The three-storey block was put up in the Seventies, a flat-roofed brick building brimming with windows and corridors, these days used for briefings and staff training, rather than anything custodial.

The room was square with six rows of seats facing a small stage. Behind it was a large poster of Amanda Brown, smiling into the camera. Lighting was set up to assist the television crews, and an engineer was testing the microphones and PA system. I arrived early enough to grab a seat on the front row. There was growing interest in the case from the national press and television, especially with the undercurrent of concern over the tension regarding immigration, and the spate of so-called hate crimes in cities across Britain.

I sat next to a couple of journalists I knew from the other newspapers in Oxfordshire, and the row behind filled with a group from London, the so-called professionals. There was a buzz of chat about everything other than the case in hand. Eventually, the door off to the right opened and Inspector Richards entered followed by David Brown then another officer, a woman. The three of them walked up onto the stage and took seats behind a long desk.

Richards saw me straightaway and smiled, a slightly

unnerving experience in front of the crowded room. He looked apprehensive and I suspected the media attention was something that he hadn't experienced before. He had obviously polished up the buttons on his uniform and cleaned his shoes, or someone had for him. I looked at David Brown. He sat upright in the chair, impassive, his face blank. He still had bruises around his eyes and his arm in a sling.

Inspector Richards took control. 'Thank you all for coming,' he said into the microphone, leaning slightly forward to make sure he could be heard. The noise in the room subsided.

'I'll pass this on to Sergeant Morgan,' he indicated the woman sitting at the table, 'to provide you with all the details we know, then I'll say something about how you can help, and David will also have a statement to read out. After that we can take a few questions.'

The sergeant outlined the facts of the case. The person next to me scribbled roughly into a paper notebook but there was nothing I didn't know already. It had been a week since Amanda had gone missing and there was still no knowledge of her whereabouts or any contact from the kidnappers, or so the police said. There was no mention of a ransom demand.

After about ten minutes, it was David's turn. He unfolded the piece of paper in front of him and spoke slowly, well briefed in the art of the emotional plea. It looked genuine, but who could be sure? So many husbands had made similar appeals for their loved ones to return, and then turned out to be guilty themselves. David must be a suspect.

'I ask you all, anyone out there who knows anything, or had any contact with Amanda to please, please come forward or call the emergency number, in confidence.' His voice faltered in all the right places but he seemed to retain an air of coldness and distance from the entire event.

Inspector Richards took control. 'We'll take questions. We really need you all to help us in this. We are appealing for any witnesses, any information or anything that can give us a lead in the case.' He looked more relaxed and commanding, tall with his fair hair neatly trimmed, his face strong.

The questions started innocently – details about the shop, the damage, the timings, the lack of CCTV. Then a voice called from the third row.

'Brian Edwards of the *News Chronicle*. Would you care to comment on Mrs Brown's former profession as a pole-dancer and tell us whether you think this has any bearing on the case?'

David Brown flinched, his cheek instinctively twitching, and he looked down at his hands.

'We're not sure. We don't think so, no. Mrs Brown worked briefly in London but it was a few years ago and we have not found any possible connection to the kidnappers,' Richards said.

'And Mr Brown? Would you care to comment on whether you think your political beliefs and activism have any bearing?'

The room went very quiet apart from the sound of a dozen pencils scribbling on a dozen pads. Sergeant Morgan slid a glass of water along the table towards David Brown and he sipped at it, clearing his throat. Richards took the initiative before he could speak.

'That's not something we believe to be at all relevant.

The word "activism" is not at all appropriate and we all have the right to any political persuasion we like. Kindly withdraw or rephrase the question. A woman is missing and that should be the total focus of us all right now.'

The *News Chronicle* persisted.

'Very well, I'll rephrase. Do you think your extreme right-wing activities of inciting riots and funding the nationalist party might cause someone to kidnap your wife?'

Inspector Richard's face reddened. Some insensitive hack was bound to bring up David's past. The murmurs were loudening into a buzz, the cameras were rolling and his CV looked threatened.

'We will leave it there. Mr Brown does not need to answer that type of question. Thank you, ladies and gentlemen, that will be all,' he said.

'Are you behind the recent spate of racist posters?' another voice shouted.

Richards looked directly at me, as if I could help in some way. I stood up to leave, encouraging others around me. Perhaps if enough of us made moves to go then it would take the pressure off, although I wasn't sure why I should be helping. David Brown's face remained flat and impassive as he was ushered from the stage.

My phone beeped with a message from Jamie, who had been listening on the radio.

<Waste of time. Need to look at the foreigners.>

***

When I reached my desk, the final version of my article

was there with a note to say it would be front page on Monday, with my own byline: a first for me. I photocopied it and posted it to Hazel, then I wrote a letter to Dad and carefully folded the article and slipped it into the envelope. I pictured him asking for Blu-Tack to stick it on his cell wall in prison.

Jamie's boss, Abigail Cadman, the editor-in-chief, called me herself, something that had never happened before, and I absorbed all her praise with a suitable level of self-deprecation, thanking Jamie for all his help. He arrived at my desk as I put the phone down, looking well-groomed with a fresh haircut and a suit I hadn't seen before.

'Let's go for that drink – you can tell me all about the press conference, not that it achieved anything. Give me a minute to shut up my office,' he said.

I heard it as an innocent. He was my boss after all and it was Friday evening. I watched him walk away from my desk, and he turned around and smiled. Why was I nervous?

***

We went to the Eagle and Child and sat in a corner booth away from diverse groups of tourists and Easter School students. Oxford changed character between holidays and term time, the gifted ones filling their three short terms and the tourists occupying most of the space between to soak up the atmosphere. What little study there was between Hilary and Trinity terms came from the various schools that put on part-time programmes aimed at developing the mind and providing one with an Oxford certificate.

'You're developing into a fine journalist, Emma,' he

said.

'I love it. And I have the perfect teacher.'

I raised my wine glass in a toast and he laughed, raising his in a slightly mocking way. Jamie didn't like to get too serious.

'What next for our lovely Miss Hawkins, then? Do you see yourself as an editor? Maybe London?'

'What about you? Time you found a good woman ...'

'You first. Time for a real man?' he said.

I sipped some more wine and sat back. 'Plenty of time for all that. Becky is leading the way on that front,' I said.

Jamie had met Becky at the *Gazette*'s summer party last year, held in the rear gardens of Trinity College, well away from the tourists peering through the wrought-iron gates while waiting for their open-topped bus tour. The sun shone and the barbecue, beers and dancing on the freshly mown lawn lasted long into the night. They seemed to get on well.

'Ah, the lovely Becky, yes,' he said.

'Anyway, I've got more than enough attention thank you.'

'I can see that you have, and you shouldn't be surprised.'

'Thanks.' I smiled.

'What sort of attention?' he asked.

I sighed, then told him most of my tale of woe with Andrei, all the accidental meetings and the little gifts, although I didn't explain the surveillance of my online shopping. It felt good to talk about it. Jamie questioned everything, and raised his voice when it came to the box with the shoes.

'He did what? The man's besotted,' he said.

It seemed like a good characterisation.

'He's sweet, but a bit weird and won't take no as an answer,' I said.

'Tell him to bugger off home,' he said.

'Only after I've got what I need for this kidnapping story. Anyway, Oxford is his home.'

'Well, I'll mark his card and we'll keep closer tabs on him.'

He didn't explain who 'we' were or exactly what he meant, but I was reassured to know that he was watching out for me. Becky was a good friend but a bit too keen on Andrei herself to be even-handed. Jamie was more balanced, if a little protective. I sipped some more wine and smiled at him.

'What about the kidnapping then? Richards is no further forward?' he asked.

'Doesn't look like it. He's not giving much away. I'll have to work on him a bit. I think he likes me.'

'No mention of a ransom demand. Looks a bit odd. The guy has plenty of money, I know that.'

I skirted around that topic and focussed on the press conference and the awkward questions raised. I decided against talking about the Randolph photograph I had found, at least until I heard from Gary, so I finished up my drink and made my excuses as quickly as I could, leaving Jamie to another pint. When he suggested meeting the next morning, I said I had to see Hazel and I'd see him on Monday.

10

We parked beside the locked gate to Florence Park, usually one of the more lively family parks of Oxford, but not at this time of day. The street was deserted except for a black cat that padded softly beside the iron railings seeking prey. David turned off the engine and a stillness descended over us. I turned to David. He looked pale in the eerie morning light. The phone call had said to be there as soon as the park opened.

'We're a little early. We should see the parks attendant come and open up soon,' I said.

'He'll be suspicious. What will we say?'

'Nothing, let's sit tight. Like we're just chatting. He probably won't even notice us.'

There was a mist hanging over the grassy picnic area beyond the gate, surrounded by neatly trimmed borders of privet and pink viburnum. The park was empty and locked overnight and I had no idea how the kidnappers expected to use it as an exchange place this early on a Saturday morning. I was sure we should have gone to the police, but it was too late to say that now.

'Will you wait ...?'

'Of course. Don't worry. You'll soon be reunited with her. This is good news,' I said.

He wiped his face with a tissue he got from his pocket,

then gripped onto the gym bag containing £50,000 in £20 notes. I had never seen that much cash until we counted it out at 7am on his dining table.

A man emerged from the gloom along the path next to the tennis club, and approached the gate with his key. He was nodding his head to the beat of his earphones and didn't look up once. When he had padlocked the gate into its open position, he ambled down the path towards the bandstand. There were at least three other entrances to the park that I knew, and presumably our perpetrators would be coming in by a different gate.

'Go on then, you'll be late,' I said.

David sat stock still, gripping the steering wheel for a few seconds, then I saw a tear appear in the corner of his eye as he stared ahead. His hand was shaking. I rested mine on his arm.

'You will be okay. I'll be here.'

Without another word, he grabbed the bag, opened the door and was gone, walking quickly through the gate. As soon as he disappeared around the corner of the wooden café, I got out and followed. I had to see as much as I could.

David crossed the open park towards the bandstand, the grass glistening with morning dew showing up his footprints as a track for him to return with Amanda. I stood behind a white rhododendron, stifling a cough and clutching my phone. It felt like I was in a movie - the clouds gathering in the distance threatening rain, an expectant silence hanging over the ground and no one to be seen. David arrived at the destination demanded by the kidnappers and stood beside the steps leading up to the Victorian platform. It had probably seen many generations of brass band players over the years, but now was largely unused and had taken on a shabby, dilapidated look.

I peered through the leaves and took a photo, then waited.

David moved from foot to foot for a while, then walked around the bandstand and returned to his starting point. It was 7:30am. There would be dog walkers soon. Was this a set-up? Just as I was considering phoning David to call it off, a man and woman appeared from the far side, along the path from the children's playground.

I could hear cars and traffic in the distance, the Iffley Road, not too far away. There was a shout of 'Puddles!' which made me jump and I looked around to see a Golden Retriever shooting past me. The owner was on the path behind me, and eyed me suspiciously when I smiled. I took out my earbuds and pretended to fiddle with them. Thankfully, I'd elected to wear my running outfit as a cover.

When I looked back, the couple was standing about ten metres from David. Even though it was the other side of the picnic ground, I could see the woman was Amanda. The man was taller and thick-set with hunched shoulders. He held onto her hand even though it looked like she was pulling away. There was some kind of conversation going on. I took another picture.

'You alright there, darling?'

I turned and yet another dog walker was passing. I waved my arm and pointed at my phone like I was sorting out my music, then started jogging on the spot. He nodded and carried on towards the gate.

When I turned back again, David had put the bag of money on the ground and had walked about another ten metres away so the bag was equidistant between them. I watched as the man, who was wearing a dark-coloured hoodie, walked with Amanda towards it and picked it up. I scanned the park quickly. The dog walkers were out of sight now and there was no one but me to witness the exchange.

Before I could step forward, I heard a motorbike. The park didn't allow them. It raced past me on the tarmac path then headed over the grass towards the scene at the bandstand. It was a powerful bike, creating a lot of noise for that time in the morning. The rider was dressed in black leathers and a black helmet with distinctive red, yellow and blue stripes that seemed vaguely familiar. It slid to a stop beside the couple and I watched the rider point something at David - it could have been a gun but more likely a stick or knife or something. I tried to capture it as a movie on my phone, although the light didn't seem too good, and I had to zoom it fully.

The person on the bike grabbed Amanda by her other arm and the first man let go, then picked up the bag of money and ran off away from me, towards the far entrance to the park. The biker pointed his weapon at Amanda then pulled her onto the back and rode off in the same direction. It all happened in an instant.

David gave chase but I could see he had no chance. He'd lost the money, and his wife.

⁣⁣*

After returning to my flat and a quick shower and

change, it was mid-morning and I waited at the window to be picked up. It was sunny and dry, just as Becky predicted, and I wore my skinny jeans and a bright yellow top with matching flat sandals. The perfect picnic for a Saturday, she'd promised, and it looked like she would be right, although I wasn't sure about spending the day with the wonderful Daniel as I had more than enough work, plus the fact that April was definitely not picnic season. Becky and I met when we were six, sitting next to each other in primary school. I had spoken to her almost every day since, meeting all her boyfriends, at least, all the ones that had lasted more than one date, so I could easily handle a new man in her life. This one looked more serious than any before.

David had said he wanted to be left alone, as he was in total shock and despair after the events of the park. All he could mumble was something about the deep voice of the kidnapper being familiar, but he couldn't be certain and the man had kept his face well hidden under the hood of his jacket. My video efforts proved to be next to useless as it was all too gloomy and too far away.

I walked back to the table to check the contents of the cool-box again. Two bottles of Sauvignon Blanc, carrot sticks, red-pepper houmous, taramasalata, pitta breads and a cheesy mushroom quiche. Ready for the park. I heard a car horn and looked out to see the roof of Daniel's car outside, so I grabbed my bag and the picnic and set off down the stairs.

When I reached the pavement, I could see him, Andrei, in the back. What have you done now, Becky? I stopped, about to turn back, when Becky leapt out the passenger door and threw her arms around me.

'Surprise!' she said.

'Indeed it is.' I said, stepping back from her hug.

'Aw, come on Em, it will be fun. And good for you.'

'Since when did you know what's good for me?' I said.

I remained as stony-faced as I could and glared at her without blinking.

'It's a beautiful day. Come on, get in.'

Against all my principles, I clambered into the back seat and sat next to Andrei. I made sure the picnic bag was secure and firmly between us.

'Hi Emmy,' he said.

'Emma.'

'Let's get this show on the road,' Daniel said as he pulled away.

The bright light meant I could keep my sunglasses on and avoid eye contact. The sharp angle of the sun gave the streets of Oxford deeply recessed shadows like the setting for a dark horror movie. All we needed were a few zombies on horseback to come riding by when we stopped at the lights.

The park in Kidlington was busy: today was one of the first opportunities for students still on Easter vacation to get out into the spring sunshine. There were a few tourists and local school kids all mixed in. I carried two blankets while the men brought the picnic bags and Becky skipped ahead to find a space near the big lonely oak tree in the centre.

'We'll need some shade!' she shouted.

I watched Becky and Daniel lay out the rugs a few metres away from an Indian family who were tucking into a feast of bhajis and pakora. I felt hungry. Andrei took the opportunity to whisper to me. He gave me an envelope.

'It has the details of that email address you gave me, it

is from Romania. I managed to extract all the emails that it has sent and received. Also, I found some information on that motif on the posters,' he said looking pleased with himself while ensuring Becky and Daniel did not notice. I stuffed it into my handbag and thanked him, squeezing his hand, deciding not to ask any awkward questions about how he had managed to unearth that.

As soon as I sat on the ground, Daniel brought out his frisbee and persuaded Andrei to join him on the open space behind the tree. Becky and I set about organising the food.

'What the hell do you think you're doing, Becky? I don't like the guy. He's not my type, and he's a contact for the investigation for me. It's not right that he is here.'

'Aw, don't worry about that. He's not helping you much anyway from what I can see. Anyway, he's lovely. I love his accent.'

'Actually, he's investigating something quite technical for me. And he's stalking me.'

'Come on Em, it's not like that. Only a few days ago, you were stalking him. He's just a bit smitten, it's all harmless. I think he's really cute.'

There's that besotted thing again, just like Jamie said. It sounded innocent, but not when you're on the receiving end.

'You fancy him yourself, don't you?' I said.

'Don't be daft. I have Daniel. Andrei has some hot features though, I must say.'

She giggled and looked at me. I knew she fancied him: lust was in her eyes.

'What hot features?'

'Well, you know, his arms – you know I have a thing for

that. And his chest, he keeps fit. His funny grin.'

I was beginning to feel a strange tug of jealousy. I'd had it plenty of times before with Becky. Men found her more attractive than me. Ben had picked up with her for a while after he and I finished when we were eighteen. If I didn't want someone, I didn't want Becky to want them either.

'Keep your hands off,' I said.

'See, you do care.'

She started to cut up the pitta bread into strips, just as the boys ran back laughing about the fact the frisbee had landed on a cow pat. I was in an Enid Blyton book, except that we had lashings of wine.

Conversation passed between Becky and Daniel, Daniel and Andrei, Becky and Andrei, and Becky and me. I ignored Andrei. We sat in a square, cross-legged, and I managed to sit at right-angles to him which, although still technically next to him, was safer than sitting opposite where he could just stare at me or smile inanely.

Every now and then he would reach across me to get the dips, allowing his arm to just touch my leg and every time I would flinch and move my leg away.

'So, are the ladies going to catch sunshine?' he said.

Becky laughed and gave Daniel a look. I lay back and looked up at the clear blue sky, imagining myself on a Caribbean beach, the sounds of happy children running, footballs being kicked and the occasional champagne bottle being popped. It was unseasonably hot.

Becky stood up and peeled off her bright pink lacy T-shirt, revealing a dark grey bustier that fitted snugly to her boobs and left her flat stomach bare, her low slung jeans helping to show off her toned abs. I glared at her through my sunglasses but she feigned ignorance and pretended to adjust the straps to ensure her modesty, just like the day when we were fourteen on the beach in Paxos on our first Greek holiday with her mum and dad, who were at the beach bar at the time if I remembered correctly.

Andrei stared intently at her. Daniel coughed.

'Come along Becky, sit down next to me. Let's relax for a while,' he said.

I just ignored them all and shut my eyes, smelling the grass and letting my hands run over the fallen bits of twigs and leaves.

'You look great, Becky,' Andrei drooled.

'Why thank you, kind sir,' she drooled back.

I sighed and turned onto my side, facing toward Andrei, and flashed him a quick smile.

'No comparison,' he said and smiled back.

I think we all must have dozed off at one point. I jumped when I heard a loud rumble of thunder and opened my eyes to see a huge, dark cumulus cloud towering high in the sky. The air had turned suddenly, with a cooler breeze, and the birds were circling and calling overhead.

'It's going to rain,' I said.

The others sat up, Becky's arms wrapped around Daniel, and we scrambled to pick everything up and make a run for the car.

The rain came heavily and I could see a lightning fork over the dreaming spires of Oxford. We ran along the path and when we reached the car, I leapt into the back, soaking wet.

'Perhaps you should take that top off?' Andrei said.

Becky had done just that, the hussy, in the front. She wrapped one of the blankets around her and proceeded to remove her top and lay it out on the dashboard. I pulled the other blanket to me and put it over my head to dry my hair, then I covered myself and slipped off my top to lay it on the back shelf. Well, at least I'd worn a modest bra that morning.

Both the boys took off their T-shirts and sat there naked from the waist up, Andrei the clear winner.

'We'll go back to my place - we can dry off properly there,' Daniel said.

He drove out of the car park, hardly able to see through the downpour and, as we headed along Sandy Lane back towards the Woodstock Road, we stopped in a queue of cars for the level crossing. I could see the red warning lights flashing and two cars waiting ahead of us. Daniel kept the wipers on the fastest speed. The rain lashed down on the road and the railway tracks.

After a couple of minutes, a passenger train raced through. I could make out people's faces watching us as we watched them. When it had gone, the red lights continued to flash and the barriers stayed down, so we continued to wait for quite a few minutes with nothing happening.

Andrei stayed quiet, fiddling with his mobile phone, presumably playing a game. At one point, he became quite animated, tapping the screen of his phone violently and making grunting and cursing noises.

The man from the car at the very front of the queue got out. He sheltered his head from the rain with his coat and ran to the barrier, then he kicked it hard causing the pole to shudder and the smaller hanging struts to shake.

'What's he doing?' Daniel said.

Andrei looked up.

'He probably thinks it's broken. There are no trains about,' he said.

'Wow, dangerous or what.' Daniel said.

Becky and I sat with our blankets wrapped around us and watched. The man continued to kick and pull at the barrier and eventually it started to rise very slowly until it stopped halfway at an odd angle. The barrier the other side of the crossing had done the same.

We all watched as the man returned to his car and start his engine. Clearly he was about to drive across.

Andrei immediately opened the rear passenger door and ran up the road. The rain bounced off his naked back and his soaked trousers clung to his bum. He stopped at the driver's door and indicated to him to stop, and to wind his window down.

Just as they started to speak to each other, another express train thundered by, the rush of air causing Andrei to hang onto the side of the stranger's car. I watched as Andrei retrieved his phone from his back pocket and tap onto the screen, then he shouted something else to the man in the car, just as the red lights stopped flashing and the barrier rose up to the fully open position.

Cars behind us hooted and the two cars in front of us pulled away. Daniel inched forward slowly and stopped to let Andrei jump back in, then he drove over the crossing.

'What was that all about?' Becky said.

'Oh, I could see there would be trouble if he tried to cross,' Andrei said.

'Wow, hero or what? You saved that guy's life, I'd say,' Daniel said.

I wrapped the blanket closer and shut my eyes. It had been quite a day and perhaps Daniel was right. Andrei was a bit of a hero.

I called David as soon as I got home and dried out.

'David, I have some information on that email address. Can we meet?' I said.

'I'm due at the police station later. Can you tell me over the phone?' He sounded as miserable as ever. I wondered whether he had eaten.

'No, it's not a good idea. We should meet. I'll be at yours tomorrow morning, first thing. Let's make it eight o'clock,' I said.

11

The roads were hushed early on a Sunday and I opened the taxi window to savour the flavours of Cowley Road at first hand. Distinctive Indian spices still filled the air from Saturday night dinner parties and remnants of handheld takeaways swirled around the pavement. Paperboys in Day-glo yellow cycled the street laden with supplements. David was waiting beside his front door.

'We'll go back to the park. I'd like to see the scene again,' I said.

He muttered something about being too busy with work as he started his car, then we pulled out into the traffic. We took the route to the other side of the park from where we had left the car before, crossing the Iffley Road and stopping beside the main entrance. There were more people around, dog walkers, joggers and a few kids running on the rain sodden grass. We headed towards the centre point from where we could see the bandstand. David walked slowly, shuffling from his remaining injuries and resistant to any friendly conversation.

'What have you found out?' he asked.

I told him that the email address was registered in Romania but the sender could be anywhere, not mentioning that Andrei had broken the password and downloaded all the emails for me.

'So what does that mean? Amanda's been kidnapped by some foreigners. I think we guessed that already.'

'I know, it's not much to go on I suppose. I was hoping we might look around the spot where the motorbike came by. Perhaps there's something?'

'Like a dropped clue, a piece of paper with an address on it. Something like that, you mean?' He laughed without humour. 'Sorry, I'm not in the mood. You mean well, but you're a friend of these people, these foreigners. I hate them.'

'Do the initials H.B. mean anything to you?' I asked.

David chewed his bottom lip as he studied the grass, as if looking for something.

'Only pencils. We sell HB's. Is that about the Romanians as well?' he said.

'It's something I'm working on. The posters plastered all over the Cowley Road.'

David fell quiet again. Asking him was a long shot and I couldn't tell whether his silence was deliberate. Was he hiding something? In the feedback I had from Andrei, all he could make out on the poster was the possible letters H and B in a flowery font.

Clouds covered the sun and I pulled my jacket closed and stepped away from him, walking ahead over the grass. I could see tyre tracks leading back towards the tarmac path in a northerly direction towards St Gregory's school. A breeze had picked up, the trees full of blossom shedding flurries of pink petals. An empty bag of crisps danced by and got caught in the black iron railings.

'I've been worried since I left you yesterday. You didn't say much.'

'I was in shock. Still am. Haven't heard anything from them since. She looked distraught when they dragged her off. And it'll be hard to get more money, even if that's what they want.'

We reached the bandstand and stood beside it in silence, scouring the ground. He was right, there would be nothing to find. What did I expect? The tyre marks were still clear despite the storm and I could picture the scuffle as the rider dragged her onto the back of the bike.

'I wish I smoked, I could do with one now,' he said, then sat down on the step and put his head in his hands. I walked around the bandstand, returning to sit beside him and put my arm around his shoulders.

'We'll find her, I'm sure. They will want something else – it's not her they want. You should get the police to help,' I said.

'Not a chance.'

Two lads were playing with a ball that landed a few metres from us. I watched one retrieve it, then over the other side of the grass I saw Jamie emerge from behind the tennis courts. I could tell straight away from the confident stride and the dark blue suit. I glanced at David then stood up as Jamie headed straight for us. How did he know we were there?

'Hey you two, what's up?' he shouted from halfway across.

'What on earth are you ...' I said. I wanted to run. This couldn't be happening.

'I was coming round to chat to David about the situation when I saw you getting into David's car, and I was worried about you. Easy to follow in this light traffic,' he said.

David pulled himself up and stared at Jamie, acting as if he was a stranger.

'You've met my editor, Jamie, you remember,' I said.

'Of course. But we don't need a chaperone. We're ...'

'I know, you're looking for your ransom money,' Jamie said.

'I'm looking for my wife. I don't care about the money.'

'What do you know about a ransom?' I said. My brain was in a scramble.

'I could ask the same. Someone needs to worry about the money, it doesn't grow on trees,' Jamie said.

I turned to David but he remained silent, his face blank.

'Well, come on. We need to get back and you've a shop to run, Mr Brown. I guess I'll see you in the office tomorrow, Emma.'

He turned and expected us to follow.

***

When I finally got back to my flat, I sat and reflected. The clock on the wall above my bookcase had stopped on four thirty about three weeks ago, and buying new batteries was one of the many domestic tasks I faced. The tap in the bathroom sink dripped unless you tightened it so hard it was difficult to turn on again, one of the kitchen cupboards didn't close properly and the window in the lounge was draughty. I needed to call the landlord. The place was clean, but not tidy. The Busy Maids cleaning company came every Thursday morning for two hours and that kept it habitable, but they wouldn't actually sort my life out, the piles of washing, the stacks of books about the Boleyn sisters, the clutter of the post, papers and magazines. The place still smelled of the takeaway curry from yesterday evening.

After a coffee and review of the Sunday papers, I started in on it. I knew I needed to talk to Aunt Hazel - it had been a week since that lunch with Andrei, and she would be fretting. She was good at leaving me alone generally and I thought about a brief visit but decided I really should get some washing done. I would call her later. Although not my blood mother, she was as close as you could get, a very special auntie who raised me from the age of six. When I was sixteen, she insisted I call her Hazel, but I never got comfortable with that and I even insisted back that she was a mum to me. Becky adored her.

I put on Blur and set about filling a bag of jumble to make some space in the wardrobe for the clothes I actually wore every day, which lay on the chair. The blue flowery blouse was last year's and over-worn anyway. The green lace was one I'd never liked that Becky had persuaded me was flattering. It wasn't; she was never a good judge for me.

I couldn't fathom the kidnapping. Yes, they wanted money, but why risk grabbing her back? It all seemed a bit staged. And Jamie and David, surely they knew each other? And why had Jamie suddenly turned up like that? He had no reason to be going round to David's shop, and David wasn't being fully open with his information.

I flicked through the snaps on my phone to find the one I'd taken of the photo from David's drawer. The four men were standing at the distinctive main entrance to the Randolph, and dressed in black tie, as if they were there for an event. The street lights reflected off the damp pavement. There was nothing to explain what event it could be, or to date it exactly but if it was Jamie he looked like a young man, so it must be a good ten years ago at least. Who took the photo? And the other two, surely I could identify them somehow, without actually asking him. Perhaps there was a member of the hotel staff who could help. It was a long shot but might be worth a go.

I sat and took the email prints out of the envelope that Andrei had given me, to reread them. There were four emails, the one sent to David, and one from Gmail authenticating the account. The other two were sent from a different, strange address and written in Romanian. Andrei had scribbled a rough translation. The first one, sent six months before the kidnapping simply said: *I've seen her, she saw me.* The other was the day before the kidnapping. *We're ready. Go-go tonight.*

I lay back on the couch to try to think. The chores could wait again.

The buzzer for my flat woke me up. I looked at my watch and it was gone seven. I had slept for over an hour. No one came to my door unannounced, and I immediately thought of Andrei - either him or another delivery. Could I pretend to be out? I could lie low. After three more buzzes, I was considering why I didn't have a view of the front door of the building with a security camera instead of this silly old-fashioned buzzer system. Another item for the landlord list. Then my phone rang. David.

'Hi David, how are you? News?' I said.

'I'm outside and need to see you.'

'Oh, sorry ... I thought ... OK, give me a moment. I'll buzz you in and you can come up.'

I went to the bathroom and freshened my face up, reapplied some blusher and combed out my hair. Then I pushed the magazine pile back under the coffee table and went to the door of the flat to let him in. He arrived breathless from the walk up the stairs.

'Lovely place you have,' he gasped.

'Thanks, I like it. Quite modern really. How did you know I was here?'

'Oh ... I'm a newsagent. We deliver papers so it's our part of our job description to know where everyone lives. Can I come in?' he said.

I showed him through to the main room. He looked just as dishevelled as this morning, unlikely to have showered and in the same clothes, under a shabby coat.

'Coffee? Something stronger?' I said.

'What do you have?'

I went through to the kitchen and rummaged in the cupboard under the breakfast bar. 'Some whisky, some gin, red wine, or tea or coffee,' I shouted back through.

'Whisky, no ice thanks,' he said.

No ice requested, no ice available, I thought as I carried it back through with two glasses. I may as well match him.

I sat on the Poäng chair opposite him.

'Cheers,' I said.

He took a drink of it, then sighed and pulled out a folded-up large brown envelope from his coat pocket, passing it to me. It was ripped open across one end and on the front was the single word *DAVID*.

'Take a look. They've been in touch,' he said.

'Shall I take your coat first, make you more comfortable?' I offered.

He stood, took off his coat and laid it over the back of the couch, then sank back down into the dark leather. He looked settled in for the long haul. My sympathies were running out, and he needed the police.

After taking a sip of the whisky, I opened the envelope and pulled out a folded sheet of paper with writing on one side. In the top left corner was a lock of blonde hair Sellotaped to the paper, then underneath was a brief note written in black capital letters. *£50,000 MORE.*

'You don't know it's her hair,' I said.

David looked withdrawn as he finished the glass of whisky and put it down on the coffee table, pushing it in my direction for a top-up.

'I'm pretty sure it is. It's the right texture and colour, and anyway, look at the photo.'

I tipped the envelope and a picture slid out. It was a photo of Amanda sitting in a carver dining chair, wearing a navy suit and white blouse that looked a little like an outfit of mine. Her arms were strapped to the arms of the chair so she couldn't move and there was a ribbon or tape of some kind tied around her head across her mouth. She looked into the camera with a look of dismay, not really fear, more shock.

'Oh, God ... Well, I guess that proves they have her.'

'Yes, if you look closely, you can see where they chopped a bit of hair off.'

I stood up and got the whisky bottle and poured him

one, then I walked over to the window to pull the curtains.

'You need to phone the police. I have DI Richards' number. You should call straightaway, from here. Right now,' I said.

'No way. Absolutely not.' His voice raised and he gripped the glass.

'You've nothing to lose.'

'I have Amanda to lose. I will do whatever it takes.'

'But we're out of our depth. You need more help than I can offer. Professional help, negotiating skills.'

'I knew it was a mistake coming here. I don't need your help. You and your liberalism. Those features in the paper have made it worse, encouraged them,' he said.

'That's not fair. They are criminals. That has nothing to do with being foreigners.'

'Ha, you think? They're all the same. We don't want them here.'

He drank down his whisky and stared at me. Then he shuffled forward to stand up, pulling himself out of the deep couch.

'No, wait. Do you have the money?' I said.

He sighed and slumped back, then picked up the letter from the table.

'Possibly.'

We finished the whisky between us, arguing the pros and cons of police involvement. David was convinced that everything would be fine this time, that it made sense to find the extra money. Any argument I put up was futile.

12

The pebbles were set close together in cement to form the cobbled surface around the Radcliffe Camera. I picked my way slowly to ensure a heel didn't get stuck. I hadn't expected to walk far when I got ready for work and the new shoes were too tempting to leave in their box. Jamie held my arm, insisting we both go to see the news story unfolding, a security alert at the Bodleian. We stopped outside the black wrought-iron fence with its collection of ageing chained bikes, their owners probably pleased by the interruption to studies. The dirty yellow sandstone walls of the library with its huge circular dome looked down onto the crowd gathering outside Brasenose College. Behind us, the viewing balcony of the University Church tower was brimming with tourists. The sky was a threatening dull grey and I didn't want to be there, but for once Jamie was turning out to be fun. He didn't mention the previous morning in the park and I thought better of it. I didn't want to talk about David's visit.

'We could get some lunch afterwards if you like,' he said.

'OK, a light salad.'

'To go with the burger, you mean.'

A man with a clipboard was checking off names of staff and we asked him for an update. Apparently we were waiting for the bomb squad. This could take a while. Someone had broken their solemn oath not to bring anything inside that could kindle flame, and a suspicious package had been isolated. Big excitement for a Monday morning.

'How about we ditch lunch and do coffee now?' I said.

'What? And miss this huge story? The place might burn to the ground while we're sipping our cappuccinos. Wouldn't look good on the CV.'

I sighed and leant against the railings in a gap between two bikes. One had a flat tyre and had probably been there for at least ten years by the look of the rust on it. Jamie tapped into his phone to track any developments he could find. Many of the crowd of evacuated students and readers seemed to disappear into the surrounding streets, off to find alternative places to write their last-minute essays.

'Have you any more on the kidnapping?' he asked.

'No. Waiting on David. He's waiting on the police. I can't get anything out of DI Richards. I think they suspect David – they always start with the husband.'

'I keep saying, it won't be him.'

'I agree, he seems genuinely shocked, but how can you be so sure? Do you know him?'

I watched Jamie's face carefully. His eyes stared a little, but he acted well.

'I know of him. He's been around the Oxford business community a few years. Probably met him at some council event at some point.'

'Well, if it's not him, it's someone and the bottom line is that she's in some danger. The pressure is mounting,' I said.

'Push harder on Richards. Use your charms.'

'My charms ... What are those then?'

'Well, let's see now ...'

He stepped back a little and pointed his phone at me as if to take a photo. I smiled and made a peace sign, Japanese-style. He moved the camera up and down like I was a model he was seeking to frame in close-up, then he came back close to me to avoid being overheard by the group of lads behind him.

'You have very attractive features, a beautiful smile, killer legs,' he said.

'Well thank you. Not sure you should be saying all that but thank you.'

'Would you come on a date with me?'

I was suddenly stuck for words. It was like he had finally summoned up the courage after all that hesitation over that last few weeks. I shouldn't have been surprised, but I was.

'Oh, well ...'

'You don't have to say now. Think about it.' He backed away immediately and looked embarrassed, something I had not seen in him before. He was quite flustered and that was cute.

'Ok, thanks. I will,' I said.

He shuffled his feet and coughed then looked down at his phone again.

'The library have put something up on their home page, warning it'll be closed for the rest of the day,' he said.

Word spread through the remaining crowd and more drifted away. The café in the old congregation house of the University Church of St Mary was also closed so there was nowhere within eyesight that we could take a break. I decided not to risk suggesting coffee again.

'So, perhaps I'll call Richards now. If I can get him, I'll try him out on what's happening here first. Not mention the kidnapping. Perhaps suggest we meet,' I said.

'Good idea. Anything to get to him, to dig out some useful information.'

'Even flirt a little, you know ... my charms.'

He laughed and put his hand on my arm. 'You see, you do it naturally ... tease.'

'I don't mean to. But anything for Amanda Brown. I'm definitely worried.'

Jamie didn't ask why I had already got DI Richards in my contact list. It rang out and went to voicemail so I left him a message to say I was standing outside the library and I would be interested in his take on the security situation.

Before I could get my phone back into my bag, he called back. I smiled as Jamie tried to listen in, so I turned away from him to ensure he could only hear my side.

'Yes, that's right, the security scare,' I said.

'Of course we could meet up, I'd like that very much.'

'Thank you Inspector .... Yes, of course ... Brad.'

I closed the call and turned back to Jamie.

'He said the device is a false alarm and they are just going through routine checks now. Someone left a bag, the usual story. There's nothing here for us.'

'OK, sounds like you got a bit more than that though. You're going to meet him? Anything about the kidnapping?'

'He asked me out. Six o'clock today.' I wasn't going to tell Jamie that he actually called it an informal meeting, not a date at all.

'Some people get instant answers then.'

'We'll see,' I smiled.

***

I arrived at the police headquarters promptly at six, having been home to change into a smarter grey trouser suit and different heels.

The North Oxford police headquarters was a long way from being an old-fashioned cop shop. It was a modern office block that had been purpose built five years ago at great, and controversial, expense to the taxpayer. I remembered the articles that Jamie had penned at the time, criticising the extravagance. Although I had never been inside it before, I had seen plenty of pictures. The outside was darkened glass and steel, reflecting back the bright evening sunshine. Smoke and mirrors was how some people described it. I walked into the reception, where the polished marble, grey floor and the light oak welcoming desk complemented each other perfectly. A line of pots along the window wall to my right contained indoor flowering shrubs, and behind the visitor area was a large map of Oxford City in relief.

The receptionist looked like a retired police officer, not quite matching up to the modern image.

'I'm here to see DI Richards. He's expecting me,' I said.

'I'll let him know. Take a seat over there,' she said.

Bradley Richards arrived looking nothing like the DI Richards I had seen at the crime scene or the press conference. He was dressed in a white shirt with a pale red stripe in it, open at the neck, and a pair of dark grey chinos.

'Miss Hawkins, good to see you,' he said.

I stood and offered my hand. 'Call me Emma. Thanks for seeing me.' I smiled.

'Well let's not disagree about who asked to see who. How about we take a walk to the coffee shop next door?' he said.

He towered over me, even in my heels, and had a controlling air that went with the job. He pulled on a brown leather jacket that completed the Brad Richards casual look, then opened the door and indicated for me to go first.

I was surprised to find that conversation flowed easily. We talked about our knowledge of Oxford, keeping fit and the culture of gyms, his love of jazz, and mine of Anne Boleyn. He used to be in the London Met but moved to Oxford for a promotion and to be near his mother.

The coffee house was busy and a local for the police so there were quite a few glances in our direction. I suspected I might be the talk of the station tomorrow. Brad, as he insisted I call him, moved on to business.

'You're not here about a silly security scare, are you?' he said.

'I'm here to see you. You invited me.'

He could see I was poking fun and didn't rise to it.

'Flattered as I am, I suspect you want to know about Amanda Brown.'

'Am I that transparent? I need to sharpen my charm skills,' I said.

'You are perfectly charming enough, Emma.'

He retrieved a card from his shirt pocket, then grasped my hand and pushed the card into it. I looked into his face and could see the lines at the corner of his mouth and a freshly shaven chin. He had prepared especially for this meeting, just as much as I had.

'Here's my direct number. You can call me at any time of day or night,' he said.

'Thanks Inspector,' I said.

'Don't tease, Emma. You're being defensive. You know to call me Brad.'

'Thanks, sorry, yes. I really appreciate it actually. And I want to do all I can to help find Amanda.'

'Just to be clear. We're off record. I will trust you Emma, I start out that way and don't ruin it. I have a one strike rule.'

'Of course. We're on the same side.'

'We're pursuing many lines as you know. There's little to go on. We don't like David Brown; he has history with us, which you could find on public record if you look hard enough. Some of his business interests are very suspect.'

It was gone seven and we both needed to leave. He was adamant the husband was the direction to look. We walked back to the car park together.

'Thanks for your help,' I said.

'Well, I still have your card so I will call if there's anything further.'

I smiled at him. 'Thanks, and I will too, and thanks for the coffee. Perhaps we'll talk soon.'

***

Jamie phoned as soon as I got back to the office. It was

late but I wanted to make some notes about the meeting.

'Just catching up on the status of things,' he said.

'You're still here? Ok, give me ten minutes and I'll meet you in reception if you like.'

I went to the ladies and reapplied my makeup, dragging my lip gloss across my mouth. I stared at myself in the mirror. What did I want? Perhaps Hazel was right and it wasn't healthy to be single. Brad was engaging, unquestionably handsome with easygoing conversation but with Jamie there was a hint of something else, something more dangerous, more attitude. I sprayed on a dash of Stella McCartney's 'Summer' perfume and walked down to the front desk where he was waiting. He kissed me on both cheeks to greet me.

'You look good,' he said.

We walked a hundred metres along the Banbury Road to the Lamb and Flag, chatting about the week's leader article regarding potholes, but I knew he was itching to find out about my meeting.

There were four tables crammed into a small courtyard at the rear with a gas patio heater. The bar was quiet and the student behind the bar offered to bring our drinks out to us. Jamie ordered himself a pint of an Oxford ale. I decided to stay dry.

'Diet Coke please,' I said.

'Are you sure? You deserve something stronger than that,' he said.

'I think I should keep a clear head with you.'

I smiled at him as he looked at me. We walked outside and took the table furthest from the door and waited for our drinks. Jamie looked like he had something on his mind.

'Would you like to join me for dinner?' he said eventually.

'Of course, that would be lovely,' I said.

When the drinks came, we both sipped slowly and a peace descended over us. Jamie was clearly preoccupied.

'What's up?' I said.

'Well, what did you find out? With Richards?'

'Oh that. Not much, he's still pointing at the husband. A bit of background information, that's all. He's very likeable.'

'Likeable? He's a Detective Inspector. Tread carefully. He didn't ask you out then? He didn't charm the pants off you, or anything I should know about.'

'Not like that. We have exchanged numbers, all very professional. Very above—'

'Hmm, so watch out, that's all I say. We should toast your first immigration feature.'

The sunlight was fading from the courtyard and I wrapped my jacket a little closer. The extractor fan from the kitchen wafted the aroma of grilled steaks, making me realise I hadn't eaten much all day. I updated him on my research for the next in-depth article and my meetings with sources including Andrei, as well as the detailed information I'd dug up on the numbers of people arriving into Oxford from various countries. I explained I was looking for the human angle on it all.

'The Romanians are integrating well in certain parts. They are welcomed in the pubs, drinking their prune *tuică* shots. A couple of the landlords have shipped it in especially. They are mostly employed and very industrious, the women also.'

'I don't blame them for being here. It's the system. They're obviously going to be better off here. But it shouldn't be allowed,' he said.

'You came from Scotland.'

'That's different. We're all British, well at least for now. And that was a long time ago.'

'You have a selective view. After all, we're all European. And anyway, what does it matter, we're all just people? We benefit from a multicultural society.'

We continued to debate the points and I enjoyed the intensity of the discussion. I couldn't be sure whether Jamie believed in his views or whether he was trying to goad me for a reaction. I looked at his face as he smiled, and the brightness of his eyes when he spoke. He was wearing a shirt with a dark blue check that suited his colouring. It fitted him well.

After half an hour, he suggested more drinks but I said we should get on with the food. We walked down into the city to the French-style bistro. The pavement was busy with commuters and sightseers, so we had to keep close together as we passed the side entrance to the Ashmolean. When we crossed the road to the Randolph, he grabbed my hand to guide me and then continued to hold it while we walked on down past Oxford's major department store where the pavement narrowed even further.

It felt natural and I didn't pull my hand back. When we reached the restaurant, he let it go and turned to me, hesitating before opening the door.

'I really like you,' he said, looking down at his shoe, striking its toe against the paving slab, as if he was trying to push it back into place.

'You've already told me that, Jamie. I like you too,' I said.

After we had ordered, the waitress took the menus away and I cleared the tea-light and salt and pepper mills off to one side to make way for the olives.

'So is this a proper date?' I said.

I think he caught the merest flicker of a twinkle in my eye and he laughed.

'How's it going with young Andrei, your other admirer?' he said.

'It's not, it's firmly not. He's just a contact.'

It seemed right to tell him all about the picnic and in the most part he found it funny, though I could sense a little jealousy creeping in – not a bad thing to keep him alert. I wasn't at all sure where this was going.

The food was delicious. We both ate steaks medium-rare, we both chose the New York cheesecake and we shared a bottle of Merlot. When it came to paying, I insisted on half, which he accepted a little too quickly.

As we walked to the taxi rank, he held my hand again. I felt like I was sixteen. I hadn't held hands with a man for a very long time. Just before we got to the cab at the front of the line, he pulled me to him and kissed my cheek very close to my mouth. I could smell his cologne and feel the roughness of his stubble on my face. I could turn away to buy time, or I could turn closer and kiss. He was giving me the choice.

13

The blurb on the website described a white stone building with Grecian portico and columns. The Ashmolean certainly appeared majestic in the rain as I looked out of the window of the hotel tea room. Its banners fluttered in the light breeze, water running off them onto the tourists below who hurried across the courtyard to the revolving entrance door. Thankfully I had arrived at the Randolph before the rain shower and before the morning rush for their selected leaf teas. The service was slow enough already with only four other tables occupied in the Drawing Room. The family in the opposite corner were arguing about what to do in this weather, the teenager suggesting the cinema while the adults were sticking to the museum theme.

I sipped at my Earl Grey and made some notes about the surroundings. The room had been refurbished and decorated in a classic English style following the fire that had devastated it a few years before. Gilt framed still-life paintings adorned the dark green walls and golden chandeliers bathed the room in a pale yellow light. I also reviewed the photo that I had printed from my phone. Surely there must be someone who worked here that would recognise it.

The waiter returned with my order of a second slice of lemon drizzle cake.

'Have you worked here long?' I said. It was a long shot judging by his youthful image.

'Na, just a couple of weeks. All I could get. Everything alright for you?'

'Yes, it's delicious. I was trying to find someone who might have worked here a long time ago, like ten years or more? I work for the *Gazette* and we're doing some research.'

'Oh, I see. Most staff are temporary like me. There's the manager I guess but I've never seen him.' He laughed and picked up the empty teapot. 'Fancy another?'

'No, that's all thanks. Just the bill.'

He wandered off, not the best representative for Oxford's most prestigious and well-known hotel, but at least he had been honest.

The rain hammered against the window next to me, a clap of thunder warning of worse to come. Three businessmen arrived with dripping umbrellas and damp trousers, the one in charge ordering toast and coffee. He took off his jacket and sat in an armchair while the other two planted themselves on upright seats across the table from him. I pondered their line of business: insurance, banking or accountancy? But it turned out to be retail and Mr Easychair talked loudly about his successful fashion store in London. I could sit here all day and write a novel set in this place, I thought.

The waiter returned with my tab and I checked the total. I could understand why the Randolph tea room was quiet, and there was no doubt I would put this on my expenses.

'Burt the concierge. Apparently he started here when they built it,' he said.

I laughed. 'You do know it opened in 1866,' I said.

'Is that when we won the World Cup? Anyway, he's been here a long time and he's behind his desk in reception and doing nothing.'

I walked back into the Gothic styled reception with its vaulted ceiling and dark mahogany panelled walls and saw Burt leafing through his copy of the *Daily Mail*.

'Can I help you miss? Looking for some suitable sightseeing in this rain?' he said when I approached.

He had a shock of white hair, a wizened, weather-beaten face and a broad grin displaying crooked, yellowing teeth. I wondered whether the tourist board realised he was the face of Oxford to the many rich guests of the hotel. I remembered staying at the Mayfair Hotel in London for a seminar where the receptionists were like supermodels and all the staff wore fashionable suits.

'Thank you, but I'm actually a local. I work for the *Gazette* and thought perhaps you may be able to help me.'

'Oh, right-oh my dear, of course I can. Take a seat.'

I sat opposite him. The desk was set away from the reception area and afforded some privacy for guests who wanted to ask him for local services or suggestions for restaurants. No one else was in earshot.

'What can I do for you? I'm sure there's plenty I know, just depends what you're after. I know all the restaurant managers, all the pubs, bars and clubs. Not much that gets past me, you know.'

'Thanks, I'm sure that's true.' I smiled.

'Yep, been here twenty years and they've been good years. Well, except for that fire. But the rest have been absolutely first-rate my dear. Helped thousands of guests - must be thousands. All sorts of questions. Did I know Morse? Was I in any films? Oh yes, I could spin quite a yarn if I chose to,' he said.

'Burt, is it?'

'Yes that's right. After my father – it was his middle name, and his father before him. Have had plenty of dealings with the newspapers over the years, they've all been here you know. I even remember Mr Maxwell, charming man he was. Stayed for a week. The *Gazette* you say, you a reporter then, are you? On a story? I'm not one to gossip you know.'

'Well, Burt, it's not a story yet. It's more background research. I'm checking on a few faces I don't recognise. I have an old picture.' I smiled my best at him and pulled the photo printout from my bag, then placed it on the desk in front of him.

He put on his glasses and picked it up, studying it carefully. He didn't frown or indicate anything at all in his face, which remained wrinkled and red just as it had been before.

'Hmmm, very good,' he said.

'I was wondering if you knew any of them?'

'Well, I might. I might not. Difficult to say really. It's outside here, just by the steps. Probably a ball, the way they're dressed, my dear. Why do you need to know?'

'As I say, it's research. I'm looking into Oxford's history of the Eighties and Nineties.'

He laughed, put the print down and stood up, then walked around the desk and shuffled over to the reception area. He rummaged in a heavy wooden cupboard standing behind the desk and pulled out a large black folder, like a ledger. I was in a Dickens novel.

When he came back, he put it in front of him on the table.

'I live off tips you know. Wages here are terrible, always have been.'

His grin was irritating; he had clearly watched too many movies where journalists paid up. How much was it worth? Did he actually have anything? I took a ten pound note from my purse and passed it across.

'Thanks, my dear. Now let's see what we have.'

In Dickens there would have been a cloud of dust as he opened it, but this was actually a printed list of events, balls, Rotary club parties, chambers of commerce and the like. He flicked through the pages.

'Yes, I thought so,' he said. 'There it is. I thought I recognised a couple of them. It was a New Year party. That one there works in newspapers, you should know him.'

'Yes, my boss,' I said, confirming my thoughts.

'Well, you should have said my dear. Why don't you ask him about it? Is there a story here? Unsavoury lot if I remember right. It was a big night and I worked through, did coats and cloakroom. Lots of booze consumed. Those were party days back then.'

'When was it?'

He returned to his printout.

'2004, the Year of the Monkey. I love all that Chinese stuff, my dear. Have you been to Brighton? Chinoiserie they call it. Beautiful place. My auntie used to live there back in the Fifties, or was it the Thirties? Well, my dear, hopefully I've helped. I'm Year of the Monkey too, you know. How about you?'

It was hard to hide my exasperation. I took another ten pound note from my purse, wondering which expense account I would put it on. General research. Three tourists walked past and stared at us, before disappearing into the bar. It was getting near lunchtime.

'Anyone else you know there, Burt?'

'Well, that one there, the older looking one. Not that any of them are my age, you know ...'

'Yes, that one?' I pointed to the man second from the right.

'He's Bob Riley.'

'I've heard of him. Name rings bells,' I said.

'Yes, so it should. I'll leave you to discover who he is. These four were part of a club if I remember. See there, the mark on the shirt.'

I peered closely at the photograph again and saw what he meant. Why hadn't I seen that before? It was an emblem of some sort, like on a uniform, but partially covered up by the jacket.

'Gosh, yes. Does that say F C ? Like a football club?' I asked, peering closely at the photo.

He glanced up at me and laughed out loud, so that the receptionist stared across and stood to come and see what the fuss was about.

'Sorry, don't worry dear, you can stay there. Me and this lady have just finished. I don't know anyone else.'

He stood to shake my hand and thanked me, then looked behind me to see if he could find anyone waiting. I put away my notebook and left. Bob Riley - that was definitely a name I should know, and shouldn't be too hard to track down.

I had been Burted, however, and I diverted to the nearest cash machine before returning to the office.

14

Finally I had arrived at season six of *Mad Men*, the final DVD in the box set that Lou had given me two Christmases ago.

'You'll love it. All that office politics and sex. It'll cheer you up,' she'd said.

For the first couple of months I'd been addicted but then life had taken over and I forgot where I'd got to, so I had to rerun a couple of episodes, then I gave up halfway through season five when Peggy left the firm.

That was nearly two years ago and I suddenly got the urge to get back into it, just by way of escaping. It was probably the new television: the picture was so good and I could actually hear what they said.

It had been quite a day. After the Randolph, I'd got sucked into helping Henry with a breaking story about possible embezzlement at the Student Union. He had me on background research and phone duty, calling as many of the committee as I could muster for quotes. There had been no time for Bob Riley or strange emblems, but at least I managed to avoid Jamie. I needed time to gather my thoughts about what I wanted after that kiss. I didn't even want to talk to Hazel or Becky, I just needed some time alone. I slipped away at six o'clock for a quiet night in with my favourite Himalayan detox bath salts.

After extracting myself from the bathroom and relaxing in the warmth of the fleece bathrobe that Hazel had given me, I entered the world of Madison Avenue and the dirty work of selling Jaguar cars and Heinz beans in Mad Men. It was gone nine o'clock and I dozed a little, catching myself missing the occasional piece of dialogue. This was not a new experience and I needed to focus, so I went through to the kitchen and put the kettle on. A strong coffee was required.

As I poured the water my phone rang. David. I had to answer.

'How are you?' I said.

I could hear what sounded like Madness or another ska band in the background and knew, even before he spoke, that he was in a happier mood.

'She's back. She's here. We're so happy, so excited. I can't believe it,' he said. His voice was quiet, and cracking a little.

I went back to the couch and sat down while he explained. He had gone to the drop alone this time, not prepared to tell me anything in advance. I suppose I had brought that upon myself with our argument about police involvement. I had missed the story, missed the moment.

'So where did you go?' I asked.

'Outside the O2, you know, that club on the Cowley Road. Two hours ago. The street was crushed full of Echo & The Bunnymen fans. It was bizarre, all that Eighties fashion. She was suddenly there.'

'That's amazing, David. Well done. What a relief for you. Can I have an exclusive for tomorrow's paper?'

'No, no. Not yet. Mandy is resting upstairs. She's had a

bath, we've had some prosecco. She is fine. No one knows.'

'Did you speak with the kidnappers? Get any details?' I asked.

'Not that I want to tell you. No thanks to you that she's back. Released from a foreign gang. But it's not important now. Not at—'

'I take it you gave them more of what they asked for?'

'Yes, all that. It's only money. It's history. We can get our lives back.'

'Is she hurt? Where did they hide her?'

'All in good time. We need tonight to recover and have some private time together.'

I scribbled notes and thought about calling Jamie. We needed to be the ones to break the story first, or all that work would be wasted. How long could it hold?

'But you must tell the police,' I said. 'There's a chance they may catch them. If you're quick. Call Richards, you must.'

'I knew you would say that. I've talked it through with her. We'll go to the station first thing in the morning. Before anyone knows. She doesn't know I'm calling you.'

'Thank you. I appreciate being the first. Could I meet her tomorrow morning? But you must promise to go to the police. It's very important.'

'After nine o'clock,' he said.

I went back to *Mad Men* for the end of the episode. Pete Campbell having yet another affair. It helped settle the story in my mind. When it had finished I sat at my laptop and wrote the entire piece ready to mail to Jamie.

***

A skinny latte, double shot was the quickest way to awaken Gary's interest. We agreed Taylor's at eight o'clock rather than our usual cemetery as it was raining again. He stumbled in at five past, shaking water from his coat before stepping over the threshold. He manoeuvred past a small queue of takeaway coffee addicts before landing on the chair opposite me in the corner. I was already halfway through my Americano, and reading the house copy of *The Guardian*.

'You again,' he said as he picked up his cup.

'Me again.' I smiled at him and could see he'd made an effort to be presentable for the day. Clean-shaven that morning, his hair combed and neat though wet. 'You're starting to look like an inspector,' I said.

'I am? Oh, that's a worry. You look your usual self-assured vision of wonderment.'

The usual Gary, but he was strangely sincere and a confidence builder. I'd have him on my team.

'I'll speak quietly,' I said leaning towards him over the table.

'Will you say it only once?' He laughed, then leaned in too. 'Sorry, serious face,' he said.

'Amanda Brown has reappeared.'

'The kidnappee. How come? Richards had a breakthrough?'

'No, her husband paid up. No police involvement.'

'Wow. That kind of thing often turns very bad. He's lucky.'

'Yes. I've promised to wait until this morning to break the story - to give them a night to themselves. She came back last night.'

Gary pulled out his phone and started to tap into it. Then he undid his coat and mopped his hair and face with a napkin. The queue at the till shuffled forward, a constant succession of people buying their morning snacks, most totally absorbed in their phones or headsets. The noise of the traffic was amplified by the water bouncing off the street. I wasn't going anywhere fast in this, not even over the road to the office.

'So, he's going to tell us eventually then. David Brown. He's coming to the police?'

'Yes, this morning. No doubt there'll be a lot of questions.'

'He's done nothing illegal. I've seen it once before, a kidnapping in London where they paid up. It happens. I doubt there'll be much follow-up. More your lot making juicy stories.'

'Well I wanted you to know first, and I've got more information about that photo I sent you,' I muttered.

I slid the print of it across the table to him, face down, and watched him as he looked it over. Gary would be the straight man in any comedy duo. He had a jovial enough face, but you could never read him. An expert joke teller, never cracking a smile at the wrong moment.

I told him all about my findings so far. Gary was the only person in the world I completely trusted apart from Becky and Hazel. I explained about Burt in the Randolph. He even knew him. And that I had discovered who Bob Riley was, owing to the power of Internet searches.

'You know anyone there?'

'I know them all. Well, no, let's say I recognise them all. One I can't quite put a name to,' he said.

'It's taken in 2004.'

'Well, I've heard Riley was a nasty piece. Not one to cross. He's retired now.'

'Yes, three years ago.'

'I never actually came across him myself. Just what I've heard. Talk around the station. He got some knighthood or something, like all chief constables do.'

He slid the picture back to me.

'An odd grouping, looks like a party. What's your angle?' he said.

'Can you make out that emblem on the shirt? Burt pointed it out. Any idea if it means anything?'

My phone rang. I indicated 'one moment' to Gary and stood up to take the call, walking towards the door. I had my umbrella at the ready.

'Hello David, how's things? I'm preparing the article,' I said.

'Well, you'd better come over. You'll need to rewrite it.' He sounded strained but I was beginning to think that was always going to be the case. I opened the umbrella and protected myself from the ongoing downpour as I stood outside the café. I could see Gary through the window, busy typing into his phone.

'I can come later this morning. It'll be really good to meet Amanda at last,' I said.

'Ha. Quite. Well, wouldn't that be great? A nice cup of tea together before we start to get this shop back into shape. Well, it's not going to happen.'

I waited for him to say more. Clearly something was very wrong.

'She's gone. Gone again. She's a gone woman, gone girl.' He scoffed down the phone. 'Taken more money, and all the stuff from her dressing table. She's disappeared.'

'I'll be straight over,' I said.

15

David made me a cup of tea, fussing over the kettle. His hand was shaking as he poured the water. Gary had laughed about Amanda Brown and speculated she had orchestrated the whole thing. Clearly that thought had not occurred to David.

'What's happened? Do you think they've blackmailed her in some way? Threatened her?' he said.

He explained how she had said very little and was very tired. She bathed and went to bed early, and he decided to sleep in the spare room to enable her to get as fully rested as possible. When he woke up at six o'clock, she was gone. The bedroom door was open, and he thought she was in the bathroom but then he found the note on the table downstairs. She had simply scribbled *Sorry* on the notepad they'd got from a stationery rep. The biscuit tin of spare change and a few tenners had been emptied.

We sat and drank the tea slowly. I made some jottings for reference. This was going to be a big story for a few days.

'You've spoken to the police now, surely,' I said.

'On their way. They didn't seem best pleased.'

'You'll not get sympathy. Did she seem threatened? Last night? Still frightened?'

He sat and pondered, in a dream, nibbling on a rich tea, and staring at the floor. There was a sharp rap-rap on the door. A knock they must teach at Hendon, I thought. David shuffled to the door and let in Brad Richards and the same female sergeant from the press conference. My back tingled and I sat up straight as if I was in a classroom.

'Emma, how are you? Here already?' he said as he walked across the room to me, so I stood up and we shook hands somewhat awkwardly. 'This is Sergeant Morgan. Sergeant, this is Miss Hawkins from the *Gazette*.'

'Pleased to meet you. David called this morning and it was too good an exclusive to miss,' I said.

David busied himself at the kettle again and a silence hung over us, as if the presence of Amanda Brown lingered in the room.

'So, sir, any idea where she has gone this time?' Brad asked.

'She came back last night, out of the blue, and now she's gone. What can I say? No explanation.'

'Did she seem harmed in any way? Injured? Bruised?'

'No, just tired, withdrawn. We need to find her.'

'Well, sir, we've seen this sort of thing before. It's looking like she left on purpose. The question is, if we find her, would you want her back?'

'Of course, she may be in some danger. Perhaps she's being blackmailed. I need some answers. I need to find her.'

'Well, we'll try but we don't have a bottomless pit of resources. Maybe the newspapers can help for once?'

He turned towards me and smiled, catching my eye. David took the note from the table and passed it over to him.

'That was all she left.'

'No doubt she's taken her most precious and useful

possessions. On the phone you mentioned her dressing table?'

'Yes, a jewellery box has gone. She always kept it locked. It has some sentimental pieces in it, a fine Cartier necklace, some rings and other stuff I don't know about, gifts from before we were together.'

'Is that the necklace in the photographs of her that you gave us. At the ball?'

'Yes, that's right. It's gold and sapphire.'

'How about her passport? Where is that kept?' Brad said.

'In the safe.'

David went to check, and of course, it wasn't there.

16

'Size five please,' I said.

The girl was chewing something, presumably gum, and looked as if the world owed her a better job. She turned and pulled the shoes from the nearest pigeonhole and dropped them onto the counter. Obviously I had the most common sized feet on the entire planet, and most of the planet had worn the pair in front of me.

'Could I have those?' I said, pointing to a box three paces away.

She eyed me and continued to chew. I smiled.

As she walked to get them, I turned to Jamie and held his arm. He looked fit, wearing a stripy brown and white shirt with matching brown cords. He had shaved and gelled his hair and smelled of his usual cologne, which was intriguing and slightly sweet. I kissed him on the cheek.

'This is exciting. Our first official date,' I said.

He ignored me and watched the girl as she returned with the replacement shoes. The place was buzzing, the coffee bar full of kids and the lanes pulsing with the steady rhythm of a heavy beat mixed with the regular clatter of balls hitting pins. Bowling in Oxford, the dream date? Jamie had suggested it on Monday, after we'd had the kiss I couldn't erase from my thoughts.

'Four-fifty,' she said.

I turned back and reached into my bag, pulling out my purse and handing over twenty pounds.

'Take for him too, please,' I said.

'There's no need,' Jamie said but he smiled as he said it.

'It's my treat, the bowling. We'll share the pizza later.'

'OK boss,' he said.

Of course, I was rubbish, I expected that, but I was surprised how good Jamie was. He had a natural style when he slid the bowling ball along the lane, finishing with a flourish of his left arm as he released it with his right. He had clearly bowled before. I played the dumb card.

'I've never been any good at this,' I said, after delivering my second of two shots directly into the gutter.

'Here, let me show you,' he said.

Jamie stood close behind me and put his left arm around my waist to steady me. Then he held my right arm and swung it back and forth. I felt the heat of his body on my back as he pressed against me.

'Try to keep your arm straight and imagine swinging the ball in a straight line. It's all about the core,' he said.

'Where did you learn all this?'

'College days, cheap daytime lanes, lots of practice.'

I turned in his arm and offered up a kiss which he took eagerly. I was conscious of the lanes around us, particularly the one with a bunch of school kids, so I pulled away and went back to the seat behind the scoring desk to my handbag and pulled out a tissue to wipe my forehead, then reapplied some lip gloss. I sat and watched him score another strike.

As we continued to play, I did improve a little. Jamie was more keen on the bowling than on me and maintained his focus despite my best efforts to distract him. He did miss the occasional shot, one time only scoring a four. I smiled as he stomped back to his chair.

'I'd like to take you out more often. Would that be OK?' he said.

'I'd like that too. Maybe not bowling.'

As we exchanged our shoes at the end, I looked up and saw Andrei arriving with Daniel. They were both talking at once to each other, Daniel totally oblivious of anything around him, but I saw Andrei catch my eye and give a knowing nod. He put a hand onto Daniel's shoulder and guided him in our direction.

'Em, how lovely to see you,' he said.

Jamie stood up, holding his pair of bowling shoes, and stared at him. I remained seated, finishing off the straps on my right shoe.

'Jamie, this is Daniel and Andrei,' I said.

'Hi Jamie, very pleased to meet you. A friend of Emmy's I see.' Andrei said.

Having finished my shoe, I stood up, holding onto Jamie and thankfully he slipped his arm around me pulling me close to him as if I was his to keep.

'Jamie is a very good friend.' I took a breath then smiled at Andrei before turning to Daniel.

'Jamie, this is Daniel, Becky's boyfriend, a solicitor.'

'Pleased to meet you.' Jamie shook hands with the two men.

'I've heard a lot about you, Jamie,' Andrei said.

'You have? Is that so? All good I presume.'

I scowled at Andrei and held onto Jamie's arm.

'You know that's not true, Andrei.' I said. I'd had quite enough of his lies and innuendos. I'd said very little about Jamie to him at our meetings. I pulled on Jamie's arm to show I wanted to leave.

'Well Andrei, actually I've heard quite a bit about you too ...' Jamie said, standing his ground as I nudged him toward the door.

'And I do think it's time you left Emma to me and returned to your own life, even your own country perhaps.'

I died on the spot and shoved Jamie hard. We started to walk away.

'Is that so, Mr Wilson? Is that so? That's what your Independence Party membership guidelines tell you to say, is it?'

Jamie stopped and stared at him, his face colour deepening and a frown creasing his forehead. I felt my pulse race and looked at the floor. Daniel found his voice.

'Come, come, gentlemen, unseemly to row in front of the lovely lady.'

After a couple of seconds delay while Andrei and Jamie stared each other down, Jamie pulled me away and we walked off to the door, leaving the bowling shoes on the bench. At least I didn't have to undergo the scoffs from gum girl.

***

'What was all that about?' I said.

Jamie took a sip from his pint and looked at me. We

were sitting in the corner of the King's Arms at a table on our own. He hadn't spoken since we left the bowling alley, simply dragging me along beside him by the hand.

'The man's an arse,' he said.

'Ha ... well, that's not news. What was all that about party membership?'

'No idea. But I shouldn't have told him to go home, I guess. I just felt protective.'

I sipped on my Sauvignon and put my hand over his on the table. There was clearly something he wasn't telling me.

'I don't need the shining armour stuff, Jamie.'

'Don't you? Why does he keep turning up wherever you are then?'

'Coincidence, besotted, who cares? We just need to focus on our work. You know, find Amanda Brown, write articles - that's what we do,' I said.

The pub was crowded and a couple took the chairs at the other end of our table.

'Pizza?' Jamie said.

'I'm not hungry, and it's busy in here. Please would you take me home.' I stood up and walked around to stand beside him, then pulled his hand.

We linked arms and made our way outside where we kissed again, then Jamie guided me to a taxi. At that moment, the world could go hang itself, I wanted to enjoy the warmth of Jamie for a while longer.

***

I woke in a daze, snuggling under the duvet on my

own. Jamie had stayed for hours, before calling a cab saying about a busy news day ahead. I lay in bed for a while pondering the night and the risks of a relationship with the boss. Could that ever work long term? It might be fun to try.

It was gone nine when my phone buzzed with the call from Gary. I was still feeling the warmth in bed, the heating having died again. I needed to add the flaky boiler to my list of woes. Apart from wanting to know what had happened with David at the shop, he filled me in on his findings about the photograph. Apparently they were an unsavoury lot and formed some kind of club like the Masons but not, possibly connected to the obscure emblem on the shirt. It was a pity we didn't have a clear image of that. Apart from Gary trying to warn me off nasty Jamie, which was the last thing I needed to hear at that moment, there was David, the Chief Constable and the fourth was a man known as Sykesy, who Gary thought had probably been in prison for the last few years.

I shivered, thinking of Dad. Why do I never visit? I should. After Gary rang off, I dove into the shower only to discover there was no hot water, so I gave up and got dressed for work, deliberating how to impress Jamie. I couldn't decide if the butterflies in my stomach were excitement or apprehension about seeing him in the office environment. Perhaps he would have meetings all day to save my blushes. I could focus on the immigration series and keep my head down.

I was just leaving the flat, coat in hand and bag over shoulder when David Brown called to get an update on Amanda, his voice cracking under the strain. He berated me when I tried to reassure him that I was doing all I could, and that the police would be too. He shouted about how useless we were, threatening never to see me again. I wasn't sure what sort of exclusivity there was left in the story anyway, but I did my best to calm him down as I walked along Marston Ferry Road, eventually convincing him to be a little more patient. The Number 13 appeared in the distance: it was time to face Jamie, and I did feel a small thrill in my stomach when I thought about him in his office. Suddenly I was looking forward to it.

17

Workstation U1-5 was piled high with books and papers, all related to the so-called immigration crisis hitting the country. The analyses by government departments were contradictory; the anecdotal reports from agencies on the front line were inconclusive. It was a sea of fudge from all sides. Another aspect the reports invited me to consider was the detrimental effect of emigration on those countries that were losing intellectual resources to Britain, and I decided that could be a good angle for my next piece.

Henry was being particularly attentive, bringing me cups of water every time he wandered off somewhere, which he was doing often as he couldn't focus on his own work. Not that I managed to get much done either. The bus ride in had been horrendous and I couldn't get Jamie out of my head. I was sure Henry could read my thoughts, so I made conversation bemoaning my boiler.

'So you had a cold shower?' Henry asked, propping himself on the corner of my desk.

'I did. I couldn't get the damn thing to light at all. More of a wash-down than a shower.'

'You should phone the landlord,' he said.

'Yes, I know. I just wanted to get something done first, but I can't concentrate anyway. I'll call now.'

Henry took the empty coffee mugs for a refill as I picked up the phone.

'Mr Desai? It's Emma Hawkins.'

Mahesh Desai was in his fifties or sixties, it was difficult to be sure. He had only been round a couple of times soon after I started renting the place. He said he liked to know all his tenants personally but I suspect it was mainly to check I wasn't filling the place with the rest of my family or friends. As soon as the maintenance challenges started, he never showed his face. I toyed with the idea of paying the rent in cash if he would allow it; that way he'd come round once a week to collect it and I could harass him about my latest issues. He insisted on a direct debit arrangement.

'How can I help you Miss Hawkins? It's about Number 20, I suppose,' he said.

'There's no hot water. Sorry to be a pain, but it's pretty urgent.'

'Have you restarted the boiler?'

'Yes, I tried to. It doesn't go. It hasn't been serviced in a while. Then there's the other things you already know about, like the bathroom sink continues to drip and the lounge is draughty.'

'Actually, Miss Hawkins, it is fortuitous timing, very fortuitous indeed that this has happened.'

I couldn't quite see what was lucky about having a cold wash. Henry arrived back with a perfectly brewed coffee with just the right amount of milk and put it in front of me. I waved a thank-you and gave a big smile and waited for him to go and sit at his own desk.

'How come, Mr Desai?'

'Well, there's good news and bad news, my dear. I have a long list of all your complaints, all the things that need doing, and I can add this one on. That's good isn't it?'

'I'm not sure what you mean,' I said.

'The bad news is that it will take three days' work and it will be really helpful if you could move out, take some holiday or stay with a friend, something like that. We'll be making some mess, but at the end of it, you'll have a much better place. What do you think?'

'Sounds inconvenient.'

'Yes, but a free upgrade. Like travelling business class. Last time I came back from Mumbai I flew in it. Very good,' he said.

'OK, I'll let you know later today. I'll see what I can do,' I said.

This was major hassle. I couldn't stay with Becky, not with Daniel practically living there, and there was no way I could take a holiday right now. Perhaps I could go home for a while. Before I came up with any ideas, my phone beeped a text message.

<Hi Emma, I thought I would let you know that we have evidence Amanda Brown has gone abroad. We let David know yesterday. Brad Richards. >

Well, he was slow to share news. I had already drafted a piece about her disappearing. I stared at my papers and struggled on with a particularly complex piece of research written by a doctor at St Antony's College who specialised in European studies, and the migration of people. I needed to focus. After ten minutes I gave up, and called Hazel, my best shot for somewhere to stay.

'Oh Emma, lovely to hear from you but so sorry, we're going away tomorrow. Of course, you could have stayed anyway but we're taking the chance to have the lounge and hall decorated. Jack has been on about it for ages and he phoned them yesterday. They start tomorrow and are working through the weekend. We'll be back next Wednesday if that's any good.'

'Oh, don't worry Hazel. I'm sure I can stay with a friend. Just thought I'd check with you first,' I bluffed, then hesitated a little before going on. 'Actually, I have a new friend for you to meet sometime.' I knew I needed to tell her at some point and it was always best with Hazel to get in early before she heard it from Becky or another of my friends. I explained a little about Jamie and she was intrigued and clearly frustrated she would be away.

'I know - come to tea today. There's still time to prepare. I insist,' she said.

There was no way out with Hazel, she insisted. Instead of solving a problem, I now had two. I returned to my work and knocked out three more paragraphs then took what I had to see Jamie, to get his perspective and to broach the topic of afternoon tea.

He welcomed me into his office, awkward in his handling of me - almost literally, as he came round from his desk to give me a hug then decided that wasn't appropriate in the workplace.

'How are you?' he said.

I talked through the research, then sat back in the chair.

'You look distracted. What's up?' he asked.

I told him about the situation at the flat and said that I had run out of options and perhaps I should actually take a few days away. He laughed.

'Well, cold showers will be good for the skin, they say. But it's good news really, if he does what he says he will. And you can't go away, you are too busy.'

'He mentioned a new boiler.'

'That's excellent. So what will we do with you?'

'No idea,' I said.

'Easily solved. I have a spare room. Come stay with me. I insist.'

'You might change your mind when you hear my other problem,' I said.

***

Two hours later, we were in the car on the way to Hazel's. I wore the top she had bought me for my birthday, a bright white one with splashes of blue and red on it as if the designer had got their paintbrush out. It was very on-trend for a present from Hazel. It was time for Jamie to meet the person nearest to being a mother to me. Fortunately Uncle Jack would be out at work.

Jamie had also changed and wore a suit. I told him not to, but he insisted.

'Emma, your auntie needs to see me like the saint I am,' he said.

We pulled up on her street in Headington, the resident's only parking meaning that we had to leave the car about a hundred metres from her front door. I stopped on the pavement and gave Jamie a hug, then straightened his tie. He leaned in and kissed me briefly.

'Thanks for coming,' I said.

'Anything I shouldn't say?'

'No, you'll be fine. Just notice her plants in the hall. She loves to dabble with indoor flowers.'

Aunt Hazel's house was pre-war, the whole street having been built in the Thirties when Oxford was expanding rapidly with the growing car industry. Red-brick semi-detached houses with bay windows and tiny front gardens and some with cute wrought-iron gates, although most of those had been removed to enable us to see off Hitler or allow cars to be parked off-road.

We stood in the porch and rang the bell. I could see her approach through the leaded art nouveau glass on the top half of the door.

'Right on time,' she said as she pulled the door fully open and walked out onto the porch to shake Jamie's hand.

'You must be Jamie,' she said.

We stepped inside and I gave Hazel a quick hug.

'Lovely flowers, Mrs Hawkins,' Jamie said.

Hazel laughed. 'Call me Hazel.'

We sat in the back room overlooking her tidy garden with its patch of lawn and borders of various bushes and a line of roses along one side. Hazel had always been a keen gardener. She poured tea from a pot and passed around a plate of sandwiches: ham and tomato with chutney, or tuna and cucumber.

'Jamie works on the paper with me. He's my editor so that sort of makes him my boss.'

'She loves it there, Jamie. Always happy is our Emma. Often mentions you,' she said.

'She's a bright young woman,' he said.

I listened to them discuss me for a couple of minutes and stepped in before they got to any of my annoying habits. Hazel looked to be on the verge of pulling out an old photo album that sat on the sideboard.

'What do you think of my latest article about the Cowley Road?' I said.

She put down her sandwich plate and stood up.

'No photos Aunt Hazel. Too soon,' I said.

'Spoilsport.'

She sat down again and smiled at Jamie.

'We'll wait till she's gone to the toilet. She's bound to go soon.'

'Hazel. Please. I'm not eight.'

'You are in the photos,' she said.

Jamie laughed and helped himself to more food. We had moved on to Victoria sponge and lemon drizzle. Hazel poured more tea.

'I think the article was very insightful. I read everything she does, you know Jamie. I always check every paper.'

'Jamie did help me with it,' I said.

'Only to get more fire into it. Your daughter's a little soft on immigration you know, Hazel.'

Hazel looked at him directly for a couple of seconds before speaking.

'She's got strong values, Jamie. Nothing wrong in that.'

'I'm sure so. But we don't want the country overrun now, do we?'

I heard myself groan inside and looked at the floor. The meet-my-auntie car was hurtling towards a solid brick wall.

'Oxford is a richer place for its multiculturalism,' she said.

'This cake is yummy, Hazel. Is it a Nigella?'

'I bought it in Waitrose. There was no time to bake.' She gave me a stare.

I smiled at Jamie and my eyes told him to change the subject. He put his hand over mine on the dining table and smiled back.

'We're spending a lot of time together at the moment, aren't we Emma, what with the series of articles and our bowling sessions.'

I laughed and looked at her.

'He's trying to turn me into a sportsperson, I think. Can't seem to throw straight.'

'Same as our Linda. It'll be in the genes. We're more arty/crafty as a family I think. Your dad's not bad though - he was a keen cyclist in his day.'

'So, we're bowling again sometime, are we?' I said.

'Of course we are, Emma. If you'll let me take you. After all, it was soured a little by the company at the end. We mustn't let that put us off.'

'He means Andrei, Hazel. Andrei turned up with Daniel.'

'Oh, he's a nice young man,' she said.

There was so much weight and meaning put into her sentence that I realised another car crash loomed ahead. I looked at my watch and indicated to Jamie we should go. He jumped up and carried the plates through to the kitchen, then asked where the toilet was.

As soon as he went up the stairs, she started.

'I don't like him.'

'Well I do. He's fun and witty and looks after me.'

'He's too old for you.'

'No he's not. He's not that old. And he's clever and funny and handsome.'

'Andrei's better for you. And better looking.'

'Jamie's more of a bad boy,' I said.

'Exactly.' She picked up the teapot and walked through to the kitchen, with me in tow carrying the remaining cake. 'I do read the papers. I know what's happening. He has a different view of the world,' she said.

'Well, we'll see. It's early days.'

'I have a cutout from the weekend for you. An ad for a job at the Guardian. Think about it.'

She opened the kitchen drawer and thrust a piece of paper in my hand. Hazel was always encouraging my career.

'It's in London. In the circumstances, perhaps that would be good,' she said.

I pushed it to the bottom of my handbag just as Jamie came down the stairs to join us and then we said our goodbyes. On the way to the car, he held my hand.

'She's not impressed, is she?'

'Give her time. She'll be fine,' I said.

We drove to the White Horse and went inside for a drink.

'When did your aunt meet Andrei then?' Jamie said, as we sat in the window, both facing inwards towards the bar. I nursed a Sauvignon while Jamie sipped an ale.

I decided to lie, it was simpler.

'She hasn't met him. That's just Hazel being a mum. I

told her about the flowers, that's all.'

'So if I give you flowers, she'll like me, will she?'

'Maybe. I guess you'll just have to test that theory.' I smiled.

'You quite like Andrei following you around, don't you?'

'No I don't. He's creepy.'

'And foreign.'

'That's not it at all. That's nothing to do with it and you know it.'

'Sorry, but well, I like you Emma. You can see that. This Andrei, I thought you wanted him gone.'

'Forget him. He's harmless. He's useful for my research but it's not like he's an ex-boyfriend or anything. You're sounding jealous of someone you shouldn't be jealous of.'

'Ok, well as long as that's the truth, I suppose. I see you as mine now, Emma. You belong to me, not Andrei.'

'I don't belong to anyone, Jamie.'

He turned to me and stared as if he was about to say something else. Then he raised his hand and slipped it around my shoulder, pulling me to him and kissing me on the cheek.

'I know. That's fine,' he said.

***

Lou-two called while I was in a taxi to work, after another sleepless night. As well as the flat renovations, Jamie and the elusive Amanda Brown were crowding my thoughts. I think I dreamt they were having sex in Andrei's café on one of the tables, for some bizarre reason. I let the call go to voicemail

– no point in the cab driver knowing all my business. The rain was coming down so fast that his wipers couldn't cope and I could hardly see the road ahead. The traffic was crawling, backed up all the way to Summertown. Water poured along the gutters into the drains and people walking on the pavements held their umbrellas at an angle against the oncoming wind.

Lou-two never called at that time of the morning, so I decided to contact her as soon as I got into the *Gazette*'s reception area.

'Hello stranger, this is a nice surprise. How's the wonderful world of Summercloud?' I said when she answered.

'Too busy. Lots of bosses over from America at the moment. Corporate entertaining.'

'Sounds glamorous.'

'Not really. A lot of boring IT blokes eyeing you up all night.'

'Not even one handsome Yankee?'

'Not really, I guess the CEO is pretty hot but that'd be like a kiss of death for my career. Anyway what about you and Jamie? How's it going?'

'Oh, good. Trying not to rush. Becky's the one who's running fast at the moment.'

'Yes I heard, but look Emma, I phoned for a reason.'

'So I guessed,' I said.

'Look, I ... well, I've been asked out on a date and wanted to pass it by you first.'

'Me ...? OK ... not sure whether I'm to take that as a compliment or not. You mean I have a good eye for men?'

Lou-two laughed. She had met and passed judgment on pretty much all my boyfriends over the years right back to

Davey, the first boy at school. Lou-two and I had been in the same year and mostly the same classes.

Gemma coughed and shuffled some papers on the desk. The lobby was empty, and there were dripping brollies in the rack in the corner where I stood. I looked across at her and she nodded towards the front door. It had to be either Jamie or the Prime Minister.

'No, not quite that reason. The thing is that it's Andrei. Your Andrei,' she said.

I was a bit stunned for a few seconds and distracted by whoever was about to appear. I felt some irritation. It seemed a strange match.

'Hang on a sec ...' I said as I walked away from reception into the big meeting room on the ground floor, not risking a look back at anyone, '... he's not my Andrei, Lou,'

'Well I know you said that. You know that night in All-Bar-One. I said I had never heard of him?'

'Yes, I remember.'

'Well it turns out I had met him, only once, a few years back. We hadn't spoken more than a couple of words at the time. He came to our company. I saw him in reception.'

'What, at Summercloud? What was he doing there?'

I began to feel a bit of panic in me. This was another of Andrei's tricks.

'He came for a seminar on Infrastructure Security. Something by one of our directors that I had to organise. He was one of the guest speakers actually. He's some sort of specialist.'

'Yes, I heard that. Well, anyway, it's fine. Nothing to do with me really.'

'I bumped into Becky's Daniel yesterday in a coffee shop in town and Andrei was there too. I recognised him from the seminar and we said hello, then realised we both knew you. Afterwards, he called me at work and asked me out.'

'Be careful Lou, he's just a bit, well ... intense I suppose.'

'Seems cute to me. I wasn't sure whether I'd be treading on your toes. I wouldn't want to do that.'

'Not at all. That's fine I think. Are you, well ... sure it's you he's interested in?'

As soon as I said it, I realised it sounded awful. Lou-two is attractive by anyone's standards. She's tall, elegant, with a short bob of dark hair and lovely long eyelashes. Always the centre of men's attention.

'Sorry,' I said. 'That came out all wrong. It's just that he got a bit clingy.'

'Did you two have a proper fling?'

'No, of course not.'

'Why did he drop you? I thought he was keen on you, but he told me he dropped you.'

'Ha. Well, that's not it. Look, he is very sweet but there was nothing to drop. It's all history. If you're asking my blessing, it's fine. Just close to home, that's all, because of my job. He gets a bit obsessive, and take care online, he seems to have a way to track that, but I guess you'd know all about that.'

She laughed, 'I'm only the assistant. But thanks, I'll be careful.'

18

Cowley Road is an integral part of East Oxford, across the Magdalen Bridge, the bridge that separates the town people of East Oxford from the gowned people of the University. The gowns had many traditional events and celebrations such as their May Day morning ritual of singing from the top of Magdalen tower at dawn, and their all-night revelling on the streets of the city.

I was more interested in finding community events for the townsfolk. These were fewer in number, the most famous being the Cowley Road Carnival on a Sunday in July, but as this was a Friday in April I needed something else. I discovered the weekly farmers' market, a traditional, community market run by volunteers, and an excellent way of understanding the cultural mix of the East Oxford area.

I tracked down Jamie in his office to discuss it and, after reassuring him that my earlier phone call was indeed with Lou-two, he suggested we should visit together. I tied my hair back and fixed my makeup while I waited in the reception for him to finish his various Friday tasks. Fortunately, the rain had stopped and a bright and sunny spring morning was emerging, a real feel of cheerfulness in the air.

Jamie brought his Mercedes round to the front door to pick me up. I found myself skipping across the pavement to jump in beside him, and as the soft-top roof opened up, it was like being in an American movie. He kissed me on the cheek, then told me to strap in for a fun day.

'You look great,' he shouted across as we drove up the Banbury Road.

'Thanks, you too.' Jamie was wearing his beige chinos and a loose fitting dark blue shirt but it wasn't his best look – I preferred his suit in the right circumstance.

It felt like we were a happy couple set for a good day out, time to relax and enjoy the vibe at the same time as gathering our impressions of the street culture of Oxford. Today there were crowded pavements of shoppers and locals mixed with friendly police and marshals directing the traffic.

We left the car in the temporary car park and started to walk back towards the street market area. Jamie put his arm around me and pulled me close to him.

'Thanks Emma. This is great. Thanks for being my girl,' he said.

I smiled at him and we walked up the side road and onto the Cowley Road itself. Even at eleven o'clock in the morning, smoke from barbecues drifted across the heads of the crowds up ahead of us, like incense hanging over the congregation of a church. A bunch of guys were standing and watching people go by as they ate some kind of hot breakfast roll, probably with sausage or bacon or both. I was hungry.

'No talk of Andrei today,' he said. It didn't sound like a question.

'We must think about work, though. I'd like to get some more interviews. I'm working on the next piece,' I said.

'OK. You should try to talk to people who've lived here

all their lives. They're harder and harder to find though.'

We wandered around the stalls of local produce, souvenirs and clothing, while we watched various busking performers and musicians who were entertaining the throng. It was approaching midday and the sun was hot, drying the pavements rapidly and causing the gathering crowds to take off their coats and bask in the unseasonable heat. I felt sorry for a man wearing a heavy clown outfit as he juggled five sticks and rode a unicycle. He must have been gasping for water under that all that makeup. A ring of people formed around him, clapping when he succeeded in stopping the bike and holding it still on one spot as he tossed the sticks into the air. Then they cheered even louder when he dropped two and stepped off the bike. Is it just a British trait to celebrate failure? Perhaps universal, I thought.

Jamie took my photo standing next to a person made up to be the invisible man with a blank head at the top of his mock captain's uniform. I gave the man a pound coin as I squeezed Jamie's arm in thanks.

We drank coffee to start but soon moved onto Red Stripe, poured in plentiful supply from the Jamaican stalls that formed the core of the market area. The cultural mix added a vibrancy, and the sun added tropical warmth and humour.

Music pounded from speaker stacks, a mix of reggae and ska with the DJ for the day seemingly high from the smoke that surrounded him as he jumped around with his headphones on. As a man tending one of the food stalls lifted the lid on a steaming, sizzling pan of paella, a heavily garlic-scented waft of air rushed past my nose and suddenly we both need to eat.

As we stood with our polystyrene containers of chilli

chicken with rice, Jamie suggested we should chat to as many people as possible about how the area had changed over the last few years. I did talk to a few, but it wasn't going to be the day for sensible responses. Most answers were excessively positive about the wonderful world. We sat in the pub courtyard to drink more beer, the afternoon sun burning overhead.

'Not going to get much today. The place is beaming from ear to ear,' I said.

'Wait till the alcohol takes hold,' Jamie said.

As if on cue, a couple of lads in England football strip approached our table.

The bigger of the two, who could not have been more than seventeen, spoke first.

'You reporters, love?'

'Is it that obvious? I thought we wore casuals today.' I said.

'Right yeah. I saw your picture on the advert. You the posh girl from the paper?'

His mate was a little shorter than him and more rounded. He had a beer in one hand and a sausage roll in the other.

'You're better looking than in the photo,' he said.

'Oh, thanks.' I wasn't sure how to respond.

'Well, stick around for the big story today ...' The first guy took a mouthful of beer and stared at Jamie.

'... make sure your boyfriend here looks after you.'

Before Jamie could speak, they walked away and I could see they were with a bigger group on the other side of the street. I recognised two of them from the gang of troublemakers that had taken a swing at Andrei.

'I don't like the sound of that,' I said to Jamie, but he was more intent on getting his camera out of his pocket and snapping a few shots of them.

We finished our drinks and vacated the table, giving it to a family with two toddlers, and a baby in a buggy. We made our way through the crowds towards the corner and the group of lads were ahead of us when one of them picked up the temporary waste-bin that had been put out for the day, and threw it onto the road into the middle of a bunch of young teenagers out with their families. It hit the foot of the girl at the front and a man, presumably her father, turned and shouted abuse at the lads.

Within a minute, there was chaos. The street switched from a revelling mass of merriment to a seething pen of angry animals all shouting and screaming at each other. Missiles started to fly; old food containers, plastic glasses, bits of rubbish from the bins. People started running and young children screamed. It was as if the surprising heat of April had addled everyone's brains. In amongst it all I could see the instigators calmly orchestrating the chaos, provoking the violent response from a rival gang of young men who looked like they might be supporters of Poland or Germany.

I grabbed Jamie's arm and looked at him. He was smiling and clapping.

'Now we've got a story,' he said.

I was appalled. I stared at him.

'It's down to you, this, you know. Your articles. You wait, you'll be headline news,' he said.

I dragged him away in disgust and we headed back

towards the car. On a side street, I saw a man starting a fire in the open front door of a Chinese food shop, using an old sheet that leapt into flames when he struck a match. He wore dark clothing, a black baseball cap and dark sunglasses. Before we could raise the alarm, I heard sirens and he glanced in our direction then ran off the other way, waving his arm almost as if he knew us. The shopkeeper emerged with an extinguisher, spraying foam on the conflagration just as a police car raced by.

'Come on, take me home,' I said, and Jamie put his arm round me and escorted me safely to his car.

19

I turned on the television in my flat. I had been awake most of the night going over the events. Jamie had dropped me off at seven o'clock and I said I had a throbbing head and needed my bed ... on my own.

It was top item on the 6am BBC local television news. They showed footage of kids throwing bottles and police lined up in protective headgear brandishing truncheons. Three people had been injured from flying objects and thirty people had been arrested. Local shops were raided overnight. All along the Cowley Road, the news report displayed a trail of wanton destruction, broken windows and damaged market stalls. The Lord Mayor of Oxford stood in front of one raided electrical shop with a microphone thrust in front of him by a local television interviewer.

'So, Mr Mayor, why do you think this has all kicked off now, at such a minor event? Who do you blame?'

'Well, it's hard to say. The alcohol. The weather was unusually hot. Who knows? We've always had such a peaceful community. This does not represent the vast majority of Cowley people.'

'Are you saying it's external troublemakers?'

'Probably. We don't know. The local paper hasn't helped with articles discussing the causes of high youth unemployment in the area. I call for calm on all sides.'

I died in my coffee. Was he blaming me? Blood rushed to my face. I stomped over to my computer and banged out a thousand words. I was there. I saw what happened with the so-called football fans. I wrote an email to Jamie and copied it to the editor-in-chief with my piece attached. I had to present the facts.

My phone rang and I expected it to be Jamie, but it was Andrei. I had opened the call before I realised.

'Hi.' I said.

'You are OK?'

He sounded so sweet, I cried. Spontaneous blubbing.

I shut the call and went back to bed under my duvet. They could all go hang for a while, although I couldn't ignore the fact my boiler was dead and I was should be getting myself ready to move to Jamie's house that afternoon.

***

An hour later, I called Gary.

'Hey, how are you? Top of the headlines,' he said immediately.

I stood wrapped in my towel with another one around my head staring at myself in the mirror of the bathroom. My head still thumped, despite the cold shower.

'Hungover. Miserable. The usual.'

I took two paracetamols while he told me how he missed me and how silly I was being.

'You're a good journalist. Don't worry about it. Man up,' he said.

'I need to. Too many men, that's part of the problem.'

'You haven't got involved with our Inspector have you?' he asked.

'You mean Brad? No, of course not, as if ... no, it's closer to home. Jamie.'

'Editor Jamie. James the Seventh of Scotland. That Jamie.'

'Of course that one. I know I'm mad but he's good for me. More than good, he's ... well, he's just perfect.'

The more I talked to Gary, the more I thought about Jamie. I needed him. I put the phone on speaker and laid it on the dressing table while I got dressed. Gary was an easy weekend chat - gossip about the force and the paper, shared views on the evils of the media. I put on denims and a long-sleeved T-shirt, keeping it low key for my temporary move, although when I pulled back the curtains, the way the trees moved in the wind looked decidedly wintry despite the strong sunlight. I teamed the look with a stripy woolly jumper.

'You're just going to have to ask him.'

'To marry me?'

'No, stupid. About the photo.'

'There's a chance it's not him. The photo's over ten years old.'

'But it is, Burt confirmed that and you'll always pick away at that. In your head. Why would they hide that they know each other? I've been asking around, subtly like, but it's all a bit of a closed book. There's some secret there. Shall I press harder?'

'No. Leave it. I'll do that. You're a star, you know. I need to go now. I'm dressed and ready.'

'In future, I insist we FaceTime our calls. It'd brighten up my Saturdays.'

20

Jamie managed to park directly outside the flat, which was a piece of luck given that it was Saturday. He had come straight from the Oxford United match and was in a good mood as they'd won two-nil, a rare occurrence. I told him I had spent the day sorting out stuff to bring with me, neither of us mentioning the riots or the TV report. Perhaps he hadn't read my email.

I put the black sack of shoes on the pavement beside the boot of his car.

'There's a few more bits and pieces in my bedroom. There's a case and a couple more black sacks. You can't miss them.'

'No problem. I'll get them in a minute, you take it easy. I want to look after you today,' he said.

Jamie pushed the shoe bag into the boot as best he could, squeezing it in between the box of clothes and my spare duvet, then he smiled and went back into the house without saying a word. He was being really sweet. I opened the passenger door and sat in the car, looking back at the front door. Happy days. Two years of living alone, now staying over at Jamie's. Would that lead to something? I had left more stuff than I was taking, boxing it and covering it in sheets, as Mr Desai said he would be redecorating completely. His estimate of three days was extending a bit. Staying with Jamie would be an interesting experiment. 'Come live with me - well, in the spare room of course. Bring some stuff of your own, make this place yours as well, see how we do,' he'd said. I think he had expected a no, judging by his shock at the bright smile on his face when I responded.

He returned with my case in one hand and two black sacks stuffed under his arm. He still looked happy; I don't think he fully appreciated what he was letting himself in for. I let him do all the work while I surveyed his car, not that there was much to review. The interior was spotless, empty, soulless. I opened the glove box and inside was a packet of wipes, special ones to clean the leather seats, and a service book. That was it, no travel mints, no pens, maps or compass ... nothing. At least there were no condoms. There was a small leather waste bin velcroed to the side of the dashboard next to the passenger, the colour of it matching the dark grey leather seating and interior. Even that was empty and clean, and the floor was spotless, presumably vacuumed that morning. There was a sweet smell of the leather mixed with a rose air freshener that dangled from the mirror.

Jamie opened the rear door and put the case and sacks on the seat and in the footwell behind me.

'Is that all of it, Emma?' He said.

He was clearly in caring and helpful mood.

'That's it.'

I got out of the car and kissed him on the cheek, squeezing his arm as I did, then I skipped in an exaggerated way up to the front door of the house and pulled it closed, then skipped back to his car and got in. He just laughed.

When we got to his place, he insisted I go on in, while he brought all the bags. Then he got a bottle of bubbly out of the fridge, opened it and poured me a large one. He held the bottle and chinked it against my glass.

'Welcome,' he said and wrapped his arm around me, still holding the bottle, and kissed me. 'Take a seat, the TV buttons are right there.'

I sat back in his leather sofa, a similar shade of grey to his car, and put my feet up on the matching footstool. The cleaner must have been in that morning, as the place was spotless. A small oak coffee table was in the middle of the room, a neat pile of *Sporting Life* on one side and three coasters on the other. The TV was huge and flat and dominated the room, which was white walled with a mirror, two prints by Edward Hopper and a poster of Ayrton Senna.

I heard Jamie struggle up the stairs with my suitcase.

'I'll put it all in the bedroom. You can sort it out later,' he shouted.

It was just gone five o'clock when he'd finished and we lay on his couch and drank the champagne.

'Happy?' he said.

I kissed him, murmuring my agreement. I could feel the heat of his body pressed against me and I ran my hand through his wiry hair, brushing it back from his forehead, where I kissed him next.

'Food. We need food before we go any further,' he said.

It was true that I was hungry. The champagne wasn't helping. I noticed he had only had half a glass and I was on my second already.

'We'll go to Bill's. I'll book us in. You go and get ready,' he said.

I scurried off to the bedroom. I'd thought I was ready enough, but clearly Jamie had ideas that I would dress up for the occasion. I spent a bit of time unpacking, hanging some clothes in the wardrobe, where there was plenty of room, and piling my shoes by the radiator under the window.

I heard Jamie go out through the front door, so I walked through to his bedroom to look out over the road. He had the vacuum cleaner and was cleaning the inside of the boot out. His bedroom was as immaculate as the spare. There was an ironing board and iron along one wall and on the bed was a wash basket with a couple of his shirts in it. I wondered about surprising him and ironing them but decided it would be dangerous to set any kind of precedent on my first day, and I probably wouldn't press them to his standard anyway. Creases in the sleeves or not? That was the question.

I returned to the spare room, which was my room now, I thought. I put on the black dress that was least creased and tied back my hair, then I sat awkwardly on the edge of the bed and tried to apply some makeup without a mirror. Giving up, I went into the bathroom and stood at the sink, then proceeded to empty the contents of my cosmetics bag onto the shelf beside the mirror.

Five minutes later, I was done and ready to go. As I walked back downstairs, Jamie came in, grappling with the cable of the cleaner. It was gone seven and getting dark. He put the hall light on, a bar of spotlights that lit me up as I reached the final step.

'Wow, you look amazing,' he said.

'Well, thank you kind sir. I'm all yours.'

He put down the cleaner and lifted me down the last step and kissed me, pulling me tight to him.

'I'm hungry,' I said.

'OK, OK. Your car awaits.'

Jamie hung the cleaner on its hook in the cupboard under the stairs and wound the cable around one of those tidy things that stops it from tying itself in knots. He was in a black shirt and dark grey chinos and looked pretty good himself. Together, we made a dark, mysterious couple going out on a stormy April evening.

He drove us down through Summertown into St Giles where he parked in a space just outside the Eagle and Child pub. From there it was only five minutes to the restaurant. We walked hand in hand, my heels causing us to take our time. There was a buzz of students all around us, hurrying out for the evening or returning from a late library session. A girl passed us with four bags of supermarket shopping, each one overflowing with provisions, presumably for her whole house. A loose orange fell to the ground and Jamie quickly stopped it with his foot and picked it up for her, returning it to her bag.

'Thanks. Good job it's got a skin. I'll make sure Maddy gets that one,' she said. Then she walked on quickly, weaving her way through the crowds.

We passed the Martyr's Memorial and I could hear snippets of talk from the guide who had a throng of tourists around him.

'Heresy ... burnt at the stake ... bishops...'

I shivered and pulled myself in closer to Jamie so that he put his arm around me. Eventually we reached the restaurant, and were put on a corner table overlooking the street.

'Happy?'

I smiled and looked up from the menu.

'Very.'

We both ordered steaks and he chose a bottle of Cabernet. I was so excited that when the antipasto came, I sneaked off to the toilet to phone Becky. Jamie was being wonderful, attentive and sexy and I was embarking on something romantic, even though there was a mystery surrounding his possible association with David.

I shut the cubicle and sat on the seat. She answered immediately.

'So you're in then,' she said.

'Head over heels in. I've taken a load of stuff there today.'

'Aww ... that's so exciting. Like when I moved some stuff to Daniel's. It feels like you're staking out some territory of your own in his kingdom, doesn't it?'

'He's Mr Clean and Tidy, all the time. Not sure I can live up to that for too long. I've already wrecked his bathroom.'

She laughed and rattled on some more about Daniel. I heard a couple of women come in and mutter something between them. There were only two cubicles and I was hogging one of them for quite a long time.

'Becky, I need to go. Someone wants to use this.' I said.

I opened the door and went outside to dirty looks, then walked back into the corridor of the restaurant, while Becky carried on talking about her day. A man passed me on the way to the gents and smiled so I smiled back, confident that

I could have fun with my life. He was slender with a small goatee beard and had a very naughty grin. Eventually I returned to Becky.

'I really must go, lovely. There's a big piece of meat waiting with my name on it,' I said quite loudly.

The guy laughed and disappeared into the gents. I put my phone in my bag and walked back to the table.

Jamie killed my mood in three seconds. The main courses had arrived and he was already eating his. He looked at me with such a stern face, I felt like I was back in the office and had submitted a complete load of rubbish as an article for the front page.

'Sorry, didn't notice the time,' I said, and sat and started on my food.

'You've been fifteen minutes.'

I beamed at him. 'Did you miss me that much? I spoke to Becky. Didn't notice the time, so sorry.'

I reached out to hold his hand but he just continued eating and looking grumpy. The steaks were sirloin, the chips were large and the whole thing was yummy. I ate quickly.

Jamie poured me some more wine and I drank quickly, nervous. When the waiter appeared he ordered a second bottle.

'Shall we leave the car in town?' I said.

'No, I'm not drinking much. We'll be fine. It's mainly for you.'

'I really am sorry. I didn't realise the time. You know what Becky and I are like when we get started.'

'It wasn't that other guy of yours then, some other suitor?' he said.

I looked at him open mouthed, put my knife down and

drank some more wine. He still looked angry, his forehead set with a frown. There was a buzz of noise around the high-ceilinged restaurant that drowned us out if we spoke quietly. Most tables were full, particularly with students and their parents. It was a popular place to bring Ma and Pa when they came up and visited for the second weekend of term. *OK, my little sweet, of course your father and I will visit you. We'll take you out and feed you up properly.*

I leaned in towards Jamie and grabbed his hand.

'Don't spoil it. I'm so happy. Don't be daft, there is no other guy.'

'What about that Romanian waiter chap?'

'I have seen him to help with the research. You know that. It's nothing more than that. Don't be daft. I can't help it if he likes me, can I?'

'I want it to stop. You're not to see him anymore.'

I gulped down more wine and stared back. He was being unreasonable and my spine was straightening with irritation. I didn't want a fight.

'It's just for the article, just professional. But fine ... I'll stop. I'll make some excuse. You're my man, Jamie.' I said.

He tried to smile and I held his hand.

My phone beeped a message. I took it out to look, thinking it would be Becky WhatsApping some joke about meat.

<Meet tomorrow at 7pm? Hope you can make it? Axxx>

It was Andrei.

'Who's that?' he said.

'Oh it's just Becky again. She's being daft. She's so into

Daniel, it's crazy.'

I quickly messaged back, putting him off to Monday morning then I turned my phone off with a flourish and put it back in the bag. Just moved in, and already living a lie.

After we had eaten, we walked slowly back to the car. I was drunk and held onto his arm tightly. He was snug and warm. I'd finished the second bottle of wine and the stress of the lie of having Andrei's text and my acknowledgement burning in my phone was killing me.

I sat back in the passenger seat, and Jamie drove us slowly back up the Banbury Road. I must have passed out, because the next thing we were parking up outside his house. I woke with a start and sat up. He came round to the passenger door to help me out, but in the time it took him to walk around the car, I suddenly felt very nauseous, and was sick all over the passenger floor just as he opened the door. I managed to move to direct the second lot out the door instead but that just spattered all over his beautifully pressed trousers and his brown shoes. His shoes were so well polished that I could see my face and hair reflected as I leaned over and was sick again on them. The red wine coming back up was the sour taste of shame.

21

I woke on his soft leather couch. My head was pressed at an odd angle against the cushion, its cotton cover soaked in my dribble. A light blanket had been placed over me, tucked in at my feet. Beside me was the smallest of the occasional tables, the other two of the set remaining up against the wall beside the television, and on it was a glass of water, half full. The room was bathed in a pale yellow glow from one of those plug-in lights that you use to deter burglars when you are travelling away on holiday. I felt deterred.

I pulled my hand from under the blanket and reached for the glass. My fingers smelt of lemons; they'd been washed or wiped. I sipped some water then returned the glass and lay on my back, staring at the line of unlit room lights embedded in the ceiling at even intervals.

I heard a door close so I breathed as quietly as I could and remained still. Then I heard the bathroom door open, close again and lock, and the seat go up and a man peeing into the toilet. My temples throbbed when I rested my fingers on them at each side. I wanted to die.

When I woke again, there was sharp sunlight through the crack in the curtains. The water glass had been refilled, the blanket re-tucked, holding my arms in its warmth. I felt my body, still wearing the black dress, still in my tights. I was untouched.

The shaft of light cut a line down the wall opposite me, highlighting the clock on the shelf above the music player. It was a clock with traditional hands and face, encased in a modern light oak stand. The big hand pointed at two, the small at eleven.

I could smell bacon and coffee combined. The smell of a Sunday. A mower whispered in the back garden. I kept the blanket close and hobbled over to the window, then pulled the curtain aside. Jamie was in green cords, tucked into green wellies. He wore a blue fisherman's smock I'd never seen before. His back was to me as he cut his way down the line of the path, the orange mower lead trailing behind him. I shut the curtain fully, the room darkening again. I could escape.

I went to the bathroom, stripped off and showered. My shampoo and gel had been placed in the small wire rack beside the shower head. His version of the same items, both Molton Brown, were standing at the base of the shower at the back, out of the way. The water was perfect and I took my time. Steam overcame the power of the extractor fan and the mirror fogged up. I was in a dream. I needed to eat. As soon as that thought hit me, I was beyond starvation. Every nerve in my body sent its pulse to my head requesting nourishment. My brain lost its sense of touch and smell, I started to see blurry spots. My whole being ached for sustenance to maintain life.

I stepped out the shower and wrapped myself in the white towelling robe that had been placed on the hook on the back of the door. I tidied my hair with my brush that had been placed on the shelf, wiping a window in the mirror with the back of my hand. I looked into my eyes, which were dead, with lines of red blood joining the irises to the corners. My mascara was spread across my lower lids and down to my cheeks.

I practiced my lines. *Sorry. I'm really really sorry. It was the second bottle. It was the prawns* (though I didn't have any). *I will pay to have your car cleaned. I'll buy you a new pair of trousers, a new pair of shoes, a new suit. A new car. I'll give you a blowjob, every day for a week. Only after I've cleaned my teeth, of course. I really love you.* I really did, I thought.

I worked out my strategy. My head hurt. I needed paracetamol. I needed coffee and food. I was hungry. I couldn't remember walking back to the car. I couldn't remember the journey. I remembered the end.

I was sick as a student when I was at university. It was on the arm of a boyfriend. I think it was Dave. Big Dave. At a party. It was rare though; I wasn't the sicky type, not like Becky, who could puke for the student vomiting team, double A-star. I was lightweight. I remembered his T-shirt that I ruined – he had only bought it that day. Three months later, I gave him a new one for Christmas and he finished with me soon after that. The replacement T-shirt was a mistake, a reminder of what had happened.

Would Jamie forget? Would he forgive? The signs were good. There wasn't a pile of my stuff in bags by the door. I crept out of the bathroom to the top of the stairs and looked down at the front door to check.

I heard the back door close and the kettle go on. If I moved, he would hear me. The radio blared. Radio Oxford Sunday morning tunes, playing an upbeat Beatles number about sunshine. I knew I had to face the music, but I needed more time so I retired back to the bathroom.

***

I heard him come up the stairs and walk into the bedroom.

'Em, I've put a cup of tea beside the bed for you,' he called.

'Thanks, I'll be out in a minute,' I croaked.

After I'd given myself a full ten minutes to freshen up and apply a bit of makeup, I returned to the spare room. Jamie was lying on the bed, reading something.

'Hello gorgeous,' he said.

'I'm so, so sorry.'

I sat on the bed beside him and then lay down, and he wrapped his arms around me. I turned and kissed him gently, then lay back. He didn't seem angry at all.

'I shouldn't have let you drink more wine, it's OK, it's mostly my fault. I rushed you.'

'Is your car alright?'

'I've booked it in for a valet at two o'clock. It'll be fine. I've cleaned out the worst of it. Leather upholstery comes into its own under such circumstances.'

He kissed my forehead and ran his fingers through my hair, brushing it back from my face.

'I can see I'm going to have to fix you. Now ... sex or pub lunch? You can't have both, too late.'

'Pub lunch it is then. Headache and starving. Lethal combination. Take me out. I promise not to drink,' I said.

Thirty minutes later we sat opposite each other at his

local, a proper roast beef and Yorkshire pudding dinner in front of us. He was drinking Guinness, and I was on water. Feeling slightly better I decided to talk about work, although I wasn't feeling brave enough to bring up the photograph. I started on safer ground.

'We need more on Amanda Brown. Why has she gone abroad? Did she go willingly? She was a dancer once. Know any gentlemen's clubs in London?' I said. I wasn't going to share my long list of names from Gary, perhaps Jamie could come up with some that were the same.

Jamie laughed. It was a lovely raucous, rasping kind of laugh that captured the essence of him. I put my hand on his across the table and smiled.

'Surely you must know one or two? All those boys' nights out? Tell me about them, I've never been inside one,' I said.

'They're seedy, dark and hot with pumping, throbbing music and a heavy overtone of sex. The better ones only take your wallet while the grimy, downbeat, shit-holes take your very soul.'

'I thought you'd know a bit. So Amanda Brown? What do you think? Upmarket? Backstreet?'

'Well, we know it was a few years ago. I'd bet she was simply making a bit of money, probably from quite selective clientele. We would need some contact from London to know more. But why bother? She's run off.'

'I'm being investigative, doing my job. I think there's a story in it still. All too easy to let it go.'

Jamie took his phone from his jacket pocket and made a call.

'Who you calling?'

'A mate in Fleet Street.'

'A fellow gentleman.'

'Something like that.'

I scoffed the roast meat and potatoes, assuaging the ache in my stomach. Given that I had puked so much last night, I guessed I hadn't properly eaten in over twenty-four hours. I looked around at the Sunday lunchers, mostly couples looking hung over plus a few extended families taking Granny out for a roastie with the grandchildren. The noise level rose as the clatter of knives and forks drowned the conversations. The British at Sunday lunch: a picture like something from a children's book.

Jamie talked quietly into his phone. I pinched a carrot from his plate as he spoke and he tried to stab me with his fork. Whoever was on the other end knew nothing useful.

I tried to interject. 'Presumably she wasn't called Amanda as a dancer. Not that easy to trace.'

Jamie hung up. 'There's no rumours, nothing remotely interesting to connect our missing woman to London.'

He paused and wiped his mouth with his napkin.

'Why don't you call your Andrei tomorrow and arrange to have a coffee. See what you can get. The accents of the attackers. It's still the only real clue I know about,' he said.

I eyed him. Was my memory playing tricks?

'But ... last night?'

'All forgotten. I was being silly. You've moved in. You're mine.'

Jamie leaned forward and spoke with what could be taken as a slight menace if you didn't know him well. I had seen this too often: he was being possessive and ridiculous.

'Are you sure?' I said.

'If we argue over every old boyfriend and girlfriend of yours, we'll be here all afternoon.'

'Andrei never was a boyfriend. You know that. He's useful to us. Anyway, you don't speak much of your old flames.'

'No one compares to you.'

'What? I bet they didn't get car sick though.' I said.

'True. No one's done that to me before.'

'I really am sorry. I'll pay for the valet, the suit cleaning, everything.'

'Just watch yourself with Andrei, that's all. He's the dangerous type. I'll sort out the rest.'

I thought about the text on my phone and knew better than to mention it. The waiter took the plates and asked about dessert. Jamie made it clear we wouldn't be having any. I could have done a blackberry and apple crumble with custard, but knew he was right. I couldn't risk feeling queasy on the way back.

'Can we go to the coffee shop, rather than have it here? I prefer their coffee. My treat, I insist,' I said.

'OK. No more work talk then. We'll review the house rules about the bathroom.' He grinned.

'Right. No problem. Let's get back to Sunday. Coffee, tidy bathroom and bed, that'll be me done,' I said.

'Perfect,' he replied.

22

I left before Jamie on Monday and caught the bus. I wanted to get to work before him and separately. I wasn't ready for any smart comments from Henry or anyone else. The Banbury Road was slow with commuter traffic as usual and I sat on the upper deck and worked through emails and Facebook on my phone.

Becky, Lou-two and some of the others had met up last night for drinks. It seems I had been the centre of their conversations, judging from a number of the comments. I fought back with little jokes about their sad, lonely lives with nothing better to talk about.

When I got to the stop for the office, I realised I ought to go back to my flat first to make sure it was alright, and to check that the workmen were actually making a start, so I stayed on and headed home.

I phoned for a taxi to pick me up from there in thirty minutes and take me to the meeting with Andrei, giving me long enough to check the place over. I stepped with care on the path to the front door, still wet from the morning dew, and put my key in the heavy wooden door that I shared with the Marsdens downstairs.

A small brown parcel and an envelope were lodged in my pigeonhole. There had been no post since I had left on

Saturday and they hadn't been there then. I picked up the parcel first. It was addressed to me, looking like it had come from some online retailer. I shook it a little, but there was no clue.

I looked at the envelope and there was handwriting on the front:

F A O Emma Hawkins

It was sealed. I went upstairs to my flat and walked through to the kitchen to turn on the kettle. There was no sign of any tradespeople yet, or a landlord.

I sat at the table and opened the envelope and took out a piece of paper folded over in two. It was a handwritten note in blue ink.

Miss Hawkins, If you value your good looks, stay away from the Brown story.

I turned it over, but that was it. A threatening letter – I had never received one before. At least it was complimentary. There was no indication of when it had been delivered. I made a cup of tea and sat to think about my next move. Jamie? Police? I didn't take the note seriously at all, a scare tactic to put me off the scent. Perhaps I was getting somewhere with my line of enquiry. I didn't even consider myself good-looking anyway. Nonsense. I looked at the parcel again and turned it over in my hand, deciding that it would be foolish to open it. I was getting paranoid; it wasn't even as though I'd written about using animals for testing. Surely it couldn't be Andrei again?

I phoned Inspector Morse on his mobile.

'Richards here.'

'I have a threatening letter. Connected to the Browns.' I didn't tell him about the parcel.

'Emma. Lovely to hear from you. I'll do everything I can to help.'

'Thank you, that would be most sweet. May I come and see you?'

'It doesn't sound like an immediate death sentence. Will after lunch do? I could see you at your office if that's OK? Two o'clock.'

He shut the call before I could. I put the letter into my bag and checked through the flat. The place was ready for the workmen but there was no sign of them yet. There was nothing else I really needed to take to Jamie's and nothing of any great value to worry about.

The taxi hooted outside and I left, double-locking and bolting the door. I sent a text to Mr Desai to encourage him along. I wanted my flat back as soon as possible.

**

I got to my coffee meeting early. Andrei had suggested the café in Marks and Spencer, or Marks's as Hazel called it. I had half an hour to spare so I browsed the clothes before going upstairs. Monday morning was quiet and I took my time to choose a couple of dresses and a pair of grey trousers that would be suitable for work, then made my way to the changing room.

'Early shopper, that's the way to do it. How many items have you got there my dear?'

The assistant was bright and helpful, though obviously bored. After I had tried them all, I selected one of the dresses and returned the rest to her.

'You'll look smart in that. For work is it?'

'Yes, I said. Thanks.'

'What do you do then?'

'Oh, well ... I'm a journalist. With the *Gazette*.'

Her face looked impressed. She stepped forward with an enthusiasm I had seen many times before. She wanted gossip. I wasn't going to oblige.

'The *Gazette*. Well, I see. And working on a big story, no doubt?'

'Something like that.'

She put the clothes that I had discarded back on the rack, but she took the dress I wanted from me. She wasn't going to give it up without more conversation. She had plenty of time, especially as another assistant had come to take over from her on the changing rooms.

'I'll take you over to the till myself,' she said, as she walked ahead of me clutching my dress. 'How about that woman gone missing? I've kept my eye out for her, not seen her though. She wears Marks, I can tell. That photo in the papers, that was one of our tops.'

'Do you think she would be able to come out and buy new clothes then? If she's been abducted?' I said, without trying to sound too dismissive.

She folded my dress carefully in some tissue paper, making sure she didn't introduce any creases into the skirt. It had a long-sleeved polo-necked top in a chestnut colour with a black skirt that swirled out when I turned. I liked the length, just above the knee. The skirt was quite full and the assistant took her time to ensure she put it in the bag properly before taking my card.

'I suppose not. You never know, though. Whoever's taken her might want her dressed up. She can't have taken any clothes with her, can she? She'll have to change her clothes at some stage.'

She had a point. What would Amanda Brown have worn? David Brown had said she was wearing a coat, but she would need to change into something. Even when she disappeared the second time, she hadn't taken any extra clothing, only valuables.

Two ladies were listening in to the conversation. They were browsing the rack behind the assistant, one whispering something to the other. I decided it was time to hurry this along.

She gave me my credit card and I slipped it back into my purse. I took out a business card and passed it to her.

'Well, if you do see her, or anything suspicious, do please give me a call. You never know, it might help to find her,' I said.

'Oh, yes, of course. Very important. I'll be sure to keep an eye out.'

She set the card down on the table in front of her and looked at it through her reading glasses. She picked it up and ran her finger over my name, then she placed it into the small pocket at the front of her uniform.

***

I took my shopping and headed to the escalator up to the restaurant to look for Andrei. He was not there yet so I ordered an Americano and took it to a quiet table in the corner.

Perhaps the assistant was right and someone had come in to buy some clothes; you never knew with these things. It was entirely possible, but I was sure they would be careful enough not to be caught, and anyway, she was abroad already.

The café was beginning to fill up. Shoppers, mostly women, and some with pre-school children or babies. I watched one young mum, no older than her mid-twenties, with a toddler and another baby in a buggy fast asleep. She balanced a tray as she made her way across to a table where the toddler was climbing up onto the seat. One day I'll get round to that, I thought. Would I still have enough energy?

Andrei arrived fifteen minutes late. He smiled his lop-sided smile and I stood to air kiss him on each cheek. He sat down opposite me and took off his leather jacket and hung it on the back of the spare chair. He looked like a World War Two pilot as he unravelled his scarf and laid it over the top.

'How is my beautiful girl?'

'I'm not your girl Andrei, Lou is. Have you been sending me gifts?'

He looked as bashful as he could.

'Ah, you found it. Maybe it was me, maybe not.'

'It's not funny. I haven't even opened it. I assume this is it?' I took the parcel out of my bag and put it on the table.

'Yes, go on - open it, it won't hurt. I can't send it back anyway. Please.'

'I'm guessing it'll be perfect. You seem to know what I like better than I do. And my size.'

'It is customary in my country to learn a lady's size very early in the courtship. And her likes and dislikes. Important, no?'

I laughed. Andrei could probably find a Romanian tradition to cover every eventuality. I pulled at the brown paper wrapping and ripped it off to expose a cardboard box inside.

'This has to stop, Andrei. I've told you before. There is no courtship. You are with Lou, she told me. I am with Jamie. I moved in over the weekend.'

'I know, I know. But he is an idiot, he has a pea-brain and he is not good for you, dangerous in fact. You need real man, a guardian angel.'

'I suppose that's you is it? A real man.'

'Of course.'

The box was Charlotte Tilbury, my favourite cosmetic company, makeup artist for the stars. It was their 'Filmstars on the Go Palette' range. There were two eye and lip colour compacts inside: 'Some Like It Hot' and 'The Spy who Loved Me'. Andrei's humour was growing on me, and I should have been totally unnerved by his intrusions into my personal life but I felt more confident now I was staying with Jamie.

'Well, much as I like them and you seem to know my tastes uncannily well, you have to stop. You know that. Jamie will get jealous, not to mention Lou-two. Did you send any threatening letters to go with this?'

'Of course not. Emmy, as if I could. Why would I threaten you?'

Andrei pulled his hurt face and looked down through the menu.

'When did you drop this off? And was there anything else in my postbox?' I asked.

'Last night, about eight o'clock. I was hoping you'd find it this morning before you went to work. I didn't see anything else. I'm hungry,' he said.

He stood and went to the counter to place his order, stooping slightly to chat to the waitress, then he glanced over at me and smiled.

'Do you want another coffee?' he mouthed and pointed at my cup.

I shook my head, then I reached in and retrieved my notebook and pen from my bag ready to talk business on his return. He walked back slowly, putting his wallet into his back pocket. I decided he looked tired, probably from late shifts at the café.

'You've been shopping already,' he said as he sat back down and spotted my M&S bag.

'I was early.'

'A little party number? Let me see.'

'A dress for work, that's all. None of your business really, is it? Now, come on Andrei, what have you dragged me here for?'

'To give you the excuse to shop, of course. We should meet here every Monday morning, I insist. You can put it on expenses.'

The waitress arrived with a large latte and two pieces of toast and jam for him. He buttered the toast from side to side in three goes, dividing the butter in half and saving the other half for the second piece. Then he spread the jam evenly, leaving a centimetre border around the edge. I watched him focus on his work, oblivious of anything around. He had a steady hand with long fingers that gripped the knife.

'What do you want, Andrei?'

'I have some information to share. You know, about the

missing lady.'

He bit off a mouthful of toast and chewed as he looked at me. I sat a little closer to the table and looked around. We were in a spy movie. Behind him, the woman with two children was feeding the baby while the older child munched on a biscuit. To our left was an old lady sipping a milky drink, still wearing her fur coat. Russian, perhaps? To our right was a businessman looking like he was waiting for an assignation to arrive. Affairs of the heart in an M&S café.

'You have some information. Very good,' I whispered, touching his hand as he put the toast down, 'You will share it with me now?'

'I will,' he said, taking another bite.

I sighed. This could take a while. I was getting hungry too.

'Come on Andrei. What information?'

'Well, it's not directly about her. I asked around like you said. At first nothing, and even now I don't know whether this is anything. I spoke to my father about it. He said that a friend of his, in the community, has gone missing. A man. A Romanian.'

'What do you mean, missing?'

'Well, my father says that he may have gone back to Romania suddenly, without a plan, overnight, two nights ago. No one is really sure, it is just that he is missing.'

'That does sound odd. Does that often happen?'

'Never. People do go back and forth to Romania of course, but it's always known about. You have to book flights and so forth. Also, friends and neighbours, or fellow Romanians from the community centre always want travellers to take or bring something, some family heirloom, some letters, that kind of thing. We never travel empty-handed.'

I wondered if Andrei ever returned. He had never talked of his life in Jilava before coming here. It was a subject he seemed to avoid. I made a few notes on my pad while I thought.

'Did he fly? Or go by car?' I asked.

'That's another thing. No one is sure but his car has gone as well. Of course, this might not be important, and he could be in this country somewhere, just hiding.'

Andrei looked sincere, like he really wanted to help me solve this. Two nights ago, that's the night she went through Dover, supposedly. Could it be a coincidence?

'You think it's connected to her?' I said.

'Perhaps. But that's all I know.'

'You have a name?'

'Sergei. Sergei Lupei. S-E-R-G-E-I. L-U-P-E-I,' he spelled out. 'He's an old friend of my father's but I have no idea why he would know your missing woman.'

'I'll make some enquiries.'

He finished his toast, then stood up and came round the table. He stooped down and took my head in his hands, then kissed me on the forehead.

'Don't worry, I'll look after you,' he said.

The businessman watched and the old lady tutted, then smiled at me. Before I could speak, he left.

23

Gemma called me at my desk.

'A policeman is here to see you, Emma.'

'Can you make him a coffee and put him in the interview room, please? I'll be down in ten minutes.'

It would do him good to wait. Especially in an interview room. Boot on the other foot. I pictured scenes of a detective movie with me watching him through some two-way mirror while he paced the room nervously. I scribbled some notes about the piece I was trying to finish. The Romanian Society was on Divinity Road and had been set up in 2008. Apparently there were two hundred members but I found it difficult to believe they were all local. No doubt Sergei Lupei must be a member, I would need to check somehow. I wrote a message for Henry asking him to do a search for me, then I raced to the toilet to freshen up my face and hair.

Brad was in plain clothes, a dark blue suit with white shirt and patterned blue tie. He was standing when I walked into the room, looking out of the window onto the Banbury Road. He turned and smiled, a warm look that completely transformed his face. His teeth were neatly aligned and very white, his hair was clipped short over his ears and neck. There was a faint smell of a familiar aftershave that I couldn't place. He reached out his hand and shook mine.

'Good to see you again, Emma. I have to say that your reporting has been very responsible ... so far.'

I wasn't sure if that was a threat, and discounted it.

'Thanks for coming, and please do sit down.'

I indicated to the chair in front of the desk. We called it the ejector seat, because that was the seat any potential candidates used in interviews, and it was also the seat used when HR had meetings to kick people out of the organisation. I took the large leather executive chair behind the desk.

I put the envelope on the table between us. He glanced at it without touching it, then looked back at me.

'Before we get to that, may I ask you about your retired Chief Constable, Bob Riley. I have a source that connects him to David Brown. Is that plausible?' I asked.

He hesitated before answering, as if considering what to share. I wasn't going to show him the photo until I had some idea whether Jamie was or was not involved with David.

'I am wary of answering. It's possible, yes. I had very little to do with him, but he was a powerful man, by all reports. Still is probably, even though retired. He had strong political views.'

'What sort? Left or right?'

'He was borderline fascist. After he retired, it emerged he supported a number of activities involved in attempting to get Britain back to some kind of Victorian set of values involving flogging and hanging. That information never reached the press, or even your average copper, by the way. Does that give you clue enough?'

The air conditioning in the interview room was like Jamie's office - cold. I shivered as I listened to him. Perhaps I should be more concerned about the threat from the letter.

Gemma knocked and came in without waiting, bringing him a cup of coffee. She flirted mercilessly, reeking of her Vera Wang perfume that she always wore to the pub, and making sure she hovered around his side of the desk as long as she could.

'Anything else I can get you, sir?' she asked.

He looked up at her and smiled patiently but shook his head.

'Emma here has it covered, thanks,' he said.

Gemma retreated, scowling at me. When she had closed the door, we looked at the letter.

'I take it you haven't shown this to anyone?' he said.

'No one.'

'So there'll be your fingerprints and that's it. I doubt we'll get anything from it, but I suppose we had better try. You can meet some pretty dumb felons out there.'

He opened his bag, a kind of hessian messenger bag that he was holding on his knee, and took out a plastic bag containing surgical gloves. Once he had put them on, he lifted up the letter and took out the note.

'And you've no idea who this is from?'

'Nope. I'd tell you if I did. Or I'd tackle them myself. It's a bit of nonsense. I don't take it seriously. It must have arrived last night at some point.'

He looked it over very closely on both sides before he spoke again.

'It is written by a woman. I'm sure of it. I will have the writing analysed by one of our guys to confirm, but I've seen a few of these over the years and I'm 90 per cent sure.'

I stood up and went round to his side and looked over his shoulder, bending slightly to get a closer look. I could feel the heat from his body. I had not really taken notice before, but the writing was classically spidery and feminine. It was hardly the work of Hercule Poirot to identify a woman's hand.

'Well, Emma, you must call me directly if you receive any more threats, or if you are worried about anything. You already have my mobile number.'

On the way out, I showed him directly to the front door of the building so that he didn't have to see Gemma.

'I'll sign you out, don't worry,' I laughed.

***

When he had gone, I returned to my desk to find a note to call Abigail Cadman, so I rang back immediately. She was a woman of few words and got straight to the point.

'It's not a demotion, Emma, simply an opportunity for you to step back a little and regroup. And for the paper to take some time to recover from all the recent incidents following your articles. Perhaps it's not in the public interest to pursue all this social justice for migrants.'

So it was a demotion ... of sorts. Had that been inevitable after the Mayor's comment at the weekend? On society weddings, an essential aspect of the newspaper's journalism as Ms Cadman was at pains to explain. See Henry for a briefing. No doubt Jamie was in the know about this. I bit my lip and took it gracefully, thinking that I would carry on with my research and investigations anyway. They couldn't stop me doing that. I sent a message to Henry about meeting the next morning, then took the rest of the afternoon off; career under review, life under threat, nowhere to live, and it was only Monday.

***

I was pleased to see Jamie leave before me again on Tuesday morning. I told him I was going to visit Henry at home and would be in the office later. It gave me chance to luxuriate in a hot bath and take time to consider my situation.

I reflected on the puzzle that was Amanda, a glamorous mid-forties newsagent and former dancer. Was she kidnapped or had she run off with this Sergei? I needed to find out more about him. And what of David Brown and the photograph and his connection with Jamie? That had to be tackled at some point.

After wrapping myself in one of Jamie's freshly laundered soft white bath towels, I wandered into his bedroom. We had shared his bed since I moved in, although I insisted on putting my clothes and other belongings into the guest room, to keep up appearances of being a temporary visitor, even if only for my own benefit and any possible conversations with Hazel.

I stood in front of his mirror with the hairdryer, brushing through the Crème Fine hair oil and pinning my hair back behind my ears, preparing for the day ahead. Reflected in the mirror I could see his wardrobe door had been left open, shirts hanging neatly in a row like proud soldiers on parade. I finished my brushing and couldn't resist the opportunity to explore more of the habits of Jamie Wilson.

I walked around the bed and opened both doors of the

wardrobe wide so I could see the entire contents. Jackets, shirts, trousers and shoes. Nothing interesting. No tatty old cardboard boxes full of snaps of girlfriends or love letters, no old stash of secret old porn DVDs, no guilty hobbies like stamp collecting. Just clothing neatly filed, his life a plain and open book. I ran my fingers over the shirts, pulling them out to see the colours and patterns. Mostly white, some striped: Hugo Boss, Hilfiger, Paul Smith, they were all there.

The one at the end caught my eye particularly because it was older than the others and had a brand label in a foreign language I had not seen before. I pulled it out fully and held it against myself. It was white with a single breast pocket on one side, and a small emblem on the other. HBFC. Of course, it was the same motif as the posters and in the photograph. This was a definite clue, but what could it mean?

My phone beeped a message from Andrei inviting me to meet someone from the Romanian community the next day. I would have to tell him I had been sidelined, if that's what I had been, although I couldn't let my work go to waste. I thought about the advert that Hazel had thrust into my hand, but decided I needed to finish what I had started on the Amanda Brown case before I got any itchy feet.

After sorting out some washing and dressing casually in jeans, given I had no intention of going to the office, I set off for my flat on the bus. Mr Desai had kindly offered me some choice of fittings and I wondered whether this was a prelude to a rent hike, but I took it at face value and when I got there I met with the plumber to review a dozen different styles of tile and a catalogue of bathroom furniture. I never realised there could be so many different styles of toilets and sink taps, and it took us most of the morning to finalise the plans. I could get excited about moving back in, but I wasn't sure what Jamie might think about that.

***

Henry lived in a three-bedroom semi on a tidy street bordering the edge of Jericho. I stood in front of the olive green door and rang the bell. A dog barked welcome. I didn't like dogs in the slightest – in fact, I had feared them since the age of eight when one bit me on the leg as I stood outside the school gate talking to Becky, leaving a small scar to ruin my left calf ever since. I heard Henry's voice call the dog back, followed by the scratching of feet on the floor then a door being shut.

'Sorry about that,' he said as he opened the door, 'She's harmless enough but I've put her in the study.'

'Thank you, you know me well,' I said.

He shook my hand and mumbled a welcome, then stood back and pointed to a door off to the side. The hallway had polished wood flooring with pale cream walls. A painting of Venice hung to one side.

'Come through to the lounge, I'll make some coffee. I know how you take it,' he said.

I perched on a large black leather couch and unbuttoned my coat, while he disappeared into the kitchen. The lounge was not huge, but was neat and tidy and tastefully decorated in a pastel yellow colour throughout. The logs for the fire were neatly stacked. Photos of the family stood on the small mantelpiece next to two silver candlesticks. Henry and his wife and two boys, both under ten, stood in various poses, all looking happy.

'Here you are then. Now, let's make a start,' he said as he put the mug on a coaster that depicted a scene in the Canadian Rockies on the small table beside me.

'It's so much easier here than in the office. You have a lovely house and family, Henry. You are very lucky,' I said.

'Oh, thanks. I don't know though. We're all a bit suburban. Boys at school, my wife out shopping at Waitrose. You're the one with the glamorous lifestyle, Emma.'

I laughed. 'I'm not a film star.'

'You date like one ... Sorry, didn't mean it to sound quite like that, I mean in a good way. You're young, fun and bubbly, and you have those bright dark eyes. Enjoy yourself, that's what I say. Live the life. I wish I had my pick of women like you have your pick of men.'

He passed me a plate of biscuits which I declined and instead pulled out my notebook from my bag.

'Well I didn't come to talk about my love life. Let's get started on some work,' I said.

'So you've been taken off immigration, then. It's my society weddings patch for you. Happy to hand that over, for sure,' he said.

'Well not quite. Abigail Cadman called me and asked for my thoughts on how the paper should position itself through the current crisis on the streets. I said the word crisis was a bit strong as there had only been a few hotheads, that was all. She sort of steered me into a cul-de-sac.' I tried to put a positive spin on it.

'Jamie will take the story up. He'll put his spin on it, some kind of xenophobic rant,' he said.

'Henry. Don't. That's not fair. You don't see his good side. He balances me well. I can be a bit self-righteous on the social justice stuff, he tempers that.'

'Temper is the right word. Anyway, we're here for you to pick up weddings. I'll go through all the ones we know of in the next three months.'

We spent an hour reviewing the various members of the aristocracy and the well-to-do who had their nuptials planned. Henry had been thorough and orderly in his research. I knew it would drive me crazy to maintain such a system, but I admired his patience.

His younger son arrived at lunchtime, back from reception class and dropped off by the neighbour. He was a sweet mini version of Henry and ran in with his pencil drawing of a dinosaur, and a blood-stained plaster on his knee. It reminded me why I couldn't deal with children, as even that made me feel queasy.

'Wants to be a paperboy when he grows up,' Henry said as he ushered him back out the kitchen to feed him a tuna wrap. I followed them in and stood and watched Henry undertake his fatherly duties, while trying to maintain an adult conversation at the same time.

'You're still looking for that newsagent woman, I presume. They haven't taken you off that as well?' he said.

'It's more of a private project. I'm determined to track down the truth. If I could find her and interview her, it would be a real scoop. Get me back on track.'

'I'll do all I can, but you need someone with inside knowledge. Someone out there will know something. That waiter friend of yours?'

'Andrei. He's very helpful. Actually, he's arranged for me to meet someone tomorrow. There's also a policeman who is showing interest.'

'In you or the missing woman?' He laughed, then passed me a tuna sandwich. 'You may as well have some lunch with young Toby here,' he said.

24

Cristina Iliescu was striking, the sort of woman no one could pass in the street without turning to look. She had dyed-blonde hair that cascaded over her shoulders in flowing waves, big dark brown eyes and a fresh, clean face perfectly made up with just the right amount of blusher and lipstick. Her slender frame and stylish coat portrayed a youthful image although she was at least in her mid-forties. She walked towards me as if she floated on the breeze. I was in awe.

Andrei had insisted that we meet her at the Romanian Society because she had some important information.

'Are you sure? You've come up with information before that got us nowhere. This is an excuse to see me again, isn't it?' I said when I phoned him to confirm the text message.

'This time, different, Emmy. Please. I'm happy with Louise.'

At the end of the Cowley Road, a community hall had been built in Victorian days for the villagers to come together and keep warm. Nowadays it was probably the coldest building on the street, especially at ten o'clock on a chilly April morning. This was where the Romanian Society met every month, a social club to help newcomers integrate into the locality.

When I got there, the weathered, peeling, blue door was locked. I could just see through the pane of patterned glass that someone was inside so I hammered on the door and waited.

Andrei welcomed me with a polite nod then I walked across the shiny wooden floor with him towards this vision of beauty, as she came towards us. There was a marked smell of air freshener as if the cleaners had been in that very morning. We met in the middle of the room, which echoed with emptiness. Piles of chairs sat at one end of the room and at the other was a small stage built of wooden pallets. There were electric heaters on the walls, not turned on, and the place was dark and shadowy.

I put out my hand in response to her delicate offer of a handshake.

'Good day, I am Cristina, you must be Emma. Andrei has told me about you.'

'Hello. Shall we find somewhere to sit?' I said.

Andrei took three chairs and set them out so we could sit in the corner of the room and chat. I kept my coat on, as did the others.

'Excuse the location. It is important we talk somewhere private,' Andrei said.

I took out my notebook and the photograph of the Browns at the Chamber of Commerce ball that had been used in all the papers.

'Just to be sure, Cristina, is this the person we are talking about today?' I said, pointing at the photo.

'Yes, that's Amanda. She looks so wonderful, dressed in her finest ballgown. And that stunning sapphire necklace, such a beautiful gift. That's her,' she said.

'So, tell me Cristina. What is so important?'

As she spoke, she came alive. Her arms and hands embellished her story, expressing the seriousness and sincerity of what she had to say. Her eyes widened at times, and closed in some distant, personal memory at other times.

'I worked with Amanda. In London. We met in the Nineties, both dancers.'

'Do you still dance?' I asked.

'Sometimes, for special occasions. Not often these days. The bones harden, the neck stiffens you know.'

If this woman was trying to say she was too old to dance, then I was positively a ruin already. She looked so lithe and spirited, her long legs crossed elegantly, her posture upright presenting a graceful confidence.

'Amanda and I, we danced together sometimes. You know, if the client requested it, and the money was right. We also competed of course, most girls did at the club. Only so many customers to share around. Amanda was the best.'

I wasn't sure how to ask the obvious question.

'And yes, of course, we occasionally got attached to certain men, certain regulars you might say. But it was always very classy, a very upmarket dance club.'

Andrei looked across at me as if he expected me to be shocked.

'It's OK Andrei, I'm a journalist, I do know about these things,' I said.

He smiled and turned towards Cristina. I think he was overcome by her. Just sitting next to her was making him blush, incapable of speech.

'I am here to help find Amanda. She is very special to me,' she said.

She explained that Amanda had not turned up on Monday to their regular get-together in London, something that David Brown knew nothing about. Every last Monday of the month, Amanda would travel down and they would spend the day together, shopping or eating and drinking together, sometimes taking in a show or visiting old haunts.

'I had no way of contacting her without alerting her husband, so I came here personally to find out whether she was ill. I didn't know any more until I met up with Andrei's father.'

I made notes as she spoke and tried to picture her twenty years younger. She must have been a goddess, a sensation at any Soho dance club. This was the side to Amanda that we wanted to understand more about.

'Tell me about any contacts from your London days. Any men that might want to do her harm?' I said.

'Those days are long gone. Yes, we had enemies. Greedy men who wanted to exploit us. But Amanda was strong, and we stuck together. We had a minder, Mr Lobb. He managed a chain of clubs and dealt in drugs, prostitution, trafficking. You name it, he did it. But he was always very protective of us. I can't see that being relevant, it was over twenty years ago.'

She sighed and suddenly looked very vulnerable and lonely.

'How do you know Andrei?' I said.

Andrei's face reddened as if I was accusing him of frequenting prostitutes. Nothing could be further from my mind; he could be so sweet and innocent, I had wondered whether he was a virgin.

'Through his father. A lovely man. I am Romanian,

from Bucharest. I believe passionately in the Romanian community and helped to set up the society in London. I met Nicolae there when he visited once and we became friends. I helped him set up the society in Oxford about ten years ago.'

'We'll do all we can, Cristina. You have no idea where they may have taken her, then? Or perhaps she ran away?'

'No idea. I don't believe it can be Romanians. That's a vicious lie. She must be in danger. What would she be running from?'

'What about the police? You should talk to them and tell them what you know,' I said.

Her face hardened, her nostrils flared a little as she breathed out. Then she laughed.

'No police. There's only one thing worse than the British police, and that's the *Politia Romậnā*, they are evil. No way. Andrei says you are good, you can help. You tell them. I ... I will go back to London to look for her.'

She stood up, clipped her wrap around her and walked over to the door. The meeting was over.

25

The next morning at Hazel's I saw immediately that the plant pots had been moved over the other side of the hall, freshly primped and pruned to display the dark red blooms. Hazel was wearing her gardening apron and gloves when she opened the door. The hall was a clean pale yellow with white wood.

'They call it Farrow's Cream. Do you like it?' she said.

I made suitably positive remarks as we surveyed the freshly decorated hall and lounge, then we went into the kitchen for some tea.

'I'll just finish the petunias in the border. Won't be a minute,' she said.

I watched her out the window and couldn't see that there was much to finish in her immaculately arranged back yard. I always thought she deserved a bigger plot but she said it was challenge enough. I couldn't have asked for a better childhood with her and Uncle Jack. Leafy Oxford. She never clung, and was always there when needed.

When she returned, we sat in the dining room overlooking the small patio area with the barbecue neatly covered and parked in the corner.

'What's up?' she said.

Where to start, I thought. Love, life, work, missing person.

'Nothing really, bit fed up, that's all.'

We munched a chocolate digestive each. I could have been dunking it in warm milk wrapped in a blanket; we had always done this. When I split from Ben, we'd had a whole packet. 'Nature's remedy,' she would say. I told her all about the problems with the immigration stories and how the paper was watering down its position, how the editor-in-chief and Jamie were set to take the series in a completely different direction. I didn't want my name associated with that.

'You're a professional journalist, you're bound to have setbacks,' she said.

'And I haven't found Amanda, so that story is dying. Looks like she's gone abroad, probably willingly, and I'm not sure who is bothered except her husband and best friend.'

She patted me on the arm, then poured another cup.

'This isn't world's end, is it? There's plenty of stories to pursue. What are you moving on to now?'

I told her about the weddings, Henry and his sweet kids.

'So that's it. Well you know the answer to that one too, you need some tough love. Stop flitting from man to man and having fun - you need to choose and settle. Man first, baby second.'

I laughed. 'You make it sound easy.'

'Well Becky's making progress, so can you. It's time.'

I told her about Jamie, the issues with the flat, and we passed by Andrei onto Brad.

'No, avoid policemen. Imagine your father's reaction to that one. No, stick with Andrei.'

'He's dating Lou-two.'

It was her turn to laugh and we cracked another biscuit. She insisted he was the right man for me in the long term.

'He'll help you with that Amanda woman too. He's got his head screwed on, that one.'

We talked long into the morning and I told her all about the ransom, the photograph, the Romanian connection, the dancing club, everything. Everything in my life from the last two weeks, except the drinking and ruination of a perfectly clean Mercedes.

'You should keep going on it. Go to London, dig around a bit. You could go with Becky if you don't want to take Andrei, but don't go on your own. Have a day out.'

It made sense. It was time to leave her to the garden. We walked out to the hall and she gave me a big hug and kiss on the cheek, like I was about to leave for school.

'When you're there, pop in the *Guardian* offices. Follow up on that advert I gave you. London's not so far.'

We both welled up at the same time as we looked at each other, then I turned and walked down the front path quickly without looking back. I sat on the bench at the bus stop, where the sign said the next one would be 9 minutes. I was full of ideas, ready to fight.

David's name flashed on my screen when the phone rang.

'Hello David, I haven't heard from you in a while. I've been a bit preoccupied, and I don't have any news for you,' I said.

'I do. She can't be abroad, they must have it wrong,' he said.

'Have you heard from her?'

'No, but she's used her Makro card, at the wholesaler. I had all her cards cancelled but forgot that one. She used it a couple of days ago.'

'Could it be someone else?'

'I got a statement this morning. I think it's her, she bought the same coffee she always buys, and other stuff.'

It did sound promising. Perhaps Brad and the police were mistaken.

**

The electronic indicator for the next bus changed to 15 minutes' delay. So much for technology. I decided to walk a few stops, to get a chance to clear my head and piece together some ideas. I continued along London Road towards the city centre, passing the art deco Holyoake Hall, an important part of the history of the Co-operative movement. The noise level from passing cars increased as the rain came harder. Puddles formed on the pavement and the gutters started to fill. I put up my umbrella and tried to dodge through the crowd as best I could.

The door of a small independent coffee shop was open as I passed, allowing the smell of fresh doughnuts and coffee beans to attract people away from the inclement weather. I decided on a takeaway drink; I didn't have time to sit and wait for the rain to stop. As I stood in the queue, my phone rang. It showed I had missed two recent calls. The noise of the town must have drowned them out.

It wasn't a number I knew, so I switched the phone to silent, then changed my mind and ordered a coffee to stay. Once I had settled into the chair beside the deli counter, a little away from all the other tables, I called the number back.

'Hello, how can I help?'

I didn't recognize her voice.

'Is that Miss Hawkins? This is the sales assistant at M&S, I met you briefly the other day when I served you and you gave me your card.'

Of course I remembered. The meeting with Andrei, and I'd been early.

'What can I do for you? Is it about the missing woman?' I said.

I kept my voice as low as I could. I was in more of a shop than a café, selling cold meats and cheeses, mostly locally produced and also from Italy and Spain. There was a strong smell of garlic at one end, and the sugary smell of pastries near the counter. The most popular lines seemed to be the home-made sandwiches and panini.

It was clear that my caller also needed to speak quietly. She seemed to whisper into her phone as she replied.

'The thing is, I think I may have seen her. Well, it may have been. You said to look out for her and I had a picture from the paper. The woman purchased two dresses. She looked nervous, like she didn't want to be seen. She paid cash.'

'Thank you. That's really helpful. When was this?'

'Yesterday afternoon.'

Based on David's call about Makro, perhaps it could be true. I should contact the store for CCTV, but that would probably involve Brad. Perhaps I could ask Andrei to investigate that as well but I wasn't sure it was worth it. I thanked her again and asked her to keep in contact with any more details. At least I had a fan in retail now, someone to help with research.

**

When I arrived at the office, Gemma handed me an envelope. At my desk, I pulled on my thin brown gloves, then I opened my top drawer and took out a pair of scissors, carefully cutting along the envelope's edge. It was bigger this time, the size requiring a large letter stamp, but it hadn't been through the Royal Mail, as there was no postmark. Inside was a small handwritten note and a photograph.

'Hello Inspector, I've received something I think you should see straightaway.' I said. I called him on his mobile and didn't wait for any niceties.

'Hello Emma. It's Brad to you.' He sounded irritated.

'Sorry, I'm a bit stressed. I have just received an envelope at work. It was dropped into the post tray on reception. We don't know who put it there.'

'Could you bring it along? I'm not really planning to be in your area and right now I'm in the middle of something,' he said.

Gemma ordered me a cab and I went immediately. The note said <Lovely Emma. Back Off ... or else> but it was the photo that was mysterious. Something about it made me really uneasy.

'I'm here to see Inspector Richards. He is expecting me,' I said to the receptionist.

I took a seat over to one side where visitors waited. A man sat in the corner, gnawing on his nails and reading a handful of papers. Beside him, a woman, presumably his partner, chattered into his ear incessantly.

'Just tell them what happened. All of it, don't keep anything back. Forget about Bill, that's his problem. Look after number one, and don't forget about me. It's no good to me if you stick up for Bill. He's had it coming for a while now. Just tell them. Hear me.'

She hardly drew breath and he continued to look at the papers in front of him as if she might evaporate if ignored.

I sat and made a few notes in my phone. Perhaps the best scoops could be scored by sitting in the police station waiting room. Then I checked a few messages and Jamie wanted my current piece about the Smythe and Johnson marriage earlier than he had said originally. Becky wanted to go for drinks ... again. Henry wanted some of my time to review his article about an escaped snake.

'Emma.'

I looked up to see Brad, neat and tidy in a plain black suit and white shirt, blue tie. He looked good, again out of uniform. I stood and shook his hand then followed him back past reception to one of the rooms. He switched the sign to 'Engaged' on the front of the door, then closed it. We could see out through the glass, but no one could see in.

'Take a seat, Emma and let's have a look.'

I put the envelope on the table. It was plain brown with my name written on the front, in what I thought looked like the same handwriting as before. Brad opened it after putting on surgical gloves and took out the photo, then the note.

He studied the picture closely. It was me, standing at the door of the Romanian Society the day before. I had my hand raised, just about to knock on the door.

'And you don't know who took it?'

'No idea. It's in Cowley. I was on an assignment.'

'The same one. The missing woman, I suppose.'

The phone in the room rang, the receptionist offering tea. He accepted on my behalf and asked for one for himself. Very civilised, I thought.

'You've all moved on from *The Bill*,' I said, as he put down the receiver.

'A childhood favourite I suppose?'

'My auntie loved it. I think it reminded her of my dad.'

He slid the photo over to me and I looked down at it again.

'The thing I don't understand, it may be a small point, but that building is on a normal street of houses, nothing else around and I don't remember anyone else being there when I arrived.'

'It looks to be taken from across the street,' he said.

'Yes. But surely I would have noticed.'

'Perhaps from a smartphone? People walk down the street with them all the time.'

'Maybe. Is it possible to tell? The camera?'

He picked it up again and turned it over and over.

'It's been professionally printed on the right paper. I'll have the lab boys examine it. They may be able to say from the resolution. I'm still waiting for more on your first note. This looks like the same handwriting,' he said.

We were interrupted by the arrival of tea on a tray. 'There's milk and sugar there. Help yourselves,' she said.

'Thanks Emily,' Brad said as she retreated from the room.

I sat back and folded my arms, hugging myself while Brad poured. Two threats in a week was getting to me.

'Should I be worried now?' I said.

'Hmmm, yes, a little I think. I will fast-track what we can. Do you have CCTV in your reception?'

'On and off. I already asked. Got a 'maybe' answer from the security company. Gemma has no recollection of who left it there. It could have been lying in the pile for hours, even a full day.'

'I'll check if there's any street CCTV in that area. It would help to narrow down the time though. Perhaps, in the meantime, you should step back from it. Work on something else.'

I could see he didn't expect a yes to that. I thanked him for his efforts and got up to leave. Just before he opened the door, he complimented me on my change of hairstyle, then he cleared his throat. I didn't need complications right now. I jumped in first.

'I'll be sure to stay with my boyfriend for a while, rather than be on my own, I think.'

'Very wise. Just for the time being. Make sure he looks after you,' he said.

I left the building and decided to get the bus back, despite Gemma having insisted I should take a taxi for my own safety. A Number 22 bus door to door, what was the risk? I had to rise above any threats.

While I waited at the stop, I phoned Gary.

'Richards. Married? Can you confirm status?'

'Don't be tempted. Not your type. Thought you were with Jamie.'

'Just checking for a friend, that's all.'

He laughed.

'OK. A friend you say. I'll text you when I've put out some feelers for an update. It's time you settled down.'

I reflected on that as I looked out on the Banbury Road from the upper deck. An impromptu chat about men with Becky or Lou-two was in order.

26

As it happened, Lou-two called when I was sitting at my desk. She wanted to complain about work – that seemed the main purpose of our catch-up. She wasn't paid enough, another girl had got a promotion, she was bored organising meetings and the printer was old and troublesome, the company too mean to get a new one.

I listened patiently, sipping my coffee and casting my eye around the office occasionally to see what life there was in the newsroom. I yawned. I didn't mean to, but it slipped out.

'Sorry. I really didn't mean to go on so much. How are you doing?' she said.

'Oh, I'm fine. Busy as usual. Nothing to report.' I said, although she obviously knew that wasn't true.

'Nothing to report, ha! What about the famous Jamie? Relationships at work ... and with the boss. Nothing to report, indeed!'

'Well, yes, it's going OK,' I said.

I told her all about the devastation I had caused in Jamie's car on the first night of staying there.

'He was very patient, but I think I have crossed a line. I haven't been allowed to drink so much since,' I said.

Before she could express her irritation at my alcohol intake being monitored, my phone buzzed to indicate another caller.

'Sorry, I need to get this,' I said.

'Go ahead, perhaps it's Jamie checking whether you'd like an orange juice.'

I looked at my phone to see the number. It looked like a central London landline. While Lou-two waited on hold, I opened the call.

'Hello,' Cristina said.

I recognised her voice immediately.

'Hello, how are you?' I said.

'I am worried Emma. Very worried. No news. Have you heard more?'

'Nothing. Don't worry, we will find her.' I stood and walked over to the window to make sure the signal was strong.

'I have something I didn't tell you. A secret. She swore me, but now ... well I think I must tell. I trust you. Amanda was having an affair.'

'You can rely on me, Cristina. Complete confidence. Please go on,' I said.

The line went quiet for a few seconds and I almost thought the call had dropped, then she whispered that someone was coming and I should phone her back in an hour. Then the line went dead.

I went back to Lou-two and said I needed to go, and we could catch up later.

'It was Jamie checking up, then,' she said.

'No, just work. Something I need to follow up on, sorry. It's an important story.'

**

Forty minutes later I was sitting on the couch in my flat. It seemed the obvious place to go to be on my own and concentrate properly. The place was soulless, like I'd let the fire of it go out by moving a lot of my stuff to Jamie's. The pile of newspapers on the coffee table were from last week and covered in dust. The vase on the window-ledge was empty. The shower had been ripped out and boxes of white tiles were piled in the corner of the kitchen, but at least the electricity and water were still on and the toilet worked, although the smell of the drain was overwhelming until I shut the bathroom door firmly.

I kept my coat on and called Cristina. It rang six or seven times but there was no reply. I made myself a cup of black tea then sat back down. My phone had a full battery and full 4G signal. I called the number again, still no reply. I threw the phone down onto the couch in frustration then I opened my laptop to see if I could find out any more information about the number. The search engine threw up the White Lace Club in Mayfair, or so they claimed, although it looked like it bordered Soho according to the map. Perhaps Cristina had gone there to look for Amanda. I remembered Gary's list and pulled out the folded pieces of A5 paper that had been in my handbag ever since. The White Lace Club, that was one of the places Amanda may have worked.

It was now over an hour since I had spoken to Cristina. She mentioned an affair. Was that hard to believe? Perhaps not. Judging by the photographs Amanda was an attractive woman, and David Brown struck me as pretty boring and unadventurous. I tried the number again and let it ring a long time.

Eventually, someone picked up. A man's voice said 'Hello, who's that?'

'I'm calling to speak to Cristina, please?'

'Never heard of her. Wrong number. This is the White Lace Club. We're closed until nine tonight. Phone back then.'

'But, she ...' He had put the phone down on me.

***

I opened the bottle of Cloudy Bay that I'd been saving for a special day. I'd left it in the fridge on its own, sitting in the door waiting patiently to be drunk by a happy owner. I poured a glass and put the bottle back to keep it chilled. The week alone in a fridge had suited it well, and it tasted delicious.

I caught up with various social media and news feeds, then topped up my wine, and sat back to reflect. My phone sat silent on the couch next to me. No one called.

I had to find out more about the affair, that much was obvious. Who could he be? The mysterious Sergei perhaps. That was the only name I had if I was anywhere near on the right track. What else had Cristina said? I turned back the pages in my notebook to the meeting with her, where I had jotted down her comments, then I looked again at the photograph. Amanda Brown was stunning, but why a lover? David surely had no knowledge of it. And that necklace, Cristina said it was a gift. From him? I would need to ask David if he knew its history.

Perhaps I should talk it all through with Jamie. Or Andrei. Andrei should know. After all, he knew about Cristina, but he probably wouldn't know the White Lace Club - that was the clue. She must have some connection with that club. I needed to go there and there was only one person that could come with me.

27

We arrived in London at eight o'clock on Friday evening and walked the full length of Dean Street, including various side alleys, stopping for the occasional glass of wine in the most disreputable bars we could find. I insisted it was all part of the research, having filled Becky in on all that I knew about Amanda and Cristina. At ten o'clock, most places were just opening their doors. We stopped to look at the posters of half-naked strippers outside one place when the black Edwardian door with its huge brass knocker was unbolted from the inside. The door swung back and a diminutive olive-skinned guy with slicked-back black hair stepped out. He stuck an A4 piece of paper to the glass poster holder next to us, using some Blu-Tack he had brought with him. He eyed us watching him, then looked me up and down and his thin lips curled into a smile.

'Interested lady?'

I looked at the paper. *Dancers wanted, all shapes and sizes. Apply within, or call Timi on 0771 2134867.*

'Are you Timi?' Why I said that, I don't know. I should have walked away. Becky just stared at me.

'Yes, you come in. Audition. Very pretty. Your friend wait at bar. Free drink,' he said in a thick Greek or Turkish accent.

Becky spluttered and grasped my arm firmly. I wasn't

sure if she was protecting me or offended by the rejection. I was flattered in some crazy way.

'OK, to talk only. My friend stays with me at all times. Just to talk and see the place,' I said.

'OK, OK.' He pushed the door fully open and clipped it back to the wall, then he turned on the flashing neon sign over it. 'Brassers' flashed in red. It seemed too obvious, but that summed up the whole street. I dragged Becky by the hand and we descended steep narrow stairs to a small room below where there was a table and money-box with a reel of tickets beside it. Timi pushed his way through a curtained entrance on the far wall and waved for us to follow him through. This was a much bigger room, low-ceilinged and lit around the edge with subdued blue and red lighting. A small bar was off to one side and in the centre of the room were two poles for dancing, surrounded by tables and chairs. The place stank of stale alcohol and disinfectant and it was empty except for a tall hairy man behind the bar who was stacking bottles into the shelves.

'I turn music on. Here, come. You dance,' he said.

'No, no, wait. We will sit at bar and talk first.'

'OK. OK. What you want to know? Pay is good. Better than others around.'

Becky and I sat on bar stools while he walked around to the back and took out two shot glasses for us. I was thankful we had decided on jeans. Becky had suggested we dress in party-wear but I wanted to keep a low profile.

'Have you been in business long?'

'Yes, long time. All above board. No sex here, only dance. Very popular. Pretty girls like you.' He took a bottle of clear liquid that was probably vodka and poured us each a drink, then slid the glasses over to us.

'You pretty too,' he said, turning to Becky.

'Oh, thank you.' She laughed and downed the drink in one so I did the same.

He went to pour another but I put my hand out and stopped him.

'We are not dancers. We are journalists. Looking for information,' I said.

'OK. OK. I guessed. Too old really.'

Our balloons lay burst open on the floor beneath our feet.

'Looks like the fall-back career is shot to pieces,' Becky said.

The guy stacking the bottles looked over and grinned, flashing a gap where one of his front teeth was missing. He looked us both over carefully, then muttered something to Timi that I couldn't hear.

'OK, OK. Maybe. Some punters might like,' Timi said, then turned to us. 'You dance together?'

I looked at Becky and could see the school trip to Austria flash before her eyes, the bar in Salzburg where we'd got horribly drunk, danced in front of a crowd of locals and fumbled a kiss with each other. After that, we were sick all the next day and the teachers banned us from leaving the hotel.

'No we don't. I just want to ask some questions about the business and the dancers,' I said.

'OK, OK. Only until first customer comes. Then dancer has to dance. You stay, watch. Maybe change your mind.'

'Were you here twenty years ago?'

'Just. Started in `99. Small room. Grown since.' He

waved his arm around the room as if he had won entrepreneur of the decade.

'Has business changed?'

'No. Pretty girls, rich men. Dancing, stripping. Simple.'

The bar-stocker left us and went through to the back. Timi poured himself a beer and seemed to enjoy the reminiscence of his twenty years. It was entirely possible that Amanda Brown had worked here, but it was also very likely she hadn't. There were dozens of clubs all offering the same and there would be no records of employment or anything that could tie her to anywhere. It wasn't even as if Timi was some kind of threatening gangster; in fact he seemed very sweet.

'Do you know the White Lace Club?' I asked.

'Yes, yes, of course. Very famous. Very respectable.'

'Could a dancer from here work there as well?'

He looked us both up and down again slowly. I couldn't help but breathe in. 'Not us,' I said.

'Only supermodels there. High class. High cheeks.'

I pulled out the photograph of Amanda Brown to show him.

'How about this woman? A few years ago of course. Do you recognise her?'

He looked at her closely.

'No. But she is classy, attractive face. Maybe one day there. Never here,' he said.

A bell sounded and Timi walked out to the front room. I could see two men silhouetted through the dirty black curtain, and could hear some kind of deal being done. The music started, deafening to the ear and killing any further conversation. The barman reappeared and poured us both another vodka without asking. I indicated to Becky that we ought to go, and just then a girl dressed in a floor-length green velvet dress appeared from the back. She walked slowly in her platform heels to the pole, held onto it with her left hand and started to sway back and forth in time to the music. We both watched spellbound. She was slim with short blonde hair and a young face, probably no more than twenty. She could dance, her hips gyrating slowly and seductively.

The customers appeared through the curtain and sat at a table next to her. The barman took over two glasses of champagne and two shot glasses of vodka. One of the guys turned and indicated to Becky and me to join them, as if we were part of the deal they had struck with Timi.

I looked at Becky, downed my vodka and reached for my purse in my bag. I put a twenty pound note on the bar before the barman could return from delivering his drinks. Meanwhile the girl had grabbed the pole and swung her legs around it, revealing a long slit in the back of the dress that went all the way to the top of her legs. While they were distracted, Becky and I hotfooted it to the stairs and out into the fresh, cool breeze of the street above.

'Don't do that to me again,' she laughed.

'Well, at least we have some idea of what Amanda Brown got up to in London.'

'That's only the half of it.'

We stopped at a noodle bar for some food, and looked at the magazine we had brought with us, a guide to the sleazier night spots. It looked like the more upmarket night spots were further down in Mayfair so, once we had finished, we walked that way.

We arrived in Jermyn Street, part of an area home to some of the most expensive shops in the land. Fortunately it was gone ten o'clock by this time and they were all closed. The pubs and clubs were alive with people, spilling out onto the street tables as the evening was cool but dry.

'This outing is another of your crazy ideas. What exactly are we looking for? I think you've done enough research for one night,' she said.

'I'm not exactly sure. The atmosphere has helped us prepare. Let's go to the White Lace. It should be open by now.'

We walked arm in arm along the street. There were too many people on the pavement, so we stayed mainly on the road where there was only the occasional passing taxi to avoid. Music spilled out of the doors and windows of The Cash Bar. A live country band was performing somewhere at the back and I could hear the singer calling for everyone to join in the chorus.

We were hit with the aromas of Chinese sauces merged with sizzling steaks, and saw queues of tourists in line for a hundred different flavours of ice-cream, even at this late hour. Flashing neon lights from every store and outlet competed to grab our attention.

When we turned the corner into York Street, I saw what I'd been looking for. On our right, next door to the first edition bookshop, there were a few stone steps leading up to an arched entrance to a nightclub. Above the open door, a black and gold sign, a little like a pub sign, hung, declaring it to be London's most prestigious and select club for gentlemen. The White Lace Club.

'This is it, we're in the right district now. Cristina could be here,' I said.

I walked up the steps without hesitation. Becky followed. We entered a small, dimly lit, modern hallway tastefully decorated in white and pastel pink. I could hear the throbbing of dance music coming from inside, both upstairs and downstairs. A bulky man in a dress suit and black bow tie met us before we could step any further. He was clean-shaven and smelled of fresh citrus aftershave. He had a shock of black, neatly trimmed, fine hair and a small scar from the hairline down to his left eyebrow, breaking the lines of his forehead neatly into two. There was no way anyone would get past him without his permission.

'Can I help you, ladies?' he said.

'How much is it to go in?' I asked.

He coughed politely and pointed to a small sign on the wall. *This is a gentleman's club. Please behave as such. Ladies to be accompanied at all times.*

I must have looked puzzled.

'We would welcome you if you had some gentlemen friends with you. Even one between you would be fine,' he said.

Becky laughed. 'We were hoping to find one inside,' she said.

'Exactly. That's why we discourage it. We're an entertainment club, not a place to meet in the way you describe. Strictly no professionals other than those we have to offer from our own staff,' he said.

I didn't bother explaining that we were not professionals in the sense he described. After all this effort, this was a frustrating outcome. Perhaps I should have brought Jamie or even Andrei. I needed to get in here to find Cristina, or get some idea of where she could be. Her phone call proved she had been here on Tuesday. The man stood large and wide in the entrance and we removed ourselves elegantly, tottering down the stairs in our heels. Becky gave him a little wave as we turned away.

Just as we were standing by the railings, discussing whether to go back and ask him outright where she was, there was a loud shout and a buzz of commotion from inside the club. Two men appeared at the top of the steps, swaying and holding onto each other's shoulders. Behind them was another member of the club's security team. He was as solid as a prop-forward with a shaved head, wearing a dark grey suit and dark glasses, even though it was night-time. I recognised him immediately, even though the photo was from 2004. It was the fourth man.

One of the customers gripped onto the handrail beside the steps and leaned over it, as if about to vomit. The bouncer kicked him hard in the rear so that he tumbled down onto the pavement instead. The other customer staggered down and tried to pick him up.

'Come on Dimitri,' he said, but Dimitri looked out for the count.

'Bugger off. We don't want your sort here. Go back to your own country,' the bouncer shouted, then threw their two overcoats after them.

Becky ran forward to help the man lift his friend from the ground. There was a small amount of blood oozing from a cut on his cheek where it had hit the pavement stone. I reached for my phone and took a picture. Then I turned it towards the bouncer, just catching the smile on his face before he turned his back and went inside.

I hailed a cab that was crawling by and Becky and I bundled the two men into it, telling them they should get him checked out at the hospital. They were foreign and didn't understand our English, and tried to get us to board the taxi with them. Eventually, we shut the door and walked away.

'Time for bed,' Becky said.

'Drink, we need a drink first.'

I put my arm round her and steered her towards the pub opposite.

'After one, then we'll go home, and come back with some men tomorrow.'

She groaned and held her head.

28

The next morning, I had a call from Brad Richards. He sounded formal but eager. Fortunately I'd had a text message from Gary while I was in London with some very useful information: DI Richards had split from his wife a couple of months ago, soon after she'd done the dirty on him with someone from her work. He was living at home but looking to move on. I hadn't had time to think that through. Was this an opportunity or a threat? He was an attractive, powerful policeman in good shape who seemed to like me. Up until now, I had assumed he was married and any flirtation was harmless fun. Shouldn't I be saving all my thoughts for Jamie?

'I have some information for you. Can you come here, or would you prefer to meet in town?' he said.

We agreed on noon at the police station. I was no further forward in finding Amanda, who was presumably hiding out somewhere in the vicinity of Marks and Spencer or Makro. And no further forward on Cristina either, though we needed to get into that club.

'Working the weekend, Miss Hawkins?' The receptionist smiled as she passed me the pen to sign in.

'Ongoing enquiries,' I said.

'I'll take you to his office.'

She led me to the lift, waving her security pass over the

card reader on the way. The office was on the fourth floor, with a small slide-in sign saying 'DI Richards' on the door. She tapped on it tentatively and opened it without waiting.

'Miss Hawkins for you, sir,' she said.

'Thanks Emily.'

She hovered a moment then pulled the door closed behind her and I could hear her heels clicking back down the corridor.

'Come and have a seat, Emma. Good to see you again. Sorry about the circumstances - we should meet under better ones sometime,' he said as he shook my hand.

'Thanks.'

I sat on the comfortable armchair where he indicated and he sat in a similar chair opposite me with a small oak coffee table in between us. His desk was on the other side of the room, laden with papers and old coffee cups.

'You have some information?' I said.

'Yes. Our boys have been busy.'

I took out a notebook but he frowned.

'I think this is better off the record, until you decide what you want to do next,' he said.

'Do you know who sent the notes?'

'Not quite. We know that the paper used was from Rymans. Not very helpful I suppose. The pen also. The ink analysis showed it to be a Ryman's own brand.'

'Narrows it down to the half of Oxford that buys stationery then.' I smiled.

'We don't know it was the Oxford Rymans, so it's worse than you think. But, yes, we might assume he or she is a Ryman's shopper. The handwriting expert has suggested it is a female writer, probably middle-aged, not old, not young.'

'This is not exactly incisive. You and I had got this far ourselves.' I said.

I put the notebook back in my handbag and sat and stared at him impassively. He moved at a snail's pace compared to the world of journalism and I could not see him standing his ground well in my work environment. By this point in the conversation, Jamie would be apoplectic.

'We have to consider all the possibilities, Emma. It all takes time. The letter is clearly written by someone with a good command of English, so does that make it unlikely to be a person from the Romanian community? We're not sure.'

'Do you have any theories? Anything based on the words used or the style? Something I can investigate?'

'Well, one, yes. It depends whether Amanda Brown is in the country. We thought we had evidence she was abroad but I'm not so sure. It wasn't an actual sighting. I do wonder whether it may be her?'

'Amanda?'

'Yes, why not? She's well educated, English speaking, middle-aged and female.'

'Well, I'd also heard she may still be around but it's a bit of a stretch, isn't it? Why would she?'

'No idea. Perhaps she doesn't like your reporting.'

He smiled and I sat back a little on the chair and smoothed a crease on my trousers as I considered it. Clearly Brad didn't know the latest development from David Brown and I was not going to bring him up to speed on that one, or the call from M&S. But it did increase the likelihood of his suggestion. Perhaps she was warning me off, especially if she was having an affair, and was still in the country. It was gone one o'clock and my stomach rumbled an awareness that I hadn't eaten all morning, given my excesses of last night.

'There's one other thing about the note. It's a little tenuous, but the Browns stock a small range of stationery in their corner shop, and they get that from Ryman's. I checked and they do stock the type of paper and pen that were used.'

'Hmmm. What about the photo of me?'

'Taken with a Digital SLR of some sort, not a smartphone, based on the quality of the image. Printed at Boots, but we haven't found out where. It will be possible to track it down from their records, but frankly I'm not sure it's worth it. I assume you haven't received any more threats?'

'No. I haven't. I guess it could be her. It does make some sense.'

'We think the photo may have been taken from the house opposite the community centre, if that helps, though we've got nothing official to go on. There's something else,' he said.

Brad pulled out a grainy CCTV still from outside our office that showed a motorbike courier with a package. He said it fitted the time of the delivery and asked that I take the picture back to show the reception staff to see if they recognised it. I saw the striped blue, yellow and red helmet and knew immediately it was the same rider as the ransom pickup. My hands felt clammy as I pushed the photograph into my bag, muttering agreement. Brad didn't expect me to answer, he was preoccupied as he stood up.

'One last thing ...'

He walked to the window, then he looked at his watch,

as if his car park ticket was about to expire.

'... can I buy you lunch?' he said.

His smile was inviting, bordering flirtatious, but I politely declined. My conscience pulled me to Jamie. I wasn't sure what Gary or Hazel would say about that decision; pleased at my chasteness or disappointed at my choice of man. Perhaps I was settling down.

***

In the taxi on the way back to Jamie's, I called Mr Desai.

'It's going well. Another week,' he said.

'But it's been a week already. That will make two.'

'Yes, yes. Of course. Not long now,' he said before closing the call.

I sighed and sent a text message to Jamie to update him. Would he see it as good news? Why wasn't I happier with the situation? Would I ever be happy? My phone rang. I thought it was Mr Desai again but it was different number.

'Emma Hawkins,' I said.

'Miss Hawkins. This is Maria Reeves. I got your number from your receptionist at the paper. She said it would be alright to call you.'

'How can I help?'

'I live next door to Cristina Iliescu. I haven't seen her since Tuesday and this is most unusual. If she goes away, I look after her cat. She always asks.'

'I see. Well, I am looking for her as well. But why did you think to call me? Perhaps you should call the police?'

She laughed. Did no one go to the police these days?

'I have a key to her place. There was a note on the table with your name and the name of your paper. There was a smiley face by the writing so I decided you must be a good person. Can you help find her?'

'I am doing all I can Mrs Reeves. I will let you know if we do find her. Please call me if she turns up.'

29

Aunt Hazel stood still beside me, waiting for the crush to move by. Becky was jumping up and down, trying to see the end of the street. I had my arms around both of them in an Emma sandwich. We could have been drunk had it not been five-thirty in the morning. It was Becky's idea of course.

The High was bursting, mostly with students in black tie and party dresses. The girls looked forlorn, pitiful and bedraggled, shivering without coats. Some of them had trusty steeds who had lent their jackets, looking dishevelled themselves in wet-through white dress shirts and striped trousers.

May morning in the rain. Why bother? I couldn't get past that thought.

The noise on the street at this time of the morning was accentuated by the rain beating down on our umbrella, the large golf umbrella with YourBestCar.co.uk emblazoned across it, that Jamie had given me 'just in case'. Well, that case just happened: a huge thunderclap had heralded the start of the big downpour. We stood with our backs to the wall of Coutts bank and watched people scurrying for cover.

'I used to come here with your mother,' Hazel shouted.

'Was that before the war?' Becky shouted back.

Becky knew my entire family history. Mother dead,

father in prison. Not many people did, especially Jamie. But I met Becky at the school that Hazel took me to, the Monday after Mum died, twenty-five years ago, so we had some history together.

Drinking appeared to be the most important tradition I could see enacted in front of me. The students had attended their college balls the night before and the long-held tradition was to stay up all night and keep the alcohol flowing. Certainly the girls were happy, but the boys seemed more fussed about making sure they got their photos taken with the right girl draped around their shoulders. The noise was a deafening cacophony of shouting and singing, and the aroma of fried onions and bacon drifted from the street sellers and coffee shops.

'Did Mum enjoy it?' I asked.

Hazel looked up at me. She was a good ten centimetres shorter than me and fitted so comfortably under my arm, and in that moment as I looked at her, I could see my mother's smile. As sisters, they weren't really alike. From the photos I had seen, it was obvious my mother was the better looker - taller, slimmer with long wavy black hair. I had inherited her eyes. Hazel was the more comfortable, more homely one.

'Your mother loved everything she did. A proper party girl. This was right up her street,' she said.

'Well, good to see that has passed down the genes,' Becky shouted, just as a new wave of undergraduates squeezed by.

As it approached six o'clock, the mass of people moved slowly down the street towards Magdalen College and we followed along, arm in arm. I could just see the choir boys at the top of the tower, some of them peering over to see the crowd below before they broke into one of their madrigals on the dot of six. The crowd fell silent and there were a few minutes of magic, as they sang like songbirds.

Almost as soon as it had started, it was all over. An hour of standing in the rain for that. Another year done. Time for jumping from the bridge into the Cherwell for the brave or drunk few.

For us, it was a hot coffee and teacake. Jamie was waiting by the door of the nearby café and took the umbrella from us, then showed us inside to the table he had been keeping. My face reddened when he kissed me in front of them. Hazel scoffed and Becky shook his hand.

'Not much of a story this year. Too wet,' she said.

'Oh well, we had to come. It's not over yet. There could still be a riot, you never know. There was a bit of a skirmish in 2003 but nothing since,' he said.

As soon as we sat at the table, a thick-set man in a long, black leather jacket walked by, on his way to the rear entrance of the restaurant. His head was shaved and he wore the same distinctive dark glasses even though it was raining. I knew who he was: for the second time in a week, the fourth man.

'Alright Jamie, how's it going?' he said. His voice was deep and growly as he spoke quietly.

Jamie looked up, shocked, but he obviously recognised him. He couldn't look more like a gangster, carrying a small black case. Jamie turned back to the three of us.

'Don't ignore me, Jamie boy. We got nowhere today. Too much rain. But we've held her,' he muttered.

Jamie took off his coat and walked to the back of the

restaurant to hang it on a hook by the rear door. Sykesy, as Gary had called him, followed and I could see them having a short conversation, then the man walked out the back and Jamie returned. I looked over at Becky but she hadn't been watching. How could Jamie still be in touch with a bouncer keen on kicking people down the steps from the White Lace Club?

'What was that all about?' I said when Jamie returned.

'Oh, nothing really. Just some old mate of mine. From the old days. He's gone now. Amazing who you bump into, isn't it? In a crowd like this. I once saw my cousin at the Cowley Carnival totally unexpectedly. You do get coincidences like that sometimes. Who wants a bacon sandwich?'

The smell and talk of breakfast blew away any further conversation. Becky looked the least bothered by anything, whereas Hazel just glowered at Jamie like he was from an alien planet. The food arrived quickly despite the crowds and I ordered extra coffees all round.

'So that man is a friend from school?' I said.

Jamie looked at me before he answered.

'No. Not school.'

'So where do you know him from?' I sounded quizzical, trying to strike a light note.

'Look, you can't know every friend I ever met. Life's too short. It's ages ago, a previous life.'

A group of students came in through the front door of the café, dripping water everywhere, totally unaware of their impact. The windows steamed up further and people crammed ever closer around the few tables, huddled for warmth. It was March in May, at least weather-wise.

But we've held her. Did I hear that right? What did he mean?

After we'd all finished, Becky had to go to work. I went with her to the doorway, leaving Hazel and Jamie to glare at each other.

'Did you see that man? It was the one from London,' I said.

'No, and you're probably mistaken. They all look the same, that type. Good luck with those two,' she said.

We hugged and I returned to the table.

'How about we take you home, Hazel? I'm sure Jamie won't mind. We can give her a lift, can't we?' I said.

'Sure we can. It'll be an honour.'

Hazel tried to smile, the briefest of thanks escaping on her breath.

***

After we dropped Hazel off, Jamie insisted he come with me to see Andrei. I had a morning coffee meeting planned, this time at his workplace because they would be closed.

'Don't tell him I'm coming. Let's surprise him. Good cop, bad cop.'

I didn't need to work out which of us was going to be which. We went to Cowley in Jamie's car and parked behind the supermarket. Shoppers were emptying trolleys into their cars, and kids were racing around chasing each other. It was busier than a normal Sunday as it was May Day weekend. Jamie parked away from the store in the far corner beside a tree, then called the car-cleaning team over when we got out.

'Make sure no one scratches it. And give it a thorough clean. We'll be back in an hour.'

We walked over the pathway by the Boundary Brook and along the back of the cinema to a shabby building on the corner, with faded grey rendered walls and wooden window frames that had once been black. I knocked on the door and Andrei's dad opened it wide, almost pulling my hand off as he did.

He didn't say a word as he stood to one side and pointed to the room at the back, indicating that we should go in. He stared at Jamie, his face questioning his right to be there.

'Hi Emmy,' Andrei said, bounding towards me. Then he also saw Jamie and stared, narrowing his eyes and crossing his arms.

'Why did you bring him?' he said.

'We need all the help we can get to find Amanda,' I said.

Andrei towered over Jamie as they both stood tall and looked at each other, glaring. Andrei's dad offered tea and retreated to the kitchen leaving them to face each other down. I simply sat in the first chair I could and got out my notebook.

'Have a seat, children. Let's begin,' I said.

They both sat at once, Jamie on a chair at the table and Andrei on the easy chair beside the unlit gas fire.

'Now, we're here to discuss the situation and share any knowledge we have.'

Neither one spoke. I waited until eventually Andrei's dad returned with three steaming mugs and set them down on the table. He said he was tired and went out the room, shutting the door. I could hear the creak of the stairs as he went up.

'I will tell you both that Amanda Brown has a past,' I said.

'Dancer, part-time singer, probably a prostitute. Tell us something we didn't know already,' Jamie said.

'Not prostitute. All a long time ago. Not relevant,' Andrei said.

'Well, what's it to you? She's a British woman, abducted from a British shop.'

I opened my iPad to show them the photograph of Cristina.

'Who's that?' Jamie said.

'This is Cristina Iliescu. She used to work with Amanda, at the same clubs. Now she is missing too. Her neighbour called me, concerned about her cat,' I said.

'You think kidnap. Same people?' Andrei said.

Andrei stood up and walked around, circling us where we sat, squeezing by the space where the table was close to the wall. He stopped and banged his hand on the back of a chair where Jamie sat.

'Probably Romanian thugs have taken her too,' Jamie said.

'Why you so against Romanians? We do no harm to no one. You have no proof.' Andrei turned to me. 'Take him away from here.'

I glared at Jamie to be quiet.

'Look, we need your help, Andrei. We all want to find these women. There's some connection to your community, that's all.' I said.

'For you Emmy, I help. Not him.'

'Have you found out any more?' I asked.

'Nothing useful. Perhaps she knew some people. That is all I know. I don't want to say any more.'

'Amanda was having an affair,' I said.

They both turned to look at me. I could tell at once that Andrei already knew. Perhaps Cristina had told him too. She had told me that no one knew but Andrei simply shrugged his shoulders as if to say 'of course she was'. It was Jamie I was more surprised by.

'How do you know about that?' he said.

'I found out from Cristina. When she phoned me after our meeting.'

'You promised her never to mention that,' Andrei said.

'I'm a journalist Andrei, sorry but things have changed. Cristina is missing. I'm worried.'

I looked at Jamie and he stared back at me as if I'd unearthed some big family secret.

'We should go,' he said.

'Can you ask around people you know, Andrei? Perhaps someone knows something. Your dad? Your friends? Cristina was Romanian and knew some people in Oxford. Someone must know something. It's too coincidental that these two friends have disappeared at the same time. Ask them to check out the White Lace Club.'

I put my notebook and iPad back in my bag and stood up to leave. Andrei came over to me and gave me a hug, right in front of where Jamie was sitting. I heard him snarl, then he stood as well and pushed past Andrei to leave the room.

'Take care of yourself, Emmy. I will see what I can find out and call you,' Andrei said.

On the way back to the office, I turned to Jamie while we were waiting at traffic lights.

'Did you already know she was having an affair?' I said.

'I guessed as much.'

'You never said.'

'Well, it was a hunch only. Didn't want to influence your investigation.'

'We should tell the police,' I said.

'Maybe. But we want to keep selling papers. It's good to have an exclusive angle.'

'Two women are missing. That's big. You should have said about the affair. How were you so sure?'

'I wasn't. I said ... I guessed.'

I rested back in the leather seat. The car was immaculately clean, pristine inside and out. I couldn't smell the vomit anymore. The incident was forgotten, though I wouldn't be drinking and passengering again any time soon.

**

'This missing woman. What's happening?' Becky said.

So Becky was interested in life outside Daniel after all. She was driving us to the cinema and I was holding on to the dashboard of her Mini as she took on another roundabout. We were going on her insistence to see a new romantic comedy without our men.

'Well, she's still missing. She went in the middle of the night, leaving a note saying sorry. I was hoping the White Lace Club might help.'

'Have they asked for a ransom?'

'They did but no one else knows that. Her husband paid up and they also took money from the safe.'

'Well, they either want her for money or sex.'

She sat forward in the driver's seat, then hooted at a car who was slow away from the lights.

'The film won't start for at least half an hour,' I said. However, she had the car, and I had the bus, and we were best friends, so I hung on gracefully.

'She's a good looking woman. Sex trade?' she said.

'Not really. You think? No, she's too old anyway. I think it's the money,' I said.

'We'll eat afterwards, there won't be time before. Fancy pizza or something like that?'

'Sure, and a glass of wine to help us with the film review.'

'No wine. Not tonight. I promised Jamie I'd look out for you,' she said.

I glared at her. 'Worried about your car?'

'Don't be daft. No, he said you could come to the cinema as long as I didn't let you drink.'

'The man's an arse. Who the hell does he think he is?'

'He's your man. I'd do that for Daniel. Perhaps he's got a surprise shag planned for you and wants you sober.'

She couldn't be serious. We were not in 1952. Anyway, Jamie didn't do surprise shags, although I wasn't going to tell her that.

'Perhaps he'll be wearing his Emperor's *trabea* when I get home,' I said.

'Spartacus?'

'No, I'm Spartacus.'

'I'm Spartacus too.'

We both laughed and came to an abrupt halt at the entrance to the car park.

'I'll take that ticket and pay for it when we leave, it's the least I can do,' I said.

***

After ordering our customary Vegi Supreme with a side of tomato salad, we settled on Diet Coke to drink.

'Well, I thought Dakota Johnson was better than she was in *Fifty Shades*,' I said.

'I can't get past Ralph Fiennes. That was a hot and tasty movie wasn't it?' she said.

A Bigger Splash certainly was a little raunchy compared to our usual taste, sizzling with undertones of jealousy and tension. I loved going to the cinema with Becky because she was so innocent, believing totally in the characters and becoming deeply involved. She always cried, whatever the story. I hadn't concentrated on it that well, unable to get Jamie out of my head.

'The odd thing is that Jamie knows something about the investigation that I don't. We're supposed to be working on the story together so I can't see why he'd hold back,' I said.

'Daniel's like that. All mysterious at times.'

'Do you think it's because he's trying to protect me from something?'

'I doubt it. You're the last person that needs protection. You happy staying in his house?'

'I love it actually. Just being with him there. It suits us,

Summertown. It's the problem of relationships at work, though. One minute lover, next minute boss. I should move job.'

'Where would you go?'

'Oh, I don't know. But it's too claustrophobic. London maybe, you never know. I should try. Hazel suggested it too.'

***

As she drove me back to Jamie's after the meal, I started on it again.

'I don't like him having secrets, not work ones, professional ones. There's something wrong.'

'You need to tackle him on it. Or maybe find out some other way. Why don't you come to dinner with me and Daniel? Let me talk to him. You never know, I might weasel something out, I'll put on my best flirt.'

'That'll do it,' I said.

30

Jamie accepted my proposal of the dinner party at Becky's with such a deadpan positive response I couldn't tell whether he was genuine or not. I knew he actually liked Becky so I took it at face value, explaining we would keep it short as it was a Monday. We arrived at the office together but did not see each other all day and it gave me time to think, as well as get some writing done.

Gary emailed me at lunchtime with a snapshot of part of Sykesy's criminal history. He'd been inside briefly about five years ago for assault causing actual bodily harm when he'd attacked someone outside a nightclub, although he'd always claimed it was aggravated by the victim. That sounded like the Sykesy I'd seen in action. He'd also done some petty thieving, but recently he had been quiet with a clean record.

Henry sustained me with cups of coffee until mid-afternoon when I left early to get changed. I considered ringing Brad to enlist his help in the search for Cristina, but decided to give myself and Andrei a few more days, and any call to Brad might be taken as a signal that I wasn't sure I wanted to offer.

***

There was a water jug on the table and white wine

wrapped in a cooler, coasters for the glasses and Becky's best knives and forks. This was Daniel's influence. Since they had got together, Becky had progressively gone upmarket, equipping her kitchen with new paraphernalia such as an egg whisk and a garlic crusher. Daniel liked to cook and loved entertaining. They seemed to be busy every weekend with a dinner party, seating six at their table comfortably, and they had introduced various members of our set to random friends of Daniel, slowly integrating us all into a homogenous whole that would form the backdrop for their future together. I could see them imagining the wedding favours already.

'Well, this is nice,' I said.

Daniel was in the kitchen while Jamie, Becky and I sat, nibbling at olives and dipping bread into the oil and balsamic vinegar. Jamie was being civil, even refined, using a stick to prod at the olives as he sipped his Sauvignon Blanc. A candle burned in the centre of the table, flickering a shadow over Becky's sheer white top, cut outrageously low so that flashes of her lacy-edged bra held Jamie's attention.

'We're having coq-au-vin, apparently. One of Daniel's specials. More vin than coq from what I remember when we had it with Louise and the Mumfords – they're his friends from Leeds. He went to school with Callum,' she said.

'You're looking so hot these days, Becky. He's doing you good,' I said.

'Indeed you are,' Jamie said. He sat back in his chair and swirled the wine glass, holding it out to the uplighter in the corner of the room that gave the whole place a slight air of sinfulness.

'Well, thank you both. One has to try to look one's

best.'

Jamie glanced at me and I automatically tidied my hair then fiddled with the buttons on my blouse. Becky poured us all more wine, leaning forward over the table towards Jamie as she did. She gave one of her giggles when he put his hand over the glass to stop her, indicating he didn't want to drink too much.

'And not too much for Em, you know she doesn't travel well,' he said.

'OK, OK,' I felt the heat in my face.

'Well, you guys can always crash on the couch if you want. By the time we've eaten, it'll be pretty late. We can put some party music on.'

I could see Jamie's mind close to that suggestion. He had his morning routine to consider. Anyway, I wanted to get him home to bed for myself, so Becky was being out of order.

'We'll see,' I said.

'Aww, go on. We can both keep Jamie here warm, Em. Daniel has to go because he's got to drive down to his mother's first thing so he's heading back to his own flat. So I'll be here all on my own. It'd be fun.'

She flashed one her most wicked grins at Jamie, just as Daniel called from the kitchen for her to help. She stood up and walked slowly, her denim jeans clinging to her fabulous figure.

'We're going as soon as,' Jamie said when she had gone.

'Good. I don't want to share you.' I smiled.

Daniel and Becky brought in the plates of food: chicken in a sauce, mashed potatoes and broccoli. Daniel looked resplendent in his apron and hat and we all toasted the chef. He wasn't going to miss the moment of fame, before we started into the eating.

'So, Jamie, how's this famous case doing? Found her yet?' Daniel said.

'Well, you'd be better directing that question at Emma. Emma's the one at the sharp end,' he said.

'Not really. The police have got nowhere, and the latest theory is that she's done a runner, not been abducted at all. Her location is a mystery,' I said.

'What about all these damn Romanians?' Becky said.

Daniel and I stared at her.

'Exactly,' Jamie said. He poured himself another glass of wine and finished the bottle. Daniel noticed and went to get a new one.

'You think it's them? The immigrants,' Becky said.

I could see the look in her eye, the merest hint of a smile on her face, but Jamie didn't notice.

'I know it,' he said.

'They probably took her abroad. I've heard of that. Sex slavery. Maybe the Arabs.'

'No. You think it's Romanians, don't you Emma?' he said.

'Don't bring me into this. As I said, there's no evidence of anything for certain, but it is all very odd. David Brown appears to be very rich but no one can explain why.'

'He has right-wing political views, doesn't he?' Becky said.

She indicated her glass at Daniel when he walked back in with a fresh bottle and we all nodded agreement to another.

Perhaps we would get a taxi.

'One's views on right and left depend on where you're sitting,' Daniel said.

'I can't find out much more than that. He's not on Facebook or any other social network. He's been in business for ten years, that's about it.' I said.

'I bet there's dark secrets there. We'll have to get you on the case, won't we Daniel?' Becky said.

Daniel explained he had many connections through his law firm and could get the low-down on anyone we cared to mention, through a network of somewhat shady organisations. Becky gazed at him as he spoke about his passion for the truth and his desire to expose fraud or corruption wherever he could.

Jamie continued to drink and stayed quiet.

'How about you Jamie? Do you know much about the shopkeeper?' Becky asked.

The open style of her innocent question went straight to the heart of the matter and I waited to hear the answer. An explanation of the photograph.

'I know a little,' he said. He looked at me as he spoke while I remained silent and smiled at him.

'Come on Jamie, do tell,' Daniel said.

'Well, Emma has uncovered most of this. I suppose I was reluctant to say that I did know David before. We used to be acquainted a few years ago but had not been in touch lately.'

I frowned at him. Here was something he could have told me days ago.

'So Mr Witness, you knew the Defendant already. An acquaintance you say, please do elaborate. May I remind you that you are under oath.'

We all laughed and Jamie shuffled a little in his seat. 'I knew him in college, that's all. We met up a few times when we realised we were both in Oxford. That was years ago. Mostly lost touch since,' he said.

'Were you in a gang with him?' I said.

'We weren't fifteen. It wasn't like that. Just the occasional beer.'

'And you didn't think to tell me?'

'It wasn't relevant, not to the story you were working on.'

I didn't want a public row but the wine boosted my courage to continue.

'What about the initials HBFC? Do they mean anything?'

Jamie folded his arms and his face reddened. I could see a pulse on his temple. The room fell quiet for a few moments, filled only by the background music of one of Mozart's piano concertos. Clearly a favourite of Daniel. Jamie frowned before he spoke as if considering the initials carefully.

'I think they do, yes, a bell is ringing. It could have been the uni football club, I think. That's a strange question, Emma. All a long time ago and we should be focusing on Amanda Brown.'

The setting was wrong for further interrogation. I could see that none of us believed Jamie's answer but that didn't make it connected to the investigation or important, more likely some student hijinks. Becky shot me a glance and steered the conversation back to the choice of dessert. I had some thinking to do; we had made a start but were a long way short of knowing Jamie's life story.

***

Gemma brought the brown envelope through to me at U1-5. It was A4 and bulging, containing a folder of some sort. Surely not another threat?

'Where did this come from, Gemma?'

'Some guy left it on reception desk. Definitely not that motorcycle courier that you told me to look out for. This one was a hunk with lovely blue eyes.'

Andrei. She dumped it on my desk and stood with her hand on hip, watching me. I had just finished a coffee and was trying to type up a piece about the effect of the rise in council tax on the East Oxford community. Yellow Post-it notes were scattered across my desk and my handbag lay open beside my laptop, makeup box and pencil case spilling from it. The fan of the laptop hummed in anticipation of my acerbic writing skill.

'Thanks, I'll open it later. On a deadline here.'

She looked disappointed; another round of office gossip thwarted. I looked at the envelope. Red marker pen had been used to write 'FAO Ms Emma Hawkins' on the front in capital letters. Was it another embarrassing gift? I hadn't had one of those in a while. All the more reason to wait.

After Gemma eventually wandered off, I eyed it for ten minutes, sitting there in the makeshift in tray which was an empty cardboard box labelled 'For Emma' in my craziest italic writing. Council tax rates were causing talk of protest marches and I wanted to get the article finished for Friday's paper, but the package gnawed away at me until I eventually pushed away my laptop.

I pulled out a dossier of papers and photos with a handwritten sheet on top. One of the sheets of paper was sticking out from the top of the manila folder and I could see Jamie's name typed across the top. My pulse picked up and I glanced around the room to check no one was looking.

No one was, of course. Everyone at the paper focussed on the screen before them. Even fun interaction was usually conducted online rather than through office banter. Twitter had seen off most of the office jokes, taking them to a new global level of journalistic sarcasm.

I opened the folder and a photo of a woman was attached to the paper. She looked about forty with a pretty face and long wavy blonde hair. She was standing outside a church and next to her was a suited and very handsome Jamie with his arm around her shoulder. It looked like they were at a wedding.

I scanned the papers and there was a listing of Jamie's academic qualifications, followed by a series of jobs and newspapers he had worked at. It read like a resumé of his life. I turned it over and more personal details were shown.

Date of birth. 18th July 1970. What? That didn't make sense. He'd told me he was 41, and that date would make him 45. I pulled up Google and LinkedIn on my laptop and scanned for Jamie Wilson. All the information I could find said he was born in 1974. This must be wrong.

There was no covering note, nothing to indicate it was from Andrei. Perhaps I had assumed wrongly; plenty of handsome blue eyes around. There were a couple of photos of Jamie in his twenties, looking like he was at university, one in a mortar board and gown on his own, and one with a group of mates. I looked closely and David Brown stood at the end of the line.

I picked up the one of him with the woman again and turned it over. On the back was written *Jamie and Alice Wilson*. Sister? Married? What?

A rush of red came to my eyes. I stared at my screen, then back at the photo. I could feel the heat in my face giving away my heartbeat. I carefully put the papers back in the folder and stuffed it into my bag, then stood up with the photo in my hand, along with a printout of an article I was working on.

Without further thought, I walked the thirty paces to Jamie's office. His door was closed but I could see through the glass that he was alone, typing and looking at his screen. I opened his door without knocking and walked in.

He looked up and smiled.

'Emma, how are you?'

I shut the door behind me and walked to the chair beside his desk.

'Fine thanks, Jamie.' I breathed slowly to control my voice. I kept my face straight, not smiling, focussed on the row of boxes on the bookshelf behind his desk, each containing journals of Oxford court proceedings. I sat in the chair and held the article on my knee, hiding the photo beneath.

'What can I do for you? I am trying to get this finished before lunch,' he said.

'How old are you, Jamie?' I looked at him directly, trying to identify any familiar tic or movement of his facial muscles. He was focussed on the screen in front of him, continuing to type.

'Forty-one. I've told you that before, darling. Why? Do you think it's a problem? You're thirty-one, I know.'

'When did you get your first degree?'

'1995, London.'

'I could look that up.' I continued to stare at him, willing him to look at me. He remained impassive.

'You could, of course. What's bothering you?'

I studied the lines around his eyes, the few grey hairs in his brushed-back, dark locks. Was he forty-one or forty-five? Who could tell? Did it matter anyway? He stopped typing and glanced at me, folding his arms. My resolve weakened.

'Nothing. Just doing some research,' I said.

'I'm not a good study. Boring life. Steady rise up the pole.'

I could hear Hazel. *I told you he was trouble. That Andrei is a sweetie.* I sat forward and pushed the photo onto his desk in front of him.

'Who's Alice?'

This time he did respond. He sat upright, grabbed the picture and stared at it. His face paled to a dull grey.

'Where did you get this?'

'Who's Alice?' I repeated, not looking away.

'She ... Look darling, we're still getting to know each other aren't we? I was going to tell you about Alice. I just hadn't found the moment yet.'

I stood up, and leaned onto the desk so my face was near his.

'Bastard. You're married.'

'No, no I'm not. It's not like that. I'm divorced.'

By the time he'd said the word 'divorced', I was at his office door and shutting it behind me, a little too loudly so that a murmur of interest rippled through the open office outside.

31

Jamie decided we needed a few days away together, some time on our own, and I could see his point. The row about the dodgy dossier had gone on all evening as he tried to put together plausible excuses for every topic I raised. Eventually he wore me down and I couldn't be bothered anymore. What did it matter? We both had a past. It was the secrets - that was his nature. I felt hollowed out inside and conflicted. I needed time to think.

I went to my own flat afterwards, where the refurbishments were almost complete so I could start to believe Mr Desai's latest promises. The bathroom was fully back in action and looked magnificent with glossy white tiles and a brand new shower. I lay on the couch and talked for an hour to Becky. Apart from really listening this time, which was wonderful, she actually offered some practical help, saying she'd get Daniel to put some of his magical investigative powers and connections to good use and prepare his own summary of Mr Jamie Wilson. I also said I was worried about Lou-two as she was close to Andrei and perhaps he was a little dangerous. Of course, Becky was having none of that, but she did agree he may not be a truly reliable source.

Perhaps a short break away together would help. After that, my flat would be habitable, so I could make my own choice of the next steps.

We left the very next day for Madrid. Jamie said he knew it was short notice but he'd cleared it with Abigail and it was fine. In fact, she was very supportive of the idea. He said it would take me away from the front line and would give us both a chance to unwind. I loved his spontaneity and ability to organise such a trip in under two hours. It would have taken me days to decide on flights and hotels.

We flew from Heathrow. Jamie was enthusiastic all the way and in a very romantic mood. He held my hand at the right time, carried all the baggage, and gave me the window seat on the plane. It crossed my mind that he might be thinking of some rash romantic proposal, but I quickly banished that thought and concentrated on the free wine.

The city centre was a short taxi ride from Adolfo Suárez airport, and by Wednesday lunchtime we were in our hotel. Madrid was hot, steamy and full of tourists from all over the world. The street cafés were filled with people eating tapas and drinking wine. We sat in St Ana's square right outside our hotel and ordered prawns and garlic mushrooms for lunch.

'Let's shop,' I said.

'You can shop at home - we should look at the art galleries. Madrid is famous for its art. Don't you like culture, Emma?'

'It's famous for its shops as well.'

I sipped on the local Sauvignon Blanc and looked across the table at him. He'd done well to bring us away. I could see him in a new light. Work had been stressful lately, the attentions of Andrei and Brad Richards, the ransom notes, the death threats. Jamie wasn't the only one with secrets.

I watched a jazz band of buskers standing beside our café, the lead saxophone belting out 'What a Wonderful World'. I sat back and felt relaxed.

'Art it is. It's time I got educated,' I said.

Jamie paid the bill. He had insisted the entire trip was his treat, which certainly was a character trait I'd not seen before. We walked slowly through the old part of the city, down narrow streets with quirky shops such as one specialising in collars for dogs and another selling only Iberian ham. The pavements were narrow or non-existent and we had to stand to one side every time a delivery van came by.

At the crossing with the main boulevard, Jamie stopped me and held me in his arms, while the little red man flashed and cars raced by.

He kissed me briefly then he whispered into my ear.

'I will show you some of the most beautiful paintings in the world at the Prado. Paintings of love,' he said.

We crossed the Paseo del Prado hand in hand and joined the short queue which moved quickly. The Prado was a huge gallery, well-practised in managing many thousands of tourists every year. I picked up a guidebook and scanned it. Art was not my thing at all, but I could see that Jamie was excited. Could I love this man? Could I trust him?

We toured a few galleries before taking a break in the café, then picked up where we had stopped and walked through some more. I didn't need an audio guide; Jamie was perfect. He was able to explain the context of many of the paintings and clearly was well-read on the subject. Of course, I didn't understand *Guernica* and I'm not sure he did either but it was fun listening as he talked me through the huge black and white canvas. That had been the busiest part of the tour; it was like the *Mona Lisa* of the Prado – not that I'd been to the Louvre either.

'Come, let's move somewhere quieter. This is war. We need peace,' he said.

He led me through to nineteenth-century portrait art. The room was empty and we sat and stared at a picture of the Countess of Vilches, painted in 1859.

'She is beautiful, much like you. Can you see the likeness?' he said.

I had to admit there were similarities in the hair and the eyes.

'Well, she is smiling like I am. But I hate the hairdo,' I said.

We laughed and he kissed me on the cheek. Oxford was forgotten. As we walked through to the next gallery, we came face to face with Andrei and Lou-two. Hell froze over, and the air turned cold in an instant.

'What on earth ...?' I said.

'Oh my, you two. That's bizarre,' Lou said as she hugged me, clearly as shocked as I was.

After mumbling a greeting, Andrei just looked at the floor. Jamie was speechless.

'You must be Jamie. I'm Louise,' Lou-two said and put out her hand to shake his.

He turned that into a polite hug and continental cheek kissing, and put on a broad smile.

'I've heard a lot about you,' he said.

We all stood there staring at each other as a few other tourists wandered by. Nineteenth-century portraits were not the big draw.

'We've been looking at the beautiful Countess over there – she's so like my Emma, isn't she?' Jamie said as he pointed.

Lou-two dragged Andrei by the hand to take a look and laughed when she saw it.

'Love the off-the-shoulder look, Emma, that's so you,' she said.

Jamie held my hand and I could feel it trembling at little. This 'coincidence' did not look accidental.

'Well, surreal though it is to bump into you, we should move on. We're on a short break,' I said.

'We could do dinner?' Lou-two said, though it sounded hesitant.

'Yes, why not? We could,' Andrei jumped in. He stared at Jamie with a small grin.

'No, thanks anyway, that's very kind, but no. I have other plans,' Jamie said. He let go my hand and put his arm around my waist, pulling me closer. He kissed me on the cheek, then turned back to Andrei.

'I've booked a special restaurant. And tomorrow, we're shopping. Perhaps another time when we're back, we may have more to talk about then anyway.'

Lou-two laughed. 'That's fine. Well, small world. Let's go, Andrei,' she said.

We walked away before they did and Jamie strode quickly towards the gallery of modern art.

***

Outside the museum, the day was cooling as we walked back up the Calle de las Huertas. We did not hold hands. Jamie simmered until we got to the hotel room to freshen up for the evening. Then he exploded. He stood by the window, staring at me with the setting sun behind him, so I could hardly see his face.

'You invited your admirer as well as me, then. You're playing with me,' he said.

I sat on the bed with my head in my hands and kicked off my shoes, then rubbed my feet. I had mistakenly chosen the black heels for that day. We had walked a lot and I was tired.

'Not that again. You're paranoid,' I said.

'You told your friend Lou, I suppose.'

'No, I didn't.'

'Presumably I'm meant to believe they just happen to be art lovers.'

'Actually Lou-two is. Always has been.'

He scoffed and turned to look out over the square below, buzzing with early evening bar-hoppers.

I sighed. 'It does look odd. I have no idea how they knew or if they did. I don't believe Lou-two did.'

'He's a little shit. Scheming his way into your knickers. Thinks he'll have a piece for himself. That's what this is. Doesn't accept you're mine.'

Jamie turned again from the window and strode over to me, snatched my hand and pulled me to my feet. He put his arm around me and pulled me close to him, so my face pressed against his neck. Then he gripped my bum with his right hand and pressed me against his body, while grabbing me firmly between my legs with his left. I could feel his hardness against me. I was thankful for wearing jeans, as he squeezed tightly and violently.

'This is mine. Do you understand?' he seethed.

I struggled free of him and stepped back.

'Don't be ridiculous.'

He took my hand again and held it against his trousers.

'I love you, I want you all.'

'This is not the way to show it. There's nothing to worry about. Andrei is helping us with enquiries. He's dating one of my best friends. Be reasonable.'

'You're being naive. Don't play the innocent,' he said.

'You're seeing monsters where there are none. I'll speak to any man I want.'

Here we were, arguing again, despite the attempt at a romantic getaway. He had such a short fuse, and I doubted I could cope with such jealousy. I sat back down and rubbed my feet some more. Jamie knelt in front of me and tried to help but I pushed him away.

***

The flight home was painful. We were delayed for an hour on the stand, waiting for clearance from air traffic control. Something to do with a strike in France. Just what I needed. There wasn't anything to say. I buried my head in the *Hello* magazine that I had purchased in the terminal. It was surprising how I could make it last so long, studying pictures of the wedding of a television presenter.

I wore the same jeans and top that I'd flown out in, and the air in the cabin was hot and sticky, adding to my discomfort. Jamie had offered me the window seat so I scrunched up my legs and tried to make myself as distant from him as possible, turning towards the side panel of the plane.

Not that it really made any difference. He sat straight with his head back on the headrest and made out he was asleep. Perhaps he was ... and just as well. There was no excuse for his behaviour.

When the captain finally announced departure, he stirred and rested his arm against mine, so I moved away and peered out the glass to watch the take-off. The city of Madrid spread below us like a checkerboard patterned with criss-crossed black lines, the buildings melding together in the sharp sunlight to become varying shades of grey.

I had a sense of dread, entrapped in an endless tunnel with a man I was beginning to doubt, the man who said he loved me.

We didn't speak for the entire flight of three hours, not about Andrei or any other men. When we touched down, Jamie took down my hand-baggage and smiled sheepishly at me when he handed it to me while we waited to get off.

'Thanks,' I whispered.

'You're welcome. Thanks for the company,' he said.

I missed his arm around my shoulder, his close proximity as we walked out with our suitcases to the car park bus. He pushed the trolley and behaved the perfect gentleman but without any sense of intimacy. We could have simply been work colleagues. *He's a bad-un*, I could hear Becky say. Perhaps she was right.

The M40 was quiet and Jamie's car purred smoothly through the miles to Oxford. He played some Spanish flamenco music on the hi-fi and I sat back and closed my eyes.

When I felt his hand tentatively reach over to mine, I allowed our fingers to touch, to try to find a spark. Perhaps I just needed to sleep.

'Shall we stop to eat?' he said.

'I'm not hungry. You get something if you want. I suppose there's not much in your fridge,' I said. I sounded like the wife I wasn't.

He turned off at Marston. I wanted to head to the solitude of my own flat and a long soak in my new bath, but he pulled up outside the fish and chip shop. Hunger took priority. I agreed to a bag of chips and I watched him walk across the pavement and enter the shop.

Perhaps it wasn't all his fault. After all, Andrei was acting very strangely. Perhaps I did like him. Perhaps Jamie realised. I was the one who should apologise. Perhaps not. He'd said too many things I couldn't agree with. We were too different in outlook. He didn't own me like that.

He looked purposeful as he walked back with the bag of food, a man in charge, a man on a mission.

I held my breath when he sat in the driver's seat. An apology was coming.

'I'm sorry Emma. I really am,' he said.

The smell of cheeseburger and chips prevailed over the fragrance of roses from the car freshener and my stomach rumbled in response.

He put the food on the back seat then took my hands. He pulled me to him and leaned forward so his lips touched mine. I was surprised by my response as I kissed him back. My body accepted him despite my head saying no.

When we arrived outside my flat, he passed my food to me, then retrieved the bags from the car boot and carried them to my front door, where chivalry stopped.

'I'll leave you in peace, and to enjoy your food and a bath, and your newly refurbished flat. See you tomorrow,' he said.

I thanked him and watched him drive away then dragged my luggage up the stairs, along with my bag of chips. Then I collapsed on the kitchen chair while the kettle boiled and I devoured the food.

I phoned Becky while I drank the tea, and she sympathised and tutted and said she'd chase Daniel on his investigations. Talking it through made it all sound a bit more reasonable from his side. I could understand his jealousy and it was sweet.

I lay in the bath thinking about his saying he loved me. There'd only been three men in my life who had said that. I shook myself as I dried off in the towelling robe and sipped at some wine. Maybe I should call Brad, or Gary, or Andrei to give him a piece of my mind.

Instead I called David Brown. I had not heard from him in a while.

'I haven't made you beans on toast in a while,' I said with a smile.

'Yes, we should do that again soon. I like your company Emma.'

'Any news on Amanda?'

'No. I take it you neither. I've all but given up, although I'm really irritated about the money and want it back. I'm assuming she was having an affair now, but I've no idea who with. Never an inkling.'

'It looks that way, yes,' I said.

'I still want to track her down. It's theft. Fraud. Call it what you will, they made me give them £100,000, after stealing £50,000 from my safe. That's a crime and I want it back. She can have her man. I deserve an explanation.'

I had to agree and said I would continue trying, but Jamie and the paper had taken me off onto other stories and it was difficult to pursue, especially as Jamie kept a close eye on my work.

'I heard that. Him keeping a close eye on you. Good for him,' he said.

'You knew him at college?'

There was a few seconds gap before he answered, and I wished I had actually gone round to tackle him on this, to see his face.

'I did, yes. He told you then.'

'Not much.'

I left the silence, until eventually he carried on.

'I was in the same band. What did he tell you?'

'Do you still have regular contact, then? It looked like you two were pretending you didn't know each other.'

'Oh, not really. Just didn't seem relevant, that's all. We were a gang of four and it was a long time ago. Similar interests, that's all.'

I lay back on the couch in my towelling wrap and talked to David for another ten minutes. It helped take my mind off the events of Madrid, although I did recount the Prado and the various artworks we saw. He listened well. I told him that Jamie and I had a romantic time.

'He can be romantic, I believe. As long as you see the romance his way,' he said.

'He likes most things his way.'

'He does. He wants the money back too. Very cross about my wife and the Romanians.'

'It wasn't his money, though?'

I made it sound more like a question than a statement, by accident really. I had no inkling or thought that there was a connection of that sort to Jamie, so I was surprised by David's response and sat upright as he spoke.

'Well, strictly between us, he did have some stake in it. Mutual friends, mutual funds,' he said.

'May I come and talk to you about that sometime?' I asked.

'Perhaps, but I may have said too much. I should go now anyway. Take care Emma.'

32

When I arrived at the office on Friday morning, Jamie was waiting in reception for me. Gemma was on her own and on the phone. She watched me push through the double doors and rolled her eyes at me, nodding her head towards Jamie who was sitting with his head buried in the *Telegraph*.

He had to be waiting for me. I wondered if I could sneak through but I decided to brave it out, so I walked up to him and tapped him on the shoulder.

'Emma, my sweet,' he said.

He stood up and grabbed the two carrier bags of clothes I was carrying, putting them on the table. I had brought them in to take to the charity shop up in Summertown at lunchtime. There were three short-sleeved tops that I'd had no business buying in the first place and a whole heap of T-shirts.

'I've bought you a coffee.'

He thrust it into my hand and looked into my eyes with a soulful, searching look. I remained silent and sat down, taking the lid off the cup, sipping at the drink.

'Flat white,' he said. He sat down beside me, so that our backs were to reception and sipped at his own coffee. Eventually, he turned to me.

'Emma, I am so sorry, so, so sorry. Please forgive me,' he said.

I sighed and looked at him. He looked so forlorn it was hard to maintain my resolve, but I wanted to hear back from Becky and Daniel, and then there was the money connection to David. Surely that stuff couldn't be right.

'None of that in Madrid was my fault. I didn't know they were coming,' I said.

'I know, I know. It doesn't matter. I just get so angry with him. I want to protect you and I just can't. I need to learn.'

'You don't own me,' I said.

We sat quietly drinking our coffees. I didn't want his apology to end, but I could understand why he'd got so angry. Andrei was stalking me and getting inside my head.

'You need to ignore him like I do,' I said.

'I get so jealous. I feel so strongly about you.'

He talked quietly. I turned around to look at Gemma. She was sitting behind the reception pedestal, perched on her stool, leaning on the desk and painting her nails a deep purple, the same shade as her top. She looked up and smiled at me. Then she put her thumb up and indicated to Jamie as if she approved and I should forgive him all sins. I looked back at him.

'You know I love you, don't you Emma?' he said.

I felt myself blush. This was not the place to have this conversation. Did he think I'd come round with a free cup of coffee and a declaration of love? I didn't want this today and definitely not in front of Gemma.

I kissed him on the cheek.

'Save it buster. Let's go and make a paper.'

I smiled as I grabbed his hand and stood up, dragging him with me and we made our way through to the offices.

'Be good,' Gemma said.

Forty-five minutes later he came and stood beside my desk. I was busy typing a piece about the perils of online ordering and returns management, one of the so-called business articles that Henry wanted help with. In reality, it was more of a guide to consumer rights, but anything was better than society weddings.

'I'm busy,' I said.

'Do you still want me?'

'I'll think about it.'

He glanced around the office and once he was happy that no one was watching, he leaned down and kissed me on the forehead.

'Thank you,' he said.

'It's only thinking, it's not a yes. I need time.'

'Thank you,' he said and walked away.

I continued to type.

***

The next day I caught the bus to work and sat upstairs. A fresh new day with a fresh new, optimistic start and a quiet Saturday office ahead, most of them watching the afternoon football. The paper never stops. I wanted to get back to proper journalism, especially the piece about how the eastern European countries were suffering from a brain drain. I decided Henry might help.

The bus was slow and the windows were steamed up so I wiped away the condensation to stare outside. Tourists were in the majority on the pavement. I could smell bacon from somewhere near the back of the bus. I seemed to be hungry all the time - I needed to return to the diet wagon.

My phone buzzed and I opened the call. It was Andrei.

'Emmy, how are you? You okay?' he said.

'I'm fine. Unhappy with you. Unhappy with Jamie. Getting back to work. On a bus,' I said.

'I know. I understand. We meet soon. Drink, chat.'

'Not a good idea,' I whispered.

'I have information. About the email address. The David Brown ransom. New things emerge.'

I propped my phone to my ear, and pulled out my notepad and pen. The lad opposite me was engrossed in his headphones, his eyes shut, and the girl behind me with the pink hair and black hat was scribbling into her diary. No one was listening.

'Go on,' I said.

'It wasn't an account in Romania after all. It did go via there but traces back to England, to Sergei indirectly. Not him, but same server. Same provider,' he said.

'I can't talk now.'

'OK, no problem. You see though.'

'I do. Meet me in Marks café at eleven.'

'I love you saying that, Emmy. I speak you later.'

Two minutes later it was Lou-two's turn.

'Emma, you must be angry with me,' she said.

'A little.'

'Meet me after work. For a drink. Let's talk properly. We're more important than any of these men,' she said.

She was right, we needed to talk about it all. We agreed on six o'clock in All-Bar-One. It would be a busy Saturday after all.

**

Andrei and I sat and drank slowly, nibbling at our free shortbread. He looked smug, teasing out the information for me and enjoying his hold.

'Sergei is the registered owner of the email address but not the actual sender. I can tell by tracking it all the way back to MAC address of device used. It took a while to get that information. It's not his computer,' he said.

'Well, I guess that helps a little, but not really,' I said.

He leaned forward over the table to me and grasped my hand before I could withdraw it.

'I want to help. Really I do. You are so important to me. But you're not concentrating. You are better,' he said.

I pulled my hand away and looked around at the usual crowd of ageing shoppers and young mothers struggling with multiple toddlers and babies. It was another world.

'What do you mean?'

'The world needs Emma Hawkins to shout. Tell our story. How our families help Britain be successful. How we escaped oppression to a better land. The evil Ceaușescu. I will help,' he said.

I sighed and explained again how the paper paid my salary and they had decided in their wisdom to point me in other directions, at least officially. Not that it was any of his business.

'And another thing, you tease. Too many men distract you. You only need me to look after you, keep you focussed,' he said.

'Don't be personal. This is none of your business, especially my love life. Tell me more about Sergei,' I said.

'I have discovered he has relationship. A long time, years. With Amanda,' he said.

He sat back and put his cup down with a flourish and that grin.

'How do you know all this? Another of your theories?'

'I spoke to my father. Eventually he told me. Sergei and he are best friends, agitators together in 1989 – on the streets of Bucharest. They have no secrets.'

'Wow, now that is a story to investigate. So Sergei and Amanda – how did that happen?'

'Many years ago. Very close, in London. Before all this shop business here.'

'Was the kidnap a set-up?'

'I think so, yes. The email was likely from her. I don't know why.'

'Money of course.'

'Probably,' he said.

He looked agitated as we checked the time and started to get ready to leave.

'And Cristina?' I asked.

'I don't know. She is still missing.'

'And Madrid. How did you know?'

He looked down at his empty cup, hesitating.

'Sorry. I traced the booking. I wanted to make sure you were safe. Keep on with the investigation, my Emmy.'

Then he stood up, grabbed my hand and kissed it before pacing down the gap between the tables towards the exit.

***

Despite it being lunchtime, Henry was at his desk and typing quickly with a half cup of black coffee sitting beside his computer. He smiled and said he would chat in a bit but wanted to stay in his zone until he'd got two thousand words done.

I unpacked my bag and made myself the closest approximation to a double-shot skinny flat white that I could manage at the machine. I checked through emails and Facebook and tidied my hair by tying it back loosely.

'Good trip?' Henry looked up at last and stopped typing.

'Not really, I would have been better off here I think.'

He snorted and complained about the weather and the sport, and the lack of anything cultural happening in Oxford on a wet weekend at this time of year.

'Henry, can you help with some of my investigations?'

'Of course, Emma. Whatever I can do, just shout,' he said.

'How's your Romanian history?'

'Ceauşescu, that's about it. When was it, Seventies? Eighties? Something like that.'

'Yes, he fell in '89. Shot by firing squad on Christmas Day.' I said.

'They have a blue, yellow and red flag. Good one to know for pub quizzes,' he said.

The helmet, of course. Surely proof of a Romanian

connection, I thought.

'I need more background on the communist history, the impact on the current day. How people might be affected, that kind of thing,' I said.

'Like sympathisers. There's bound to be people still out there who are supporters of the cause, despite the fall of the regime.'

'Exactly. How would we know? How would we recognise them? What are they up to?'

'The age-old story. The Left vs the Right. The commies,' he said.

He stood, picked up his coffee and walked around to my desk. He'd had his usual spicy chicken sandwich for lunch.

'I was wondering whether there could be problems with Romanian immigrants, some of them old enough to remember the Ceauşescu days, having a different outlook to the traditional British residents where they live,' I said.

'The neo-fascists, you mean.'

He smiled when I looked puzzled.

'Let's kick out all the immigrants and have ourselves a nice jolly one-party state,' he said.

'Well, anyway, I need to have a whole background piece on it, and maybe try to get an angle on why the Romanians, in particular, are being singled out as the bad guys.' I said.

'Sorry, yes. I didn't mean to get too carried away. Starting to sound like Jamie, aren't I?'

It was easy to see, and even Henry knew it. Yes, Jamie was extreme in his outlook. I wondered if he was in his office, and what he was working on. Should I go and see him?

'Talking of fascism, tell me about Madrid,' Henry said.

I told him about the art galleries, not the fight, and bragged about my knowledge of Picasso, which Henry saw through straightaway. Then I moved him on to the spate of posters that had happened and said I thought the emblem or logo at the bottom of them might say HBFC and could he investigate that. I didn't tell him about the shirt. He said he enjoyed getting involved in a puzzle and would get on it immediately.

I left him to it and wandered past Jamie's office. He wasn't in and I couldn't decide whether I was relieved or irritated. There had been no messages this morning, no more grovelling, just silence. It was hard to concentrate on any work and I kept checking my phone.

I went to the gym in the afternoon and that helped. I worked hard on the cross-trainer, playing Blur at full blast and maintaining a high tempo until I could feel a sheen of sweat on my forehead. The man was a prize idiot. My mind drifted to Andrei's comments about how the world needed Emma Hawkins, and Hazel's view of my career.

When I got back into work, I tried to focus on the facts, but after five minutes at my desk, finally I decided to make contact with the *Guardian*.

33

York Way headed north along the side of King's Cross station. I crossed Railway Street and the *Guardian* offices emerged ahead of me, towering over the tracks. The façade of the building was a wall of curved glass, reflecting the bright sunshine and scattering shards of light across the dirty red brick of the station buildings.

Cars and taxis hurried by me while I hesitated on the pavement, staring at the revolving doors. I could hear train noises thrown back off the building, the sliding of doors, the whistle of the train manager, the surge of the electric engines. London was a dirty city; smelly, crowded and noisy. If I moved here, I would have to run the washing machine every day. I would be tired, irritable. The Tube was sticky, people were grumpy. There were no aspirations here.

But the *Guardian* was the *Guardian* and I was convinced my future was inside these doors, the advertised post of journalist a natural progression for me from the *Gazette*. I wasn't at all sure Jamie would see it that way.

'I'm here to see Mr Woodward,' I said to the receptionist.

I clutched my bag too tightly. I was wearing my best business casual outfit, carefully selected on Saturday after coming home from drinks with Lou-two. We had talked about

Andrei, about Jamie, about work and men in general but I hadn't told her about this. No one knew I was here, not even Hazel. I'd spent a quiet Sunday rewriting my CV twenty times.

The blue jacket, the matching trousers. I was overdressed.

'I'm Emma,' I said.

'I'm Patsy. Pleased to meet you. I'll take you through security and up to his office. He's on the top floor overlooking the canal. Remember to mention the view, it's his best perk apparently. That and the fact he's the only one with an actual office.'

She gave me a tag to wear and walked with me to the lift. We chatted about the traffic and the Tube lines. She lived in Balham and had worked there three years and loved it. I wanted the job.

Mr Woodward stood up as soon as she ushered me into his office.

'Miss Hawkins. So pleased to meet you,' he said, shaking my hand.

'Pleased to meet you too, Mr Woodward.' I said.

I walked over to the window.

'You have a lovely view,' I said.

'Call me Doug. No doubt Patsy told you to say that, it's her party trick.'

I had stumbled at the first.

'She did. I figured it was a no-win set-up. If I ignored it, I would be rude. The trick was to sound genuine. And it is a great view,' I said.

I smiled at him.

Doug Woodward was in his forties and dressed in an

open-neck striped shirt with dark blue trousers and red braces. He invited me to sit on a low chair beside a glass-topped coffee table. The trousers had been the right choice. He sat at right-angles to me with a big pile of loose papers in front of him and started to leaf through them. Just then, the door opened and a second man strode across the office to us, carrying his tablet. I stood and shook his hand. He introduced himself as Pete from Talent Development, saying he was responsible for preparing the job description for the role of senior reporter in the UK Society department. We settled into our chairs around the table, them relaxed, me braced for a grilling.

'You have a strong sense of right and wrong, Emma?' Doug Woodward said. Straight in with a tough one.

'I do. From my mother I think.'

'Are you a radical?'

'Not politically, no but I thrive on change.'

'Did you support the austerity measures applied by the previous government?'

He didn't even look up at me as he rattled through the questions. Occasionally he scribbled on his notepad and often he rummaged through his paperwork as if the right answers were buried in an appendix somewhere. He was forthright and thorough, just as I could be, I thought. I felt ready and prepared. I could work for this man. Pete remained silent throughout, tapping into his iPad as he seemed to eye me suspiciously, although no doubt that was all part of the act.

After an hour, Doug walked me back to the lift.

'We have two others to see. You're a strong candidate Emma, although Pete would kill me if he knew I told you that at this stage. I'll be in touch next week.'

His hand was hot when we shook. The air conditioning was fighting a hot British day outside. I gave him my best smile and returned to the ground floor.

'Told you he was alright,' Patsy said.

'Thanks, you were lovely. Are they all like you here?'

'No, they're a bunch of arsehole journalists. I'm the only friendly face, that's why they put me out front.'

We both laughed.

'I'll aim to be the second then ... and be on the inside,' I said.

***

Becky called the next day before I could call her. I was just drying my hair, grappling with the comb to rid myself of tangles in front of the mirror. Long hair had been my thing since secondary school, sometimes a little more than a bob, but mostly down below shoulder level. It was eight o'clock on a fresh new morning and the world was good, whether I got the job or not.

'I was in London yesterday,' I said.

'Dancing I suppose,' she laughed.

I explained all about Mr straight-faced Woodward, and my doubts about whether I would actually take up the post even if they were to offer it to me. There was a lot to consider, especially Hazel's feelings.

'Look, we can talk about that later, I'm calling because of Daniel,' she interrupted.

'What about him?'

'He's got more details on your Jamie. Sordid stuff.'

'He's not really *my* Jamie as such, especially since Madrid. I need to know what details,' I said.

'Well he's got form. Not actual prison form, but "dodgy past" form.'

'Define dodgy.'

I sat down at the dressing table and grabbed my notebook and pen as she spoke.

'I can give you the notes when we meet, but there's been suspicion of violence against ethnic minorities. It's quite a list, I'm afraid, from verbal abuse all the way up to street fighting.'

'How did he find all this?'

'We're not to know, but I was told it is accurate. Daniel was very thorough and has many connections with the security services.'

'Wow, he sounds like a member of *Spooks* or something. We should watch the box set of reruns sometime. Rupert Penry-Jones, those were the days.'

Becky laughed and I could tell she was enjoying this new-found dimension to Daniel, but my stomach turned and I felt like I was going to be sick. I drank some water and gripped the dressing table, digging my nails into the wood.

'There's more. He is banned from the Arsenal football ground for life,' she said.

I didn't even know he was a fan but apparently he had been banned in the Nineties, caught on CCTV shouting racial abuse at players and throwing coins and nuts. He was turning into a brute.

'That HBFC thing is some sort of secret right-wing club apparently, aimed at eradicating immigrants and taking back control for the British,' she said.

There it was again. HBFC. Surely this couldn't be Jamie, but the shirt said it had to be. It sounded far more fanatical that I could believe of him. There had to be some explanation.

'But he can be a real softy,' I said.

'Perhaps that's an act for you.'

'Maybe. I'd like to see the evidence before I overreact. And thank Daniel for me. He's a diamond sweetie. I'll buy him a bottle of his favourite red,' I said.

Becky laughed.

'OK I'll tell him. He's OK isn't he?'

'He's the best you've had. Better still, he's the one to keep.'

***

Auntie Hazel always taught me to count to ten before taking any action I might regret. I had never really understood why because I was the type to follow through with something anyway, whether there was a ten second delay or not. But this time I needed to think. What was Jamie involved in? Surely all this in his past wasn't right? But I couldn't just ignore the whole thing.

I sat upstairs on the bus again, trying to think about the impact of the rich and privileged international students. How did they affect the culture of Oxford and what were they leaving behind? I called it 'The Foreign Feed', playing on the feeding of Oxford's economy from the high fees paid by overseas students, but it was difficult to assess any influence on the local community.

I watched the pedestrians on St Clement's from the window, walking with purpose, living their lives, on their phones or listening to the world through headsets. I couldn't get Jamie from my head. He was strong, charming, caring. He was witty, fit, attentive. He was assertive, demanding, infuriating. He took what he wanted.

When I got to work, I kept my head down and typed. I had notes from interviews with students from all over Eastern Europe, and academic research papers from Bucharest and Warsaw. Henry had left me some initial findings about Romania under Ceaușescu, and how the Soviets put pressure on the state, reducing subsidies and causing bread and fuel lines. The *Securitate*, the secret police, were seemingly everywhere. It wasn't any more than I could have got from Wikipedia but Henry had catalogued it perfectly, including rare photographs of Nicolae and Elena Ceaușescu at formal functions, displaying their taste for fine quality clothing and Cartier jewellery.

After half an hour and much twirling of my hair in my fingers, I gave up and grabbed my folder of notes and marched into Jamie's office. My counting to ten was up. His door was open and fortunately he was on his own.

'Emma. How lovely to see you.'

He could patronise with the best of them.

I stood at the side of his desk and he quickly put his screen saver on and looked up at me a little startled, as if I was about to steal his idea or, more likely, catch him looking at something he shouldn't.

'I need a minute of your time,' I said.

He smiled then and indicated the seat so I deliberately put the manila folder on the desk and then walked back to the door and shut it. I knew he'd check out the title of it. I had scrawled *Jamie's dirty secrets* in big black letters across the top.

When I came back, I sat down facing him across the desk, crossed my legs and took the folder onto my lap.

'If we're to last, I need some answers to some questions,' I said. I had practised that first line a hundred times, but I wasn't sure where I was going next.

He looked a little flustered but quickly recovered.

'Of course. What do you want to know? I have no secrets from you, darling, we've been through all that,' he said.

He smiled and tried to put me off my game.

'Really, how old are you?' I kept the stare straight, the question short.

'Not that again. I can see you're not to be fobbed off. As far as the world is concerned, I'm forty-one, it's better for my career. I never found the moment to confess and bluffed it out last time.'

'Forty-five then, not forty-one'

'Yes, yes I am.'

That's one-nil to me, I thought. I could see he looked nervous and I wasn't sure that I wanted to go through all the information like this.

'Still married?'

'Oh Emma. No, no I'm definitely not married. But, well, I was at one time as I said. We're divorced.'

'Sure?'

'Yes. But the papers did only come through last month.'

'Why didn't you tell me?'

'It didn't seem relevant really. We've got serious very quickly and I didn't get the opportunity to raise it and I knew the papers were imminent. I'd have told you eventually. Sorry.'

He took a mouthful of coffee and sat back, a little more relaxed, like I had lifted the weight off him.

'You've been checking up on me then? Perhaps I should be flattered.'

'Only doing my job. Using all my sources.'

'I'm glad you're taking me seriously. I want us to work. I really do.'

I tried to remain impassive; I didn't want him charming himself out of it again. I sifted through some more papers in a show of professionalism, keeping hold of his attention like he was being interviewed.

'What about Arsenal football club. Are you a fan of them?' I said.

This time he laughed.

'Thierry Henri. Best player in my lifetime,' he said.

I just stared at him and waited. Not a time to blink.

'Actually I was, yes. But a long time ago and I got in a lot of trouble. I was young and impressionable. I was violent, there's no excuse.'

'A lifetime ban is quite a punishment. It must have been bad,' I said.

'Well ... Yes and no really. It was bad, but lifetime bans were common then. The police just blanketed everyone together, no matter what your crime was. Arsenal also wanted to show they were tough and there's always a long line of people waiting for tickets so lifetime bans did them no harm.'

I could see he was getting a little impatient now. More

on the front foot, like I'd thrown the worst at him and he'd survived. None of this really mattered if it was all behind him. The phone rang and he answered it quickly, giving himself a break and allowing me to regroup too. I fidgeted in my seat, crossing and uncrossing my legs as he watched me while he talked to someone about a meeting tomorrow. When he finished, he carried on.

'Where did you get all this from? I thought it had all been buried. I know that sounds bad but my career needed a clean and innocent past. I worked hard to hide all that.'

He sighed and stood up and walked over to the window. It was getting on for midday and the sun was streaming in through the upper part, casting a dark shadow over his face when he stood to one side. He adjusted the blind to shield out some of the heat. I watched as he stared out of the window onto the lawn and surrounding trees. In the background there was a constant drone of traffic heading in and out of town on the Banbury Road during another business day.

'It doesn't matter how I found out, it's what you believe in that matters to me, like this HBFC. It's not a football club is it?' I said.

'I was twenty. Thatcher had just been deposed. I was in my first year of an English degree in London surrounded by radical thinkers, lefties and communists, but I'd grown up through the Thatcher years. We needed to be strong against Europe. I was an isolationist. I needed to find like-minded thinkers, that's all.'

'And now?'

'Now I'm calmer, older, more rounded, in love with a

beautiful girl.'

I closed the folder and put it on his desk as I turned to leave.

'You can keep that,' I said. I still needed time to process my thoughts about him. Could I trust what he said? Had he really changed? Somehow I doubted it.

34

Back at the flat that evening, I stood in my bedroom reviewing my wardrobe again. It was my way of escaping. I piled anything more than a year old onto the bed. Anything - with the exception of all the exceptions I always made: favourites, items that provoked memories, fancy dress possibilities, the short blue sheath number that barely covered my bum which I'd worn to a distant cousin's wedding and flirted mercilessly in with the best man, who was married at the time, the pin-striped wrap dress I'd worn to Royal Ascot, which had got me a series of dates with the son of a knight of the realm. These were classics to be kept.

But somewhere in here was another bag for the charity shop and I was determined to fill it. It was time to say goodbye to jeans that I had worn on anti-Iraq War marches, and a top I'd worn when I saw Busted in Hyde Park. Happy memories of those enthusiastic uni years. All this was more recent than Jamie's student years. I had never been an idealist like him, more an investigator, a sponge, learning to be a polite person who asked rude questions. I hoped we could give it a go - after all, he said he had mellowed and I liked mellow. The door buzzer interrupted my thoughts.

'Come up, Andrei,' I said. I sighed. There was no point in trying to avoid him.

He looked wet, soaked from the rain. I got him a towel
and a can of beer and continued with my charity work while he
sat at the dressing table and watched.

'Moving in with Jamie?'

'Clearing some stuff out, that's all. Maybe thinking I'll
move out of here at some point, you know, there's always the
possibility.'

'I see. Well, good luck.'

He smiled and I didn't perceive bitterness. Perhaps he
meant it. He'd had plenty of time to get used to the idea of me
and Jamie. He was with Lou-two now.

'That's a lovely blue outfit - let's see you in that,' he
said.

'What do you want, Andrei?'

'Just wanted to see you. I was hoping to catch you at
home. Do you like Mumford and Sons?'

'"I will wait ..." It's your song, Andrei.'

'You're teasing me, that's cruel.'

'You have Lou now.'

'I know. My Lou-one you know, not two.'

'I saw them live once. They are a great band,' I said.

He undid his jacket and pulled an old CD from the
inside pocket and passed it to me.

'I wanted you to have it. I played it a lot when I had my
thing for you. You still have CD player?' he said.

I dropped it on the bed in front of me, then walked
over and kissed him on the cheek. He was being really sweet,
looking shy as he sipped his beer. The room was tidy and the
bed made. Thankfully I had cleaned up that morning before
work. It was the first time he'd seen the room and I thought we

should go back to the lounge before his mood changed.

'Let's go and sit. I need a beer too,' I said.

He sat on the couch while I put the CD on play, then settled into the Poäng.

'You need to stop coming to see me, Andrei, you know that. Jamie will find out.'

'You're allowed friends.'

'You can't do just friends.'

'Of course I can. It's you that strings us all along. It's your way. You talk the moral high ground about society but you don't act it.'

He stared at me and I could feel my pulse throbbing in my temple. There was a harshness in the air.

'Did you come for a fight? I'm not in the mood,' I said.

'For my family, I'm imploring you to work on society. You're clever, you write powerful stuff. I'm your friend, not enemy.'

I raised my beer can to him. 'I will try,' I said.

'Then, I will wait for you,' he laughed. 'Would you wear something for me?'

'You've asked that already. My wardrobe is off-limits. I'm not doing some fashion show for you, you perv.'

'Perv, what is perv?' He said with an exaggerated accent.

'Stop teasing.' I put on a shocked face and laughed. He could always surprise me.

'I have a serious gift for you, not just CD. Something more memorable, to show friendship.'

'What now?' I said.

He stood up and walked over to me, standing squarely

in front of me so I shrank back in my chair. I felt a shiver of fear down my back all of a sudden.

'What are you doing, Andrei?' I said.

He grabbed my hand and pulled it to him and kissed my fingers.

'Don't be afraid. I'm not here to attack you,' he said.

He held my hand tightly and reached into his pocket with the other one. Then he pulled out a bracelet and quickly slipped it over my hand. It was three solid interlocking rings of silver forming a bangle that exactly fitted over my wrist. It was beautiful.

'It's a Russian wedding bangle, traditionally the trinity, but I think of it as Faith, Hope and Love,' he said.

'It's beautiful, Andrei. Thank you.'

Without thinking, I stood up and kissed him gently on the lips.

'Wear it for me. I still live in hope,' he said.

I sat back down, feeling really embarrassed, and admired it on my hand. It looked amazing. I had a drawer full of bangles, always my favourite accessories, but this one was more beautiful than any of them. He walked across to the lounge window and pulled open a gap in the venetian blind.

'I can't keep this. You know that, don't you,' I said.

'My father met my mother on 21st December 1989. You know that date?' he said without turning around.

'Ceauşescu. The rallying speech in the Plaza of the Republic.'

'He was in the crowd. With Sergei. Demonstrating. My mother too. That was when I was started. That night or in the days following. The euphoria, the passion. I existed before

Ceaușescu died, though my mother didn't know until the sickness in the following months.'

I held the bangle and turned it around on my wrist. Andrei stared out of the window as if he was looking for the *Securitate*.

'Was this hers?'

'Yes, before that my grandmother in Jilava.'

'I can't keep this Andrei. It is special.'

'There was hope back then. Excitement, anticipation, a thirst for change after years of misery and austerity. My father knew how to queue for bread. Can you imagine? Cowley Road length queue for bread.'

'You've never talked about your childhood.'

'It is too painful, but if I squeeze my eyes tight, then I can remember, people waiting, sometimes all night, waiting in front of shops whose shelves were empty, on the rumour of a delivery of meat or cheese.'

He stood beside the window and peered out into the night.

'It's stopped raining. I should go,' he said.

***

The morning at work was torture. Henry had researched the entire history of Nicolae and Elena Ceaușescu and the events of December 1989, starting earlier with the rise of the Romanian Workers Party, then the food hardships of the Eighties, and leading right up to their executions on Christmas Day. He was a sweetie for sure, laying out his research in logical sections all the way to the current day but I couldn't stifle a yawn.

'Too much partying last night?' he said.

'Actually, I had a quiet night in, although Andrei did visit, so this really helps. Puts his life into some context, and his Dad.'

'So Jamie? Andrei? A bit confusing for an innocent bystander like me,' he said.

'Andrei is a mate, that's all.'

Fortunately I wasn't wearing the bangle that he wouldn't take back. Too risky at work.

'This does help to explain the history of Romanian migration since they joined the EU in 2007. You're a marvel,' I said and squeezed his arm as I smiled at him.

We were in a meeting room just off the corridor leading to Jamie's office and he had already walked by twice and stared in at us. Surely he couldn't be jealous of Henry, of all people. Probably just wondering what story we were on. Henry caught me looking apprehensive.

'Ten more minutes, then I'll head him off for you while you escape if you want,' Henry said.

I smiled and grasped his hand in thanks, then listened intently as he outlined his findings on the poster logo. He couldn't make anything of the initials but he had discovered the printing company that probably had prepared them. Apparently a whole pile of them were discovered in a waste skip near their premises but there was no definite proof. When he scrutinised their filings on Companies House, he discovered that David Brown was a non-executive director and shareholder.

'Well that is interesting. Thanks Henry. Nothing on the meaning of HBFC then?'

'No sorry. Perhaps you should ask Jamie,' he said.

I sighed and told him I'd been down that road already. We stood and I kissed him on the cheek before we left the room.

'You're a star, Henry. I need to go. I'm seeing my friend Louise for lunch and my Aunt Hazel. Time for a proper chat and moan about men,' I said.

'Don't include me. Remember I'm one of them.'

'Aww, not really, you're too nice.'

'I can turn if you wish.'

He sighed and nodded, before heading in Jamie's direction. There were any number of weddings he could choose from that he could assail Jamie with by way of deflection.

Thirty minutes later I was walking down the Banbury Road towards the Ashmolean. Lunch and Hazel beckoned. Brad called as I waited to cross the road, heading towards the Martyrs' Memorial. There was a heady smell of kebab in the air from the temporary van just setting up for the rest of the day.

'Hello Detective Inspector. To what do I owe this call on a pleasant Wednesday afternoon?' I said.

'How are you? Not a word from you in days. I feel used,' he said.

'Not used, I'm just busy. I haven't forgotten you. How could I?'

'Well I have an interesting piece of information. If I didn't know you better, I might need to interview you formally. We've trawled through all the CCTV from the unrest at Cowley market last week.'

I stopped by the wall of St John's College to listen properly. Oxford's heritage stared at me from all sides. Apparently the police had sifted through all the images and found one of the man who set fire to the shop front. I remembered seeing him. The image had caught him lighting the inflammable rags at the moment Jamie and I are walking by.

'It's clearly you. I'd recognise that back view any day ...' he said and I detected a note of humour in his voice, '... and actually it's even more clearly Jamie Wilson holding your hand.'

'Busted,' I said.

'Quite.'

'We did make a statement at the time.'

'Oh, I know. No problem. I wanted you to know that we have managed to do a match on the face of the man, and he is known to us, through criminal records. He is one William Sykes, better known as Sykesy.'

I gasped a cough and said there was passing traffic so didn't quite catch what he said. He repeated himself and went on to ask me to keep that off the record for now while they tracked him down. He reassured me it wouldn't take long, but he wanted me to pass the information on to Jamie as well.

'Certainly Brad. We'll do some of our own investigations but won't print anything yet. Thanks so much for the call.'

'You're welcome Emma. Stay safe. Speak soon. I'll be waiting for your call,' he said.

I carried on walking in a daze, trying to understand all the connections in my head. Every avenue seemed to lead back to that photograph outside the Randolph.

***

I glanced at the famous hotel over the road as I entered the Ashmolean museum, half expecting to see the four men standing outside. When I got downstairs to the restaurant, Lou-two and Hazel were already waiting, sitting at a table near the entrance of the long vaulted room, with a large pot of tea and three cups. A very sensible choice of venue for a sober afternoon chat. The place was quiet, with a few visitors chatting and reviewing their guidebooks. I gave them both a hug then plonked myself down beside Hazel.

Hazel had made an effort.

'A dress? You look wonderful,' I said.

'I thought we might go clubbing later,' she said.

Lou laughed and gave my arm a squeeze, then passed me a cup and poured tea into it. She was looking suitably businesslike in dark blue trousers and a matching jacket.

'So, you two been talking about me?' I said.

'Men, that's the topic for today. Men and men,' Hazel said.

I looked at the tables around us and at the queue for hot food. There were a few local office workers as well as the usual tourists in the mix.

'Sorry to disappoint but I can't see any available at the moment. There's two on that table behind you but I think they are a couple,' I said.

Hazel took a sip. 'You're not here to look, you have enough already,' she said.

'Your auntie is funny,' Lou said.

'I know. She thinks I'm Mae West.'

'Except you can't act,' Hazel said.

Images of drama lessons at school flashed in front of my eyes.

'OK, but we're not here to talk about Jamie,' I said.

'I think that's exactly why we're here. Him and all the others. And to eat, I'm hungry,' Lou said, as the order for three soups of the day and slices of lemon drizzle cake arrived.

When the server had gone, Lou-two grabbed my hand and gave me a big smile.

'I love you, Em,' she said.

'Me too,' Hazel said.

My eyes flooded for the first time in ages, overcome with the thought that here was my friend since the age of eleven, as near as you could get to being a sister, sitting next to the closest person I had to being a mother. We didn't need to talk. But we did. First it was Uncle Jack, then Jamie, then first boyfriends, then first kisses, then desert island dreams (David Beckham), then we got to Andrei, leading back to Jamie.

'What should I do, then? I'm over thirty now,' I said.

'You're not sure about him, are you?' Hazel said.

'I think Jamie could be good for you,' Lou-two said.

'I think Brad,' I said.

They both looked at me with mouths open. There was a moment of silence between us, drowned by the clatter of cutlery and the buzz of conversations around us, then they looked at each other and laughed.

'Who is Brad?' they said in unison.

We devoured our cake and ordered more tea. Hazel was caring, Lou harsher, calling me a slut, though in a good way, she explained. I couldn't quite work out what a good slut was but I think she meant well. There was enough background noise making sure adjacent tables couldn't hear us, which was essential for our professional reputations.

Through it all a decision emerged about my future conduct. I was to firmly decline all men except one, that was rule one. No flirting, that was rule two. Why this had to apply to me and not the others, I wasn't sure. They both said I should stick with Jamie for a while yet because he was all I ever talked about, both good and bad, although I hadn't given them the full story about the bad, as I was still trying to get my head around all the facts, if they were true. Whatever facts I presented him, he always seemed to conjure up alternative facts.

I took the opportunity to visit the ladies to clear my head, and when I returned the subject had moved on to Andrei. Lou-two was saying how sweet he was but I explained some reservations, like his uncanny ability to stalk me, or that's how it seemed.

'He's just a bit naive. He's seriously clever,' Lou said.

I felt I had to come clean about the bangle so I took it out of my bag to show them. I'd held back enough about Jamie and didn't want to let them walk away with a false impression of Andrei.

'Wow, that's nice. Is it new?' Hazel said, taking it and turning it in her hand.

'That's why I needed to see you.'

She looked puzzled and I struggled to find a way to get into the subject.

'It's Russian traditional. Three bands inter-locked. You know bangles are my favourite - especially silver,' I said.

'I know. I love that Victorian one you have with the engravings all over it, Indian styling. Where did this one come from?' Hazel said.

'That's the problem, it's from Andrei,' I said, looking at Lou.

'You're joking. Oh God no,' she said.

'You should have it,' I said.

'Oh no. Look, about that Emma. It's not what you think. We just kinda hang out together, that's all. We're just friends. He's lovely.'

'Looks like he stills holds a torch for you.' Hazel said.

'A torch? It's a bloody beacon. The guy's totally mad about you,' Lou-two said.

'What am I going to do?'

'Take your time. Think it through. Just don't let Jamie see it, for God's sake.'

I tried to smile but was not at all certain what step to take next.

'Look, I work in a company full of experts in computers, proper nerds. But I can tell you, none of them are as expert as Andrei. He's a real specialist apparently. I don't think he means harm.'

'I'm not so sure. Can you find out more about him? His background. What's so special about him?'

'I suppose so. I'll get on it this afternoon. Sounds a bit like snooping, but why not? You're more important to me than anything, that's for sure, Andrei included. Isn't that right Hazel?'

Hazel nodded and looked on the edge of tears, so we clinked our empty teacups and got up to leave, hugging each other, and I promised to go and see Uncle Jack very soon.

As I walked to the bus stop, I ran my fingers over the bangle in my pocket and resolved to speak to Andrei about it again, or send him some sort of cowardly text message. I couldn't keep it if I was to be with Jamie. Maybe I could escape all this by commuting to the *Guardian* – if they ever got back to me. I wasn't sure what I wanted, but I'd take a second interview if I got the chance.

35

On Thursday morning Becky called. She was distraught and I spent ten minutes of my valuable morning trying to calm her down. Firstly her washing machine had broken down and they couldn't come until next week to fix it. Then Daniel had called to cancel their date and she'd already gone to the expense of getting her hair done and spent hours on selecting an outfit. Apparently he had some urgent business which she made out to be a big mystery and suspicious, but was probably genuine. To cap it all, she had fallen out with her mother about the birthday present for her father. All this put my man problems into perspective, I suppose, and it did take my mind off things but I could have done without it on that morning as I was trying to prepare for a big meeting at eleven.

Eventually I got her to admit she was being a tad overanxious and managed to steer the conversation onto my career.

'What time do you see the big boss then?' she said.

'Eleven o'clock. Jamie will be there as well which probably makes it worse. He can be lovely and attentive but I don't need that when we're at work, and he can also be very boorish.'

'Boorish or just a bore. I mean, come on Em, you can do better.'

I didn't have time for this. I looked across the office at the intense and professional journalism under way at every desk – well, almost every desk. I had my own stack of yellow Post-it notes of follow-up calls to make. I could see Pete's coffee cup on the next desk, steaming with fresh ideas. I could smell the roses arranged in a vase perched on Jackie's neat filing cabinet, the one she'd purloined from Ed when he left. I need to focus on my own world and Becky was sowing doubts.

'I need to go. Wish me luck.'

'You'll be fine. Knock 'em dead. See you at the weekend.'

I sighed relief and returned to my preparations. The meeting was about business fraud in Oxford. I had no idea about business or fraud, so when the assistant had called at nine to insist on my presence, I couldn't see why they wanted me there, but I could smell an opportunity. I dug out all the archives I could and tried to think what my dad would want me to do. Whatever it was, it would be exciting. I went to the ladies and fixed my eyes and lipstick. I stared into the mirror and repeated 'You can do this'.

Jamie was waiting, jacket on, file of papers under arm. I hadn't seen him since Tuesday and our latest showdown in his office, so I felt awkward. He gave me a hug and we walked through the main office to the stairs at the back. People didn't stare at us any more. When Ed had a fling with Jackie before he left, everyone knew and everyone watched every move they ever made – when they went for lunch, when they walked to the toilets, everything. It lasted a week before we all got bored. Ed and Jackie had lasted even less time. But Jamie and I were carving out couple territory; we'd moved beyond the fling to the relationship. We didn't hold hands at work, but everyone thought we'd probably done it on his desk. We hadn't, nor would we if I couldn't start to trust him.

The editor-in-chief's office was on the top floor and was lined with dark wooden panels on all the walls. The lighting was modern and subdued, lots of little spotlights highlighting the dark corners. Fresh yellow roses were on the window ledge, no doubt put there by Gemma or Julie every morning. The desk was unassuming and cluttered with coffee cups, two keyboards and three screens. Abigail Cadman was an online wizard; she was more geeky than the geeks in IT in the basement and you would never want to challenge her on her social networking skills. Half of Oxford followed her Twitter account.

'Come in Emma. Take a seat. And Jamie.'

We sat before her.

'You're our rising star, Emma.' She smiled.

I blushed and remained silent. This was an about-turn from being sidled off to weddings. Did she have the right Emma?

'No, I mean it. Truly. You put your own stamp on everything you do. That reflects back on the paper.'

She was ambiguous. A good reflection or a bad one? Jamie shuffled his folder and looked anxious. I sat serene, at least on the outside. There was a pause which I wasn't going to fill.

'She's produced a series of excellent and incisive articles,' Jamie said. We both looked at him and wondered why he was there. I could see it in her face.

'She certainly has. It's just what we need, some

controversy. Although the paper takes a somewhat different political view at times. I sense you are a little left of us, Emma.' She smiled as she said it and I had to laugh as well. Ms Cadman was twelve years older than me and had moved through various regional newspapers across the south of England after the early part of her career at the *Mail*. She oozed control and sophistication from every pore in her body, her nails immaculate, her suit probably Chanel and her hair restyled every three weeks. Clearly, the *Oxford Gazette* was not the final resting place of her career, but nor was it of mine.

I looked out the window to the tree-lined avenue that was behind the Banbury Road. A suburbia of readership who only really wanted to know that their world was safe, their house prices protected, their pensions secure. Theirs was not to worry about the impact of immigration on the Cowley Road or other unsavoury parts of Oxford or the South. Two weeks in Cornwall and a week on the Algarve - that needed protection, and the private health hospitals in Headington and the quality of education in fee-paying schools: what else mattered? Perhaps I didn't fit the *Gazette*.

'I have some views, but I like to research well and try to present a balanced analysis.' I said.

It was her turn to laugh. 'Balance and the press aren't really good bedfellows,' she said. 'Balance doesn't sell, and your sense of balance may be different to mine, or to Jamie's here.' She looked across at him like she had him on a lead. 'Actually, no one has the same balance as Jamie,' she said and laughed again.

'So, business fraud in Oxford. How do I fit into that?' I said, deciding it was time we moved on to the agenda.

'I want you to head up a brand new initiative,' she said.

She sat forward in her chair and tapped on her keyboard, looking at one of her screens. Jamie coughed and shuffled his folder again.

'You're allowed to be pleased. It's a promotion. We want you to stay. Diversity of view, that's what we need.'

'An initiative about fraud?'

'Yes, the impact of corporate crime on sleepy Oxford academia. On this project, you'll report directly to me. Everything else comes through Jamie here.' She waved her hand at him as he seethed, I could see it in his hand grip.

I wasn't sure what to say or where this was coming from. A promotion? Better title? More money? It didn't seem the right time to ask.

'Thank you, but why me?' I said.

'Diversity and opportunity. Better here than the *Guardian*,' she said.

She looked at her watch, then picked up her phone and spoke to her assistant. 'Send in the twelve o'clock,' she said. We were dismissed.

***

When I got back to my desk, there was an email from Lou-two with a full review of Andrei. Born near Bucharest in 1990, the year after the fall of Ceauşescu, he had gone to school in one of the suburbs and then to the University of Bucharest where he studied Mathematics and Computing. He was convicted in 2009 for hacking into the Romanian state security system, a five year sentence reduced to one when he was placed in a state-funded computer network company. After that, he moved to the UK to be with his father and family, helping with their catering business, although Lou said that was probably a front for his ongoing computer security work. 'The guy is seriously clever, my boss says he's the best Summercloud have ever known.' And if Lou-two says that, then she has done her research and means that.

Jamie hovered as I scanned for any other important emails.

'Pub drinks? We should mark the occasion of your new opportunity and celebrate,' he said, although his face looked like he had sucked on a particularly unripe orange.

I packed away my laptop and grabbed my bag, then we walked through reception and down towards town. Jamie was quiet and my mind was occupied by Andrei. Could the waitering in the café be a front for something else? If so, then what? What was he up to? I knew that it was possible to track people's online activities much more than they realised so it was no surprise Andrei was watching my every click, and Jamie's for that matter. But what else was he doing? I shivered a little at that thought and Jamie put his arm around me as we walked. I looked across at him and smiled and he squeezed my shoulder without speaking. This promotion, if that's what it was, was hard for him to take. I needed to tread with care, even if I wanted to do the job.

We sat in one of the small rooms of the Eagle and Child for a change, as it was very quiet. Usually thronging with tourists, and not the most accessible of pub bars, we often avoided it and preferred more mainstream places. I sipped slowly at my half of lager for a change as Jamie drank steadily through his first pint of a rich red Oxfordshire ale, clearly intent on downing more than one.

'You've done so well,' he said grasping my hand across the table.

'Thanks, couldn't have done it without you.' I squeezed his hand back and looked into his eyes which were their usual dark brown but troubled.

'I don't want there to be any kind of problem between us. We have enough already. This is just a job and I'm not sure I even want it,' I said.

I wasn't sure if the editor-in-chief's comment about the *Guardian* was innocent or if there was some knowledge of my interview. It seemed unlikely they had contacted her for a reference without asking me first. I didn't want to mention it to Jamie.

'You should take it; it's a promotion and if you turn it down, they may not offer again.'

'Did you know about it?'

'Yes, but only just before. She called me first thing this morning, and I said it was a great idea, not that she gave me any choice.'

I sighed and let go his hand and drank some more lager. He went for his second drink and I watched him closely. I knew I really cared for him, but there were so many questions. When he came back, he wanted to know about the immigration series and what I had planned to do with it. That was another problem – it seemed like they really wanted to quash it now. Was that why I was offered the fraud opportunity?

'I spoke to Andrei about it. He's very keen that I continue to pursue it, and that Oxford needs to understand more about the positive impact that immigrants can have.'

'I bet he does, the bastard,' he said.

'Oh don't start Jamie, not as soon as I mention his name. I found out some more about him anyway. He's a product of the post-Ceauşescu Romania, when the early shoots of democracy were just taking hold. He's not all bad. He's actually very, very clever, especially with computers.'

'Well, he's a crook and a con-man and his whole family want to bleed us dry, and he has the hots for my woman.'

Jamie's face turned a deep red and he spat his words out with more venom than I'd seen. I liked his passion but it was always in the opposite direction to mine. I was much more on the same page as Andrei. It was time to take stock, because I couldn't see how Jamie and I would ever resolve our differences.

'Jamie, do you think we have a future? We see the world so differently,' I said.

'Of course we do.' He cracked his cheeky grin and leaned over to kiss me on the cheek, 'I just need to keep working on you, that's all.'

I pushed him away. I'd heard that line too often.

'Well, I'm not sure. You get so jealous and controlling. I am not yours to own. There's so many questions in my mind about you, and your past.' I finished my drink and Jamie still had half a pint left. I knew I needed to leave before I said too much, but couldn't stop. The time had arrived. I opened my bag and searched for the print of the Randolph photo, while he simply stared at me. I took it out and put it face up on the table in front of him.

'I need to know about this. And no flannel,' I said.

Jamie baulked at it and drank some more before speaking. His face was impassive.

'All in the past. I admire your investigative skills, my love, but it's all in the past.'

He took another mouthful of beer as if that was the end of the matter, and I seethed. Was that the best he could manage? I picked the picture up and put it in my bag without saying another word, then I got up and put my coat on.

'Thanks for the drink. I really need to go. I have a meeting,' I said.

'With him no doubt. Stay for one more, I love you, and you love me, not him.'

'Thanks but I'll leave you to enjoy your beers and think. Our trust is broken. Only you can fix that.'

I walked to his side of the table, quickly squeezed his shoulder and kissed him on the forehead.

'I won't be back until late afternoon, if at all today,' I said and walked out quickly onto St Giles, heading toward town.

36

I phoned Andrei as I walked towards the taxi rank. He answered immediately and I arranged to meet him at his café. He was surprised by the call and eager to see me.

'We'll have a nice talk. It's often quiet on a Thursday and I will close it early. My father won't mind.'

'Make sure you have your laptop,' I said.

'Yes of course. Should I call Lou? She may be able to come too,' he said.

Perhaps he did like Lou more than I realised. 'No, this is not a social visit. I have some questions for you,' I said.

We stood in the main area beside one of the tables. Chairs were still stacked on most of them where the floor had been cleaned at the end of the day. Andrei had made a black americano for me by the time I walked in. He looked relaxed and smarter than usual in a pair of dark brown chinos and a beige check shirt. He kissed me on both cheeks, overwhelming me with his aftershave, which must have been recently applied. He locked the door, then came and sat at the table with me.

'Now then Em, what can I do for you? You sounded businesslike on the phone.'

'I want to admit something, Andrei, first. I had Lou-two help me do some investigations ... about you.'

He grinned that annoyingly attractive lopsided grin

again and waited for more without comment.

'You are not quite all you say you are. In fact, you are more,' I said.

'Light under bushel. Isn't that it? Something from Bible? Am I hiding a light? A torch perhaps, that's true.'

'Stop teasing. I mean about your computer wizardry. You are seriously clever,' I said.

'Well, thank you. I like to think so.'

'Tell me about yourself, Andrei. I'm interested.'

I sipped at my coffee slowly, looking across the table at my second man of the day. Perhaps this one would be more open. His father and mother met at the Ceauşescu rally in December 1989 and he was the result of the passion they felt that night. There was something romantic in that, he said. The intensity of the revolution for change, erupting into the creation of him. But then reality, and his childhood through the Nineties was very challenging, a lot of poverty and hunger and social change as Romania adjusted. He had become very passionate about his country from an early age.

'Then you excelled at computer science,' I said.

'Mathematics really, leading into research on security in the early days of the Internet, how to protect privacy, and of course, how to break into it. That led me into trouble,' he said.

'So I understand: a year in prison.'

'Yes, I served half of a lenient sentence. You've done your homework, or Lou-two has - although it's not so hard to discover. I made a name for myself. My father was used to the *Securitate* in the Eighties, so he was actually encouraging, but I did break into some state secrets. I learned that was not a good thing to do.'

I told Andrei I wanted to see some evidence of what he had been up to lately, so he opened his laptop.

'Sit my side of table, Em, I will show,' he said.

We looked at the screen together and he immediately brought up a page of information about my shopping habits. I had a basketful of plain underwear in Marks & Spencer as an unfinished transaction, three books about modern art in my private Amazon wish list (a hangover from Madrid), and he showed a full listing of my most recent delivery from Tesco supermarket, including all the embarrassing items you hate to take through the checkout.

'That's the easy start. You already guessed I could do all that from the shoes I sent you,' he laughed and I could tell he liked to show off, so I encouraged him some more. He moved his fingers rapidly over the track-pad.

'OK, what about this? Let's see,' he said and pulled up a screen showing some grainy images from a CCTV camera. I peered at it closely; it was the inside of a shoe shop that I had visited at the weekend with me holding a pair of heels.

'Shame you didn't buy those red shoes, you would look very hot in them,' he said.

'This is not legal, is it?' I said.

'No. Not here, not for me. Legal for the security forces but technically they need permission from magistrate,' he said.

'Can they track you doing this?'

'Yes, probably, maybe. I cover well. IP address masking. It is cat and mouse. Who is watching who, watching who. If I was on other side, I could track me. It is about being the best,' he said.

'You've been stalking me, no other word for it.'

'At beginning yes, and I'm really very sorry. I got carried away. I went too far, but now we friends, I think, at last. So now not so much stalking, more protecting. '

He put on his sorry face and squeezed my arm.

'Now it's Jamie I track,' he said.

'I could tell the police,' I said.

'You could. Perhaps your friend Brad ... or Gary. But please, not until I tell you about Jamie.'

I sat back and looked around the café. The blackboard of specials was wiped clean and all the salt and pepper pots were neatly stacked along the counter.

'I do think you have a good heart, Andrei. That you want to do good. I thought that before, like when you saved that man at the railway crossing. But the stalking scared me.' I said.

'Ah that, yes the crossing. I wanted to impress you.'

'You mean you actually made that happen? Oh God, why? How?'

'I took over the signal system. I wanted you to like me, see me for good. There was no danger really,' he said.

'OK, enough. I need to take this on board. I'm not sure,' I said.

He jumped to his feet and went to the cupboard beside the door through to the private area, taking out a bottle of clear, pale yellow spirit.

'Ţuică, you will need it,' he said. He poured us a shot glass each and we drank it down in one. It was like a fire in my throat and I coughed, causing him to laugh. He tapped into his computer and brought up a photo of Jamie.

'I helped Daniel with his report about Jamie. Here's the

research I did, and some more since,' he said.

As he took me through various screens of photographs and images of information, he described Jamie's life all the way back to his childhood in Glasgow. I sat quietly, absorbing what he said.

A car pulled up outside, the driver stopping suddenly so there was a small squeal of the tyres interrupting our conversation. I couldn't tell the make through the frosted glass but my stomach flipped when the driver got out and a shadow loomed at the door of café. It was Jamie, I was sure of it. There was a loud banging as his fist hit the wooden frame.

Andrei walked over to the door.

'We're closed,' he shouted.

'I've come to see you,' Jamie said.

Andrei turned and looked at me with concern. Then he waved me towards the rear door.

'My father is through there. Go to him. Don't be seen here with me, you will be in trouble with boyfriend. Take computer,' he whispered.

I picked up the laptop, grabbed my bag and coat and hurried through to the back, hoping Jamie could not see anything clearly through the glass. I pulled the door behind me but left it slightly ajar so I could watch Andrei unbolt the café door, allowing Jamie to step inside. I could hear my heartbeat whooshing in my head.

In the back room, Nicolae Constantin sat in a shabby leather easy chair reading a book. He was wearing a scruffy grey shirt tucked into black jeans, his bushy grey hair uncombed. The air was filled with the pungent aroma of boiling cabbage. I indicated to him to remain quiet when he was about to speak to me, so he stood and hugged me like a bear.

'Where is she?' I heard Jamie shout.

'Who? What do you want?' Andrei responded.

'Come on, don't mess me about. She's here isn't she? And Sergei, he's here too. Get them.' Jamie's voice was raised and harsh. I peeped through the gap in the door and saw his face a dark red in the shadows of the café.

Andrei moved to offer a chair but Jamie put out his hand to stop him.

'Don't waste time sitting, get me Sergei now. This is over,' Jamie said.

Nicolae had stood up behind me so he could hear the interaction. At the mention of Sergei, he pushed me aside and went through to them. I stood behind the open door, unsure whether to make my presence known, but certain that I would only aggravate the situation if I got involved.

'You're here for trouble,' Nicolae said.

'If that's what it takes ...' Jamie said, stepping forward. 'I want my woman, and my money. Where's Sergei?'

'Never heard of him,' Andrei said, glancing across at Nicolae.

Jamie moved towards Andrei and grabbed his arm. Nicolae took a chair from the table, turned it over and sat on it, wheezing and spluttering.

'Now listen, you silly boy. This is not a game. You lot all need to go home, back to where you belong. Stop your sponging off us and give us our money back,' Jamie said.

Andrei pulled away from Jamie then waved both arms in the air, shouting something in Romanian. Before I could think what to do or say to try to stop them, the café door burst open and in walked the bouncer from London, Sykesy. He was wearing a black bomber jacket and black trousers, and heavy Doc Marten boots. The sheer presence of the guy filled the threshold of the door, and he was carrying some sort of metal bar. My hands were shaking and I felt sick; this man could hurt people. I leaned against the wall to stop myself passing out.

'What's to do, Jamie?' he said, his accent heavy from London.

He walked towards Andrei, who immediately pushed into Jamie. Jamie raised his fist and punched Andrei hard on the mouth and nose. Blood poured from his nose immediately, which sent me into meltdown. I began to choke back the raw sour taste of vomit in the back of my throat and brought my hand up. Nicolae stood up and put his arm around his son to stop him falling over.

I heard the crunch of another punch, then a shout from Jamie as Nicolae crumpled to the floor. He lay still, as if out cold. Sykesy crashed the metal bar onto the table beside him, then grabbed a chair with his other hand and threw it towards the counter, sending plates and pepper pots smashing onto the floor. I watched Andrei wipe blood from his face then raise his foot and try to kick Sykesy in the groin. He hit his upper thigh and the guy simply laughed and stepped forward, using the bar to crash against Andrei's arm. I heard the crack of a broken bone.

'Want to have a go, foreigner?' he shouted, then he threw the bar aside, knocking more chairs to the ground, and stepped forward and swung a punch at Andrei, catching him in the chest, then another one under his chin. Andrei fell to his knees.

Nicolae stirred and reached out to his son, grasping at his leg.

'Get away, son!' he shouted.

Andrei struggled to his full height, then tried to punch Sykesy, but had to hold on to his broken arm. The bouncer hit him in the stomach, then kicked him on the upper leg and into his groin. Andrei immediately struggled towards the front door and staggered outside.

My bag and the laptop were on the sideboard at the back of the room where I had left them. I turned away from the door and silently ran over to it, my hands shaking uncontrollably as I fumbled to open the zip to retrieve my phone.

'Where's the man we want, Jamie?' I heard Sykesy shout.

'The old man knows,' he said.

'We need the police. Now,' I whispered to the operator.

'No police, call ambulance,' Nicolae said behind me. His face was bright red and he was sweating profusely. He had lurched in through the door to the back room, I wasn't sure whether to get to me or to escape his assailants. Before I could say any more, he fell to the floor, clutching his arm.

Sykesy followed him in and towered over him. Instead of helping him up, he kicked him in the face, his heavy boot crunching against his jawbone. More blood. I coughed and gagged, then vomited a mix of coffee and țuică over the floor, dropping my phone

Nicolae howled, then cried.

'Where is he?' Sykesy shouted.

But it was no good. Nicolae passed out again, this time frothing at his mouth and making a small gurgling noise. Jamie came into the room as I was on my knees, spluttering an explanation to the operator, saying we needed an ambulance really fast.

'Sykesy, that's enough. Go,' Jamie said, staring at me with a face of sheer panic.

Sykesy did as he was told, stumbling out of the room into the café. I heard the front door glass smash as he left the building, no doubt swinging his metal rod as he went.

Before I could take a breath, Jamie turned and ran without saying another word.

37

The storms overnight had cleared the air, and bright sunshine welcomed the next morning, at least for a while. It was Friday 13th. Was that auspicious or unfortunate? Gary was late. After the chaos of the evening, I had been on the phone to Hazel for almost an hour, Becky for half an hour, but most importantly, Gary the rock. He always knew what to do, and if he didn't, he made it up so confidently that it gave me belief to go on.

'Sleep on it and we'll meet tomorrow, usual place, 8:30,' he said.

***

The gravestones looked shiny wet from the overnight rain and I had to put a Sainsbury bag on the bench to sit on it while I waited with the two coffees in hand.

I had not seen or heard from Jamie since he turned and ran from the café, but the image of his deathly pale and shocked face was etched on my memory. Nicolae had been taken in the ambulance and I'd spent an hour giving statement after statement to various police officers, before going home in a taxi and eating three rounds of toast. I was angry with myself for not taking photographs or getting involved in some way to stop some of the injuries.

There had been no word from Andrei either and I wondered where he may have gone. The damp cold of the bench brought me back, and I called Lou while I waited.

'Emma, early-bird, how are you?' she said.

'Have you seen Andrei? Since last night?'

'No, actually Emma. I told you we're not that serious. He's only stayed here once and that was on the sofa,' she said.

Wherever he was, clearly Lou wasn't his first choice of friend for support. St Giles' Church stared down at me, as it had surveyed the scene since the thirteenth century. It was no longer in open fields, and the noise of traffic on the Woodstock and Banbury roads made it hard to hear what Lou said.

'Well, he's gone missing. Can you meet me this morning? Get out for an hour? It's urgent,' I said.

'I will have to clear it with my boss but it should be fine. You sound stressed. Make it ten?'

'OK. I'll come to your office. Got to go now. Gary's here.'

'I can't keep up with you,' she said and was gone.

I stood and kissed him on the cheek and we sat drinking our coffees together. Suddenly the place seemed calm and welcoming. I sat close enough so my arm pressed against his.

'I've already acted on what you told me last night. I've spoken with the officers you saw and I've been in touch with DI Richards. We need to find them all, especially that thug Sykesy. Him and Jamie are bad news,' he said.

We talked through the potential evidence and I told him all I could remember and how pathetic I'd been.

'Still got that blood thing, then,' he said.

I slapped him on the arm and kissed his cheek again.

'So you thought it was just your blood? That time you cut your finger in my kitchen. No, it's all blood.'

'And I liked to think I had that effect on you. Caring at the time.'

'Sorry to disappoint. Ever since childhood. Sight of blood makes me either pass out or vomit. Of course, the țuică didn't help.'

'You need to rest today. That's an order. Someone needs to look after you.'

'I'm off to the hospital first. To see Andrei's father. Then I'll call Brad.'

My phone buzzed and the screen lit up with a text from Jamie.

<Sorry, I love you.xx>

Not a surprise he didn't have the nerve to call. But where was he? Gary suggested I call Brad immediately since they may be able to track his phone but I insisted I had to see Nicolae.

After hugging Gary, I caught a taxi to Summertown and met Lou in her reception area, where the dazzling white lights meant the receptionists needed even heavier foundation than our own Gemma and Julie.

'We're going to the hospital. I've got a taxi waiting,' I said.

On the way, I gave her a run-down of what had happened. She hadn't heard anything from Andrei, so we shared our worries and tried to work out what to do.

'We could check the café. Maybe he came back,' she said.

'Perhaps, but I doubt it, too risky. Perhaps his dad can help. Who knows, Andrei may even be visiting him. He certainly needed an A&E visit himself,' I said.

The Marston Ferry Road was slow-moving with school traffic. We crawled past one of the best OFSTED-certified secondary schools in Oxford and watched all the young adults amble slowly into their futures.

'Queue to the JR will take a while. No alternative,' the taxi driver said.

'It's OK. We're visiting a friend. He's not going anywhere,' I said.

When we reached the double roundabout, Lou suggested some food first, so we could talk some more, and then we could walk up the hill from there. It would save crawling in the queue for the hospital car park. It wasn't as if we had to see Nicolae urgently, since there wasn't much we could do. The police would be looking for Andrei as well as Jamie and Sykesy. I paid the taxi and we stepped into the local deli, ordering drinks and a sandwich, which came quickly as there was no one else there.

'Guilty pleasure – panini with melted cheese and ham. Not had one of these in months,' Lou said as we sat in the window and tried to absorb all that had happened.

'Andrei looked really scared when he ran off. Well, more like staggered really,' I said.

'Lucky to come out alive by the sound of it. That heavy brute of a thug with an iron bar. How come Jamie knows people like that?'

We spoke quietly and sipped our hot drinks. She was right, how on earth did Jamie get mixed up in this in the first place?

'They've known each other a few years. Some sort of club.' I said.

I took out the photo from my bag and showed her the four outside the Randolph.

'Isn't that the newsagent?' she said.

'Yes, they all go back a long way and have done some very nasty things, but Jamie said it was all in the past. We've all done things we've regretted I suppose - I know I have.'

Lou was quiet after that and we finished up our food, commenting to man clearing the tables that we would definitely be back, next time we were visiting someone in hospital. Then we walked up the hill towards its main entrance.

In the modern entrance lobby there were a number of small stalls selling newspapers, coffees and food before you reached the main reception. I bought a copy of the *Oxford Mail*, our main rival, and a bunch of grapes for Andrei's dad, although I wasn't sure they would be allowed.

'We're here to visit Mr Constantin. We're friends that he is expecting,' I said to the professionally-smiling woman behind the countertop who was staring at her screen, which she tapped away at.

'Visiting starts in 15 minutes. He's in ward 3A,' she said and pointed to the lift.

Lou put her arm round me as we went up. She could tell I was shaking; she knew about the blood thing too. Silly really.

The nurse that received us looked severe and stony. Was that her poker face? She spoke to us before letting us into the private room where they had put him.

'You can stay for thirty minutes, no more. I doubt he'll say anything. We have him on various drips and he has many injuries, he's barely conscious,' she said.

'Injuries?' I said.

'He must have had quite a thumping. You can go in now.'

She stepped to one side and we walked into the room where there was a single bed in the middle of one wall. A monitor at the side showed his heartbeat and beeped steadily. I walked up to the bed and saw immediately that it was Andrei, not Nicolae. The top half of his head was covered in dressings, one arm was strapped and plastered, and his feet were elevated. I could see deep bruising across his whole face and it looked as if his nose was bent at right angles. His right eye socket was swollen and the eyelid almost clamped shut. There were small cuts and grazes on his cheek. I held my throat and suppressed my usual instinct at the sight of it all. His injuries were much worse than the last time I saw him.

'Oh God, it's Andrei,' Lou shouted and rushed to the other side of the bed to grip his hand.

Andrei nodded with his eyes, just slowly, as if recognising us but unable to process exactly who we were. I went and got us both a chair from the stack behind the door, and we sat down at the sides of the bed, holding a hand each. His two women, it'll spark him to life, I thought. As I squeezed his hand, he mumbled some sort of greeting, then his fingers opened and reached forward to stroke the bangle on my arm. I could see his smile.

'Who did this?' I said, although it seemed pretty obvious.

Andrei groaned and closed his eyes. As he did, he muttered two words, only one of which I could understand and that didn't make any sense anyway.

***

Nicolae was in a general ward behind curtains. The duty nurse was kind enough to allow us in for a few minutes, even though visiting time was over and we were not family. She realised it was her mistake in the first place that we had been able to see Andrei, especially as there was a special note on his file that he was to have no visitors until the police were able to question him fully about the attack.

The general ward had four beds, of which one was empty and the other two held elderly men asleep, so we would be able to talk freely with Nicolae if he was awake. Lou pulled the curtain aside and walked through, and I followed.

He was sitting up in bed reading a travel magazine with a picture of the Grand Canyon on the front. He looked pallid, but wide awake. There were no drips, just a wire connected to the monitor on the table beside the bed, presumably keeping an eye on his heart.

'Miss Hawkins, Louise, good to see you,' he said.

'You too. You gave us quite a scare, How are you?' I said.

'I am alive. It was heart scare. No damage. Good people here in the hospital say I am OK.'

Lou-two took it upon herself to tidy and arrange the table beside him which was scattered with old teacups and papers. She opened the bag of grapes and put them neatly on a clean plate, then she clasped his hand and leaned over and gave him a gentle kiss on the cheek.

'My Andrei, he's so lucky to know you two. To have two girlfriends,' he said.

We laughed. 'Not much wrong with you then, is there?' Lou said.

'My Andrei. He has not visited yet. I have not heard. He ran off.'

'Well, it wasn't really a run, was it? He stumbled out the café door to escape that thug.' I said.

Lou held onto his hand and looked up at me, seeking a nod about what to say. I smiled at her.

'Listen, Andrei's wonderful dad. We need to tell you something,' she said.

He lay back and sighed. 'He's dead, isn't he?'

'No, no, nothing like that ...' Lou's voice faltered and she coughed, then, against all regulations, she sat on the bed, continuing to hold his hand. 'But he is badly injured. He's in this hospital.'

'He's going to be fine,' I said, although I had no idea whether that was true. A sheen of perspiration covered his forehead and he started to breathe slowly and deeply with his eyes closed. I wondered whether we should have told him, but he had a right to know.

'We'll ask the nurse to arrange for you to go and see him. He's on a different floor, but he's well cared for and he's stable,' Lou said.

We took turns to describe some of Andrei's injuries and how we had been in to see him and held his hand for a few minutes. We joked that the nurse had muddled up the two handsome Constantins who could be brothers. He opened his eyes at that and smiled weakly.

'You are good girls,' he said.

The food trolley arrived with a drink for him of tea or coffee. He chose water, and we took it as an opportunity to leave.

'We'll come back, but you should rest now,' I said.

'These are my son's English girlfriends,' he said to the trolley attendant but she didn't seem to understand enough English to follow that thought.

'Look after him. I will see him soon,' he said.

'We will,' we both said as we walked out and returned to the nurse's station to leave. We cleaned our hands with the alcohol gel as we left.

**

'That was sad,' Lou said as we walked along the corridor towards the escalator. The League of Friends café was downstairs and we needed a hot drink. I was also very hungry again. Lou stepped onto the down escalator ahead of me and we descended slowly.

I glanced across to the up escalator and watched a steady stream of people on their way to visit loved ones, and uniformed doctors and nurses going to work. A dark-haired woman caught my eye, mainly because she was holding hands with a man and they were standing side by side, so no one could walk past them on the escalator. I studied her carefully as we passed. She was familiar. Definitely a face I had seen before. The man was taller, with a slight stoop. It was over in an instant and although I glanced back, I didn't want to stare and cause offence.

When we reached the ground floor reception, we joined the coffee-house queue, clutching plates of cake. It was difficult to talk openly so we didn't speak. I watched Lou as she observed the various patients and visitors around us, like a small town of misfits who all collected in one café. Eventually, we ordered our coffees and sat at a table for two beside the window, looking out onto the busy entrance road where no one was allowed to park except ambulances. A half-dozen smokers were gathered by the pillar near our window, sucking on their cigarettes, chatting with each other in the camaraderie of a shared guilty habit.

'I saw someone,' I said.

'Who? What do you mean?'

'Just now, on the escalator. Someone I know, or should do.'

I sipped some coffee then took out my mirror and makeup bag and set about fixing my eyeshadow. Lou sat quietly pondering. Who was it? Someone important. Once I'd finished I flicked through the photos on my phone, cursing what a terrible journalist I was. I should always recognise a face.

'Was it someone to do with your job? Or a friend of Hazel perhaps?' Lou said.

'I don't know,' I said as I idly continued to examine my photos.

Suddenly I saw her there at the Chamber of Commerce ball. Of course.

'It's Amanda Brown. She's dyed her hair, or wearing a wig or something. But definitely her.'

'The one who was kidnapped. No, really?'

'Yes, really. The man with her, he must be the kidnapper. Sergei. I've never seen him before.'

'Wait here. I need to find them,' I said.

I abandoned my coffee and stood up quickly. The tables around us thought we had some kind of emergency or argument. I was shaking as I picked up my bag. Amanda. Sergei. Where were they going? To see Nicolae. It had to be that.

An ambulance arrived outside, its siren still sounding, and the nursing staff rushed to its back door to open up to a new medical emergency. It was enough of a distraction for our surrounding tables that I could make my escape quietly. Even Lou didn't wave any kind of acknowledgement. I walked quickly to the escalator and rose back to the upper level, watching out for them. I wasn't sure what I would do when I saw them: claim an exclusive interview or make a citizen's arrest? I barged past the nurse's station, where luckily the duty nurse was on the phone and didn't react quickly enough to stop me. The ward had woken up; the two old men in adjacent beds were chatting about the price of petrol. It seemed an odd conversation. Andrei's dad's curtain was still closed and I pulled it aside. No visitors. He was lying back, eyes closed, and sat up quickly.

'Back again already?' he said.

'Did you have other visitors?' I asked.

He lay back and shut his eyes, indicating with his hand for me to go.

'Mr Constantin, this is important. Was Amanda here? Amanda Brown?'

'Never heard of her,' he said, without opening his eyes.

Whatever he was hiding, I was losing time. I turned and retraced my steps back to the corridor and walked along to the other end where the staircase up to Andrei's ward was. If they had been going there, they would not have used the escalator in the first place. It didn't make sense. They had to have been here for Nicolae. I ran back to the top of the escalator. A doctor approached me with a look of concern.

'Are you alright?' he said.

'No, I'm a rubbish reporter. A stupid hack.'

'But you're not ill?'

'No, just brainless. I didn't even take a photograph.'

'They're not allowed on the premises.' He smiled a cute smile and I laughed. 'Doctor Gilmour,' he said and put out his hand for me to shake, which I did.

'Emma. Emma Hawkins. The *Gazette*. I saw Amanda Brown with a man on the escalator and now I've lost her.'

'It's a big location. We lose patients all the time.'

'Well, she and her companion are of interest to the police and my paper. Any suggestions how I find them?' I said

'You don't watch *Casualty* then? They'll either be outside smoking or in the toilets hiding. Actually, the best thing we can do is to go to security and get them on the case – they have instant rewind CCTV.'

'I'll do that, thank you. Good idea. I'll go to reception.'

'I could take you straight there. It would save time,' he said.

Andrei came to my mind, lying there almost unconscious. You tease, he had said over an M&S coffee. Why did I remember that? All he could do now was mumble. One word I understood. 'Brook.' What did that mean? Focus Emma. Rule two, no flirting, I thought.

'Thanks, but I'll be fine. You go and save some lives.'

I walked away quickly without looking back.

As I stood on the escalator again, going down to rejoin Lou, my phone pinged a text message. Another contact from Jamie.

<Will come back for you when I'm finished. x>

38

Lou was waiting by the hospital reception, on the phone. I hopped around her but she ignored me until she had finished, then we both spoke at once.

'I've ordered a taxi,' she said.

'We need to go to security for CCTV,' I said.

Lou grabbed my arm and gave me a hard stare, not blinking. The high-ceilinged reception amplified the cacophony of waiting patients and a busy A&E.

'We're going to the police station now. A taxi will be here in three minutes. Call your police friend,' she said.

She was right. Even if the CCTV showed them, Amanda and Sergei had gone by now whether they'd visited Nicolae or not, and he wasn't going to say.

'We should talk to Andrei first,' I said.

'No, it's time for the police. Andrei's going nowhere in a hurry and we need to find out who did that to him. We need police help. It's probably that thug of a bouncer that you keep talking about. Caught up with him and gave him round two,' she said.

Rain ricocheted from the pavement as the taxi drove through Summertown towards the police station. Brad said he would wait for us in the entrance. I gazed out at the passing streets of North Oxford. It had to be Sykesy, the bouncer. And what about Jamie, where was he? The idiot. Lou was right, we had a lot to talk about, and Brad would know where to look next. It was time to show him the Randolph photograph as well, I'd waited too long, protecting Jamie.

Having Lou with me gave me comfort. I couldn't face Brad on my own. What had Andrei meant by 'Brook'? What was Amanda doing there at the hospital? Presumably that was Sergei? And what about finding Cristina?

The taxi pulled into the entrance area, but two police cars were parked exactly where he needed to drop us off, so we had to stop further away and run to avoid the rain. Lou paid and ushered me ahead. As soon as I walked into the lobby, Brad was there as promised, casually dressed as if he'd come in specially for us.

'Hey Emma, come on in, let's get a quiet room where we can talk. You looked stressed,' he said.

I introduced Lou-two and we followed him to an interview room. It was sparsely furnished with a table and four chairs. He didn't offer coffee and got straight to the point.

'Do I need to get the force out fast?' he asked.

'No, not yet. We will go through what we know and share everything with you. Louise is Andrei's best friend and Andrei is in the JR, badly beaten up,' I said.

The story tumbled out as Lou and I took turns to explain different details. Brad sat quietly with a pad and pencil although he didn't write anything down. He looked businesslike and calm; this was his professional side.

'When we came out from seeing Andrei, I spotted Amanda. It was definitely her. It took me a while to realise and by then, it was too late. She was with a man. He wasn't familiar but I would recognise him again. We're thinking it must be Sergei.'

I said I was worried about Jamie and showed him the text messages that I had received.

'I can't find him now. He won't answer his phone.'

'We have a couple of officers checking his house and your office, just in case he is there. We're also trying to track his phone but that takes more time. What did he mean by "when I'm finished"?' Brad said.

'I have no idea,' I said.

Lou leaned forward and stared closely at Brad. She was more concerned than me.

'We think Andrei was beaten up by this bouncer guy that was there. It seems obvious,' she said.

'Well it may look like that but it's not really possible. We arrested him quite early last night, soon after he scarpered from the café. We will question Andrei Constantin when he is well enough to answer, but it looks like the attack was after we had already arrested William Sykes.'

Lou and I glanced at each other, both with the same thought. If not him, then who? Who could possibly want Andrei beaten to within an inch of his life?

'Andrei managed to say one word to me. It didn't make any sense. He whispered "Brook". It was soft but very clear. There was a word before it that I couldn't catch, so "something Brook". Do you have any idea what that might mean?' I said.

'None at all.' Brad stood up and paced around, then sat back down. He put his hand on mine. 'Don't worry, we'll get this sorted.'

I opened my bag and took out the photograph again. It

had been a while since I'd considered its relevance. Jamie, David, Sykesy and the Chief Constable at the time. Brad studied it, running his finger over it.

'A secret band,' he said.

Then he stood up again and walked towards the door.

'Come on. Let's go and see David. There must be something he knows. Some kind of link to all this. Let's put him under some pressure,' he said.

'You two go. I'm going back to the hospital to sit with Andrei. I have a bad feeling and prefer to be there,' Lou said.

***

In all my years, I had never been in a police car. We even had the siren on. Brad became DI Richards again, sitting in the back with me while he had one of his sergeants drive. We raced down St Giles and turned along Broad Street, then into Holywell Street. This was a route that normal traffic could not take. Traffic lights didn't bother us. It felt like the entire city watched as we sped by.

'When we get there, DS Hodgson will stay in the car while you and I go in to chat to David. We'll be friendly, at least to start with. He has to know more than he's saying,' he said.

I gripped the hand-hold on the door as we cornered the Plain, wishing I had turned on my voice recorder that was in my handbag. I would do that when we reached the shop. When we started along Cowley Road, DS Hodgson turned the siren off, so we wouldn't draw David's attention. Brad opened his door as the car came to a halt outside the front of the shop, then he walked around the back of the vehicle and opened my door for me. The pavement was slippery from the previous rain shower, and he held my arm as if I was either a wife or a criminal, I wasn't sure which.

'I can manage, thanks,' I said.

'This is where we first met. You were prickly then.'

'Ha, looks who's talking.' I laughed and held my coat and bag close as I followed him to the door of the shop. All signs of the recent closure had gone and David Brown was standing behind the counter staring into space. There was no one shopping. The stock had been replenished and looked fresh, the magazines stacked neatly and the window display was no longer a line of fluffy toy bunny rabbits. He had cleaned it all and stacked dummy jars of sweets to attract customers.

'Good morning ... Oh, it's you two,' he said.

David came round and walked to the door, slipping the lock across and turning the sign to say *Closed*.

'Don't worry, it's quiet anyway,' he said.

'We have a few questions,' Brad said.

We walked through to the room at the back and David offered a cup of tea, which we declined. He put the kettle on anyway and put a teabag into his *READ A NEWSPAPER* mug.

'What can I do for you?' he said.

David looked calm, better than the previous time I had seen him. Either that, or he had improved his poker face; having a Detective Inspector in the room didn't seem to bother him at all. We sat at the table and watched as he poured the water.

'Well, amongst other things, we're looking for Jamie Wilson, you know, your friend Jamie.'

'Not sure I would use the word "friend",' he said.

'Anyway ... he's missing. Also, of course, your wife is still missing, her "friend" Sergei is missing, and a lady called Cristina is missing. That's a lot of missing people and we believe they are all connected. We want you to explain everything you know.'

I smiled at David to encourage him. Brad was being gentle.

'No idea what you're talking about.'

Brad stood up and his frame of almost two metres towered over David. I remembered my recorder and rummaged in my bag for it, then switched it on and left it inside. I didn't want to make this into something official and on the record, if it was going to be a simple chat.

'Come along, Mr Brown. You can do better than that. There could be lives at stake. This missing woman Cristina, she could be the key and may be in some danger now. And this secret club of yours. Tell me about that,' Brad said.

'Nope, don't know.'

'Jamie already admitted it to Emma here. A club from university days was it? A musical group? Tell me about it. You know a man called Sykesy?'

'Heard of him a long time ago. Not in years.'

'We have him in custody for causing bodily harm. He had a go at Andrei Constantin and his father in the Romanian café up the road from here.'

'He always was a thug, but that's nothing to do with me.'

'True. But Jamie. He was there too. Shall we say that he orchestrated it?'

I took off my coat and wiped my forehead. It felt as if

David had deliberately put the heating on maximum, and the place smelled of burnt toast.

'Where would Jamie hide out? If he wanted to disappear? He's not at his house, or in his office and he won't answer his phone. You must know where he could be,' Brad said.

David drank some of his tea and walked over to the door to check on the shop.

'You're starting to cost me money. I don't see how I can help. Yes, I wanted my wife back but I've given up lately and not sure I do any more.'

'How about the money? Surely that's important to you,' Brad said.

'Of course it is. We've been conned. I borrowed some of it.'

'From who?'

'You know that already. From Jamie.'

'So let's start again about your friend Jamie then. Tell us how you know him.'

David sat down and sighed. He put his mug on the top of the bookcase and looked up at Brad who stood over him.

'OK, well, yes, we knew each other years ago. And Sykesy as you call him, though he was Billy then. We played together in a musical group, a band, back in the Eighties.'

'A local fascist band, was it?' Brad said.

'We played rock, not politics, but we did have similar views on things, yes.'

I walked over to the kettle and switched it back on. We were getting somewhere and I thought a cup of tea might buy us more time.

'Help yourself,' David said.

'Thanks. So, this band? Presumably it was local to Oxford.'

'Yes, pubs and local bars. That kind of thing. We just enjoyed playing together, never made much money.'

'And you had a common bond, similar opinions,' Brad said.

'Yes and we worked hard. We played together well. We enjoyed getting together for all the rehearsals as much as the performances. '

'Where did you practise? Annoy the neighbours, did you?' I said.

David sighed and looked across at me.

'I suppose this has to come out. We used the barn of a farm near Horspath, some mate of Jamie's. He had mates everywhere back then.'

'And the farm was called?' Brad said.

'I think it was Hollow Brook Farm,' he said.

Brad looked at me and smiled. Then he picked up David's mug and took it over to the small sink.

'You look like you've finished that, sir. We have a spare seat in our car and I think you should take us to see this barn. Relive your youth; I'm sure you'll remember the way.'

39

Blue lights again. Down the Cowley Road out of town, passing uninterested locals who saw police cars all the time. Brad sat in the front this time, leaving me and David to hold on in the back.

'Should we be informing the Cowley Road station about this, sir?' the sergeant said.

'Let's see what we find first. Possibly a waste of time.'

The built-up city of Oxford ended abruptly after the car factory and turned into green rolling countryside at the foothills of the Chilterns. There were mixed farms of livestock and crop production covering the ground between tiny villages that would have housed farm workers at one time, but were now occupied by commuters into the city or down to London. The car took a sharp left-hand bend into the lane of Hollow Brook Farm, although there was no official sign to say where the track went. There was an old wooden post leaning at an awkward angle that had the faded letters H B F C painted on it vertically. Of course, the Hollow Brook Farm Club, I thought. David gave no indication whether he had been here recently and it was difficult to tell his mood as he remained silent throughout the journey except for the brief directions he gave.

'Hollow' must have been the other word that Andrei had mumbled, but how could Andrei have known about it? The track to the old farm was rutted from tractors, and the recent rain had caused puddles of mud to gather in the deepest crevices. Our driver maintained a steady speed, and we had to hold on tight to the seats in front of us. I looked across at David to reassure him but he just gazed out of the window looking across the fields of sheep. The land was being actively farmed, but as we approached we could see that Hollow Brook farmhouse at the end of the lane was derelict.

The sergeant navigated through two large granite gateposts and turned immediately right in front of the farmhouse to follow the track around the back. The front door of the house hung on one hinge and most of the panes of glass of the windows were broken. A dark green ivy covered the walls and had spread onto the roof. The gravel track that went around the side of the building crunched from our tyres. I could see tracks of previous vehicles. As we passed the back corner into the farmyard behind, I saw Jamie's car. The side that I could see was spattered with mud and the tyres caked in dark red earth. He would not be pleased with that, and I envisaged a trip to the car wash later. A wave of relief came over me. Whatever awful things he'd done, I still wanted to see him, if nothing else but to understand what was going on. He was here somewhere.

We stopped alongside and Brad told David and me to stay in the car while he and the sergeant investigated.

'I'm going to have to lock you in; we can't have David here making his escape,' he said.

I muttered disagreement and irritation but Brad was commanding. It wasn't up for negotiation. David remained quiet and we watched them walk across the yard into the barn on the far side. It was a rectangular stone barn with no windows and two brown doors at one end big enough to drive a tractor through. They hung on a sliding rail so Brad could pull one sideways and it moved easily, as if it had been recently oiled. Brad and the sergeant disappeared inside with their bright torches.

'What will they find here?' I said.

'I don't know. I really don't. I have not been here for at least ten years. I promise. All I care about is finding Amanda.' David said.

'Would you take her back?'

'Yes, of course. She's the love of my life, but I see now that it's not reciprocated. I could bring myself to forgive. Move on together. But this Sergei, I don't know. They must have known each other back in her London days.'

He stared at the barn. There was light from the flashlights coming through the door, then someone turned on a main electric bulb. They were taking some time, presumably interviewing Jamie.

'Jamie has a problem with Romanians and others living here. And he gets jealous,' I said.

'He has the strongest views of the club, the most active member.'

'Did he lend you the money? For the ransom?'

'Yes, most of it. I only had five thousand pounds. But Jamie provided a considerable sum as a friend, and then she disappeared the second time with her jewellery box. He wanted the money back. The fact Sergei is Romanian made it worse.'

'Presumably the jewellery was valuable?'

'Yes, I think so, and sentimental from her time before

me. Gifts from him, no doubt. She often wore the necklace.'

'Well, matters reached a head last night in the café, but there was no Sergei,' I said.

We fell silent when Brad reappeared from the barn and approached the car. He was speaking on his phone. After a couple of minutes he unlocked the car and asked me to get out, leaving David behind. He walked me part-way towards the barn so that David could not hear what was said. He took my hand and looked into my eyes quite deliberately.

'Emma, I have some terrible news for you. We have found Jamie inside that barn. I'm sorry to tell you that he is dead.'

My world tilted violently and I wobbled on my feet, almost slipping on the farmyard mud. My knees simply gave way and I grabbed onto Brad.

'Take a minute,' he said.

My brain went into a dream-like, surreal state. I could not absorb the information. I closed my eyes for what felt like a few minutes, although it was probably just a few seconds.

'I need to see him,' I said, and I pulled my arm away from Brad and ran toward the barn. He came after me but slipped and fell onto the floor. At any other time, I would have laughed, but I didn't look back and charged through the open door. Inside, the sergeant was taking photographs with his phone. The barn was almost completely empty. Straw was strewn around as if in readiness for a herd of cows but it didn't look natural, even to a non-farmer: there was a small stove in one corner with two chairs and various detritus from someone living there. Jamie lay flat out, face down on the ground in front of the oil-burning heater. The back of his head was battered in and caked in blood. More blood surrounded him, soaked into the straw to make it red.

I wobbled on my feet again and bent over and heaved vomit in front of me. This time it wasn't over my poor Jamie's trousers and shoes. The sergeant ran to my side and held me, and the light seemed to fade in front of me until it was completely dark.

***

I opened my eyes to see Brad sitting next to me in the back of the police car, holding my hand. David was in the front and Brad was talking to him.

'This is now a crime scene, Mr Brown, and we will be taking you in for questioning.'

David was holding his head in his hands and moaning very quietly, as if in a trance.

I sat up straight and looked across to the barn door. The sergeant stood at the entrance, stretching blue and white tape from one door to the other.

'We have full back-up on the way. Forensics, the works. I'm sorry about this Emma. I really am. This is a murder, we have no doubt. It also looks like someone has been held here against their will; there's ropes and rolls of tape. Whether that is Amanda, or Cristina or both, we don't know yet, but we will find out.'

I sipped from the water bottle that Brad had found somewhere, hopefully not taken from the barn.

'I need to talk to Lou ...' I said, 'and Hazel, Becky, Andrei, the editor at work.' I started to cry, and sobbed uncontrollably.

'All in good time,' he said.

40

Two hours later and Lou was encouraging me to eat. No chance of that. I sipped on a cup of weak tea and held her hand. The JR café was strangely comforting, with its now familiar counter of cakes and sandwiches, and smiling serving ladies steaming milk into lattes. The place was thronging with afternoon visitors so it was easy for us to talk without concern for being overheard.

'I can't believe it. Jamie. Why?' she said.

'I don't know. I can't think straight.'

We sat and stared around. A snippet of conversation about a man with liver problems, a couple holding hands whispering, an old woman eating a biscuit. The world was running along without us. We didn't need to talk. Brad had stayed at the farm while the sergeant dropped me back. I had nowhere else to go, not at this time. I needed to talk to Andrei, and hopefully Nicolae too.

'Andrei will meet us in a room they have agreed to lend us. It's like a relative's room on the same floor as the ward. He's just having some of his wounds re-dressed. You should eat something,' she said.

'Have you told him?'

'Yes. I had to. After you phoned I was in such shock. It just came out. He was overcome.'

Lou looked worse than me, probably because I hadn't actually looked in the mirror yet. She bought two ginger biscuits in a cellophane wrapper and we nibbled on one each. Then I went to the ladies to freshen up. I couldn't face Andrei yet. Standing at the mirror, I did my best to brighten my face. As I glared at myself, I tried to work out what had happened. The violence of the café fight seemed a long time ago. The escalation so fast. Who could have done this? Surely it couldn't be Andrei? Could it? He had known about the farm. Brad had been vague on timings and said he wouldn't know more until after a further examination of Jamie's body. I shuddered and tried to apply some lipstick and look presentable.

Lou was waiting at the bottom of the escalator and we went up to meet Andrei. She held my hand all the way. He was already waiting in the private room, sitting with his leg in plaster and outstretched onto the bench opposite. He shuffled when we walked in, as if to get up, but I hurried over and pushed him back and kissed him on the cheek.

'Andrei,' I said, tears rolling.

'My Emmy, how are you?' He gripped my hand and looked into my eyes with a depth of comfort that I found surprising and reassuring. I could tell instantly Jamie's death wasn't his doing.

Lou and I sat across from him and we all took a minute of peace. The relatives' room was decorated in a pastel mauve colour with pictures hanging from a rail: two photographs of the spires of Oxford, and one of a college quadrangle which could have been any one of a number of them. There was a kettle and mugs on a table in the corner, but no tea or coffee to be seen.

'There's so many questions,' Lou said.

'We need to find Cristina. That is the key,' I said.

'And Amanda. And Sergei,' Andrei muttered. He could speak softly and was much brighter than when I had last seen him.

'Who is Sergei?' Lou asked.

'Before we get to that, I think there's something more urgent, Andrei. You know you mentioned the farm to me. I pieced it together with Brad when David spoke of it. How did you know about it?' I asked.

He sighed and looked from one to the other of us. 'You don't think it me? Me who did this?'

Lou grabbed his hand, 'No of course not, Andrei,' she said without evidence or thought.

'We don't, no. But you muttered the word "Brook", "something Brook". How did you know about the place?'

Andrei closed his eyes and was quiet for a few minutes.

'What happened after you left the café?'

'I walked around Cowley streets in a daze. My arm was broken but I was not bleeding anymore. I made a makeshift sling from my belt. Then I went back to café and watched from across road. It was empty. I was worried about my father but didn't know where he could be. I went back inside and made coffee. There was loud hammering on glass. I don't know why I opened door but I did. Stupid. Jamie burst through with weapon like hammer or bar or something. He set on me, shouting about foreigners like he does, but also about Sergei and Amanda and money, wanting to know where they were.'

'Jamie. My God. I assumed he had run off,' I said.

'He shouted about you too, saying he loved you. Then

he went crazy, not making any sense. I think he had followed me back. We had big fight, but I didn't tell him anything. He hit me many times. After that, I don't remember. I remember lying on café floor.'

He put his hand up to his head and rubbed the side of it. His other arm was in plaster and his face and mouth were still swollen. It looked painful to talk.

'I woke up in boot of car. Dark. Bumping along roads. I could hear traffic noise and we swung wildly around corners. I could see a small amount of light through to the back seats of the car. It was big boot. Then I heard Jamie's voice. He was talking on the phone.'

I looked at Lou and she was crying. We needed Brad again, Andrei needed to report this quickly. But we had to find out about Cristina if we could.

'Have you told all this to the police?' I said, trying to smile at him.

'No, no police. Very important. He was arguing with someone. I heard the word Cristina. Also Hollow Brook Farm. I have good memory. Then car stopped. He got out. I shut my eyes and waited. Boot opened. I pretended to be unconscious. He dragged me from boot and threw me onto ground at side of car, then he raced off. It was a lay-by.'

'What a monster,' Lou said.

I had been a fool. Jamie was a monster. At last I could see that.

'So, where is Sergei? Where is Cristina?' Lou said.

'For that, we need my father,' he said.

***

A hospital porter brought Nicolae in on crutches. The porter was smiling and offered to bring us all some fresh tea. 'You all look like you need it,' he said.

Nicolae sat down slowly next to his son. They had the same mouth, despite Andrei's swelling, but no lopsided smiles today. Nicolae sat and looked around the room with expressionless eyes.

'Oxford is a beautiful city. Such architecture. It is a pity about the people,' he said.

'Some of us are good,' Lou said and smiled at him.

'You are. True. Such history here. Even more than my city. Bucharest – 1459, so young.'

'Tell us about Sergei. We urgently need to find him and Amanda. And what has happened to Cristina,' I said.

'I don't know how to help. They are gone.'

'They came to see you. I saw them. Amanda with her new dark hair. And a man, presumably Sergei.'

'They did. To say they were leaving. To Romania.'

'But we must find them first. Where is Cristina?'

'With them.' He looked across to Andrei before speaking further. Andrei gave a nod.

'Cristina is Sergei's sister. Cristina and Amanda are friends. Amanda is Sergei's lover from long time. Sergei is my lifelong best friend. My only true friend. Sergei is the radical, I am more moderate, more with-the-flow. We stood in the same queues for food, we studied at the same engineering university, we worked together to convert buses to methane after the diesel ran out. We stood together in the crowd and watched the helicopter escape, then the euphoria of the capture of

Ceauşescus and their fall.'

I held Nicolae's hand and studied his face. He was in anguish, ashen with concern, tired.

'Nicolae, Jamie is dead,' I said.

There was a long pause, then he said, 'I know.'

'What is this about? Why has this happened?' I said.

'The world is full of hate. Where we were once welcomed, we no longer are. The long twentieth-century war of Europe that some say started in Sarajevo and ended in Târgoviste in my country on that Christmas Day, it has solved nothing. So we go on.'

Andrei shook his head and raised his good arm to silence his father. A stillness came over the room.

'Yes ... what you say is true. The likes of Jamie and his gang. But this is more, this is different. There's love, passion ... and money,' I said.

'We need to find these people fast,' Lou said.

'I agree. You cannot hide them, Father. They must be caught,' Andrei said.

I looked at Nicolae again. 'Nicolae, did they kill Jamie?'

He slumped back into his chair and nodded. 'Sergei. He told me. It was accident, in a fight at farm. Sergei was trying to untie Cristina. She was bound and gagged,' he said.

'How did he find the farm? Find Cristina?' I said.

'He followed Jamie there.'

'And where are they now?' I sat forward as Lou stood up and paced around the room.

'In a car to Romania,' he said.

We sat silently while the porter returned with four mugs of tea on a tray, together with a bowl of sugar and a plate of biscuits. He had no idea of the conversation that had occurred in his absence.

'Let's get some hot tea inside you,' he said.

We looked at each other and laughed, then thanked him and the air became a little more relaxed after he had gone.

Andrei spoke first. 'Emmy, you have laptop with you?' he said.

I reached for my bag and pulled out the red sleeve containing my Ultrabook and passed it to Lou. She opened it up and held it for him on her knee as he typed one-handed.

'He is expert,' Nicolae said.

Lou and I looked at each other and laughed. How many times had we been told that?

Andrei tapped quickly and we waited. He frowned and then grinned and looked up, telling us they were booked on the Eurotunnel, in a Ford car under Amanda's name.

'We are too late?' I asked.

'No, there are some delays, but I can also move them onto a later train. If we go now, perhaps we can talk to them,' he said.

Nicolae was in no fit state; he was wheezing as Andrei spoke. Andrei himself was mobile enough but awkward with his leg and arm in plaster. Apart from that, we didn't have a car.

'We should call the police right now,' I said.

'No police. Not yet. Please let our community sort this out first,' Nicolae said.

There was a chance of a big story here that I didn't want to miss. I knew we should call Brad but perhaps Nicolae was right. If we got there first, we might persuade them to give themselves up. If they escaped over the Channel, it could take forever to get them back through the international courts or extradition. It was worth a shot. If Andrei could delay them long enough, we might get chance to talk to them, get the real truth and convince them to go to the police voluntarily. We had to get there before they got away.

41

Hazel insisted she would drive and come with us, but I managed to persuade her that it was better for her to be at home as a contact point, and that I would drive very carefully. Even though I didn't own a car, I had passed my test at first sitting at the age of seventeen and driven many hire cars since. I was a natural, I told her. She slowly handed over the keys to her black Volkswagen Golf, her pride and joy.

'It will be fine,' Andrei said as he stood in her hallway, propped against the wall.

'You're not reassuring me, Andrei, you're really not. How will you get in, anyway?'

'I will sit in back. Emmy will drive,' he said.

There was no time for further explanation. We had left Lou at the hospital to be with Nicolae at my insistence. At the very least, he was an accessory to murder, but he also needed someone to care for him.

Driving down the M40, I kept the speed at eighty. The evening traffic was heading out of London and the roads were dry.

'Andrei, I am sorry for what Jamie did to you,' I said.

'It is not your fault. None of this is. You are fighting for good all the time. Jamie was bad.'

'Not all bad. He didn't deserve to die. No one does,

not like that. He had his head bashed in by a spade or hammer or something.' I started to feel sick and focussed on the BMW ahead, keeping pace with it.

'He and his gang were neo-Nazi fascists orchestrating many acts of mischief such as the postering of shops, and some violence to inflame anti-immigration passions. They were backed by powerful rich people.'

'And Sergei, what about him?' I said.

We slowed a little as we moved onto the M25. We were at least an hour from Folkestone and Andrei kept an eye on the departures from Eurotunnel on his phone. There was still time.

'Sergei looked after my father. They suffered under Ceauşescu and wanted to see him gone. They were carried by the crowd, the mob baying for blood. Communism was dead. They wanted change, but they didn't know what to. Sergei became greedy ... and he wanted the love of his life.'

Andrei fell asleep as we passed the junction for Gatwick and I let him rest. The lights of oncoming traffic held my gaze. I needed to expose David and the bouncer and the former Chief Constable; they were all connected to this. I wrote the headlines as I drove as fast as I dared. *Dead man part of a Nazi plot. Racism funded by secret society. Evil exposed by unfortunate death of talented journalist.*

By ten o'clock we were two miles away and I leaned into the back and nudged Andrei awake.

'We will need a ticket to get in. Had you thought of that?'

He coughed and spluttered, then held his bad arm for a few seconds as he came round.

'Yes, I did a booking. Just drive up. There should be

recognition of the number plate.'

I kept to the speed limit through the entrance lanes of the Eurotunnel and approached the departure booth. A ticket spewed from the machine, I took it, and the barrier rose so I could drive through to the car park by the departures terminal.

'Their car is still here somewhere, so they must be inside,' he said, after checking his phone.

I parked in the far corner away from other vehicles and helped him from the back seat. He hobbled across the tarmac as I supported him. Floodlights gave the terminal building an ethereal glow in the cold evening air as we approached.

As the automatic glass doors slid back, we were hit with a wall of heat and noise from the waiting passengers. There was a strong smell of fried food. I needed coffee. We walked slowly around, Andrei hobbling, and people stared. If they were here, they might see us first, so I persuaded Andrei to sit on a chair at the end of a long table, propping his leg up onto the chair opposite.

'I'll take a quick walk around, and if I see them, I promise to come and get you first,' I said.

I walked through the duty-free shop, scanning the whiskies and gins, then I made my way from one fast food outlet to the next, checking the queues. The terminal building was trying to be an airport but was more like a ferry building, small and all in one open area. There was no room to hide, even if you were trying. After fifteen minutes, I had searched the entire area, so I started again. Perhaps they had been in the toilet? But surely not all at once? I stood beside the coffee outlet and looked around carefully. There were tables of travellers checking their bags and chatting about their holidays.

Then I saw them. Clearly. On the end table nearest the central area. I recognised Cristina instantly, and Amanda had the same new dark hair. They were sitting with empty cups. Sergei was standing behind them, his shoulders hunched and hands in his coat pockets. I skirted around the back of the queue for the fast-food chicken and hurried to Andrei. He started to get himself on his feet as I approached.

'You've seen them. Let's go,' he said.

I put my arm around him to help him walk and we headed directly for them. We were about five metres away when they saw us and stared, speechless. Cristina rose to her feet, looking pale and exhausted with no makeup, and even thinner than I remembered.

'Andrei, Oh God you look terrible, and Emma, the journalist. Oh my. What are you doing here?' she said as she approached and went to greet Andrei with an air kiss as best she could. Sergei looked as if he was going to run, so I walked around behind him to head him off.

'We're here in peace. Please. Let's all just talk,' I said.

**

I pulled up three chairs, two for Andrei, so we could join them. They were not due to board for forty minutes, although no one would actually be travelling anywhere, I thought. I had my phone ready to call Brad.

'You are a journalist, no?' Sergei said.

'I am, and I'm a friend of Andrei. We want to know what has happened. Andrei's father is not well. He is your friend. Why are you running away?'

Amanda gripped his hand. Her hair did not suit her fair complexion.

'I have done a terrible thing,' he said.

We spent twenty minutes listening to their full story. Amanda explained how she met Cristina when she was a dancer in London and they became close friends, and had always kept in touch. She met Sergei at one of Cristina's parties in the Nineties, and they became lovers, but eventually he returned to Romania and she left London to go to Oxford to care for her sick mother, and set up a dance school with the money she had made. There she met David through the Chamber of Commerce and they married quickly. She'd thought she loved him at the time, but Sergei reappeared a year ago.

'I wanted Amanda, to start again. For years I couldn't get her out of my head. I begged her,' Sergei said.

'I was disenchanted by then anyway. David was a monster. I didn't agree with his politics and his petty games. I found out about his little club causing mayhem for any overseas settlers in Oxford. The Hollow Brook Farm Club, they called it. That was the end for me,' she said.

'We hatched a plan to steal his money. We didn't tell anyone except Grigore. He helped us,' he said.

'What? My brother? No way. He said nothing to me,' Andrei said.

'He drove his motorbike when we picked up the ransom.'

I thought back, picturing the scene in my mind, the rider in black with the red, yellow and blue helmet.

'I should have thought. The flag of Romania,' I said.

'When I ran that first night, I stole all I could, then we got the ransom money, but I forgot my jewellery box,' Amanda said.

She laughed and looked at Cristina, then at Andrei.

Cristina sat forward and filled in her side of it before Amanda could continue. Cristina had been genuinely worried about finding out what happened to her, so she enlisted my help, thinking I would get to the bottom of it. She thought Amanda had been kidnapped.

'I had death threats because of this,' I said.

'That was us. We were trying to warn you off our trail. We were hiding out in a house opposite the community centre. We knew you were a formidable force,' Sergei said.

Andrei smiled. 'She's a crusader for modern justice, for good over evil,' he said.

'I hadn't even told my sister what we were doing,' Sergei said.

'David's money was from Jamie and their club. It was money for bad deeds, and I wanted to take it away and make them stop. But I had to go back for more, to get my jewellery. That's really why I came back,' Amanda said.

'The Ceaușescu sapphire necklace,' Sergei said.

I gasped and gripped his arm.

'You mean the necklace in the photograph. The one you wore to the ball,' I said looking at Amanda.

'Well, we're not totally sure of its source. But it is a pretty necklace and it did come from Cartier, and maybe it was worn by Elena. Who knows?' Cristina said quickly.

'Whatever the story, it is worth a fortune. More than the ransom money, so I couldn't leave without it.'

I sat back. Now there was a headline. The Ceauşescu necklace. It was a romantic story but my stomach turned. The money might have been from a group who were morally wrong, but Sergei had inflicted extreme violence. He had killed.

'Jamie is dead. My boyfriend is dead,' I said.

Sergei reached out with both hands and held mine. He was shaking.

'I am very sorry. I followed him to the farm, I had been keeping an eye on him for some time, following him up and down the Cowley Road. He often went out on that country road, and I watched him turn into the track. When I got there, we fought.'

'That thug of a bouncer had snatched me first,' Cristina interrupted, 'then Jamie took over. They held me there trying to find out where Amanda was. I never told. I couldn't tell, whatever they did. I didn't even know myself.'

She looked white-faced and her hands were shaking as she spoke, more from anger than fear.

'When I tried to release Cristina from her ties, he came at me with a big bar and then a spade, but I was stronger than him. It was self-defence,' Sergei said.

There was a long silence then. We all looked around the terminal and watched as people gathered their belongings and made their way on vacation, or drank their coffees.

'What will you do?' Sergei said.

'I believe in justice. Jamie was a bad man, yes. But you have killed him. You cannot run. I plead with you to go to the police. I know someone. I think he will believe your story. The evidence will support it too. You will be OK,' I said.

'And the money?' Sergei said, glancing down at the

tatty leather holdall sitting between Amanda's feet.

'It might be tainted money, but it's not your money,' I said.

Amanda jumped to her feet and I thought she was going to escape as she picked up the bag, but then she came around to my side of the table and pulled me to my feet as well. She hugged me tight.

'Thank you. That is what I want too. I have said this already to him. We must stop the fight. We should return the money,' she said.

She kissed me on the cheek, then she knelt down to the bag and unzipped it to expose the bundles of notes to me.

'Perhaps it should go to a charity. I know someone who works in law, on cases of fraud. He may help, but we should take it to the police first. That's what we do in this country,' I said.

I waited and looked at them all. After another minute, Sergei smiled and nodded slowly, and Cristina grasped his hand.

'That's what we do too,' he said.

I took out my phone and sent a text to Brad.

42

As we drove back, I felt intensely tired but my mind raced and the excitement of the last few hours kept me awake. Andrei rested in the back of the car, while I talked incessantly about Jamie and how I had not seen the truth about him staring me in the face all along. He truly was a monster. Andrei murmured agreement in all the right places. I had secured an incredible scoop and wondered how I would break it to the paper or how I would approach the nationals. I played out all the events in my head and how to structure the article.

Then my thoughts turned to the necklace. I kept thinking that Cristina had said it was a Cartier. Was it really connected to the Ceauşescus? That truly was big news, I thought. Could they be right? There was something in my memory about it, something in Henry's research. His notes were still in my bag in a folder. I turned quickly to Andrei in the back and nudged his leg, to waken him.

'Andrei, can you pull out the brown folder in my bag? There are some photos and an article in there.'

He shuffled himself over to it and pulled out the report, then he started to hunt through the pictures.

'What am I looking for?' He said.

'Anything with Elena Ceauşescu. There's a few there of her in fine ballgowns. I remember a necklace.'

Suddenly, Andrei shouted and leapt forward to grab my arm as I drove, despite his injuries, and almost pulling us off the road.

'That's it. She's wearing the same pendant. I've never seen that photograph before,' he said.

'Well well. How about that? I guess Amanda can keep that. It's been hers for a long time. Who knows how Sergei got it? That sounds like a whole new story,' I said.

***

I dropped Andrei at the hospital to see Nicolae and Lou. It was nearly dawn, the sky streaked with soft pink and orange. I needed sleep. I kissed him on the cheek as I left and promised we would be friends for life, crusading for social justice. That would do for me. I needed to give up on dating men, at least for a while.

'We make good team,' he said.

I took the car to Hazel and she hugged me tight and was thankful we had come back in one piece, the car more than me. She stroked my hair as I wept and she brought out a new packet of chocolate digestives and a pot of tea. I talked and talked about Jamie, about his trickery, his apparent evilness, but even so I couldn't get rid of the image of his lifeless body lying in the barn with such hideous injuries. He hadn't deserved that.

'No one should see that twice in her life,' Hazel said, but I was too tired to ask her what she meant by that. I went to bed at her house and fell asleep immediately.

***

Later that morning, my phone pinged with an email notification.

I could see it was from Doug Woodward at the *Guardian* with a subject line *'Reference your application for the role of senior reporter'*.

Would I be excited or disappointed? My destiny determined by the contents of that email. As I steeled myself to click on it, I wasn't sure which outcome I desired. It was beginning to feel like there was plenty of dirt to investigate right here in Oxford.

THE END

Acknowledgements

I am very grateful to all the people who have helped and encouraged me over the years. This is my first novel and I am sure most of my family and friends have begun to doubt whether this book would ever exist. You have all inspired me, but you can also rest assured that all the characters in this story are entirely fictional.

I would like to thank my wife, Meryl, who has read numerous drafts and commented and helped me very patiently as always.

Thank you to Laura Callaghan who has professionally and painstakingly edited this book, both at the detailed level of ensuring my grammar and punctuation are correct, and more importantly has helped with the structure and pace of the story, providing me with great insight in a constructive and tactful way.

My writing career has gradually picked up momentum, with long periods of inactivity interspersed with spells of boundless enthusiasm and I have taken encouragement from the numerous creative writing courses that I have undertaken. I would like to thank all my tutors, especially Jan Henley(Rosanna Ley) for the summer schools at Missenden, and Morag Joss at the University of Oxford Department for Continuing Education.

I would like to particularly thank Joanna Penn (www.thecreativepenn.com) whose teachings and podcasts have sustained me and cajoled me into action. Joanna was the person who inspired me when I started listening to her podcasts back in 2008, and when I met her in 2012 she commented that one of the most important aspect of writing novels is "Shipping". Well, it's taken more years than it should, but I am finally "Shipping".

Thanks to all my friends at the Turl Street Writers; Birte, Charles, Jenny, Julie, Neil, Penny and Rob. Our regular meetings keep us all writing and it is scary to think we have been creating stories and books for ten years.

Thanks to all the clever people at Literature and Latte for creating Scrivener. Without that software, I could not possibly have managed the many versions of the manuscript that existed throughout various drafts.

Finally, thanks to all the staff at the Bodleian Library, especially the admissions staff, for allowing me to use their wonderful Upper Reading Room, where I have spent many an hour sitting in U178 (or nearby) to write this book.

Thanks for reading this to the end, and if you enjoyed this book, please let me know. I need the encouragement! Positive reviews are always welcome.

You will find all my books on your local Amazon site.

If you didn't enjoy the book, also please let me know… maybe as constructively as you can. Thanks!

You can contact me through my website www.grahamdinton.com

or directly by email to graham@grahamdinton.com

On my website, you'll find a link to download the first chapter of my next novel. It's called *The Home Signal* and features Emma in a brand new mystery and investigation.

Best wishes,

Graham

Printed in Great Britain
by Amazon

21356792R00209